GLADIATOR, GODDESS

GLADIATOR, GODDESS

MORGAN H. OWEN

London · New York · Amsterdam/Antwerp · Sydney/Melbourne · Toronto · New Delhi

POMPEII

1. Taberna/Gia's House
2. Gladiator School and Barracks
3. Amphitheatre
4. Forum
5. Temple of Fortuna
6. Forum Baths
7. Road to the Villa of Mysteries
8. Brothel

To Mount Vesuvius

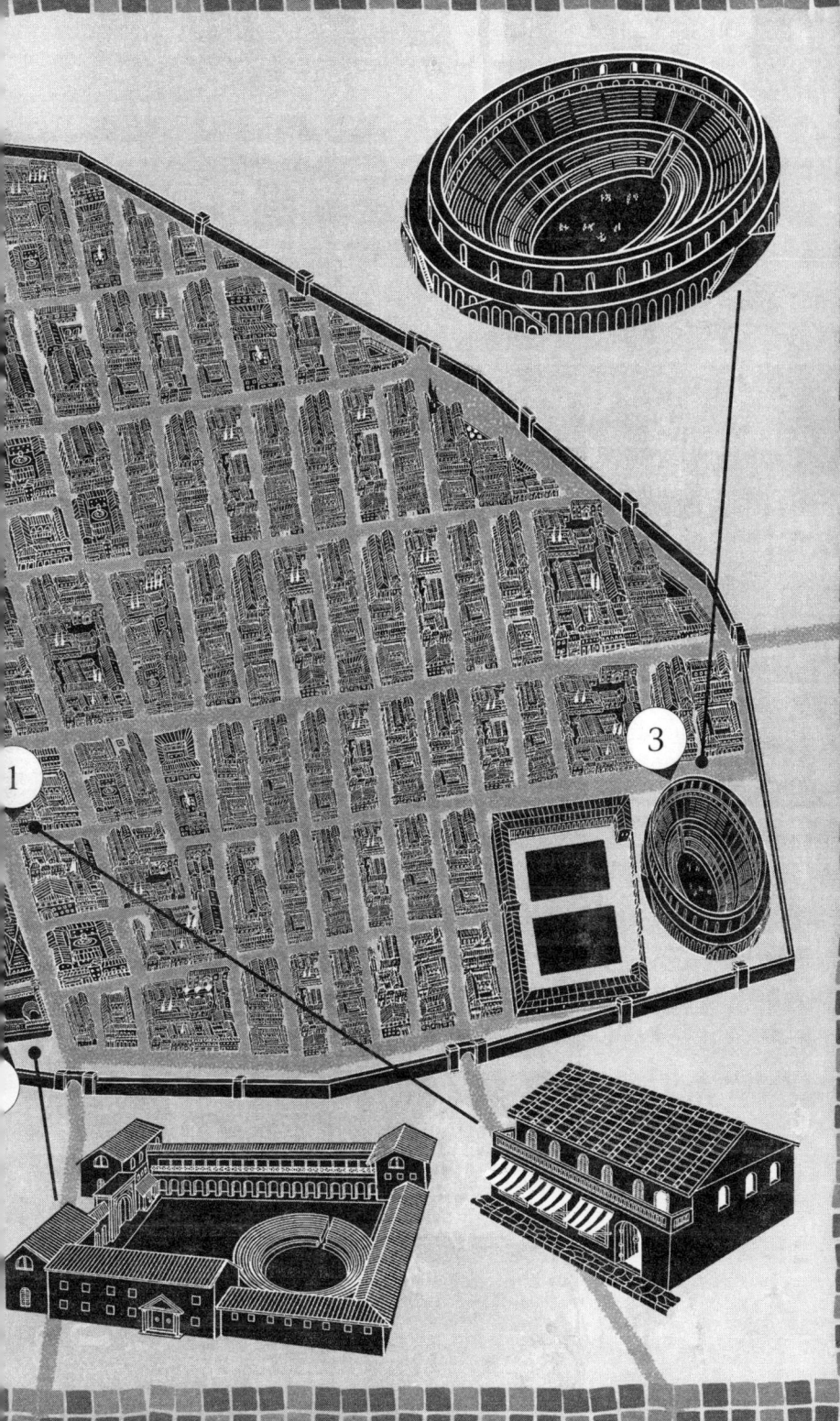

First published in Great Britain in 2025 by Gallery YA,
an imprint of Simon & Schuster UK Ltd

Text copyright © 2025 Morgan H. Owen
Cover illustrations © 2025 Tom Roberts
Map and interior illustrations © 2025 Patrick Knowles
Cover designed by Holly Macdonald

This book is copyright under the Berne Convention.
No reproduction without permission.
All rights reserved.

The right of Morgan H. Owen to be identified as the author of this work
has been asserted by her in accordance with sections 77 and 78 of the
Copyright, Design and Patents Act, 1988.

1 3 5 7 9 10 8 6 4 2

Simon & Schuster UK Ltd
1st Floor, 222 Gray's Inn Road
London
WC1X 8HB

www.simonandschuster.co.uk
www.simonandschuster.com.au
www.simonandschuster.co.in

Simon & Schuster Australia, Sydney
Simon & Schuster India, New Delhi

The authorised representative in the EEA is Simon & Schuster Netherlands BV,
Herculesplein 96, 3584 AA Utrecht, Netherlands. info@simonandschuster.nl

A CIP catalogue record for this book is available from the British Library

HB ISBN 978-1-3985-3851-1
eBook ISBN 978-1-3985-3854-2
eAudio ISBN 978-1-3985-3852-8

This book is a work of fiction. Names, characters, places and incidents are either
the product of the author's imagination or are used fictitiously. Any resemblance to
actual people living or dead, events or locales is entirely coincidental.

Typeset in the UK by M Rules
Printed and Bound in the UK using 100% Renewable Electricity
at CPI Group (UK) Ltd

To the girls with endless rage inside them

For whenever I look at you even briefly
I can no longer say a single thing.

SAPPHO

CONTENTS

	Prologue	01

ACT I

1	To Be Burned	27
2	Not Until I Win	54
3	Viatrix the Victorious	77
4	We Who Are About to Die Salute You	90
5	The Princess and the Gladiator	102

ACT II

6	The Gods Demand Their Sacrifices	126
7	In Her Eyes	145
8	A Woman of Wealth and Power	163
9	I Choose You	186
10	A Mountain of Bones	201

ACT III

11	Protect Yourself	218
12	A Dangerous Game	233
13	Enter the Labyrinth	251

14	The Games We Played in the Heavens	268
15	Murder is its Own Vocation	288
16	All My Heart Longs to Win	297

ACT IV

17	Every Emperor's Last Words Are a Lie	319
18	You Are the World	332
19	Decimalia	347
20	You Never Forget How to Kill a Man	364
21	A Monster of a Different Nature	378
22	A Corona of Fire	394

ACT V

23	Making History	412
24	The Amphitheatre of the Gods	419
25	A Merciful Death	430

Epilogue   448

This book contains scenes of a sexual nature and dark content that may be triggering for some. For a full list of warnings, please turn to the end of the book.

PROLOGUE

Ten years ago

Gia ran ahead of her brothers, waving an imaginary trident, a wreath of flowers draped around her neck.

'And then Salinator said, "UGH"!'

Acting out the gladiator battle she'd seen at the amphitheatre, she mimed thrusting a weapon at an opponent.

'But Thaddaeus said, "not today, shades of the underworld"...' She spun on her heels, ducking the invisible weapon, driving down with her own invisible sword before she stumbled, tripping over her own feet.

'Watch out,' her mother said, yet her warning went unheeded.

'Because Salinator wasn't done yet. Though he was hurt and bleeding, he swapped his trident to his left hand and – BAM! Right in the eye!' She mimicked the roar of an imaginary crowd, pumping one fist at the sky.

'Perhaps it was a mistake to let an eight-year-old watch,' mumbled her father, walking behind her arm in arm with her mother.

'It's just a game,' said her mother. 'The earlier a girl learns about the world's brutality, the better she can prepare for it.'

Gia continued, undeterred.

'But the eye was stuck on the prong of Salinator's trident, so he pulled it off and stepped on it!'

The way the eyeball popped had made her skin tingle with horror, but there had been something thrilling about it too.

'At first, his opponent was in shock,' said Gia, 'rooted to the spot as Salinator laughed, but when he was distracted Thaddeus took advantage and ran at him, driving the sword right into his guts.'

'We *know*,' groaned her eldest brother, Cassius, long-haired and knowingly handsome. 'We were there too.'

'I'm just excited,' said Gia, hopping up and down. 'I want to make sure I remember it all, every last disgusting little bit.'

She mimicked clutching at her stomach before collapsing like a log onto the ground, recreating the death of Salinator. She scraped her palms and knees in the effort, but it was worth it to make Cassius laugh, shaking his head in amusement.

'Get up, idiot,' said Atticus, the younger of the two brothers, while the elder hauled her upright. Atticus grimaced apologetically at the passers-by who watched on, his face pinched, his dark brows sloping. 'You're embarrassing us.'

'People will be talking about the feral child of Via Stabiana if you're not careful,' said Cassius.

'Then let them talk. It isn't every day you see an eyeball pop.' Gia sighed.

'It is Floralia, I suppose,' said Cassius, swirling the daisy he'd been given by a pretty girl near the docks. 'The goddess wouldn't allow the violence if she didn't think it part of nature worth celebrating.'

They passed a mural advertising an upcoming gladiator match: one contender broad, bald and wielding a sword, wearing what looked like a bird helmet; the other dark and tattooed, holding a spear, with a stoic expression.

Gia pulled up in front of it curiously.

'Why are there no female gladiators?' she asked.

'Don't be stupid, sister,' said Atticus.

'I'm just asking a question.'

'Men are made for war; women are made for love,' he said, staring lustfully at their neighbour Rhea. Like them, she was walking home from the day's festivities with her family, draped in flower chains. When he caught her eye, Atticus waved enthusiastically, but she merely pulled a face and returned to her conversation.

'What Atticus means to say is that women are precious,' said Cassius. 'They are jewels and not weapons.'

'I could be a weapon,' Gia said.

'I don't doubt that, sister. You would be a most delightful dagger, I'm sure. But the world is the way it is and it won't easily be turned upside-down.'

Gia turned to Atticus, who was in training at the local gladiator school.

'What do they teach you at the ludus?' she asked.

'It is not for you to know.'

'Will you show me how to fight?' she begged.

'Not a chance.'

'I want to learn. Violence is in my blood; I can feel it.'

She snarled, striking a fighter pose and trying to look as fearsome as possible, but Cassius merely laughed.

'No,' said Atticus, drawing out the sound as he pursed his lips for emphasis. 'You should focus on learning how to be a young woman. You're not doing a very good job of it so far.'

'Oi!' she said, elbowing him sharply.

'Ouch.'

Though Gia was just a child, she already knew her options in life were limited. She was a girl, and a girl's life was smaller than a boy's – there was no avoiding it. She wasn't taught to read like her brothers, though she picked it up by reading signs and stealing scrolls. She wasn't taught to use a sword, though she taught herself by watching the gladiators.

She would grow up to be a wife or a courtesan. Those were her choices.

'But I want to poke people's eyes out and stab them in the guts.' Gia pouted, clutching at his tunic. 'Please, brother, teach me.'

'You'll never find a rich husband like that,' said Cassius.

'Who says I want one?'

'Everyone wants a rich husband,' he said. 'Even I wouldn't mind being the playboy of a wealthy Roman.'

Gia looked to him, giggling. Cassius wiggled his shoulders coquettishly, eyebrows dancing.

'Then maybe we should swap,' she said. 'I'll go to gladiator school and you can be a courtesan.'

'Stop it, Gia,' came her father's voice, but only half-heartedly.

'I'll wear the helmet and you will wear the robes,' said Gia.

Cassius burst out laughing, tossing his long hair and shaking his head at her audacity.

'A girl gladiator,' he chortled. 'Whatever next.'

'We may as well have flying pigs for senators,' said Atticus.

'It would surely be an improvement,' said Cassius.

'Is that really so ridiculous?' said Gia in a quiet voice.

The blush of humiliation coloured her cheeks.

'The world is ridiculous, that's not your fault,' said Cassius.

'Maybe the world can change.'

'I suppose stranger things have happened in the history of time. It's good to have dreams.' He smiled at her kindly.

'Women aren't meant to fight. The gods made them soft and warm for a reason,' said Atticus, with a sniff.

'The goddesses aren't soft and warm,' argued Gia, picturing Diana the hunter with her bow, or merciless Fortuna spinning the wheel of destiny. 'The goddesses are fearsome warriors.'

'You are not a goddess, little sister.'

'No, but I could fight like them. Please, Atticus, just show me a few moves so that I might use them against the neighbourhood boys. They're always bothering me. No one needs a boot in the rear more than Maximus Marius.'

'Who?'

'The garum seller's son. He's always pulling my hair.'

'He's probably just sweet on you,' said Atticus.

'Well, that's no way to show it,' said Gia. 'It hurts. I hate him. Next time, I'll pull his arm right out of the socket.'

'Gia, that's enough,' her mother's voice cut in, accompanied by a worried look. 'No more fighting today, please.' She rubbed at her temples, then the bridge of her nose. 'I have a headache coming on.'

'That would be from all the wine,' whispered Cassius.

Her family continued on along the road towards their home as Gia hung back, sulking. She stared up at the lavish mural on the nearby wall that depicted the emperor's eight-year-old daughter, Claudia, paid for by the imperial cult. She and Gia had been born just three months apart. Claudia was already dressed like a miniature woman, golden-haired and green-eyed in a jewelled headdress, smiling serenely as if she knew something that Gia didn't, which she probably did.

There was something irritating about her face. Her ridiculously pretty face. Gia could just tell that she was supremely annoying.

'I bet the emperor's daughter would be allowed to fight, if she asked,' she said, running to catch up with her brothers. 'She probably wouldn't want to, though. She probably sits on her arse all day long, combing her hair and looking in the mirror.'

'Probably,' said Cassius. 'I'm sure she gets everything she asks for. But you're not really on the same level I'm afraid, sister. Too bad you were born to a humble wine peddler instead of an emperor. Such is life.'

They approached the villa on the corner of Stabiana and Menandro. The taberna her parents ran was on the ground floor, its lively noise raging night and day, though it was closed today for the festival. The taberna was a rectangle on top of a rectangle, a dull tan colour with a thick red stripe painted on the bottom and a mural of the food served inside on the eastern wall. On the ground floor, three arched windows were topped with red-and-white cloth awnings and lined with brown wood shutters.

Gia and her brothers often snuck out onto the balcony after dark, leaning over the stone-carved balustrade so they could listen to the curses and bawdy talk from the customers who filed in and out, their voices getting louder with every pitcher.

In this fashion, Gia saw a new side to their parents, a facet that was unfamiliar: the wide-smiling hosts who flirted and made jokes, proffering bowls of olives and baskets of bread, fawning over the senators Gia had previously heard them complain about.

The arched door was open, leading into a tiled restaurant area with a stone counter and a crumbling mosaic of Gia's parents on the wall. Inside the building, past the burning-hot stove where food was cooked for customers, was an atrium, open to the sky, full of plants and a fountain featuring Neptune's face.

Gia and her brothers ran in and collapsed onto benches. Petals floated on the breeze and drums beat faintly in the distance as her brothers told stories and made jokes about spoiled little Claudia, imagining how the rich lived.

'They say she sleeps on pillows full of goose feathers individually plucked from living beasts,' Cassius said.

'Eight years old and she already has a staff of forty.'

'Must be nice,' Gia grumbled.

She slept on starchy sackcloth hand-me-down sheets covered in sinister stains left behind by her brothers.

'They say she has her own choir who follow her around all day long, singing songs of her glory.'

'And a servant specifically to wipe her arse,' said Cassius.

Gia pulled a disgusted face.

'I think I'd rather do that myself, no matter how rich and powerful I was,' said Atticus, 'if only for dignity's sake.'

'I don't know,' mused Cassius, 'if they gave me a little spritz while they were down there, that could be refreshing.'

The boys laughed. Gia giggled too, although she didn't really understand what they were talking about.

She sat on the bench, listening to the steady trickle of the fountain as she imagined standing in the amphitheatre, thrusting her weapon to the sky as the crowd chanted her name.

She would call herself Viatrix the Victorious. Her skin would be oily, her muscles defined. People would ask for her signature and paint her likeness on walls.

'It's not fair,' she said, turning to face her brothers.

'What isn't?'

'That some people are so rich while others are slaves, that men can fight and women cannot.'

'Those are two different problems.'

'Maybe all the problems are actually just the same problem.'

'Is this your first day on earth, summer child?' said Cassius.

'Don't be bitter, sister,' said Atticus.

'There are far worse things in the world to worry about,' said Cassius. 'Like what will happen if the empire is invaded.'

'Invaded?' Gia echoed.

'You should hear what the generals of the army say when they think we're out of earshot. They'd have us thinking Rome will fall in a day.'

Gia scoffed. She'd never been to Rome, but she'd seen paintings of it. It looked sturdy, as if nothing on earth could move it. Any disaster that had ever befallen it had merely caused cracks that could be easily repaired. Rome was unshakeable. With every catastrophe, it was rebuilt stronger and more formidable in her view.

She aspired to be as immovable.

'The gods will protect us,' said Atticus, 'just as they always do.'

But Gia didn't trust the gods. She wanted to be able to protect herself.

'Atticus,' Gia said cloyingly.

'What?' he grunted, sensing her intention.

'If you show me what you've learned at gladiator school, I'll do your chores for a week,' she tried.

'Do you not understand the meaning of "no", sister?'

'I do, but I don't like the sound of it,' she said.

'Too bad. I'll get in trouble.'

'*Two* weeks, and I'll talk to Rhea next door for you, tell her what a great brother you are,' she countered.

His expression shifted, considering.

'Talk to her first, then maybe I'll think about it.'

Atticus departed, leaving Gia alone with Cassius. He stood up, looking her up and down.

'What?' said Gia, touching her face as if she had something stuck there.

'I might not be a gladiator, but I am a soldier.'

He waited for Gia to catch on, opening her mouth in delight.

'I don't see the harm in showing you some of the moves I was taught, if you're still interested,' he said.

'Am I ever,' she said, bouncing on her heels. 'Let's go.'

Standing six feet apart, Gia watched his feet dancing nimbly as he stretched out his arms and legs. He wasn't bulky like Atticus, but he was speedy and agile with a sharp mind. Gia could not – would not – underestimate him.

She pulled back her messy black hair, catching it with a hair tie to form a ponytail as fraying strands danced around her face. Cassius did the same.

'The first thing to learn is how to defend yourself. If you're lucky, you'll have a shield, but if not, you'll have to use your arm. Hold it up like this, as if it's in a sling.'

Gia copied him, eyes narrowed in concentration. Her face was stony and serious, but her dark eyes glittered with excitement. Up close, she mirrored her brother's determined expression.

'First, make a fist. Keep your thumb on the outside, like so.'

'So I can punch with it?'

'If you have to, but you're better off using your elbow. You can do more damage with an elbow. When your opponent gets close enough, you can move your arm like this, see?'

Gia copied the sharp, jutting movement as Cassius guided her arms into the right position.

'An elbow to the nose hurts like a son of a bitch,' he said. 'If you hear it crack, it's broken. That'll give you time to make your next move.'

'Got it.'

'I'm going to take jabs at you and you're going to fend them off, okay?' Cassius said. 'Don't elbow me in the face, though. It won't help my reputation if I get a black eye from my baby sister. Ready?'

'Ready.' She nodded.

The first hit took her by surprise, striking out like a snake's head. She shimmied backwards, but too late to spare her arm.

When the second strike came, Gia was ready. Her elbow shot out and bumped his jaw, pushing him back. As he nursed it instinctively, Gia ducked and tripped him up with one skinny leg, causing her brother to sprawl on the ground.

Cassius flipped over, sitting on his rear.

'That was ... that was actually pretty good,' he said, grinning.

'Told you I could fight,' said Gia, though she was also surprised.

'Perhaps you're the real warrior of the family. Don't tell Atticus I said that.'

'Try again,' said Gia. 'That was too easy.'

She watched her brother's lips purse, his brow wrinkling, knowing she was baiting him. Gladiators goaded each other in the ring, insulting each other's mothers in the hope that they would be distracted. Perhaps what she lacked in size, she could make up for in spite.

Gia and Cassius resumed their positions, dancing gently on the upper soles of their feet.

'All right, let's try something tougher now,' he said. 'I'm not going to tell you my move in advance this time, so you'll have to react fast.'

'React fast.' She nodded, studiously. 'Got—'

Before she had finished this sentence, Cassius was already upon her, wrestling her to the ground. She pushed back with all her might, locked in a stubborn embrace, but she couldn't break free. Their legs tangled together until she toppled, smashing her chin against the stone bench.

'Shit!' Cassius pulled her upright, inspecting her face. 'You okay?'

Gia's pride was most wounded, but a dribble of blood trickled from the gash in her chin. 'Oops,' she said, unbothered.

'Mother won't be happy,' said Cassius.

'Then don't tell her,' said Gia. 'I'll say I fell down the stairs instead.'

'You are pretty clumsy,' said Cassius.

'I'm not clumsy. It's these sandals,' she protested. 'The soles are all sweaty and slippery. Stupid things.'

'It's not the sandals, it's your skinny girl body,' said Cassius. 'Men have more muscle to protect them.'

'On their chins?' Gia retorted.

'What do you know of physiology, sister?' he said, though his eyes were light, his lips curving at the corners. 'If you want to stand a chance at beating a boy, first you need to train – build up your strength.'

'Let's try it again. I'll beat you this time. Watch me.'

'No, no more,' said Cassius. 'My heart can't take it. Mother will never forgive me if I kill her only daughter.'

'You're not scared, are you?'

'Of Mother? Absolutely.'

She was no warrior, and yet she was fearsome in her own way.

'Well, well,' said Atticus, appearing in the doorway with a smug expression. 'If it isn't the consequences of your own actions. Didn't I tell you it was a bad idea? Now look at you, sister.'

'It's nothing,' said Gia stubbornly.

'You're getting blood on the floor,' said Atticus, indicating the scarlet drops that spattered the stony ground.

'What do you care?' Gia grunted.

'I just don't want you to break a bone or lose a tooth. That won't help with your whole –' he gestured airily – 'problem.'

'What problem?'

'You look like father.'

'Atticus!' scolded Cassius.

'I'm sorry, but it's true. Plain girls have to work even harder to catch men's attention. That's just the way it is.'

Cassius tutted. 'Harsh, brother.'

'And certainly no man wants a wife who threatens to kick him in the balls.'

'Father did,' said Cassius.

'Well, he's the only one.'

Gia had never noticed before, not even when she gazed at her reflection in the fountain's pool, but, now she thought about it, she did have knobbly knees and a nose too big for her face, with scraggly hair that fell about her shoulders. She'd heard what people said about ugly girls. Pretty girls got favours and fortunes in life that others didn't. Doors opened for their charms. People were more forgiving. She wanted to be pretty, like the princess of Rome.

'You think I'm ugly,' she said.

'I didn't say ugly, I said plain,' said Atticus, softening slightly when he noticed her distressed expression.

'Don't listen to him,' said Cassius. 'Atticus is hardly an expert on the topic of attractiveness. He's a beast. I got all the looks in the family, evidently.'

'You got too many looks, I think. It's making your head too large for your body.'

If Gia couldn't be pretty, she'd have to be something else. She needed a different kind of fortune on her side, if she was to survive. No one would mess with her if they were scared of her, if she could fight like men did.

'Let's go again,' she said, more determined this time.

'No, absolutely not,' said Cassius. 'That's enough now.'

'You barely showed me anything.'

'Yet still, you are injured.'

'You really won't help me?' She pouted. 'My own brothers? But how will I become a famous gladiator if I don't practise?'

'You don't want to work a job so dangerous anyway,' said Cassius.

'You'll be a soldier,' Gia protested. 'Soldiers die all the time.'

'It's different.'

'Atticus will be a gladiator.'

'It's different for girls, I mean.'

'But why, though?'

'Be serious, sister,' said Atticus. 'If it were so easy, the streets of Pompeii would be full of female gladiators. There's a reason there are none.'

'Being born a woman has its own privileges,' said Cassius. 'At least you don't have to fight the emperor's wars for him. You should marry a rich old fellow who's not long for this world, wait until he dies and spend your days lazing in the sun, kept full and happy by the denarii he left for you.'

'Sounds dreadful,' said Gia.

'When the time comes, many years from now, just close your eyes and think of Rome,' said Cassius.

'Who cares about Rome?' she said.

'It's just an expression.'

They silenced, listening to an argument erupting between their parents from within the villa. Even though their mother ran the taberna with their father, it was his name painted above the door. It was him people called the owner. People thought of it as his business and her as his employee, even though she handled all the deliveries and accounts.

'If you can't find a husband, you'll have to sell yourself in the wolf den,' said Atticus, as if it were nothing. As if *she* were nothing.

Gia knew what happened in the Den. Not exactly, not the specifics, but she knew it involved men paying women to spend time with them. She'd learned as much from listening to girls talk on corners, or eavesdropping on her brothers.

Gia recalled the screams of the girl who'd been beaten in the street six weeks past, dragged out of the Den half-naked by a customer. Gia had watched from the balcony, too frightened to move or even look away. She'd heard them arguing about money. He'd hit her once, and again. He wouldn't stop, even when she ceased protesting.

Cassius had come out and found Gia, watching in horror as the screaming sound echoed.

'Men take what they want,' her mother had said, when Gia told her about it. 'You must never sell yourself like those girls. You are not a jar of garum or a basket of bread.'

Back in the present, Gia met Cassius's eye.

'I don't want to end up like that brothel girl,' she said.

'What girl?' asked Atticus, but Cassius didn't need an explanation.

He knew. He remembered. It was why she wanted to fight, and it was why he wanted to teach her.

Gia was young, but kids grew up fast in Pompeii. Even then, at the age of eight, Gia knew she would rather die a fighter than give away something she didn't want to. She would kill a man if he tried it with her. She would slit his throat if she had to, and spare him no pity, just like a gladiator.

Gia signalled for Cassius to move back into place.

'Again,' she demanded. 'Fight me again.'

Long ago, Hannibal of Carthage advanced towards Rome with a plan to conquer the eternal city. The known world hailed Hannibal as a military genius and he had sworn Rome as his enemy. The Romans were outnumbered. The Carthaginians had almost one hundred war elephants. The public feared that Hannibal was unbeatable.

The Emperor and the Senate had no solutions, so they turned to the scholars for guidance. Professors at the College recommended a direct appeal to the gods. Twelve human sacrifices were offered, in the form of criminals and virgins.

Twelve harmonious gods appeared to claim their souls, turning them into constellations which they wore as crowns. They showed themselves to the Senate as colossal shining figures with molten eyes, who spoke in voices that echoed for millennia. The gods agreed to aid Rome, but in return they instructed the people to honour them.

The Senate hastily arranged a feast in their name. Beautiful and divine, the gods dined in human form before a select audience of noble mortals, but even in the flesh they were colder than the infinite dark from which they'd been born.

A three-day festival was subsequently held. Many thousands of citizens travelled to the city to worship them, chanting and burning incense as they begged for divine protection in the face of certain defeat.

Yet Hannibal never reached Rome. His advance was halted by the Roman Legion, and his army was forced to retreat.

The Romans understood that the gods had assured their victory, directing from the unknowable heavens. The belief that the gods were their allies gave the Romans the confidence to go forth and conquer the world, and so the Republic became an Empire.

The gods had ruled the world ever since.

The city commissioned gilt statues of the deities in six male-female pairs: Jupiter and Juno, Neptune and Minerva, Mars and Venus, Apollo and Diana, Vulcan and Vesta, Mercury and Ceres, to stand in front of the Pantheon of Rome.

The temple to all gods was closed to the public on holidays when the divine pantheon it was named after were said to gather there. Crowds often congregated in the Forum outside, hoping to catch a glimpse of Venus's girdle or Neptune's trident. Everyone had a favourite deity, and who it was said as much about a person as which senator they supported. The gods too were said to have their favourites: mortals of interest whose lives they influenced.

But the Pantheon was guarded by soldiers, while the deities themselves took various precautions against being spied on.

It was said that whoever was caught trying to intrude on their business would be transformed into an animal, a flower or a tree – if they were lucky.

It was inside the Pantheon that Fortuna, the ancient deity of destiny, requested to meet with the goddesses Diana, Minerva and Venus.

Fortuna was unremarkable at first glance. From one angle she appeared youthful, with the light of Juvenalia shining in her clouded eyes, but from another she was aged, her hair silvered. Her head was shrouded by a filmy grey palla: a long, billowing silk shawl that covered her entire body. She was neither beautiful nor ugly.

She simply was.

Inevitable and unmoving, she stood beneath the coffered concrete dome – a central opening bared wide open to the sky – and dramatically pulled down her hood.

Three other women appeared from behind columns. One tall and armoured, wearing a plumed helmet. She was stern and scholarly, bowing to the woman in the palla. The other was young, pretty and barefoot, wearing only a belted chiton. She issued a wave, less reverential than the first. Finally, came the short-haired huntress in sandals, with a bow and arrow at her back. She officiously circled the perimeter then saluted the elder like a Roman soldier.

'All clear,' she said, with a nod. 'We are alone.'

'Thank you, Diana.'

'Why did you summon us here, Fortuna?' said the youngest, suppressing a yawn. 'And so early? I have yet to eat my ientaculum.'

The helmeted one gave her a sharp look. 'There are things in this world more important than breakfast, Venus,' she said.

'Then I am yet to hear of them, Minerva.'

'That is enough, girls. Pay attention now,' said Fortuna.

Fortuna was not one of the Twelve. She was far more ancient and powerful. She had existed before the idea of them, and she would continue to exist long after they ceased to be: the living embodiment of destiny itself.

'I wished for us to meet before the rest of the Twelve arrive, so we may speak in private. You three are the only ones I can trust, and even then, with considerable reservations,' said Fortuna, her eyes lingering on Venus.

'You wish for us to keep secrets from Jupiter?' asked Diana.

'I have spun the wheel,' said Fortuna, in a voice that echoed through the colossal building. 'I have had a vision. I have glimpsed through the veil of time and space and seen a grave warning, a dark portent, of things yet to come.'

Fortuna moved her hand just so and patterns formed in the dust, caught in the rays of sun that poured through the oculus. The motes spun and swirled, forming the face of a balding man wearing a crown of leaves.

Fortuna's eyes were unseeing. She couldn't perceive him physically, but she traced the dust with the lightest graze of her fingertips, reading him in her mind where her vision was intact. She saw a vision of his last moments, clutching at his neck, foam slipping from purple lips as a stretched shadow cast over him.

The others watched as his face emerged, the dust gathering until it became solid like a bust of marble, suspended in the air and revolving slowly before it crumbled into dust once again.

'The emperor will be murdered,' summarized Fortuna.

'Not again,' said Minerva, with a world-weary sigh. Ever since Julius Caesar, the mortal empire had been a never-ending bloodbath.

'Tiberius will be betrayed by one of his own,' said Fortuna.

'Aren't they all?' said Venus. 'It is an occupational hazard.'

'What's the issue? Don't tell me you feel sorry for him?' said Diana.

'I pity all mortals, for their lives are short and miserable, but Vulcan is the emperor's patron,' said Fortuna. 'This betrayal will enrage the god of fire ... even more than usual. Vulcan has long been at odds with Jupiter. The premature death of Tiberius, the mortal he has guided since childhood, will finally cause him to blow his top. His anger shall bleed from the Earth. There will be war.'

Venus rolled her eyes. 'He is all smoke and no fire.'

Vulcan had pursued her aggressively, but she'd resisted, drawn instead to the toxic charms of Mars, god of war. According to Diana, her taste in men was appalling, but then Diana was a fan of no man.

'I think the expression is, there is no smoke without fire,' corrected Minerva.

'Vulcan may be an insufferable old hermit,' said Venus, ignoring her, 'but he isn't foolish enough to start a war with Jupiter.'

'Do not speak too soon,' said Minerva. 'We all remember what happened in Etna when they last quarrelled. Jupiter burned down his forge. Vulcan had to rebuild it in Pompeii. He has been holding a grudge ever since.'

'The emperor will be betrayed, you say?' asked Diana, turning to Fortuna. 'By that terrible son of his, I presume?'

Fortuna paused, closing her eyes and looking inward.

'Yes, the emperor's son, Decimus, is sponsored by Jupiter,' she replied. 'When Emperor Tiberius is murdered, Vulcan's era will be over. Jupiter will ensure that Decimus inherits his father's position, with the help of the imperial cult. Vulcan will see it as a deliberate attack against him, reigniting the feud between them.'

'So Vulcan and Jupiter will argue and the world gets another terrible emperor,' said Venus. 'What else is new?'

'It is far more serious than that. If Decimus rules, it will set in motion a series of cascading events. Jupiter's arrogance makes him an unsuitable patron, and Decimus is void of any sentiment. The combination will be disastrous for Rome. Jupiter will push Decimus to advance the empire beyond its bounds, causing it to collapse. I see a future in which us gods are absent from the world entirely.'

'Gone?' gasped Venus. 'Where would we go?'

'We are Roman deities. If Rome should fall, we will be forgotten. We only exist for as long as there are people to believe in us.'

The goddesses paled and fell quiet. They couldn't imagine not existing, just as it was difficult for mortals to conceive that they were once unborn.

'We would be unable to influence human society, for better or worse.'

It was unthinkable. Humans weren't known for their great wisdom.

'When?' asked Minerva. 'When will the emperor die?'

'For as long as Proserpina spends under the sun each year. For half a turn of Anna Perenna,' said Fortuna.

'Why must we always talk in riddles?' asked Venus.

'In six cycles of the moon; just a heartbeat in immortal time.'

Another moment of silence filled the chamber.

'This could be the beginning of the end,' said Fortuna. 'The fury of Vulcan. The rise of Decimus. The fall of the empire. The great wastes of the dark age. A war in the heavens that will sever the pantheon in two and destroy the mortal realm.'

'If it is so, then we cannot stop it,' said Venus. 'How are we to stand against destiny and the king of the gods?'

'This is how I know you pay no mind to my teachings,' said Minerva.

'Not true. I listen ... occasionally.'

'Fate is not set in stone like the pieces of a mosaic,' Fortuna said. 'Fate is malleable, like clay. There is yet time to rework it.' She smiled at the gathered goddesses. 'We are deities, after all.'

'What do you suggest?' asked Minerva.

'The emperor is sure to die, but we can prevent his son from seizing power,' said Fortuna. 'We goddesses must form an opposition. We must have a contender to challenge Decimus . . . and Jupiter, too.'

'But who?' Diana queried.

'Minerva, are you not the patron of the emperor's daughter?' asked Fortuna.

'Claudia. I am indeed. She has prayed to me on many nights.'

'What do you make of her? Tell us honestly.'

Minerva hummed, tilting her head back and forth. 'She is brighter than the gods would give her credit for, and she would be a far better ruler than her brother.'

'But?' said Diana. 'I sense a but.'

'She is hungry for power, believing herself superior to all the men around her. She could be ruthless. She is kissed by Venus, as they say,' said Minerva. 'The men of Rome worship her as if she is one of us.'

Venus gave a little envious huff, turning her back.

'The gods are certain that a woman will never rule Rome, yet I see a future in which she could be its empress instead,' said Fortuna.

'You are serious?' said Minerva, rapt.

'A woman would rule Rome?' said Diana.

'The first empress of the empire. The vision is faint, but it is there. She may lead our world into a better era, but she cannot do it alone. She is powerful in her own way, but she is not a fighter. She will require a warrior to battle for her. A warrior of great name and stature, like you, Diana.'

Diana's cheeks coloured with pride.

'A warrior who would give their life to save hers. A warrior to kneel at her feet and give her their very soul,' said Fortuna, 'just as Venus herself would.'

Venus perked up at this, looking back over her shoulder with interest.

'A soldier of the Legion?' asked Minerva.

'No ... a gladiator,' said Fortuna, as if the vision she saw was clearing, like the sky after a storm. 'I can't see their face, but I see victory, grief, fire, blood and ... love.'

'Love?' said Venus, clasping her hands together in excitement. 'All right, fine, now I'm listening.'

ACT I

DIANA

FORTUNA

MINERVA

VENUS

1. TO BE BURNED

Twelve days after her brother Atticus died, Gia washed and dressed in the bathroom, pulling on the thin undergarments of her fascia and wrapping her body in a plain wool tunic, cinching it with a leather belt.

She was ready to greet the world again.

Gia had grown into her face. If ever she'd been ugly, as Atticus had once claimed, it was a thing of the past. At seventeen, her nose was the perfect size. The hair that had once been straggly was scraped back into a neat braid. Though she still dreamed of cutting it short like the goddess Diana's, she grew it out in memory of her other brother, Cassius. When she tossed her long locks in the polished metal mirror, she briefly saw his face in hers. She feared that one day she might forget what he looked like, or that she might forget herself in turn.

Unintentionally, she had taken his advice, building her strength through the weight of responsibility. Her knees, though cut and bruised from weeks of labour, were no longer knobbly, but in line with her calves and thighs. Her legs were shapely from running back and forth at the taberna. She was tall and fit, and her biceps were hard, but she was still a woman, and that was all that mattered in Pompeii.

Gia had spent her whole life in the city, and she loved it with all that was left of her heart. She loved the chorus of animals and drunkards that rang through the night. She loved how busy and bustling it was at any given hour, and the calendar of festivals that broke up the annum. She even loved the rancid smell of sewerage mixed with grilling meat from the smoky corner stalls. But Pompeii was also the setting of her life's tragedies. Every street reminded her of her losses, every pavestone reminded her of the world's shortcomings.

Pompeii was still a prison for a woman like her. There were no female senators. Only the goddesses wielded true power and they didn't reveal themselves, perhaps because they knew some plebian would insult them with a cat-call.

The men of Pompeii would harass Venus herself, if only they had the chance.

It was just Gia and the living ghost of her mother now, with no one to spar with. She kept fit by lugging sacks of grain and legumes up the cellar stairs, by sweating in front of the burning fornax, by ferrying back and forth between the tables of red-faced, loud-mouthed customers who were never satisfied, no matter what she did. At dawn, when the taberna closed, she'd smoke and drink and play knucklebones with the other employees. They'd crack jokes and tell stories about the gods misbehaving. But they were not friends, and they were not brothers.

Nothing was the same, nor would it ever be again.

Gia was so lonely she reconsidered her opinion of the Den. From a distance, the workers were a welcoming sisterhood, arms around each other as they walked the streets looking for clients. They fed vagrants and stray cats. On one occasion, they comforted her as she sobbed for her brother on the stoop outside. On another, a girl named Berenice had given her a slice of the cake she'd made for her own birthday. If she joined them, she would have a new family to love and protect her.

But she'd promised her mother that she'd never be a Den girl. Being a man was dangerous enough – to which her brothers could attest – but being a woman was far more perilous. The thought of letting a stranger touch her made her hurt worse. She had sacrificed too much already to let wretched men take her body as well. Her desire to fight was stronger than ever, the fury inside her growing horns and teeth.

In her quiet moments, Gia still imagined herself as Viatrix the Victorious, holding her sword aloft as the audience cried her name. She kept dreaming, for Cassius's sake. 'It's good to have dreams' – that's what he'd said.

When the sun hung directly overhead, casting long shadows from the olive trees on the horizon, it was time to leave the house. Gia passed the dark room where her mother sat staring at the wall.

'I'm going out now,' she said. 'To meet Cyrus.'

Her mother nodded slightly, to acknowledge that she had heard, but she said nothing. Her robes were stained, her hair dishevelled. Gia was glad of her silence, preferring it to the slurred strings of rantings and ravings she had taken to lately.

'Make sure you're back to open up,' was all her mother said.

Lately, Gia had been running the taberna by herself, much to the dissatisfaction of the regulars who found her rude and slow, an inferior chef.

Out in the atrium, Gia sat on the stone bench as she tied her sandals, listening to the spluttering of the fountain.

She stared at two matching tombstones, one for each brother.

She could still remember the day Cassius had first taught her how to fight, right here. She ran her fingers over the scar on her chin, barely visible now. Her mother had found out, of course. Atticus had told on them and Cassius been punished for leading her astray. But they had all laughed together that night over dinner, her father proud to have such a tough little girl, he said.

Gia's eyes stung bitterly, her throat constricting as if a serpent had wrapped around it, squeezing ever tighter.

The smaller, newer gravestone was carved with a gladiatorial scene, showing Atticus with a broken neck as his sparring partner wept, still dusty from the engraver's work. An accident in the amphitheatre. It was meant to be a friendly fight, but fate had intervened, like a giant invisible hand descending from the skies to crush him.

Life and death were the domain of the pantheon. The Fates decided who would die, how and when, cutting the lengths of thread with which they spun tapestries of destiny. It was a sick and wicked world that turned people to dust in a blink, but, for the most part, Gia accepted it. Such was the way of fortune. It was cruel, but it was beyond human control.

No. It was Cassius's death that made her bitter.

The larger, older stone was engraved with a battle scene depicting the barbarian Brits who'd torn her other brother to pieces. Nothing left of Cassius but the ring his commander sent home, his blood still splattered on the brass.

The thought of it turned Gia's stomach, took her knees out.

Cassius had always been her favourite, and though she'd never have admitted it out loud, she was certain that he knew it too.

She could still hear his jubilant laughter, imagining his clownish expression as he cracked some wry joke.

Dead for nothing, dead in the name of the empire, and what difference did it make? He should've stayed and been the playboy of a rich old Roman, like he wanted. The emperor whose wars Cassius had fought was oblivious to his existence, to his sacrifice. The army hadn't even paid to bury him, leaving her mother to struggle.

Behind them was her father's gravestone, weeds already sprouting shaggily around the stone, illustrated with a carving of a decanter of wine. He was five years gone. A disease of the liver had taken him, swiftly and without mercy.

Her mother had begged the gods to spare him, but his death had already been decided, or so Gia assumed from their silence, for no attempt at summoning the pantheon to reprimand them had been successful.

She imagined descending to the underworld like the heroes of myth to retrieve the shades of her family and bring them home, but she knew they would never be the same; that their souls were gone.

Her eyes rested on the brass fixture on the wall, a wheel of fortune with the goddess of destiny atop it. Blindfolded and holding a sword, she symbolized the turn of fate, from good to bad to good and back again.

'Fuck Fortuna,' Gia murmured, hoping the goddess was listening. 'What kind of destiny did you give me?'

They were dangerous words, but she stood by them. She needed someone to blame, and the ancient goddess of fortune and misfortune seemed like a fair enough target. She didn't even know Gia existed anyway.

Squaring her shoulders, Gia stood up and marched on along Via Stabiana towards the ludus.

Her brother's tutor, Cyrus, had promised to return Atticus's things. Wishing to issue his condolences in person, he'd invited her mother to share a drink in his honour – out of guilt, probably. But her mother hadn't stepped outside in weeks, all through the sweat of early summer. She lay in bed with the shutters drawn until it was dark, waking only to buy more wine.

Gia would fetch them herself.

On her way, Gia passed the mural of the emperor's daughter, updated to depict her now-eighteen-year-old form.

She had an angelic face that reminded Gia of a cupid, her hair elaborately curled. Her ruffled dress was fastened with a girdle, her stola embroidered with flowers. A jewel hung in the centre of her forehead.

She seemed to catch Gia's eye, but her painted smile was met with a scowl.

'Fuck you too,' said Gia.

Her father had ordered Cassius to be sent to Britannia and she had probably benefited from it, somehow. His blood had paid for her luxuries. His life had been the cost of her bliss. She symbolized everything Gia despised.

Picking up a sharp-edged stone, Gia carved a vulgar word in the cracking paint underneath her portrait.

ORAPUTIDE. *Mouth-stinker.*

She probably did have bad breath too, from eating all that rich-person food. It was childish, but it made her feel better.

The emperor and his heir were painted on the wall opposite:

one red-nosed and balding like Bacchus, the other young and handsome in a gaunt and ghoulish way, with the flat gaze of a dead fish.

The emperor's wife had died the year before her father, but Gia felt no empathy. The imperial family did not suffer as she suffered. They did not grieve as she grieved. Their power and money protected them from the worst of the world.

RUCTABUNDE, she carved beneath the boy. It meant *gas bag*, or *full of burps*. If Claudia was spoiled, then Decimus was rotten. Rumours told that he tortured his servants.

She began to carve another rude word beneath the emperor's portrait, one so rude it felt illicit even to speak it in her mind, when she heard a sudden voice.

'What are you doing?'

Gia turned to see the shopkeeper, staring at the jagged stone in her hand. His eyes drifted to the words she'd carved.

'You little shit!'

She was gone before he could scold her, long legs striding down the street and hurtling around the corner. She disappeared into the stink and din of the city.

Ass-pulled carts rumbled over the uneven pavements, loaded with bruised fruits. Sellers called out from open doors, advertising the imported wares of merchants, like tins of poppyseed and rolls of linen. On the corner, women in gaudy orange togas huddled on corners, inching up their hems as a group of soldiers walked past.

'Gia!' One of the younger girls raced over, almost being mown down by a chariot. 'Whoops!' Her curly black hair was piled up on top of her head, and her eyes were ringed with kohl.

'Hello, Berenice,' said Gia. 'How's business?'

'Not so bad.' She jingled the bag thrown over her shoulder as she fell in line with Gia, walking at pace. 'Last night's customer was a famous wealthy Roman.'

'Who?'

'I cannot say. He swore me to secrecy.' She clutched at her chest, giddily. 'But he paid me thrice as much as the thieves around here *and* he gifted me this lovely shell necklace from Phoenicia. Isn't it pretty? See? See?'

She held it up for Gia to admire, and though it wasn't her sort of thing, she was happy that Berenice seemed so pleased with it.

'Nice. Did he treat you well?'

'He was gentle after. He even wept.'

Gia didn't know what to think about that.

'He confided his secrets in me. You wouldn't believe me if I told you.'

Berenice was a runaway whose history was a mystery. She said only that her family had hurt her many more times than she could live with. Gia quietly suspected that she might be insane, but she liked her anyway.

'Where are you off to?' asked Berenice.

'The ludus,' said Gia. 'The master wants to give my brother's things back.'

'Oh. That's . . .'

'Depressing? I know.'

'How's your mother?'

'Terrible.'

Berenice gently patted her shoulder. 'I'm here for you, friend.'

'You should steer clear.'

'Never.'

'I wouldn't blame you,' said Gia. 'I'm not the best company right now, nor am I in Fortuna's favour.'

'Fuck Fortuna, right? That's what you told me when I was heartbroken over the hunk from Gaul,' said Berenice. 'What has she ever done for us?'

'We're alive,' said Gia.

'Is that all?'

For the rest of the walk, Berenice talked about her mysterious new lover and how she was drawn to him on a deep spiritual level, how this might be the good fortune she was overdue. Gia was just glad for something else to think about, even if Berenice did have a habit of repeating herself.

'This is it,' said Berenice, when they pulled up in front of the modest building known as the ludus. 'I'm going to the shrine of Venus. Maybe if I venerate her enough, she'll make me pregnant with the Roman's baby and I can quit work.'

Gia frowned and scratched her head.

'I know,' said Berenice with a shrug. 'Just let me have this.'

It was a bad idea, but off she went to do it anyway, skipping down the street. Gia watched her go, sighing and feeling older than her years. She couldn't imagine acting so heady over some silly boy, but maybe her heart was all dried up from grief. It seemed that way sometimes, like it was difficult to feel anything at all.

The gladiator school comprised of several small buildings, set back in a dusty courtyard. The street-facing front had a triangular pediment painted in faded red and gold with murals of famous fights on either side. To the right, a terraced gymnasium with an upper walkway looked out onto the courtyard, where boys in gladiatorial gear practised sword fighting.

The ludus hadn't been repaired since the last earthquake. Dusty, with a broken shutter out front, its walls were daubed with graffiti even more explicit than the insults Gia had scratched. She crossed the courtyard, towards the stone arch that marked the entrance.

A group of boys stood out front, blocking the door.

Gia groaned inwardly.

There were four of them, including a tall, broad-shouldered youth with a shaved head who stared at her. She had seen those looks before. She knew what happened next. Gia hesitated before pushing forwards, listening to the end of their conversation.

'So then she said, "can my friend join us"?' announced a red-haired boy with the exuberant presence of an actor.

'She did not.'

'She did, so I said, "sure, the more the merrier" and screwed them both. At the same time.'

'You're such a liar, Felix,' said a boy with black skin as he folded his arms.

'You sound jealous, Dominic.'

'I'm not jealous because you're full of shit.'

Red-haired Felix whistled at Gia as she passed. A chubby boy with curly hair made obnoxious kissy noises. Dominic pulled what Gia interpreted as an apologetic face. But the boy with the shaved head stood in her path.

'Hello,' he said menacingly.

Gia ignored him, trying to push past, but he stepped right and blocked the way again. 'Not going to say it back?'

'Hello,' said Gia, in a very unenthusiastic voice.

'Rude. Why don't you stop and say hello to my friend here?' He clutched suggestively at his crotch. 'He's pleased to see you.'

If this idiot wanted to play, then Gia was ready to play.

Staring in the direction of his groin, she said, 'Oh sorry, my mistake. I didn't see you there, *little* guy.' She gave it a wave. 'You're so small, so easy to miss.'

The boys whooped and hollered, flashing wide-eyed looks.

'Watch out, lads,' said the curly-haired boy. 'We got ourselves a shit talker.'

'I like them angry,' said Felix.

'Now, get out of my way,' said Gia.

'We're just being friendly.'

'Is that what you call it?'

Gia pushed him to one side, hard enough that he staggered.

'Watch it, bitch,' he warned.

She glared at him, reminding herself that murder would be inconvenient, messy. She was halfway through the door when she heard:

'Hey, isn't that Skidmark's sister?'

'Who?' asked Dominic.

'You know, the gladiator who died in an accident,' said shaved head, with a note of disgust.

Gia paused just out of sight, flushing hot and cold.

'Oh yeah,' said the curly-haired one, nonchalantly.

'Got his neck broken in a friendly, didn't he? I recognize her now. I saw her at one of his matches.'

'That's too bad,' said Felix.

'It figures that she's just as stupid as him.'

'Why did they call him that?' asked Dominic.

'Because he had a skid mark in his loincloth one day and everyone saw it. One of the boys ripped it off and passed it around for us to laugh at,' said Felix.

'He was a chicken shit,' said the shaven head. 'He fought like a girl anyway.'

The grief and rage of Atticus's death reared up inside Gia like a wild horse's head, baring its teeth, dark eyes manic. Without warning, she spun around and launched herself through the door, grabbing the boy by the collar of his tunic and slamming him against the wall.

'Say it again,' she said.

She wasn't sure which enraged her more: her dead brother being called a skid mark, or that girls fighting was considered an insult.

Shocked, the boy swung at her, scrapping, trying to pry her off, but she was unnaturally strong, as if the presence of a goddess had momentarily entered her. The others fell silent, though Felix suppressed a grin at the corners of his mouth.

'Say it again,' Gia demanded, pulling back one arm. 'Say it again and I'll wipe the words off your lips with my fist.'

'Get off me, ass-face!'

'What's his name?' she said, turning to Felix.

'Don't tell her,' said the boy she'd pinned.

'Fabius,' said Dominic quickly.

'Listen to me, *Fabius*. If you speak to me like that once more, you'll have bigger problems than the empty wasp's nest you call a head.'

A chortle of laughter rang out from the curly-haired boy.

'I don't know what your problem is, but cross me again and you'll be the one leaving skid marks,' she said.

Fabius hissed at her through his teeth. 'I'll slap that smirk right off your face.'

'Go ahead, and I'll tell all the local girls how terrible you were in the sack. I'm sure they'll have no trouble believing me.'

Fuming, Fabius swung at her again.

Gia ducked, stepping aside so he fell flat on his face. When he scrambled up, she grabbed his neck and pushed him down, but Fabius caught her ankle, twisting it and pulling her with him. As they rumbled on the floor in thrashing movements, Gia managed to free one leg, kneeing him hard in the groin as he pulled at her hair, both of them grunting and snarling.

Impulsively, Gia jutted out her elbow, thinking of Cassius as his nose cracked. Fabius yelped and twisted out of her grip, hands cupping his face as blood trickled through his fingers.

'You broke my fucking nose.'

The other boys goggled at her, surprised. Gia expected to feel regretful but instead she felt that same glorious revulsion she'd experienced after watching Thaddeus's eye being popped out.

'How does it feel, loser?' she said.

'I didn't lose yet,' said Fabius.

He lunged again, both of them rolling on the ground as the boys formed a circle around them, fists and feet flying. The curly-haired boy started clapping.

'Break it up!' came a voice.

The others shrank backwards at once.

'What's going on here?'

Gia looked up, wiping dirt out of her eyes, to see the man she knew as Cyrus. She had only seen him from a distance before, cheering on Atticus during fights. Muscular, with dark skin and short, tight curls, he had a face much kinder than she'd expected, with dimples and tender eyes. He wore a short woollen cape around his shoulders, with rusted armour beneath, and he walked with a slight limp.

Cyrus was not just a former gladiator and a teacher at the ludus, nor just the boys' trainer and mentor. He was also the one who placed bets on gladiators.

If they lived, he made money, and if they died, he went hungry. The ludus was afforded by such windfalls, allowing them to train another generation of boys into fighting men. Some would even go on to protect the imperial family.

'Gia?' he said.

She nodded, shamefully.

She guessed Cyrus to be about thirty or so, though he could've been younger, aged by the tribulations of life.

He gripped the back of Fabius's tunic, pulling him up and throwing him aside. The boy slumped against a pillar, cradling his face.

'You will stay behind after class and clean the latrines as punishment for your lack of discipline,' he said.

'But, Cyrus, she—'

'I don't give a rotten fig. She's here as my guest. If I can but teach you one thing, Fabius, it's to treat others with respect.'

'What about me? She broke my damn nose!'

Cyrus looked him over, casually.

'It will give your face character,' he said.

'Godsdamn. My mother will be furious.'

'Then I'll tell her what you said to deserve it. I know your mother and, despite the way you turned out, she's a fine woman who wouldn't stand for it.'

Fabius swallowed, averting his eyes.

'Go fetch some cold meat from the cellar and hold it up to your face to reduce the swelling; Lucas will help you. Go on.'

He nodded at the chubby curly-haired boy, who groaned. Fabius grumbled something inaudible, muttering all the way down the hall as Lucas followed behind.

'Gia, please come with me.'

Cyrus crooked one finger at her, flashing a friendly smile. She followed. Inside, the floor was tiled with mosaics depicting fighting figures. He led them into the room that served as his office. This was the room with the broken shutter. There were gleaming trophies on shelves and in alcoves, and many hand-drawn portraits of gladiators painted on the walls, each one signed with their name.

Cyrus took a seat on the wicker couch piled with cushions and throws, which formed a right-angled nook with another couch. He gently fondled the leaves of a plant, which hung in a basket suspended by woollen strings.

'I do apologize about Fabius,' he said. 'Bit of a mad dog. Mostly bark, but also a little bite.'

'I'm not scared of him,' Gia replied.

'I see that ... I'm sorry about your brother,' he said, softly.

'Me too.'

'I feel responsible.'

'Why? You didn't force him to fight.'

'No, but he was always trying to prove something. He never felt good enough. I don't know who he was trying to impress, but I don't think he ever succeeded in it.' Cyrus shook his head. 'Maybe there was something I could've done to prepare him better. More training, a better speech of encouragement, nicer lodgings ...'

He rubbed his face wearily, showing off the marks on his wrists. They were manacle scars, marking him a freed slave.

'I let him down,' he said.

'It was an accident,' said Gia.

'The worst kind.'

'Then there's nothing for you to cry over.'

'Here,' he said, pulling out a wooden box and handing it to her. Gia looked down, as the room seemed to tilt and groan beneath her feet.

It was full of her brother's belongings. His sandals and tunic, a bag of coins, and ... her name, engraved on a stone.

Her eyes filled. Gia bit her bottom lip, holding the tears back, and reached into the box to pick it up. She tossed the smooth pebble up and down, too scared to hold it tight.

'Oh,' she whispered.

'I'm so sorry,' he said.

The engraving on Atticus's tombstone flashed behind her eyes, his opponent weeping because he hadn't meant to kill him. None of it was on purpose. But that only made it worse. He could've lived.

He *should've* lived.

'I watched him die, Gia,' said Cyrus, as if mirroring her thoughts. 'I've seen men die before, plenty of them, but ... not like this. Young boy like that with his whole life ahead of him ... such a waste. Even his opponent was destroyed by it. He hasn't fought since. Fortuna wasn't feeling merciful that day.'

His hands were shaking. Up close, she could see the dark half-moons beneath his eyes. He reached out for a clay decanter and poured himself a chalice of wine, then he nodded at the second, empty, cup.

'You in?'

'Sure.'

Gia had a complicated relationship with the vine. She'd developed a taste for it, but it was also the poison rotting away her mother.

No good. The worst side of her won out. She was hurting and she wanted to forget the pain. She wanted to be a kid again, spying from the balcony, fighting with her brothers in the atrium.

She downed the glass Cyrus poured for her, warmth rushing to her cheeks, then held the empty glass out expectantly.

Cyrus smirked, impressed. Gia felt her head lightening. It was much stronger than the watered-down stuff her mother sold at the taberna.

'Got yourself some moves out there.' Cyrus raised one dark brow, downing his wine before refilling the cup immediately, and hers.

'You think?'

'Who taught you?'

'My brother, Cassius,' said Gia, sipping slower now.

'Interesting,' said Cyrus.

'But also from watching the gladiators at the amphitheatre. Mostly on holidays,' she added.

'Who's your favourite fighter?'

Gia didn't need to think about it. 'Celadus.'

Cyrus chuckled into his chalice.

'Celadus the Handsome, huh? All the girls like him best – fancy that,' he said, after taking a long drink. 'I hear even the emperor's daughter favours him.'

'Not like that,' said Gia, face souring. 'He's not as big as the others, but he's graceful. It's admirable, how he weaves like a reed. Watching him fight is like dancing. It makes me think …' She chickened out of ending this sentence. 'Never mind.'

Cyrus watched her carefully. 'You want to fight?' he intuited.

Gia squirmed. 'What did Atticus tell you?' she said.

'Nothing. Just a feeling I got.'

'Don't laugh,' she said, staring down at her lap, 'but when I was a kid, I wanted to be a gladiator. It always seemed so stupid to me that women aren't allowed to fight when so many of us have this rage inside us. Endless rage. The kind men shall never know or understand.'

Cyrus said nothing, waiting for her to finish her train of thought.

'Sometimes, I'd hang around the amphitheatre after a match and ask the winner to teach me. They usually just laughed at me, honestly. Some of them had some more colourful words to share. I tried the losers instead, but even then ... I never had any takers. So it goes.'

She grew anxious waiting for him to respond. Gia began to wish she'd never said anything, but the wine was making her careless.

'What about now?' Cyrus said.

'What *about* now?' she replied.

'Do you still want to be a gladiator?'

'I have bigger problems,' she said, 'like how I'm going to keep the taberna open and look after the wreck of my mother.'

'Money's tight, huh?'

'Tighter than Lady Lando's purse strings.'

Cyrus chuckled again at this reference to the brothel owner, a coin-counter and corner-cutter. They called her the Mother Wolf.

Everyone knew: you didn't fuck with Lady Lando.

'You were really beating Fabius's ass out there,' he said. 'I admit, I waited for a moment before I called it off. I was impressed.'

'You were watching?'

'You picked up a thing or two from young Celadus,' he said, 'if not a burning lust for his sculpted abs. You dance when you fight too. Did you know that?'

'I don't know ... It's not like I've watched myself.'

'Okay, then how do you feel, when you fight?'

Gia wet her wine-stained lips, her head swimming. Her tongue was loose and she was off-guard.

'Like I'm floating ... like I'm free.'

'So you enjoyed hurting him?' asked Cyrus. 'Fabius.'

'Can you blame me?'

'Not at all. Smug little shit. He's not usually too bad in the ring, but I think you threw him off.'

'He's afraid of little old me?'

'He was shaken, quaking in his sandals.' Cyrus said this lightly, but there was a ring of truth in his voice. 'He definitely wasn't expecting you to break his nose. Not normally something I'd condone, but I think I can make an exception on this occasion.'

'What's his problem?'

'How long do you have? His father was a brute, his mother works at the Den. He has a chip on his shoulder. I try to hold pity for him, but ... he makes it difficult. He doesn't see women as equal in nature.'

'Does anyone?' Gia asked.

'Me,' he said. 'That's why I want to give you a chance.'

'A chance ... to do what?'

'To fight.'

A breath caught in Gia's throat, causing her to cough, splutter and choke.

'You okay?' Cyrus clapped her on the back as she attempted to gain control of herself, eyes watering.

'Fight? In the amphitheatre?' she croaked.

'If we get that far,' Cyrus said. 'We'd have to see how training goes.'

'Are you mad? Has the moon goddess converted you to lunacy?'

'A little, but not right now. Right now, I have never been saner,' he said.

'Just because I punched that idiot in the face doesn't mean I'd last a minute in the arena. I don't know the first thing about fighting.'

'Your best chance of staying alive is staying upright. Can you do that?'

'I guess?'

'Then you're no different to any of the boys who turn up here with legs like a stork's, still warm from their mother's bosom, begging me to shape them into the world's greatest warrior. Perhaps the flash of brilliance I witnessed outside was a mere fluke, or perhaps you are a natural, destined for great brutality. There is but one way to find out, don't you agree?'

Gia waited for him to laugh and say he was just teasing her, like her brothers used to, but he didn't.

'You can train here in the day and return to the taberna by night. I won't charge you a fee, and, if you win a match, you'll get a cut.'

'Why would you do that?'

'Which answer do you want?' Cyrus asked. 'The encouraging one, or the selfish one? Both are true.'

'The selfish one,' said Gia.

'I think I can make money from a woman gladiator. Times are changing. Soldiers returning from around the world tell stories of women warriors. It could be the new fashion. Perhaps at first you will be nothing but a novelty, drawing a crowd who merely see you as a spectacle, a curiosity, but eventually the battles of women gladiators could become a recognized sport. You can show the world that women can fight just as hard as men, as I know they can.'

Gia luxuriated in the idea. It still seemed like a trick, too good to be true, but she was falling for it. Tempted. She could feel that same bubble of hope swelling in her chest and sticking in her throat, just like when she was a child.

'And the encouraging answer?' she asked.

'You seem like a good kid, you can fight, and I want to help you. I want to see women do all the things men can, if only to share the load of the world's weight.'

'So, what do you say?' pressed Cyrus.

'I ... I don't want your pity,' Gia said. 'If you're lying to me because you feel sorry for me, I would ask that you didn't.'

'No pity. Merely seizing the opportunity. Let us say that your brother owes me some money and you're here to work off the debt.'

'Did he really?'

'No, but we can tell people that, if it makes you feel better that way. If you need an excuse, let this be it.'

Gia considered it. What else did she have to hope for? Being the first female gladiator in Pompeii was something to aspire to. Maybe the world could change, after all. Maybe she could help to change it. It was good to have dreams, Cassius was right about that, but what distinguished a dream from a delusion?

'When you are ready, you must take the Gladiators' Oath.' Cyrus stood up, fishing a knife from a drawer as Gia stiffened.

'Don't worry. We used to give our blood as a promise, but it's fallen out of favour these days. The knife is just for effect.'

Gia had never expected to receive such an offer, and likely never would again. Her childhood fantasy was on the brink of coming true and all she had to do was say yes. There was nothing to stop her, no fear to tame her, nothing she dreaded more than the loss she had already lived through, not even her own death.

She could go out fighting.

That was her choice.

Legs shaking, Gia stood up, her head thick and heavy.

'I'm ready,' she said.

Cyrus nodded, clearly pleased. 'Then you must repeat after me: I endure to be burned...'

'I endure to be burned.'

He placed the knife on her left shoulder.

'... To be bound,' he said.

'To be bound,' she echoed.

Her heart pounded as he moved the blade to her right shoulder.

'I endure to be beaten...'

'I endure to be beaten.'

The words came out course, hushed.

He lifted the point of the knife to her head, holding it up to her forehead but not touching the skin.

'... And to be killed by the sword.'

'And to be killed by the sword,' she whispered.

'Uri, vinciri, verberari, ferroque necari.'

'Uri, vinciri, verbarari, ferroque necari.'

Rome may have been the eternal city on Earth, but, in the heavens above, it was Elysium. The capital city of the gods was so colossal it made Roman monuments look like wooden building blocks. Its statues were built with an iridescent gold that reflected the rainbow spectrum, studded with gemstone eyes in every colour. Its domes were the size of moons, its stony towers as tall as mountains.

Here, each deity had a palace of their own, with the residences of the Twelve forming a ring around the giant colosseum known as the Arena. Diana's palace was situated in a sacred woodland grove roamed by centaurs. The palace of Venus was built of many glimmering shells with glittering pools where she was waited on by sea nymphs. As the goddess of wisdom, Minerva's palace doubled as a library. Its walls were shelved with an infinite matrix of books. Even its pillars were shaped like scholars, holding scripts and scrolls like weapons. Owls flapped in the rafters, while her desk was cluttered with maps and battle plans.

Minerva watched the Earth for signs through a polished shield, waiting until the mortal sun sank below the horizon and the human moon rose high and round and bright to take its place. A deity like her could not simply appear in the flesh. Many had lost their minds at such a sight. She could only communicate through visions, through hallucinations and dreams.

Only when the human consciousness drifted through the liminal world between life and death, wake and sleep, could she reach out to them.

Minerva passed through the archway at the rear of her study, stepping into pitch darkness. She followed the shining trail ahead, a road of glittering stardust.

It led her to Claudia, daughter of the emperor Tiberius.

The princess was dreamwalking through the fields of pallid, ghostly flowers that carpeted the underworld. Human souls travelled here as they slept, roaming the in-between in search of signs or meaning, though they rarely recalled it when they awoke.

'Claudia Caesaria,' said Minerva.

The princess turned, her face soft and shining with rapture.

'My goddess,' breathed Claudia.

Minerva slowly approached her as the scene around them wasted away, replaced with dunes of black sand beneath an ever-twilit sky.

'My child.'

'You have shown yourself to me at last. I have prayed to you.'

'You always knew that I would come,' said Minerva. 'You have always known that you were special, destined for greatness.'

'I have wanted, and yet I have doubted,' said Claudia. 'I have waited for ever, for as long as I have known your name.'

The landscape around them changed again, trees sprouting and withering, rivers flowing and receding. Elysium was always shifting and stirring, the sands of time rising and falling to form new architecture.

'We do not have much time, Princess, so listen to me well,' said Minerva. 'The moment has come for you to take your place in history, as you have long desired. You have dreamed of seizing the world from the hands of men, and I am here to help you. A great danger awaits humankind should your brother come to power, as the gods have planned. Tyranny. Cruelty. The abandonment of all decency. Wars will be waged for millennia. The Earth itself shall rot and burn. But when we goddesses gaze into the future, it is your face we see instead... and you are wearing your father's crown.'

Claudia did not appear surprised, her eyes shining in awe.

'You honour me, my goddess,' Claudia whispered.

'Your father is not long for this world. His death cannot be prevented,' said Minerva. 'But the world can still be saved, if you should take his place.'

'I am not worthy,' said Claudia. 'No one takes my ambitions seriously.'

'They will, when you are ruling over them all. I have seen.'

'I want to be the ruler the people deserve,' said the princess.

'You will be better than any man who came before you,' said Minerva. 'You must rise, or all will fall.'

'What must I do?' asked the princess.

'You must prevent the ascension of your brother, Decimus.'

'I already desire it with all my heart, but how?' asked Claudia.

'We cannot show you,' said Minerva. 'We cannot see. Only you can stop him. Only you will know. But your life will soon be in danger. You must seek the warrior who will spare you from death.'

'I have many warriors who say they would die for me.'

'And most of them are lying,' said Minerva curtly. 'It cannot be just any warrior, dependent on the empire for survival and serving out of duty. It must be one who stands at your side willingly, one who gives their heart to you as they lay down their sword for you.'

'They will love me?' asked Claudia.

'And you them.'

There was a hunger in Claudia's expression now, a curiosity.

'Where am I to find such a warrior?' she said.

'Pompeii. Home to the first and finest gladiators. You will find a reason to visit soon, Fortuna will make sure of that,' said Minerva. 'When you do, you must seek the warrior there if you are to fulfil your destiny.'

When Minerva held out her arm, spectral figures moved around them like spirits, slightly translucent and blurred, echoes from the future.

A figure in armour and a helmet promenaded, kneeling at Claudia's feet and saluting before springing up to battle a series of shadowy foes. As before, the scenery shifted, forming a run-down ludus where other gladiators were being trained, a villa with fallen pillars, and a statue of Venus, which toppled to the ground. Blood dripped from the sword the gladiator held, a dead man at their feet.

The visions took a more sinister turn, depicting a man ripped apart by lions, a sinister banquet in a black-painted room, a severed head rolling down a series of steps. Claudia saw her father in bed, surrounded by flowers, choking on his own vomit. She saw a mountain with fire bursting from the top.

Hordes of invaders surged into the amphitheatre before disappearing.

The final vision was of Claudia herself, crowned by the rays of the sun, as the gladiator in armour kneeled before her...

But their face was still obscured by their helmet.

'When I find him, how will I know?' asked Claudia.

'You will know,' said Minerva. She raised Claudia's hand to touch her own chest. 'You will feel it.'

The princess watched as the scene before her wasted away like sandcastles in the ocean tide, until she was alone in her bed beneath a canopy of blood-red silk.

Her heart pounded fiercely at the idea of loving someone.
It felt even more terrifying than ruling the world.

2. NOT UNTIL I WIN

When Gia was born, she waited eight days to be named. After her cord was cut, her parents hosted the nominalia, inviting friends and family to a banquet. She was presented at the domestic altar to the Lares – familiar spirits who were said to guard the villa – while offerings were made to Jupiter, king of the gods, and to Diana and Apollo, who represented the spring. Only then was she given her name: Gia.

It meant 'the gods are gracious'.

Though she couldn't remember it, Gia knew from retellings that her brothers had been present to poke her (Atticus) and coo over her (Cassius). She had known them from the very moment she came into the world. Though they were now gone, she felt their presence as she dressed for her first day of training with Cyrus, rooting through their old clothes to find a tunic fit for fighting in.

One still had a spot of blood on the hem.

Gia pulled it on, speaking to her brothers without words as she put her sandals on in the atrium. She lit incense in the lararium and left a fig for Diana, touching the stones that represented her loved and lost.

Outside, it was still early and the air was fresh with newly-cut flowers. The large villa nearby had recently been purchased by a wealthy Roman, probably a senator. He had hired someone to prune the peristyle garden, which was bordered by a maze of hedges.

Gia wondered if he and his family would frequent the taberna, being situated so close. They could certainly do with the money. Word had spread that the place had gone downhill and last night there had only been a handful of customers. Once again, her mother had been too drunk to do much but talk the patrons' ears off about her problems. They soon cleared their plates of Gia's cremated cooking.

Though Gia was tired and aching, she was hopeful – something she hadn't felt since Atticus died.

Over at the ludus, Cyrus was waiting in the rear yard. 'Gather round,' he called to the other students as she approached. 'I want to introduce you to someone.'

An open, dusty square rimmed with short chunky pillars, with a barracks for sleeping and bathing at the rear, this was the real training ground, where boys battled straw-stuffed dummies, fired arrows at targets, sharpened their weapons on stones and wrestled each other in circles of chalk. The half-circle of a small amphitheatre served as their aspirational backdrop, a model version of the larger one where gladiators fought professionally.

'All right,' said Cyrus, as Gia hung behind, 'listen up.'

'What is it, sir?' asked Dominic.

'As of last night, I've taken on a new student. I know some of you are going to shit yourselves over this –' he looked pointedly at Fabius, whose eye was starting to bruise – 'but I'm going to give you the chance to grow up and be real men. So, everyone, please give a warm and, most of all, *appropriate*, welcome to Gia Valerii.'

The boys gawked at her as she stepped down off the porch to stand at his side, trying not to look self-conscious.

'You're teaching her to fight?' asked Dominic.

'That's right, Dom.'

'You're fucking kidding,' said Fabius, scowling.

'What's happening?' said Lucas, looking confused and a little scared.

They all began talking at once but for Felix, the pale russet one, who grinned at Gia as if he wanted to eat her.

'You can't. It's an insult to the honour of the fallen,' said Fabius.

'Since when can girls fight anyway?' asked another kid.

'Since Gia here gave Fabius that shiner yesterday,' said Cyrus.

Fabius muttered under his breath, something about how he'd been trying to go gentle on her.

'What's the problem, boys?' said Cyrus. 'Are you worried she might beat you at your own game?'

'No,' scoffed Fabius. 'It's just not right, is it?'

'I don't think it's wrong.' Dom shrugged. 'Why shouldn't girls learn just the same as us? Give her a chance.'

'But, sir, if all the women are fighting in the ring, who will care for the children?' asked Lucas earnestly. 'Who will clean our rooms and make our food?'

'We're just talking about one woman for now, but perhaps you can learn to clean your own room, Lucas?' suggested Cyrus.

Lucas appeared shaken to the core, as if the idea had simply never occurred to him before.

'Women are already fighting all across the world,' said Cyrus. 'There are women soldiers in Britannia and in Gaul. I'm sure you've heard the stories. The men who have returned have spoken of them with great fear and admiration. They are not just fighting, but winning battles.'

'Women aren't allowed in the Roman army,' said Fabius.

'Not now, yet they battled in civilizations that came long before us,' Cyrus said. 'Even the goddesses themselves battled. They carry weapons and wear helmets in ancient statues and reliefs. Minerva the wise strategized her father's wars. Diana the huntress rarely missed a shot. Even Juno the great mother has been known to wield a spear from time to time. If men can do as gods do, then why not women?' He turned to Gia. 'Anything you want to add?'

'Not really,' she said, folding her arms over her chest. 'But, if you're all so sure you're better than a woman, I'll take any one of you on, any time, any place. Let's go.'

'That . . . wasn't really what I had in mind, but okay,' said Cyrus.

'She will make a mockery of us, sir,' said Fabius.

'The only person who can make a mockery of you, is you, Fabius. It seems you have quite the gift for it too. Let us be open-minded, like the great philosophers, and think of the possibilities. Naturally, people will cause a fuss to begin with, as people always do when faced with change, but they will soon come to understand that the presence of women will invigorate the game. I hope to attract a new audience to the amphitheatre, for a new kind of sport.'

Fabius glowered silently.

'I wouldn't mind watching two women go at it, to be honest,' said Felix, after a moment. 'I saw two courtesans fighting outside the brothel. They were fierce.'

Dom and Lucas laughed.

'My aunt and my mother had a fight once,' said Lucas. 'They

went outside and came back with cuts on their faces, but they never fought again. They were the best of friends after that.'

The others were quiet; Gia couldn't tell what they thought of her and she wasn't sure she wanted to know.

'Is that all?' said Fabius. 'Can we go now?'

'One last thing. I hope you can keep this between us for the time being,' said Cyrus.

'Why? Is it a secret, sir?' asked Dom.

'You know what Pompeii people are like. One wrong word and your dirty bed linen is on display for all the city to see. We're doing something daring here, so let's not advertise it in advance. If I catch wind that you've been telling your uncle's cousin's wife, you'll be on latrine duty until you can learn the art of discretion. I have faith that we can all be supportive of each other, like a happy little family. Do we have an understanding, boys?'

They grumbled resentfully as Cyrus turned to Gia again.

'I think that's as good as you're going to get,' he said.

Cyrus directed them all to run laps around the yard. Gia wasn't muscular like most of the boys were, but she'd been run off her feet at the taberna lately and all that grunt work had paid off. She was as fast and light on her feet as she was when she was a kid, back when she'd thought she was immortal.

'Is that what you call running?' jeered Fabius.

'You look like one of Diana's deer!' shouted Felix.

'If you want to act like a man, you'd better run like one.'

Gia struggled behind as the boys made fun, but after a few laps she found the right groove, letting energy flow through her freely. She began to overtake them, one by one. As she passed, she imagined that she was slaying them all with a sword. Down.

Down. Down. She didn't look at them, for they barely existed in the mindset she was in. She focused only on the ground ahead.

Her long legs came in handy when it came to running, oiled and shiny in the sun, as did the endless rage inside her. Her braided ponytail thwacked annoyingly against her back, reminding her to wear it up next time. There *would* be a next time, she could promise herself that.

It was almost as cathartic as kicking a rude boy's butt.

After overtaking Dom, who slowed to stare at her, Gia kept her eyes on Fabius some way ahead. She would show him what a woman could do, or die trying. But he had the endurance of a marathon runner, barely breaking a sweat. When he heard her coming up behind him, he ran faster, leaving her in the dust.

Gia leaned into her last strength, pushing herself to the limit in an attempt to catch up with Fabius. She ran until her chest hurt, until she felt sick, until her face was so hot it felt like her skin was boiling.

By the time Cyrus called for them to stop, Gia was in the lead.

Gia hadn't told her mother about her training yet, uncertain of how she would respond, but she intended to turn up each day, work hard, and hope that the gods were entertained enough to spare her suffering. She would make the best of the opportunity destiny had given her.

Over the coming weeks, Gia received a rapid schooling on the gladiatorial world. In between training sessions, where she lifted weights and practised swinging a sword, she learned the long, bloody history of gladiatorial games in a small damp room that smelled of sweat and bad breath. Cyrus acted as teacher behind a podium, his face rapt as he described a flute-playing bear who once performed before matches. He seemed to enjoy giving lectures more than he enjoyed instructing his students in action, as he was often troubled by his leg.

'There are many different types of gladiator,' he explained. 'The murmillo, the retiarius, the secutor and the thraex, the hoplomachus and the cestus. The cestus fights with spiky wrappings around their hands. The hoplomachus has a shield and a spear. The equites enter the arena on horseback. The essedarii battle from chariots. The dimachaerus carry two swords at once. Then there's the noxii. The noxii aren't gladiators, technically speaking. They're criminals, forced to fight by the emperor as punishment. They carry no weapon.'

Through Cyrus, Gia learned that the earliest gladiators were captured slaves who brought their native weapons to the fight, and that each gladiator had a scorecard to keep track of their victories and defeats.

Cyrus drew one up for Gia in his office, to encourage her.

'Look, you're a real gladiator now,' he said, holding it up.

But Gia shook her head. 'Not until I win,' she said.

The students of the ludus fought each other daily, with mixed outcomes. On one occasion, Gia had delivered a devastating blow to Lucas, while she had received a bruised rib from Dom in the next session. She had brought Felix to his knees with a wooden sword one afternoon, but Fabius had her face down in the dirt just an hour or two later. So it went, back and forth. Win or lose.

The students also took day trips as part of their training. They visited an armourer to learn his trade, crowding around the heat of the forge. Elite gladiators like Celadus the Handsome wore ornate plates made of gold or silver. Some were highly decorative, bearing the symbols of the gods. The plumes of their gladiator helmets were topped with tassels or peacock feathers. Even their loincloths were ornately embroidered, to be revealed in their post-victory celebrations. The ludus students enjoyed no such luxuries, wearing worn tunics and fraying leather, dented plates of brass that had seen far better days.

The boys were already experimenting with different weapons, trying to decide if their fighting method favoured the net and trident of the retarius, or the bow of the Sagittarius. They spoke with equites and bestiaries, who fought with horses and wild animals, and took their sage advice. Every time Gia thought she had memorized each kind of gladiator, she was introduced to another one.

A month in, the boys had still not adjusted to Gia's inclusion at the ludus. Felix was still openly lustful, earning himself sharp reprimands from Cyrus. Fabius, her mortal enemy, was always snarling and sullen, never missing an opportunity to voice his opinion that girls didn't belong in the ring. Lucas looked at her as if she was a rare creature recently discovered by scientists, never quite comfortable in her company. Only Dom made an attempt to be friendly, helping her with training she had missed, though he still joined in with the jokes.

One afternoon, they went to the Pompeii amphitheatre nearby, running through the tunnels that real gladiators entered through, their whooping voices amplified. They huddled in the centre of the ring, looking out over the rows of seats that seemed to stretch up into the clouds, trying to imagine what it would feel like to stand there when they were full.

'One day, you'll be fighting here for real,' said Cyrus, as the boys nudged each other excitedly. 'I'm sure you've all attended before as spectators, but you'll get a very different perspective from down here, believe me. Split into twos and practise sparring, to get used to the space and the views.'

The boys paired off, until only Felix was left. He grinned wolfishly and licked his lips, raising his wooden practise sword. Gia grunted and met it with her own, but Felix was dominant, keeping her on her toes.

'You'd win every match if you flashed us,' said Felix, as they fought each other again.

'I don't want to win like that.'

'If I had breasts, I'd bare them like weapons.'

'Then thank the gods you are not a woman. I simply wish to be treated as an equal,' Gia said. 'I want to win for the glory, just like you.'

'A win is a win,' Felix said.

The *clack-clack-clack* of wooden swords rang through the sunken circle.

'A gladiator battle is as much a performance as it is a sport,' said Cyrus, his voice carrying as he watched them. 'Always think of the audience and position yourself so that they get a clear view of the action.'

The amphitheatre was ringed with tiered semi-circular stone benches that looked down on the entertainment below, stretching back to the raised outer ring. At ground level were private entrances for the wealthy and powerful, who sat close enough to be splashed by blood. Commoners climbed two sets of stairs at the front entrance, which stood back-to-back like warriors, filing into the upper benches near the rear.

It was built for action, for spectating.

Though the arena was empty, save for her and the others in training, Gia had the strange feeling she was being watched. She stared out at the stone benches, but there was no one to be seen.

Perhaps she had drawn the attention of Diana or Minerva, both women who knew how to fight. She imagined them critiquing her footwork, encouraging her when she got the movement just right. As she fought Felix, she pictured Minerva taking notes, Diana cheering with her maidens.

'No one enjoys watching dust clouds and ungainly thrashing,' Cyrus was saying. 'The crowd are here to be entertained and the better you succeed in that goal, the better your chances of winning.'

'What do you mean, sir?' asked Dom. He was the most studious of the boys, and the most eager to please. 'How can the audience influence who wins or loses?'

'If the audience takes a disliking to you, they won't hesitate to heckle you. They will cheer your opponent and call for your loss. *He's had it*, they'll say. *Kill him*, they'll say. With every swing of your sword, you will become less assured of your ability. You will doubt yourself and that doubt will leave you weak. The audience senses fear. The fear of failure so often leads to real failure, you see. You and Gia will face more hostile reactions than the rest, so you must work against it.'

'Why me?' asked Dom.

Cyrus looked from Dom to Gia and back again.

'You having dark skin, Dominic, like me.' He pointed at him with the tip of his sword. 'And you being a woman.' He nodded at Gia. 'You will face the harshest judgements. As I did.'

'But you were a great fighter,' said Dom.

'*Were?*' said Cyrus, with a comically furious look, tapping his leg self-consciously. 'Still am. But trust me – I know how hard it is to win over the crowd.'

'How do we do that?' Gia interjected, still fending off blows from Felix.

'The mood of the audience ebbs and flows. You can lose them, but you can also win them back with one smart move. One entertaining act. Show them your personalities in the arena. You can be good, bad, serious, funny, but whatever you do, it must draw their attention. They will be more forgiving if you entertain them. The battle for your life is a show, so make sure it's a good one.'

Cyrus ambled back and forth, inspecting their moves, adjusting an arm here or repositioning a shield there.

'There may be influential people in the audience too who can sponsor you, should they favour you. They may pay for better weapons, better armour, or pay for you to travel to fight elsewhere. When I was a gladiator, I had many patrons. I fought in Sicilia and Macedon, in Corsica and Sardinia. I listened to the roars of different crowds. I came to understand which moves worked best with which audience. Every region has their preferences. Knowing your audience is key.'

He paused. Fabius had knocked Lucas to the ground and booted him in the side. Cyrus shook his head, disapproving.

'We fight with honour, until we have no choice but to get dirty. It is, after all, a game of survival. A dance of death. When the thumb goes down in a kill-to-win game, you'll have only seconds to contemplate your life's meaning before your opponent will finish you off.'

Gia shuddered.

'How did you get injured, sir?' asked Lucas, scrambling up from the ground and motioning to Cyrus's leg.

'A trident in the thigh,' he said. 'That was the end of my fighting career, but the beginning of my career as a trainer and master. I make no complaints. Fortuna has kept me alive this long.'

Gia thrust out her weapon, driving Felix back, his heels kicking up dust.

'Good, Gia,' said Cyrus. 'Just make sure to keep your feet apart. You're less likely to lose your balance that way.'

Gia nodded, distracted. Her mind kept wandering, worrying what her mother was doing in her absence. Drinking, probably. She yawned, exhausted from working the taberna by herself the night before, barraged with complaints and forced to refund the meals that were either cold or incinerated. One of the employees had stolen a casket of wine, though she wasn't sure which and didn't know who to let go.

She'd slept for less than an hour before the sun rose—

A sudden jab in her side drew her attention back to her sparring partner, who grinned devilishly.

'Looks like you're dead,' said Felix, and so she would've been if it had been a real blade. 'Too bad.'

'Guess so,' she said, rubbing at the spot.

'It's always the beautiful who die young.'

'I'm never going to sleep with you, Felix.'

'If you say so.'

'I'm never going to sleep with *any* of you,' she said, looking around at the other boys, paired off into twos. 'Think of me as one of the men. I'm here to fight and make money, same as you.'

'Why not?' asked Felix.

'Yeah, why not?' asked Lucas nearby. 'What's wrong with us?'

'Don't be a beg, Lucas,' said Dom, cringing. 'You can't just ask a girl why she won't sleep with you.'

'I'd rather fight you than go to bed with you,' Gia said. 'It's nothing personal.'

'You think you're all that?' said Felix.

'No, but I've seen courtesans and their clients going at it and that's not what I'd call a good time. Count me out.'

'So you're a virgin?' Fabius smirked.

Before Gia could answer, the sudden blare of a horn startled them all to attention. A messenger in armour marched into the arena, saluting in greeting. He walked up to Cyrus and murmured something, his back to the students. Gia and Felix ceased sparring, watching on curiously.

'A message from Rome,' Gia said.

'How do you know?' asked Felix.

She pointed out the seal on his golden shield, thinking of the last day she'd seen Cassius, all dressed up in armour at the Bay, waiting to board a ship. She recalled hugging him goodbye, holding on so tight, as if she'd known it would be the last time.

Whatever the stranger said, Cyrus appeared excited, clapping his hands together in gratitude and bowing.

'We will be there,' he said.

The messenger bowed his head in response, retreating.

'Boys!' Cyrus called, before remembering his new student. 'And Gia! Come, gather over here. I have news.'

The students all ceased fighting, taking seats on the lower benches, which were crumbling in disrepair. Some of the arches had fallen in the last earthquake too, leaving single standing pillars, some broken off at sharp angles.

Cyrus waited until they were settled before he spoke, looking barely able to contain his glee.

'I just received a message from my acquaintance at the Ludus Magnus, the finest gladiator school in Rome, where I myself was trained. They bring word that Senator Cornelius is having a birthday party this Saturn-day, at the Villa of the Mysteries just outside the city walls.'

The Villa of the Mysteries, so-called because of its mystical rites and mysterious cult gatherings, was the most luxurious location in Pompeii. Everyone clamoured for an invite to an event there.

'I thought it was still being repaired,' said Dom.

'The banker Iucundus has been busy restoring it for sale. He and his associates use the place to store their wine preserves, but it will be fine for a party. The frescos are undamaged, as are the hanging gardens. It's still a sight to be seen, and Cornelius is a fan of the place.'

'Senator Cornelius? The lech?' asked Felix.

'The very same, though word has it that he's been on his best behaviour since he took a mistress to supplement his wife. He's looking to hire some gladiators to fight as entertainment and he's too cheap to pay for professionals. Looks like we're in luck – my friend from the Ludus Magnus recommended us when the senator objected to their big-city prices. You're all hired, so clear your schedules this weekend.'

'Even me?' asked Gia.

'Yes, although I'd like to keep it a surprise, if we can. It will get the people talking if your first appearance is at such an important social event. Consider this a test run. It will give you a taste for how an audience will respond to a female gladiator, for better or worse. And there's more news.' He was practically giddy. 'Can you guess who'll be in attendance at the party?'

The students looked at each other, unsure.

'His mistress?' suggested Felix.

'Well, probably yes, but that's not who I meant. Listen to this: the imperial family are travelling to Pompeii as we speak.'

'The *emperor* is coming?' said Dom.

'Indeed.'

'What about his daughter?' asked Lucas.

'Her too.'

This news was met with jubilation, inspiring a chorus of whistles and whoops, the boys clutching at each other. Gia met eyes with Cyrus and shook her head in amusement, as if watching over a group of merry children on Saturnalia.

'Claudia's even more beautiful than Venus,' swooned Felix.

'Finally, Fortuna has answered my prayers,' said Lucas.

'Dear gods, I'm going to regret this, aren't I?' said Cyrus, burying his head in his hands and moaning. 'Please, boys, promise me, you must be on your best behaviour at the event. Do *not* harass the dear princess of Rome, whatever you do.' He looked to Gia. 'At least I don't have to worry about you on that count.'

'You have my word,' said Gia, confidently.

'Let us finish training early today, so I can begin preparations for the event. You all need new armour, for one. But tomorrow we shall meet at an hour past dawn, to practise our routines. You will fight each other, but no one shall die. There will be no bloodshed for a noble woman like Claudia to see.'

'Maybe she likes a bit of bloodshed,' said Felix thoughtfully. 'She probably watches men die all the time.'

'Perhaps, but this is a birthday party. There will be children present as well, so keep it clean. Maybe the senator will wish to make a charitable donation to our school after a few glasses of wine. For now, why don't you enjoy a drink and some food at the taberna to celebrate? On me.'

He pressed several coins into Gia's hand, some of them blackened with scum, as if he'd dug them out of a sewer.

'Go, enjoy yourselves.'

The students filed out of the amphitheatre, walking back to the ludus under the midday sun and piling into the taberna on the corner. It was nicer than Gia's taberna; its murals fresh and detailed, its floor tiles unbroken, its tables clean with working legs. A delicious smell wafted into her nostrils, making her stomach clench with hunger. How she longed to eat something she hadn't cooked herself.

'What can I get you?' asked the owner, eyeing Gia as if she might be a courtesan, the sole woman in the company of men.

They ordered a platter of fruit and bread with goat's cheese and wine to dip it in, talking over each other about their favourite gladiator matches. Gia turned to see Felix staring at her intently.

'What?'

'I don't get it,' he said.

'Get what?'

'Why you're here with us, and not out with your boyfriend?'

'I don't have a boyfriend,' she said.

'Exactly.' He grinned. 'Maybe we can fix that.'

'Stop, Felix. You don't want to end up like poor Fabius, do you?'

she said, inclining her head to where he sat alone, nursing a drink. She and Felix had gone to the bar to collect more wine. 'He had a shiner for a week, remember?'

'I wouldn't mind, if I got to experience your pleasures first.'

'Do you not think of anything else?' she said, annoyed.

'Not really.'

'Felix, I'm not having this conversation with you again,' she said. 'How many ways can I tell you, there's no chance?'

'Why not? I'm not bad looking,' he said.

'If you say so.'

The owner lined their drinks up on the taberna counter, as Gia moved them onto a copper tray one by one.

'What did your last man look like?' he pushed.

Gia avoided his eye, uncomfortable.

'There is no last man? I could be the first.'

'Not a chance.'

'Why? Are you a vestal? Afraid they'll bury you alive if you betray your vow of chastity?' he said.

'No, dickhead.'

'There must be something wrong with you. You're not ugly. You can take a joke. But I don't see you hanging around with any other guys.'

'That's not an accident,' she said, turning back to the table.

'You don't seem to like us very much either.'

'Also not an accident.'

'Are you like Sappho?' said Felix, taking the tray.

'Sappho?' she asked, as they sat back at the table.

'You know, that poet.'

'Greek poet,' said Dom, his mouth full of bread.

The others looked at him blankly, including Gia.

'The only woman poet I know, actually. From Lesbos. She preferred the company of women, they say.'

'You read poetry?' scoffed Felix.

'What of it?' Dom shrugged.

'You can read?' said Lucas, impressed.

'You can't?'

'My father taught me a little,' said Gia.

'Lucky. I never learned. My parents never did neither.' Lucas pulled a face. 'Never did either? Is that right?'

Gia's mind was stuck, tracking back to what Dom had said.

'What do you mean, she "preferred the company of women"?' Gia asked. 'Like Diana and her companions?'

'No, more than that,' said Dom. 'She fancied herself the lover of Venus, instead of Mars.'

Gia blinked.

'She liked the sheath and not the sword,' clarified Felix.

He made an obscene gesture, darting his tongue through the V of his fingers. It took Gia a minute to work out what he meant.

A deep, infernal heat spread through her body, burning her skin, its energy pulsing beneath the leather folds of her skirt. A picture most illicit filled her mind. She shook her head, trying to scatter it before it fully formed, but her curiosity won out.

'Don't men do that?' she asked, faux-casually.

'Sometimes, but you can do more with a sword,' said Felix.

'But only if you know how to use it,' replied Dom.

'Which I do,' said Felix sternly.

'So, are you?' asked Lucas.

'Am I what?'

'One of those sapphics?'

'No!'

'Are you sure about that?' asked Felix.

'I swear to gods, Felix, I will murder you.'

'Ooh, go on, please.'

'What I like and what I do is none of your business,' said Gia, still hot in the face. 'But also, no. I have never done that, or thought of that, nor even heard of it before. End of conversation.'

The boys exchanged glances. Gia was flustered, but she wasn't lying. She had never considered a woman in that way. She was just embarrassed that these idiots knew more than she did, that they thought it something to laugh about.

'How do you know what women get up to when they're away from the eyes of men, anyway?' Gia asked of Felix, still scowling.

'I slept with two lovers of the female form once,' he said. 'Both as beautiful as the bay of Naples. They let me watch before I joined in.'

'No they didn't,' she said, deadpan.

'No,' he said wistfully, 'but I hear stories.'

Gia sighed, wishing she had somewhere better to be. She'd had so many friends as a child – friends with whom she ran through olive groves and drew pictures with chalk. Now she wondered where they'd all gone. Some had died, some had left for Rome, others were engaged to whichever boy their parents preferred, some had become courtesans and vanished from sight overnight. She had Berenice – but Berenice was flighty, prone to disappearing mysteriously for weeks at a time.

Gia had only these ridiculous boys for company.

When they ran out of money, the taberna owner threw them

out, leaving them to weave their way back to their villas along Via Stabiana. Fabius skulked off into the darkness alone, no longer part of the friendship group.

They staggered by the colourful mural of Claudia, pausing to admire her as Lucas took a piss up the wall.

'I hope she's as attractive in real life as she is in her picture,' said Felix. 'You know how flattering imperial portraits can be.'

'I bet she's even better,' said Lucas.

'We'll probably only glimpse her from a distance,' said Dom. 'They won't let you anywhere near her.'

'They probably shouldn't,' said Gia. 'If she could hear you all, I'm sure she'd call for a guard to have you skinned.'

'Do you think she'd take a commoner to bed?' asked Lucas.

'No,' said Gia, without consideration. 'I'm sure she has the finest men in the empire lining up by her bedchamber at night. Generals. Senators. Princes.'

She couldn't help but roll her eyes at the idea of it.

'Fine ladies in high places like a bit of rough and tumble,' said Felix. 'Many a senator's wife has come calling for me after dark.'

'No, they haven't,' said Dom.

'No, they haven't,' echoed Gia.

'You don't know. They could. They might ...' His confidence paled. 'They don't know what they're missing.'

Gia and Dom exchanged a look that was halfway between a brow raise and an eye roll, before shaking their heads in sync.

'Has the imperial family ever come to Pompeii before?' Gia asked.

'Not all together,' said Dom. 'The emperor comes for business. Decimus is said to visit several times a year, for the pursuit of leisure, I presume, since he doesn't seem to do anything else. But Claudia? Not that I know of.'

'Maybe she'll need someone to show her around,' said Felix.

'If she did, you'd be the last person she'd pick,' Gia said.

She stared at the mural. The Roman princess was coming to Pompeii. It was like the beginning of a story. Perhaps she would stand on this very spot, admiring her own portrait as servants flocked around her.

Though Gia had defaced her picture just weeks earlier, though she despised the princess and all she stood for, though she disliked that insipid painted face that smirked at her perpetually, she was still curious to see the reality.

Yet Gia would be at the party as a gladiator. She would be a novelty, like Cyrus said. She could be the punchline of a joke, the laughing stock of all Pompeii.

How embarrassing.

It would be bitter, to be humiliated in front of a princess. Perhaps it would serve her right for calling Claudia a mouth-stinker, but it was too late to take it back now. Her words were still there, etched in the wall for anyone to see.

'Gia! Look!' came a voice, disrupting her thoughts.

Clutching her sleeve, Felix pointed past the crowded taberna on the corner, where teenage courtesans sat with elder senators, indicating two young lovers crushed against the wall nearby, the man's head up his girlfriend's skirts. She threw back her head in delight, eyes closed, mouth hanging open as he gripped her thighs.

'Now that's what I'm talking about. Lucky dog,' said Felix.

'Don't be disgusting,' said Dom.

'There's nothing disgusting about sex,' he said. 'Isn't that what we're all on this earth for?'

'Not me,' said Dom. 'There must be more to life than ... *that*.'

The boys walked on, but Gia was transfixed by the scene unfolding before her. She knew she shouldn't watch, but she couldn't help herself. They were doing it out in the open. It was almost an invitation to witness.

As if hearing her thoughts, the girl caught Gia's eye and ... smiled.

They parted ways on the corner, with Dom headed home and Felix headed to the brothel, though his pockets were empty.

Gia realized how late it was and that the taberna should've opened hours ago. The shutter was down. No light inside. Without her, there was no business. Her mother hardly seemed to care whether they lived or died any more.

She crept inside, fearful that her mother would be conscious and furious that she wasn't home, but she was passed out cold on a lectern. Gia covered her with a blanket and went into her room. She'd hear all about it in the morning, she was sure, but for now she held on tightly to this fleeting peace.

Gia sat on the bed and hugged her knees, missing the days when her mother was a friend, before so much grief made her a stranger.

Would it ever be like that again?

One night of the taberna being closed wouldn't make much difference, she told herself. Their takings were ten times less than they'd been when her father was still alive. Business had been declining for a while. She'd open up tomorrow.

Still giddy from the drink, Gia closed her eyes, too tired to think. The wine made her mind heavy. Between wakefulness and sleep, she found herself pulled into a sweet, silken dream.

Venus, the goddess of love, was being chased through a grove of forest nymphs by Diana, goddess of the hunt. Struck with one of her own Cupid's arrows, Venus fell to the ground. Diana caught up with her, catching her prey, but Venus merely laughed, flipping over and smiling invitingly, holding a sprig of wildflowers. Diana crawled on top of her, still wearing a bow at her back. A silent deer watched on, breaking its unjudging gaze occasionally to munch grass.

Suddenly, the dream shifted. Now Gia had taken Diana's place, leaning over a prone Venus, but when she looked, Venus turned into Princess Claudia.

'I've been watching you, gladiator,' she said.

Claudia reached out to embrace Gia's face, and all the world exploded.

BOOM.

A river of fire flashed through her mind.

Gia bolted upright, dizzy and confused. That heat was still emanating. Her skin was hot to the touch, as if an inferno had started deep inside her, burning through layers of flesh.

Her thoughts swirled in a violent maelstrom.

Claudia's voice seemed to echo in her mind, calling out to her in a honeyed voice of desire.

The idea enchanted and repulsed Gia in equal measure.

3. VIATRIX THE VICTORIOUS

The Villa of the Mysteries was painted with exotic scenes, many depicting a Bacchic initiation rite. They showed a young noble woman approaching a priestess, who was seated on a throne. A small boy carried a scroll, his mouth wide open in song or in fear. A serving girl held out a tray of cakes. A Silenus played a lyre, while a satyr played the panpipes. Gia stared at it, scratching her head, trying to make sense of these peculiar events and failing miserably.

'Gia! Over here.'

Felix waved at her from across the room. Dom was beside him.

The boys were dressed in matching armour, strapped and sandalled, equipped with helmets. Gia wore plain white robes; it was still a secret that she was the night's entertainment. Like this, she was all but invisible. She had already been mistaken for a server at the entrance.

The noise of a large boisterous party filled in around her as she pushed on, through the columned peristyle and into the main atrium. People in fine, fashionable robes filled the halls, drinking from bone-cut chalices, dripping in exotic feathers and foreign jewels. Characters too large and fabulous to be true.

Many acrobats and fortune tellers had been hired, along with chefs and musicians and high-class courtesans who represented each of the nine muses, singing and playing instruments.

Beyond the triclinium was a portico with a wide sunset view of the Gulf of Naples. Vesuvius loomed powerfully in the distance, the primordial forge and earthly residence of Vulcan.

Out in the landscaped gardens on the other side of the villa, Lucas and one of the other boys fought each other in a makeshift ring, as the birthday senator and a group of nobles watched on. Cornelius was seated in his own personal veranda, with his wife on one side and his mistress on the other. His mistress looked glum, her face painted like Berenice's.

Drums beat steadily as the boys circled each other.

It was obvious that their moves were rehearsed, too slow and apprehensive. It was easy to anticipate where they'd step next, waving their swords with soft arms like corn dollies. The audience quickly turned, booing until the boys picked up pace. They clapped only when Lucas submitted, face down in the dirt. The other boy held up one arm triumphantly, but no one seemed to care.

The ocean breeze cooled Gia's skin, drying the perspiration that had settled after walking to the villa on the outskirts of town. She was sick with nerves. She had rarely been nervous in her life, for she'd had little reason to be. She had been sad, angry, sick, regretful, anxious, but not nervous in the way she was now. Part of her hoped the emperor wouldn't come and that her performance would be cancelled, but when she saw Cyrus pacing back and forth anxiously, shaking his head at the boys' poor show, she willed the opposite. He needed something to go right tonight.

She would put on a show for Cyrus.

As if on cue, someone called out: 'The emperor is here!'

Whispering and giggling, the boys pushed to the entrance, trying to get a look at the princess of Rome, dragging Gia along with them.

'She's just a girl,' she muttered.

'Best-looking girl in all the empire,' said Felix.

'You've not seen them all yet,' said Dominic.

'I don't have to. Just look at her.'

Through the haze of heat, she made out the figures pulling up in front of the villa. Claudia was hard to mistake, graceful as a palm, her gold hair shining in the sun, her fine silk dress revealing her curves.

Her smile came so easy, her wave a blessing.

Annoying.

Her brother, Decimus, walked beside her, dark-haired where she was fair, sallow where she was peachy. He looked as if he'd rather be anywhere else, while Claudia appeared to be enjoying the attention.

Like the spoilt brat she was, Gia thought irritably.

The emperor came last, small and bald, ringed by guards in gold armour and plumed headdresses. The crowd gave a half-hearted cheer, reverent and fearful, as the imperial family moved towards the house. People applauded as they passed, holding out flower wreaths and baskets of delicacies as gifts.

Felix gave a low whistle.

'You can barely see her.'

'Jealous that I might prefer another girl?' teased Felix.

'She'll never have anything to do with you, you know,' said Gia. 'You're wasting your time wanting her.'

'Looking at beautiful things is never a waste of time.'

The emperor drew closer, and so did his daughter.

The princess paused to bless a servant's baby. Claudia accepted a bunch of flowers and moved on, brushing past the crowd.

She was so close, Gia could smell her perfume. She could see the oils that glistened on her skin, and her glittering chain necklace with its green glass pendant.

Gia paid close attention to the enemy. The way the purple silk of her stola draped over her hourglass body. Her thick shining hair, held in place with a thin gold headband. Dark brows, fine nose, a strong jaw. Pale green eyes, dark-lashed and penetrating. She noticed it all.

The dream flashed through Gia's head, making her sweat, but she pushed it down, deep beneath the ground, where the emperor and all his kin should be buried.

Felix was right about something, though.

She really was the best-looking girl in the empire.

The imperial family passed them by as if they were invisible, headed to the table that had been set up for them outside. Laden with food and pitchers of wine, it was shaded from the heat by a red canopy.

Gia and the boys were just peasants to their rulers, not even worth half a glance. Gia found herself strangely disappointed. She might've had the chance to scowl at her, so Princess Claudia would know how much she loathed her.

Hate. Yes, that's what was making her chest feel tight.

Cyrus appeared, emerging through the crowd. 'Felix, Dom, you're on,' he said. 'And, please, I beg you: make it a good one.'

'Now? Right now?' said Dom.

'Right now. Remember what I told you about putting on a

show. Keep the audience on their toes and they won't throw food at you.'

'Does that really happen?' asked Dom, eyes wide.

'You'll be lucky if it's just food,' said Cyrus.

Felix looked to Gia, and for a second all of the bravado he wore as a mask slipped away.

'You'll be fine,' she said.

'How do you know?'

'I don't, but it's just a friendly match,' she said. 'You might feel bad if you lose, but you'll walk away alive at least.'

He nodded briskly, squaring his shoulders before he and Dominic trundled off into the garden, slow and unsteady on their feet.

Cyrus turned to Gia.

'You'll be next,' he said.

'Who am I fighting?' she asked.

'Whichever of those two wins.'

'I might have to fight *Felix*?'

'I think you can take him,' he said. 'Don't you?'

'Maybe,' she said thoughtfully. 'I did once before.'

'Well, I need you to believe that you can. I need you to walk into the ring as if you're Celadus the Handsome himself.'

A cheer arose from the garden, drawing back her attention. They moved to the balcony just in time to see Felix raise his arm in triumph as Dominic lay sprawled on the ground. Dom was playing it up, groaning and writhing around, pretending to be more injured than he was, while the crowd seemed to delight in his pain.

Gia swallowed, her dry throat swollen and sticking.

'I can't do this,' she said.

'Yes, you can,' said Cyrus. 'Believe in me when I say I believe in you.'

'You could be wrong.'

'There are a lot of people relying on me,' said Cyrus, gripping her shoulders and fixing her with a serious stare. 'The money I make keeps people fed. I wouldn't take a risk to my reputation by backing you if I wasn't confident that you can change the game. So go out there and kick that boy into the dirt.'

Gia took a deep breath.

She had to trust Cyrus. She *did* trust him. Mostly. But this was a cruel world, she knew that well. It was hard to believe in good things.

'You can get ready in the washroom over there,' said Cyrus. 'Your armour is in the chest, hidden beneath a throw. Lock the door behind you and don't let anyone in until I come for you.'

He handed her a rusted key, patting her back gently.

'Dear gods,' he said, scouring her face. 'You look absolutely terrified.'

'Shouldn't I be?'

'Yes, but try not to let it show.'

Her belly gurgled dangerously.

'I might actually shit myself, Cyrus.'

'Just the nerves, although if you have to crap, make sure you do it where no one can see you,' he said. 'It will taint your image if the audience has already seen you squatting over a bush.'

'Great advice, thanks,' said Gia.

Cyrus smirked and hurried off to console Dominic.

In the cool quiet of the monastic washroom, with its cracked walls and the smell of rising damp, Gia pulled on the uniform Cyrus had sourced for her. Leather-strapped bronze body armour with a short brown woollen cape like his; shin and shoulder guards, arm bands and knee pads. Her long black hair was already greased, scraped back into a neat fishtailed braid, but now she pulled on a helmet, its visor partially concealing her face. It was heavy and slightly too big, obscuring her vision. Finally, she armed herself with a dented sword and a rusted shield, flexing her arm and groaning at their combined weight. It was hard to even carry them both, let alone wield them with intent.

There was no mirror, but when she looked down on her body she realized she didn't appear much different from the boys after all. She had never been blessed with curves. Her muscles were more defined now from the hours of training, but she was still skinny, straight.

No one would know she was a woman from a distance. That must've been the point. Cyrus's idea, of course. Hide what she was until he was ready to announce her. He did say he wanted it to be a surprise, and so it would be.

Gia felt suddenly faint, imagining how the audience might react to the unexpected revelation.

She thought of Cassius again, telling her to toughen up if she wanted to fight and win. What would he think if he knew what she was about to do? She thought of Atticus too, and how he might feel if he saw her taking his place. Were they watching from the beyond? Would they be cheering her on?

Her thoughts were frantic and violent, a muddled mix of flashbacks from games she'd watched and nightmarish imaginings of how Atticus died, so she sat awkwardly on the bench and stared out at the calm sea, breathing deep and even, filling her nostrils with the scent of salt and fish. The fertile folds that surrounded the villa were speckled with oleander and mallow, with fig trees and pomegranates growing in the orchards nearby.

Gia watched the sky darken. A moment of peace.

The door handle rattled, interrupting it. When she unlocked it, Cyrus was standing there, smiling too hard.

'Ready?' he said.

'Can't wait,' said Gia, gritting her teeth.

'I'm choosing to believe you mean it.'

'Me too.'

'Then follow me. It's your time to shine, baby.'

She trailed him through the villa, past Lucas and Dominic, both commiserating their losses. Dom flashed her a thumbs up for luck. Lucas merely stared gormlessly. Fabius was surrounded by girls, but he made sure to mouth something vulgar as Gia passed. Several people held her visored gaze as she navigated the straggling clumps of servers and partygoers, but she moved on before their curiosity could settle. Soon, everyone would know. Gia's fate lay more in the hands of the audience than her opponent.

Outside, a group of musicians performed for the senator and his special guests, with acrobats who somersaulted and waved silks. Cyrus pulled up on the steps leading to the lower part of the garden, waiting for them to finish their performance. Felix stood waiting on the opposite side of the ring.

'Now, remember what I told you ...' Cyrus began.

His voice faded as her eyes drifted over to the imperial table. The red-faced emperor had fallen asleep in the heat, gently nudged awake by an attendant. He awoke with a piggish snort as the attendant pushed a fresh goblet into his hand. Prince Decimus threw food, heckling the dancers. Claudia watched attentively with a performative smile, applauding when appropriate.

Gia's eyes rested on her a moment, watching as she twirled a fork in slender fingers. What must it be like, to want for nothing? To care about nothing? Gia might've been envious, if only the sight of her didn't incite such irrational dislike.

Cyrus was right: from a fighter's point of view, looking up at the imperial family, she had a new perspective on the people who ruled the world.

They were even more terrible than she had imagined.

Nearby, the birthday boy, Senator Cornelius, and his two women looked uncomfortable, upset. As though an argument had taken place.

'Gia?' said Cyrus, drawing her back. 'Did you get all that?'

'Not really, sorry,' she said.

The band ceased playing their instruments, inspiring a chorus of subdued applause. The heat was thickening. More people were starting to doze off. Gia watched as a wave of yawns spread through the crowd. The audience were tired, their plates and glasses empty. They were in need of more wine, more water, more bread, more cake. More of everything. Some of the nobles were already drunk.

Cyrus signalled for them to move forwards.

If she couldn't win them over, she'd be finished. In boredom, men were often cruellest. She hoped she was enough to wake them up.

Cyrus approached the enormously tall man who was announcing all the acts, handing him a bag of coins and a scroll of parchment.

They had a short conversation, which Gia couldn't make out over the sound of the restless crowd, but the announcer looked confused. The tall man Cyrus was talking to looked Gia up and down, his face a buffet of mixed feelings.

'On your head be it,' he said to Cyrus.

'Don't I know it,' said Cyrus.

With a wave of one arm, the man signalled for the blare of trumpets as the band reassembled to bang their drums.

'Now is your moment,' said Cyrus, turning to Gia. 'Think back to every creep comment. This is your chance for payback.'

Gia exhaled and squared her shoulders, trying to make herself feel as big and broad as possible.

'You can do this,' he said.

It was just Felix. Just that idiot Felix.

'Normally I wouldn't say anything, but since it's a friendly match and your first performance,' said Cyrus, leaning in and lowering his voice to a rumble, 'you should know that Felix's Achilles heel is his right shoulder. He broke his collarbone as a kid and a strike there will take his breath out. Don't tell him I told you.'

'Got it,' said Gia, wondering if he'd done the same thing with Felix and what he might describe as her weakness.

'Whatever happens today, you're my champion.'

But that only made the possibility of losing feel worse. An image of herself sprawled face-down in the dirt popped into her head, with everyone laughing and pointing in mockery.

No. She could not lose. She would not lose.

Cyrus nodded at the man he'd given coins to, who nodded back. The tall man walked into the centre of the makeshift ring and raised one hand, causing half of the gathered guests to quieten. With the other hand, he held a horn made of bone, which amplified his voice over the sound of chatter.

'Our next match is between another student of the Pompeii gladiatorial school ...'

The way the gardens were designed, in undulating levels, carried the sound of his voice for half a mile as people casually ceased their private conversations and turned their attentions back to the centre of the arena.

Drums rumbled. Feet stomped.

'Felix the Fortunate,' called the announcer.

Gia bit down on her lip, watching her pale, red-headed opponent flexing his muscles, blowing kisses at the girls in the audience as rowdy boos sounded.

'Doesn't look too fortunate to me,' said a man standing nearby.

'I could snap that lad like a twig.'

'His opponent has come all the way from Amazonia,' bellowed the master of ceremonies, 'to take revenge against the men of Pompeii.'

'What?' said Gia.

Cyrus looked to her guiltily.

'Just a little character – for promotion. It's also ... security. In case they react very, *very* badly. You don't want to be run out of town.'

'For gods' sake, Cyrus,' she said, but there was no time.

'So please put your hands together for our very first gladia*trix*, Viatrix the Victorious!'

The gathered crowd fell silent for a moment, as if watching something drop, then exploded into a riotous chorus as she stepped out from behind Cyrus.

Gia entered the ring to a deafening drone of cheers and boos. The crowd goggled at her, their expressions comically exaggerated. One man spat at her. Mouths hung open in curdled curiosity and disgust.

Though she tried not to, she picked out several words from the din:

'Whore!'

'Dog!'

'Public toilet!'

It was as if the announcer had just told them she was a mass murderer. Even then, they probably would've been more welcoming.

Cyrus led Gia in a circle, parading her around the ring like a horse. She ignored the growing calls of the audience, staring straight ahead defiantly as if she couldn't hear their vulgarities. When they'd completed a full circle, she and Felix were urged to present themselves before the imperial table.

Dread filled every part of Gia's body. The feeling was so overwhelming that her mind rose above her body, as if to fly away. She peeped out from her low visor, watching Felix bow unsteadily before the emperor, his voice high-pitched.

'Ave imperator, morituri te salutant.'

The emperor appeared unimpressed, exchanging a raised eyebrow with his sour-faced son, Decimus.

Claudia gave him a brisk, graceful nod. 'Good luck,' she said.

Gia didn't dare to meet the emperor's eye as she took her turn, bowing as well as she could in her gladiatorial get-up.

'Ave imperator, morituri te salutant,' she said in a low voice.

For a moment, no one spoke.

'You are an insult to the sacrifice of good men,' the emperor said in a flat voice, 'but I shall enjoy watching you slaughtered. For the crime of offending the emperor, you and your opponent shall play to the death.'

The crowd rolled, calling out in shock and glee.

'What?' came Cyrus's voice, too far way to help.

The commentator stepped forwards, raising one hand. 'My emperor, this is not to be a kill to win game. We're having a party. We have agreed—'

'Cornelius will allow it, won't you?' shot the emperor.

'Oh, yes,' said Cornelius, in a voice of barely concealed resentment. 'You should have anything you ask for ... on *my* birthday.'

'Then they will fight to the death,' reaffirmed the emperor, in a voice that left no room for argument. 'It is settled.'

The commentator shot Gia a regretful look, his brows pinched, before he nodded in submission. 'Whatever you wish.'

When Gia looked to Felix, she saw her own fear reflected.

Her first fight, and her last.

She looked up to see Claudia staring right at her.

The princess had stood up behind the table to get a better view. She was distant, but Gia could still see the emotion that shone so clearly through her face.

Horror.

It lasted only a moment before the princess regained her composure, applauding dutifully for the games to begin.

4. WE WHO ARE ABOUT TO DIE SALUTE YOU

Either Felix would die today, or Gia would. One of them would not leave this place alive and she was not ready to pass into the dark night.

'Then let us begin.'

The commentator solemnly urged them forwards.

'You know, I've been thinking about what you said before,' said Felix casually, as they walked to the centre of the ring, 'about you being treated as an equal.'

'This isn't a good time for a debate,' she said.

'I just want you to know that I'm not going to hold back. I will fight you as I'd fight any man sent to take my life.'

'As will I.'

'I won't die today for your mistake. I hope you understand.'

'My mistake?' said Gia, confused.

'Your hubris, then. You should never have joined the school.'

'What?'

'Come on, Gia. You must be mad to think you can act like a man and get away with it,' he said. 'Even the emperor is insulted.'

His friendly mask had slipped. His true feelings about her were becoming visible now, though there had always been signs. Signs she had ignored.

'If you carry on like that, I won't feel bad about killing you,' said Gia, in a voice as sharp as the sword in her hand.

'It's true. You could've been some lucky man's wife and now you'll be a pretty grave instead. You would've been better off at the brothel. What a waste.'

'Perhaps it's you who should never have joined the ludus,' she said. 'You can talk big with your balls out, but you're still just a little boy underneath it all.'

'I'm no boy. You'll see, soon enough.'

Her sandals on the dirt crunched. Gia was struggling to walk under the weight of her weapons. Sword in one hand, shield in the other, she tried to assume the position of a victor, flexing her knees and leaning slightly forwards.

The insults continued to ring out:

'A woman fighting in the ring? Well, now I've seen everything.'

'Take off your clothes!'

'I'll show you how a woman acts.'

'Now, gentlemen,' said the announcer, 'please keep it in your robes. Must we behave as if we still live in caves?'

The noble men quietened, but the expressions on their faces did not soften. As the noise of the crowd reduced to a resentful murmur, something hit Gia hard in the face, catching her temple.

'Ow.'

Raising one arm reflexively to rub the spot, she saw a wooden cup rolling around her feet, its contents running in rivulets through the dirt. A warm damp spread across her chest, liquid soaking the skin between the straps of her armour. A pungent smell wafted up into her nostrils, like a blocked sewer.

It was piss.

Someone had pissed in a cup and thrown it at her.

Gia kicked it away furiously.

'Who did that?' she shouted.

A lone titter sounded, giggles catching like fire through the crowd as they realized what had happened. Women smiled behind their hands. Men slapped each other's backs in amusement. Heat bloomed in Gia's cheeks. Doused in piss in front of the imperial family. It could hardly get worse.

'No more, gentlemen,' cried the announcer, over the ruckus. 'We must all behave decently. Please, let the battle commence.'

Gia couldn't judge them too harshly. She'd stood up there once with her parents and her brothers too, delighting over the gore just like everyone else. She had never thrown piss at anyone, certainly, but she had cheered for violence. She had delighted over eyeballs popping. In Pompeii, death was theatre. It was worship. It was sport. Death was their reason for living in so many ways and, today, it had come for her.

Gia fixed Felix with a glare as he joined in on the mocking laughter. She tried to ignore the stench of urine that had permeated everything.

A steady drum beat shepherded them into battle.

'First, we must take the oath,' said the commentator. 'Repeat after me: I will endure to be burned, to be bound, to be beaten and to be killed by the sword.'

'I will endure to be burned,' Gia and Felix chanted in unison, 'to be bound, to be beaten and to be killed by the sword.'

A torch was lit as drums quickened. The monotonous sound of stamping feet filled the amphitheatre.

Gia and Felix saluted the emperor in turn.

'We who are about to die salute you,' they recited.

Gia had always known death would claim her one day, but she hadn't expected it to be so soon. She resisted it, with all her might. She vowed to herself that she would triumph and prove to everyone that women could hold their own in the ring. She would go down in history as a fighter of great legend, lavished by riches and living in Rome. This was the occasion she had no choice but to rise to.

There was no lose.

Only win.

As the commentator kneeled down to grab a handful of sand, the sound of the audience melted away until Gia could hear only her own pounding heart and her own shaky breathing. Time rushed and slowed, froze and stuttered, as the carnivore roaring of spectators gradually increased in volume.

She watched in slow motion as the sand trickled through the commentator's fist, petering out to cloudy dust. When his hand was empty, he bared his palm and bellowed through his horn so loud it startled her into full wakefulness.

'FIGHT!'

Gia danced lightly back and forth, the weight of the shield already straining her arm. Felix copied as they circled each other like wild dogs. They did this for so long that people in the audience began to boo again.

'One of us must make the first move,' he said.

'Go on, then. Show me what you've got,' she dared. 'I hope you're bringing more than you did to our practise match.'

These words seemed to stir Felix into action, setting his face as he took a run at her. She lunged out of his way, her helmet slipping. With a soft clang, the visor dropped down and obscured her vision, drawing a laugh from the crowd. Yet she couldn't stop to fix it, having both of her hands full and with Felix approaching fast for a second attack, this time grunting with false confidence.

Unable to see where his weapon was, she barricaded herself with the shield instead, slamming into him. Felix stumbled backwards, cursing, but, as Gia struggled upright, the visor slipped even lower, completely covering her eyes.

The crowd chortled and chuckled. The match had only just begun and she was already making a fool of herself.

Temporarily blinded, she thought of Fortuna, who saw nothing and everything at once to symbolize that destiny worked in darkness. She felt herself standing on the edge of her own blade, poised between life and death as the wheel of destiny spun. All she had to do was cling on.

Gia held her breath, listening intently as quick, dusty footsteps neared, followed by the high-pitched metallic whine of a sword in flight.

Now, came a little voice in her head.

She brought up her own sword to meet his with a reverberating clash of steel. She felt some fleshy resistance, as Felix cried out and retreated. She'd hit him, but she still couldn't see a damned thing.

Gia was sweltering. She couldn't get enough air. And she urgently needed to fix her helmet, which required her to free one hand.

She had to choose between the shield and the sword. Attack or defence? Which should she pick as her weapon? The shield was protection. It guarded and sheltered. The sword was strength. It empowered and enabled. She needed both, but combined they were too much for any one person to carry.

Gia made a quick decision based only on the chaotic, unspeakable poetry of her gut feelings, releasing the shield and letting it fall to the ground.

With her now free hand, she reached up to fix the visor, her fingers slippery and trembling. It was stuck, rusted in place. She could see Felix's feet and the tip of his sword dragging on the ground, watching as he moved into position again.

She couldn't win like this. Gia had no choice but to pull the helmet off, her long braid freed from its steel prison and swinging free.

The action drew a curious 'ooh' from the audience, surprised by her daring. Without a helmet, she was vulnerable. Its removal also seemed to make her womanliness even more obvious, as most of the men in the arena now called out in support of Felix.

'Get her, boy!'

'Don't let a woman beat you!'

'You can do it, son.'

No one called for Gia. If she had any supporters, they were of the silent kind. When she looked to Cyrus, pacing nervously back and forth around the ring, he nodded firmly as if to tell her, 'Go on'.

Noticing this look of allyship between them, Felix charged her with both hands on the hilt of his sword. Gia defended, using all her strength to push him back.

'You think you're his favourite, don't you?'

He had a bloody gash on his chin from her sword. Felix scowled at her, all traces of the person she'd gone drinking with now gone.

'The competition isn't that strong,' Gia said.

Only one of us can live, she reminded herself.

'Cyrus is only doing this out of pity, you know that, right?' he said. 'You're just here to give the audience a good laugh.'

Felix was trying to get into her head.

'They were laughing at you too, clown,' she said.

'It's insulting, for them to make me fight you. You should submit. They'd probably let you live if you wept and begged.'

'Not happening,' she said.

Back and forth, they jabbed nervously at each other, ducking and diving to avoid the other's hit.

'Is that it?' she said. 'All the privilege and convenience of being a man and you can't even beat me?'

'Says you!'

'Great comeback.'

'Don't you feel stupid, dressed up in that armour like a child playing make-believe?' he said. 'It's embarrassing. You're embarrassing.'

'I'm not pretending,' she grunted.

They hurled more insults than fists.

'It's no wonder you're a virgin,' he said.

'Your only experience is with your own hand,' she said.

Felix lunged. As their swords met once again, he used his free hand to punch her in the hip, kicking out her feet so that she fell forwards to meet his blade.

A last-minute twist spared most of her face but for a sharp slice of the cheek, speckling the ground with a scarlet spray of blood.

The commentator called out to reprimand him, Felix retreating with one palm bared, but the damage was already done. The crowd was entirely on his side now. There was nothing they wanted more in this moment than to watch him kill the woman who had dared to fight like a man.

Pain seared through her body, deep and throbbing. Groaning, she struggled to stand. Before she could gather herself, Felix thrust out his weapon once more, this time stabbing her in the upper arm. Gia watched the blade retract, leaving an open gash that gushed blood.

'How about now? Are you impressed yet?' he said.

With a guttural groan, she kicked him in the crotch and swung her sword into his shoulder, just where Cyrus had told her to strike, watching as he dissolved into a shrieking, submissive crouch.

'I have never been impressed by you, Felix, and I'm not going to start now.'

A scatter of muted applause. When Felix stood to face her, his eyes were white and wild, his red hair ruffled, his skin pale.

Sweat dampened the back of her neck, her palms so clammy she could barely get a grip on her sword.

Gia just wanted it to be over.

Desperate now, she sprang into action again, teeth tightly gritted to block out the hurt as she swung wildly in his direction. She gained ground as he retreated defensively, but one slow swing and he was out of her reach. She staggered after him, heavy in her armour, while he seemed to hop nimbly from place to place like a frog.

Felix's swordsmanship was sloppy, but his defence was impressive. Gia tried to keep up with the dance, performing a miraculous roll to avoid a certain strike, but he was wearing her down, hit by hit.

She had to strike now, or it might be too late.

The tables turned again, with Felix advancing and Gia stumbling backwards. Both of them were dirty and boiling in the heat, him stinking of sweat and her of piss, but she sensed that he had more yet to give.

When he struck again, Gia lashed out. Her sword snagged in the leather straps and buckles of his armour. For the briefest of moments, she was stuck in position before a rusted buckle fell off, releasing her weapon. The sword clunked to the ground, but she was still exposed. Gia snatched it up and held it out just in time to defend, but Felix pushed forwards, driving her across the amphitheatre floor with the blade of her own weapon pressing against her neck.

Her back hit the wall of the makeshift ring.

'Kill her!' cried the audience.

'Do it!'

'Any last words?' Felix said, as the crowd chanted on. 'Do you wish to make a speech about women's liberation?'

She stared into his sweaty, freckled face. Up until today, Felix had been a friend. A terrible friend, but still a friend. She would never make that mistake again. Men could not be trusted. Perhaps not even Cyrus. Hadn't he trussed her up and thrown her to the lions, after all?

'This fight isn't over,' she said in a low voice.

'Looks like it to me.'

Felix set his jaw, wincing in readiness as he pushed harder, letting the sword constrict her neck.

Blood trickled from the wound, beads of blood forming a necklace.

'Last chance to submit,' he said.

His hesitation gave her just enough time to take advantage. Pushing her weight up against the wall, she kicked out at him, pounding him in the stomach.

As he staggered backwards, Gia used her sword to create distance. She stalked after him as the crowd booed. He was finally starting to tire, his face bright red.

He raised his sword to fight back, but something stopped him, causing him to fall back again.

'I submit,' he said, taking her by surprise.

Felix turned around so that she couldn't see his face, then dropped to his knees, letting his sword fall.

'Kill me,' he begged, his shoulders shaking. 'I can't look at you. Just get it over with. In the back. Make it quick.'

The amphitheatre was silent, unsure what was happening. When the boos resumed, they were aimed at Felix.

'Pathetic!'

'You snot-nosed little coward!'

'You could've had her!'

'What kind of man are you?'

He was submitting. He was forfeiting the game.

Gia had long dreamed of being a gladiator, but she had never fully understood the gravity of taking a man's life until now. Even if Felix had been a stranger, she wasn't sure she could do it. It seemed suddenly absurd, that she had romanticized such a thing as eyeballs popping.

'I don't want to kill you either,' she said.

Instinctively, she dropped her own sword in relief, drawing another gasp from the crowd as she inched towards him.

'We can make a pact,' she said. 'They might kill us both, but we can still refuse to kill each other. We can hold onto that one last bit of decency, no matter what.'

In battle, she'd loathed him, but now, she wished to comfort him for some reason. Perhaps because he was making pitiful blubbering sounds, like an infant throwing a tantrum, or perhaps because he was trying to sacrifice himself for her.

She was nearly close enough to pat him on the back when he stood up suddenly, wiping his eyes with one hand.

'Felix?' As he turned, she saw that he was smiling and that in his other hand, he was holding her helmet.

The helmet she'd removed and left lying on the ground.

Thump.

Gia barely had time to register her mistake before he smashed her in the face with it like a boulder, using the full force of his weight.

Every single person in the audience drew a breath.

The visor sliced her nose but it was the blunt force of the strike that hurt. The pain was indescribable, a white-hot explosion in her brain. She fell backwards and hit her head for a second time, crashing onto the hard ground. Stars burst behind her eyes before red filled her field of vision.

Blood, but she wasn't sure where it was coming from.

'You . . .' she rasped, scrambling around on the ground.

The crowd roared.

'Kill her! Kill her! Kill her!'

'Sorry,' said Felix with a smirk, standing over her with the bloodied helmet under his arm, his sword outstretched. 'I just wanted to give you a good ending.'

Gia spat blood at him.

He dug the point into her throat and put one sandalled foot on her pelvis to pin her down.

'Don't be mad,' he said. 'It's just a game.'

5. THE PRINCESS AND THE GLADIATOR

As Felix shifted his arm, ready to finish her off, a pompous voice cried out: 'STOP!'

Gia couldn't see what was happening through the veil of blood, but Felix stepped back hastily, dropping the helmet.

An unintelligible swell of noise surrounded her, pulling her back to reality. Gia heaved herself upright, wiping her face and squinting through the sting of pain that caused her eyes to water.

The crowd was looking over at the imperial table, where the emperor had called a halt to the match, one hand raised.

Claudia was whispering in her father's ear. He batted his hand dismissively but she insistently continued whispering.

Gia watched him submit, shaking his head.

'As happy as I would be to see you kill her, my daughter here is amused by the concept of a woman gladiator,' he said. 'She finds it to be quite the entertainment. She wishes to see the woman live to fight again.'

Several faint cheers seemed to agree, though others protested.

'Felix the Fortunate is the victor!' called out the commentator, lifting one of Felix's arms and parading him around the ring.

Claudia had intervened to save her.

Claudia? Had intervened to save her?

Gia stood in concussed shock as the crowd began to boo her again, throwing their drinks and whatever food was left on their plates. They weren't happy with the outcome, but who could argue with the emperor. It was done.

Gia stared at Claudia. The emperor's daughter was looking right at her, right at the mess of her face.

Claudia's expression curdled slightly. She seemed pitiful yet disgusted, like Gia was some poor sick dog she'd fed scraps to and now she wanted to wash her hands. The princess had just saved her life, yet Gia had never hated her more.

Cyrus appeared at Gia's side, expertly ushering her out and shielding her from projectiles.

'That ... that was ...' she gasped, blood on her lips.

Gia was going to say, 'a complete fucking disaster', but Cyrus jumped in: 'Fantastic.'

She whipped her head around, frowning.

'Are you kidding? I got piss thrown at me, everything hurts, I must look like a bruised piece of fruit ...'

She dabbed at the cuts on her face: one on her cheek and one at the bridge of her nose, between her eyebrows.

'You won in the only way that counts,' said Cyrus, leading her towards the villa. 'Let's get you cleaned up.'

'In what way does it count?' asked Gia, swaying slightly.

Cyrus offered his arm for support.

'That was your first match, and the emperor's daughter intervened to spare your life. If that doesn't get people talking, nothing will ... I guess she's a fan.'

He winked at her as she glowered.

'You think this is funny?' she said.

'I'm just happy you're alive. I thought you were destined for the pyre for a moment,' said Cyrus.

He dabbed at his forehead with a cloth. Gia noticed the drops of sweat that had gathered along the line of his tight curls.

Alone in the washroom where she'd changed into uniform, she cleaned her face with a wet rag. With the two cuts on her face, one on her arm and an open wound on the side of her head, there was a lot of blood to be washed away, not to mention the piss, but she was alive, which seemed improbable in the circumstances.

Maybe she was in favour with Fortuna, after all.

Still strapped up in her leathers and armour, Gia sat at the window again, watching the sea wash away the stains of the day. She knew she ought to change back into her civilian clothes, but she feared that unwrapping the ensemble would cause her to fall apart, crumbling into chunks of diced flesh.

Claudia had saved her life. It defied belief. For what reason could Claudia wish to spare her? Gia tried to imagine what insidious reasoning she might have, but she couldn't think of anything. Perhaps the princess really had been amused by her. The death of a peasant was all a game to someone like her.

A soft knock scattered her thoughts. Cyrus appeared, poking his head through the door. Grinning, he handed her a small bag of coins.

'What is this?' she asked.

'Your winnings.'

'But I lost.'

'I told a couple of gambling men my plan to present a woman gladiator and all of them but one bet against you. Only I specified you had to *submit*. The words 'I submit' never left your lips – in fact, they were spoken only by your opponent – so they had to pay out on a technicality. They're not happy, but rules are rules, right? This is your cut. Your first salary as a professional gladiator.'

'Did you know the emperor would do that?' she said shakily. 'Force us to fight to the death?'

'No,' Cyrus said firmly. 'He's short-tempered and mean-spirited unless drunk, but I didn't think he would go that far. Something about powerful women must've really irritated him.'

'I could've died out there.'

'That's the game, for better or worse,' he said. 'This is a brutal business, Gia, but it's often the only way a poor man can gain his freedom or his vocation. There's no reason why women shouldn't have the same chance to make their own fate. We cannot change the world. Not now, not alone. Let us just bask in this small glove tip of glory for now, shall we?'

'I can't be glorious,' said Gia. 'I was terrible out there. Felix ran circles around me. I was humiliated in front of . . .' Claudia's face flashed in her mind. 'Everyone. How can I stand up to fight again when I almost died the first time?'

'Because that is what gladiators do and, as of today, you are a gladiator. Officially,' said Cyrus.

He held up her scorecard, which was marked with a draw.

Gia shot him a look, suppressing a small smile.

'You're sure? Even after that?'

'You'll win the next one,' said Cyrus. 'You got some good hits in. Felix played dirty, but it's a good lesson for you to learn, plus he had the crowd on his side. You see now what a difference it makes?'

At least she wasn't dead, Gia kept reminding herself. *Fortuna had spared her for a reason. It was meant to be this way.* Such incantations kept the waves of embarrassment from rolling over her so often.

Felix appeared at the arch of the open door. Gia noticed how his expression changed when he saw Cyrus. Here he was, the technical victor of the game, and his mentor was busy congratulating the loser.

'There you are,' he said monotonously.

'Ah, Felix! Man of the hour.' Cyrus clapped his hands together, sweeping Felix into a hug and patting his back. 'You put on a fine performance out there. Better than fine. It was diabolical, but I can't help but admire your audacity. You might've gone a touch overboard with the fake crying, though. Just a little note for next time.'

Felix didn't seem to be listening, staring solemnly at Gia.

'Come, I'll shout you a flask of wine,' said Cyrus. 'Make sure you keep an eye on Lucas, though. He's already had plenty, and we all know he can't hold his drink.'

Cyrus slunk out, but Felix didn't follow.

'This is awkward,' he said at last.

'For you, maybe,' she said.

'I'm sorry about ... all that.' He waved his hand, making a circular motion. 'I was just trying to get under your skin.'

'That was some act you put on.'

'Gladiators *are* actors,' he said. 'Every battle is a performance. Cyrus taught us so. I was just pretending. It's our job. It isn't personal.'

'You tried to kill me. That's personal.'

'Like you wouldn't have done the same thing if you'd had the chance?' he said contemptuously.

'I *did* have the chance, actually. I didn't want to do it and that's my mistake. Some of the things you said, I can't forget.' Gia tutted, irritated and itchy. 'I don't want to talk about this any more.'

'Gia, wait...'

She shouldered him hard, bustling out of the room. Felix didn't follow and she was glad of it. She was too tired to deal with her mixed feelings, too tired to string sentences together. She was shaking from the pain, from exhaustion and hunger.

The tables downstairs were still covered with plates of of uneaten food and full glasses, though the crowd had drifted further down the gardens to stand around a large fountain and light candles in floating lanterns. Piling up a plate, Gia filled her belly as she drifted through the villa, admiring the flaking murals and scuffed mosaics.

She found Lucas puking into a potted plant as Dom sprawled on a bench nearby, hands clasped over his chest. Lucas looked up, vomit staining his mouth, said, 'Hello, Gia' before he resumed his regurgitations.

'Where are the others?' she said, cringing in sympathy.

Dom gestured lazily out into the gardens.

'Being idiots, as usual,' he said. 'You look like roadkill.'

'Yeah, I know. Thanks for the confirmation, though.'

'I'm glad you're still here.'

She met his eyes for a moment, so dark and warm she felt at ease, and exchanged a small but genuine smile.

'Me too.'

Looking through the arch, Gia saw Fabius wrestling another man on a mound of grass. A group of girls looked on, unimpressed.

'Have you seen Felix?' asked Dom. 'I think he wanted to apologize to you.'

'He can stick his apologies up his arse.'

She poured the last dregs of wine from a vase.

'Fair enough,' said Dom.

'What about Cyrus?' she asked.

'No idea, he just disappeared.'

Gia moved through the villa, draining every abandoned glass that still had wine in it as she went. She and her brothers used to do the same thing in the taberna and at the parties her parents threw for local merchants. The villa was mostly empty but when those who lingered caught sight of her, they whispered fervently.

'That's her, the woman gladiator.'

'They should have let him kill her.'

'See, this is why you don't let women make decisions.'

In the kitchen, Senator Cornelius's wife was crying about her husband's new mistress, comforted by her handmaids. In the atrium, two men in togas fed each other grapes. A group of servants chased a chicken down the hall. Gia walked along the colonnade, passing arches where different groups of people sat, creating little vignettes. Two courtesans plaited each other's hair; three senators argued about the emperor's growing incompetence; a serving boy ate a stolen pastry in the shadows; another senator serenaded a depressed-looking courtesan who met eyes with Gia and sighed heavily.

She continued along the hallway until she reached a dead end. She passed through one arch, then another, and found herself disorientated, trying to follow the noise of the party back to the main part of the villa.

Gently pushing open a wooden door, the light fell upon Cyrus's naked buttocks as he screwed the senator's mistress. Her leg was wrapped around him as he thrust his hips, her back banging against the shelves of a pantry full of jars.

'You're a bad girl, a very bad girl,' he said.

'Yes!' she said. 'I've been so very naughty! Punish me!'

Gia backed away, trying to make as little sound as possible.

So that was where Cyrus was. Good to know.

Gia was not a virgin, as Felix had presumed – though she liked to think she was, simply because it had been so disappointing it felt like it shouldn't count. Her one and only time with one of the serving boys at the taberna had lasted for less time than it took to grill a fish. It had been painful and degrading, watching him putting his tunic right and turning away, never to look at her in the eye again.

Cyrus obviously liked to live dangerously if he was willing to risk doing the senator's side woman on said senator's birthday. Trying to recapture the feeling of being in the ring, maybe.

Gia's skin buzzed as she recalled her battle with Felix. She'd feared for her life every moment, and yet, she wanted to do it again.

As she made her way back downstairs, Gia looked out over the balcony to see two figures standing before a fountain. One of them was Claudia; Gia recognized her blonde hair and purple stola. The other was the birthday boy, Senator Cornelius, his jowly cheeks flushed, his gait wobbly.

He was standing far too close to Claudia, which set a bell ringing in Gia's head. She recognized that lean – the belligerent, entitled lean men did when they thought a woman owed them something.

She crept closer, quietly descending the covered stairs to stand behind a nearby pillar, catching strands of their conversation over the noise of the party.

'If you want me to do something for you, you have to do something for me,' he said. 'It's only fair.'

'I cannot give you that,' said Claudia.

'One day you will give in,' the senator said.

Claudia wore a fixed smile, but her body was as stiff as the marble statue behind her, guarded but not yet fearful.

'Please be serious,' she said. 'You're a good thirty years older than me ...'

'Age is but a number.'

'... and I'm not interested. Whatsoever.'

He stepped forwards, grabbing her wrist.

'Interest is of little importance. Duty is more compelling.'

'You think I have a duty to go to bed with you?' asked Claudia, attempting to break free of his grip. 'I have no duty to any man, and you already have enough women at your feet – more than you deserve.'

'I helped you fix the vote,' he said, in an even lower voice. 'I convinced the others to vote against the emperor's proposal, at great risk to myself. I can't imagine what your father would do if he found out. Perhaps he would leave your punishment up to Decimus. He might let them paint a mural with your blood.'

'We had an agreement, Senator,' said Claudia. 'This was not the agreement.'

'It is now. I'm making a new agreement, with new terms. You'll go along with it if you want me to keep my mouth shut.'

'I thought you cared about the future of Rome.'

His demeanour quickly switched from menacing to adoring.

'I do. I do, for you are it, Princess. That is why I wish to appreciate you so much. Let me show my affections.'

'You can please me more by leaving me be.'

'No one will see us. It won't take me long.'

Gia's hands curled into fists, listening as Claudia struggled against him.

'I said no,' she affirmed, pulling back.

'I didn't ask for permission.'

'You are very much mistaken about the relationship between us, Senator,' said Claudia, in a harder voice than she'd used before. 'You are an adulterous politician who can easily be bribed. There are hundreds more of you back in Rome. I am the emperor's one and only daughter. If you think you have any power over me, you are wrong. Now, step back.'

But her firm words went unheard as the senator began to drag her into the shadows, Claudia protesting, yet not in such a loud voice that it would draw attention. It was a desperate whispering, the kind of voice a person might use when they were panicked but didn't wish to be caught in such a compromising position.

What would happen if no one intervened?

Though Gia hated the princess, Claudia was still a woman, and no woman deserved such an indignity, which is why Gia moved to her aid without thinking.

She dashed forwards, following them into the alcove where the statue of Venus stood, in a small stony recess with a curved bench on either side. As she drew the sword she had the great fortune to still be carrying, she caught the senator assaulting the frightened princess, his right hand around his . . .

Hearing Gia approach, Claudia turned to stare, her face unreadable.

When the senator faced her, quickly covering himself, Gia

raised her weapon, using its point to push him back towards the statue of Venus.

'Who the hell are you?' he gasped.

Somewhere far away, a gathering of goddesses assembled in audience.

'Viatrix?' gasped Claudia, using the opportunity to spring away.

Gia ignored her, eyes on the senator.

'I think it's time for you to go home, don't you?' she said. 'Fuck off nice and quick and I won't tell everyone what I saw.'

'You're at *my* birthday party.'

'I don't care. Fuck off, or I'll use this sword on the one thing you treasure most.' She looked pointedly at his lower half.

'Listen here, man ...' He narrowed his eyes at her. 'Woman? Whoever you are, you're making a terrible mistake.'

'No, that was you, when you harassed the princess,' said Gia. 'Not sure the emperor is going to like that, and now she has a witness.'

'You ... I recognize you now,' he drawled, his hooded eyes rising up from the blade. Despite his dire situation he gave a gurgling laugh, still drunk. 'You're the gladiator girl who almost got killed today.'

'You only just noticed that? You're not too bright, are you?'

'Dare you speak to me this way? Don't you know who I am?'

'I do, but I don't give a damn.'

'Leave, Cornelius,' pleaded Claudia. 'Go back to your wife, or your mistress. Whichever one can tolerate you best when you're like this.'

'That's right,' said Gia, 'or I'll tell everyone you're chasing the emperor's daughter around with your dick hanging out.'

'No one would believe you.'

'I don't know about that. On the streets, we call you Cornelius the lech.'

'What do I care what plebians say about me? It's your word against mine, and I'm the emperor's dearest friend.'

'They might not believe me, but he *will* believe her.'

She met Claudia's gaze, but the princess gave a doubting expression.

The senator scoffed, which turned into a cough.

'Claudia? Oh, please, nobody takes her seriously. She has to scrabble on hands and knees for the crumbs of power that fall on the floor. Her father would give her to me gladly if I asked.'

Gia slowly turned to Claudia. 'Want me to kill him?' she said.

'Not today,' she said coolly. 'It's his birthday.'

'Looks like you're done here,' said Gia. 'Leave. Go back to your party.'

'You're blowing this all out of proportion,' he said, baring his palms as he shuffled backwards. 'I have committed no crime. She is of age. Who can blame me for showing interest in such a beautiful woman? I wouldn't be a real man if I didn't try.'

'Whatever helps you sleep at night,' said Gia.

His expression hardened. 'If you start gossiping, it's you who will be remembered as a tease, Claudia dear, not me. Think carefully on this.'

'Go, Cornelius,' said Claudia.

'This was all just an unfortunate misunderstanding, wasn't it?'

They exchanged a long look.

'Yes,' said Claudia, through gritted teeth.

'What about ... *it*?' said the senator, pointing at Gia. 'This abomination of nature is intent on telling lies about me.'

'The gladiator won't say anything, will you?' said Claudia, with a look that told Gia, firmly yet wordlessly, to agree.

'Not unless you want me to,' said Gia.

'See? Just leave, and we will keep our word.'

We.

Gia could never have dreamed that the princess of Rome would one day refer to them in the plural sense, even if just in passing.

Senator Cornelius departed into the dark, fixing himself before running off to meet the angry wife who called for him.

When Gia looked to Claudia, Claudia was already watching her.

'You shouldn't have done that,' she said, frowning.

Gia blinked at her repeatedly. This was not the reaction she'd expected.

'What?'

'You heard me, gladiator,' she said.

'Oh, I'm sorry, did I inconvenience you by saving you?'

'*Saving* me? That's a bit dramatic. I was handling it.'

Even as a damsel in distress, the princess was annoying.

'Were you? Because it looked like he was mishandling you,' said Gia. 'I thought he was going to—'

'I am aware,' said Claudia curtly. 'It isn't the first time he has tried.'

Side by side, they stared up at the statue of Venus, goddess of love and sex.

'Your intervention has complicated things,' said Claudia.

Gia shook her head. 'You should focus your ire on the man who just tried to force himself upon you.'

'Oh, I do. One day, I shall celebrate his departure from this Earth with the most lavish of parties – but, for now, I need him.'

'You need him?' Gia parroted, in disbelief.

'These things are complicated. You would not understand. Cornelius is an ally. I do not wish to make him an enemy.'

'How can you ally with such a monster?'

'You have no idea what monsters I have known, gladiator. I do what I have to do to stay alive.'

'Your choice.' Gia thought of Felix and all the disgusting comments she'd personally ignored for convenience. 'But a man like that can never be an ally to us.'

Us.

They locked eyes again, as Gia recalled the dream she'd had. Her skin burned hot as the improper thought took hold of her, entirely against her will.

'Can you promise that you won't speak of this?' said Claudia. 'It will do both of us harm, should people hear of it.'

'I will hold my tongue, but you should tell everyone what he's really like,' said Gia. 'He shouldn't be allowed to get away with it.'

'Even if my father had him executed to spare my shame, citizens talk,' Claudia said. 'They'll think I gave myself to him willingly. It will stain my reputation more than it will stain his legacy.'

It was true. Despite her fury, Gia knew. Even the gods were known to take what they wanted from mortal women. No one stopped to think about how the women felt about it. People just assumed they were happy for the chance to lay with a being of divinity. Who could argue with a god?

'Then I didn't see anything,' Gia said. 'Nothing at all. I just went for a walk, and had a nice, boring time.'

They fell silent.

'You should be warned, Cornelius is a petty man,' said Claudia.

'He enjoys plotting vengeance. He'll find a way to punish you for today.'

'What about you?'

'He will punish me too,' she said. 'There is no doubt about that. But, as I said, I need him ... for something important.'

She turned as if to leave, then paused, frozen in the act of exiting the scene.

'You're not really from Amazonia,' she said: an afterthought.

'No, I live down the road,' said Gia, gesturing awkwardly with one thumb. 'My name isn't really Viatrix, either.'

'I thought not. Then what is it?'

Gia paused, unsure if this information was safe to share with someone so dangerously powerful. The silence between them was growing too plenteous to bear comfortably. Finally, Gia gave in.

'Gia,' she said, gripping her sword tighter. 'Gia Antonia Valerii.'

'Claudia Imperia Caesaria,' she said, bowing slightly in response.

'Oh, I know,' Gia said. 'Your name is engraved on statues. Your name is chanted by priests of cults. There is no name in this world that I know better than yours.' Gia found that she was unable to stop talking. 'I have spent my entire life under your name. I have always known you.'

And hated you, she thought.

She was sure by the way Claudia left herself open to attack that she did not have any training in combat.

As if sensing Gia's thoughts, Claudia said, 'I must go now, gladiator. I hope our paths will not cross again.'

Gia nodded, numb. Claudia vanished into the growing dark of the gardens, leaving Gia to wonder if she had just imagined the whole thing.

She waited there, staring at Venus for a while before returning to the villa to retrieve her belongings. She walked all the way home in a daze, barely aware of the drunkards and stray dogs all around her. Still dressed in armour and covered in blood, they shrank in fear of her.

Once, Gia had believed strongly in destiny, thinking that if she found herself in a certain place at a particular time, she was fated to be there. This was how she coped with her losses.

By this reasoning, Cassius was destined to die on the battlefield. Atticus was fated to expire in the ring. Their deaths were written in the stars, which meant there was nothing to regret and no one to blame but the gods.

On the opposite side of the coin, when good things happened, the gods were responsible for these too. Gia had survived a fight she was meant to die in. She had found herself in the company of the princess whose picture she'd grown up under. Until now, she would never have thought the gods paid any attention to her. Gia was a background actor in a play, to be culled when the plot demanded it, yet what happened tonight could not escape their attention.

The gods had a connection to the imperial family. They were surely watching Claudia tonight, and Gia with her.

If the gods were paying attention, they knew her now.

ACT II

DIANA

FORTUNA

MINERVA

VENUS

Each of the goddesses had their own way of spying on the mortal world. Minerva used her polished shield, which reflected the comings and goings of humans of note: scholars and politicians she liked to keep an eye on. Venus gazed into a large standing mirror, keeping in touch with her favourites: beautiful people she romanced in dreams. Diana did her scrying through a pool in her grove, surrounded by the nymphs who lived in trees. She mostly followed mortal sports and games.

'Any developments?' asked Venus, emerging from thin air.

Diana pretended not to be startled.

'The princess has arrived in Pompeii,' she said as Venus sat beside her on the flower-scattered grass. 'She is due to attend an event this evening, at which gladiators from the local ludus will be performing. Perhaps one of them is the fated one.'

She reached into the water, skimming her fingertips upon the surface until visions appeared there.

'I do love a party,' said Venus.

An image formed in the water, broken apart into ripples that merged, revealing a scene of two boys fighting.

'Good gods, they're dreadful,' said Diana. 'I have seen better attacks from leeches and limpets.'

The images in the water carried no sound, so the goddesses didn't hear the master of ceremonies announce the next opponent.

'What are the mortals so upset about now?' said Diana, as they watched the fight. 'There's always something with them.'

'They certainly don't like this fellow here.'

As the figure removed their helmet, Venus gasped and clutched Diana's arm.

'It's the girl,' she said.

'I recognize her,' said Diana. 'She is the sister of the late Atticus the Agile. The boy is one of Fortuna's recent sacrifices. If this is how the people respond to a woman gladiator, imagine how they will treat a woman ruler.'

They watched as Felix dominated the match.

'I don't know if I can watch,' said Venus, burying her face in Diana's shoulder.

A hair away from death, the battle suddenly halted. The visions shifted to the emperor in his box, and Claudia beside him.

'What's happening?' said Venus.

'The princess called off the fight. She intervened ... to save the gladiator girl.'

'Do you think ...'

They exchanged an unfathomable look, one only possible when two people have spent an eternity together despite their differences.

In Pompeii, the party continued, until the goddesses witnessed the incident between Claudia and Senator Cornelius.

'The princess saved the gladiator, and the gladiator saved the princess,' said Venus when the visions faded. 'How romantic.'

'Hmm. I am not so certain about that,' said Diana. 'The princess said she wished never for them to meet again.'

'We can work with that. No, I think this is it. I feel it. She is the right one.'

'Fortuna said it would be a warrior, like me,' mused Diana. 'I didn't know she meant that so literally.'

'We must tell Minerva.'

The goddesses dissolved into matter, pouring into the study of Minerva's library palace like sand and waking her from her nap. An owl flapped angrily on its perch before resuming its slumber, cracking open one eye to glare at them occasionally.

'Good heavens, what's going on?' said Minerva, righting her helmet. 'Can't you see I'm busy?'

Venus and Diana exchanged a look of amusement before they both began talking at once.

'We found the warrior!' said Venus.

'The one Fortuna foresaw,' said Diana.

Venus produced a clamshell-shaped compact mirror, in which the visions they'd seen in the water reverberated once more.

'Perhaps the hero we seek is really a heroine,' said Diana.

'Our gladiator is a woman,' said Minerva, springing up so forcefully she knocked over a stack of scrolls. 'Of course she is! A female guardian for a female ruler, in a plot hatched by goddesses. Why did we not see this coming?'

'What now?' asked Diana.

'Now, we play. Now, we fight. But first, we must consult with Fortuna.'

'I am already here,' came a voice.

Fortuna emerged from nothing, as if she had been there all along.

'I hate it when she does that,' whispered Venus.

'I sense you have good news for me,' she said. 'I am in dire need of it.'

'Yes, my goddess,' said Minerva. 'We think we have identified the warrior.'

Fortuna held a golden globe, which spun without aid. 'Good, because the situation is rapidly evolving. Jupiter has heard word that some in the pantheon are working against him. For now, he suspects only Vulcan. They do not yet have our names, but they soon will. We must bring forward our plans and move with great haste. It is imperative that Claudia secures the heart of the gladiator.'

'Her name is Gia,' said Diana.

'Her?' said Fortuna, pausing. 'A woman? And you are certain she is the one?'

'It would seem so,' said Minerva thoughtfully. 'The princess spared her life at great risk to herself, and so the gladiator repaid her. But she is still in possession of free will. There are no guarantees in war or love. Even if she is the right warrior, she may not react as we expect. Her allegiances are still to be established, yet the signs are there, and they are clear.'

'What should we do now?'

'When the gods learn that we move against them, Claudia's life will be in even greater danger than it already is,' said Fortuna. 'We need for them to be inseparable, if we are to keep her safe. We need the gladiator to be at her side at all times. We must orchestrate another meeting, and soon.'

'What do you advise? They inhabit different worlds,' asked Minerva.

'We must commune with the gladiator. Minerva, you must visit *with Claudia again and persuade her to extend a hand. Until then, we must move in darkness, and tell no one of our plans. Let the gods have no reason to suspect us, or the consequences will be grave indeed.'*

6. THE GODS DEMAND THEIR SACRIFICES

Hardly a man could be seen on the streets on the day of Vestalia, while slaves and noblewomen alike flooded the Pompeii Forum, walking barefoot to the temple while singing and praying. They stood in line to give offerings to Vesta as equals, as did Gia and her mother.

'We'll be here all night,' groaned Gia, who hated standing stationary for long periods of time. 'Let's try later.'

'Don't be so dramatic,' her mother said, carrying a basket of bread bits. 'There are only twelve people ahead of us.'

'Twelve too many if you ask me.'

'Just wait.'

'All so we can light a candle in a cave,' said Gia.

'It may seem frivolous to you, but these traditions are a part of our culture. It's important to keep them up. One day, Rome might be invaded by philistines and all of this will be forgotten.'

The taberna was closed tonight. Her mother had been in a much better mood since Gia had come home with winnings. Naturally, she asked how Gia had come by the money, but Gia was vague, telling her she'd been struck by a reversing chariot and that the wealthy senator being driven in it had given her the money as recompense.

As she'd tended to the wounds on her face, her mother had quietly told her that whatever she had done, she must never do it again. Gia had pretended to agree and that was the end of the conversation.

Her mother occasionally hosted businessmen who made generous loans to her, letting them stay overnight in her chamber. Gia assumed that she thought the same of her. This bleak realization seemed to shake her mother out of her fugue, compelling her to get up, get dressed and go to work, fearing that her only daughter would soon be earning denarii by the same means.

Not all of the courtesans in the empire slept with men, but they all sold their time and energy. Some poured drinks, performed poetry, danced or even played board games, never revealing too much skin. These were the richest, most powerful courtesans in Rome, the ones who entered all the rooms other women couldn't. But, for most women, the work was much more rudimentary: a squalid room in a rotten brothel, flesh slapping on flesh before the faded murals of orgies.

The wait seemed to last for hours, queuing under a parasol in the baking heat. Gia and her mother talked in lapsed conversations that came and went, picking up where they'd left off a quarter-hour ago.

'Did you hear about this Viatrix?' her mother asked.

'No?' said Gia innocently.

Dressed in a tunic and a robe that covered her hair, she had yet to be identified in person, though she knew it was only a matter of time.

'You'll never believe it,' her mother said. 'A woman, fighting a man at the Villa of the Mysteries. I heard it from Lady Lando's new girl. She battled a boy from the ludus down the street, but Claudia Caesaria called a halt to the match just as he was about to finish her off. They called it a draw. People lost money betting against her. They're very upset.'

'Sounds like a real spectacle,' Gia murmured, mouth dry.

Her mother clucked her tongue. 'I don't think it's right. Women are meant to be better than men. We're the brains and they're the brawn.'

'Father was the brawn?' Gia joked, arching an eyebrow.

'Father was ... the heart,' said her mother, putting her arm around Gia. 'He would've been very upset to hear that young girls were putting themselves in the ring.'

'You don't know,' said Gia. 'Maybe he would've found it exciting. I don't think there's anything wrong with it.'

'I don't like it. If we act like them, we'll become like them. Women should be above all that violence and gore.'

'You enjoy the games just as much as anyone,' said Gia.

'But it's different to be down there in the pit, going head to fist with some brute. This Viatrix doesn't stand a chance. She'll be dead before the end of the year, even if Fortuna favours her. Why the emperor's daughter intervened, I have no idea.'

The line moved, inching forwards.

'You'd best not get any ideas. I remember how you used to be when you were a kid, thinking you could fight like your brothers.' She gently tipped her chin. 'That's how you got that scar there, I remember.'

Gia averted her gaze, not wanting her mother to look through her as she sometimes did, but her eyes rested on Gia's fading bruises.

'I don't want you thinking you can be like some Amazon woman,' she said. 'You wouldn't last a minute in the ring, and I'm not about to lose a third child.'

Silence followed, shrouding them in the grief that defined their relationship now, but like a dark cloud it soon passed over and they pretended it hadn't happened at all. It was easier. Atticus had been a gladiator. Atticus had died. It was no wonder that her mother was so opposed.

'Promise me you won't do something stupid like that?' she said, taking Gia's hand in hers. 'Thieving. Walking the streets. Gods know what. I know this world can be tough for a girl, and that death comes for us all, but don't throw your life away like that.'

'I'm not,' Gia said. 'I won't.'

'Don't put your mortality in Fortuna's hands to do what she wills with.'

But Gia was already on the wheel. She was aboard and she couldn't get off, riding it until it stopped.

Her mother sighed. 'Okay, all right, that's it. I think you've been lectured enough now.'

A group of people pushed their way out, past the flamen, or fire priests, who guarded the archway, allowing Gia and her mother to enter the small cavernous temple. It was crowded with barefoot women holding infants, offering skinny, sick-looking livestock, and occupied by three donkeys dressed in flower crowns. The animals lazily ate the straw scattered on the floor, eyeballing Gia as she lit a waxy candle stub and reignited the pungent spicy incense.

Vesta was rarely pictured in human form, more often taking the shape of the ignes aeternum or sacred fire: a large torch in her temple, its fixture made of intricate brass mouldings. Her vestal virgins swept away the ashes of spent offerings. Their job was to keep the flame burning. A simple enough task, but they were sworn to chastity for thirty years for it.

'Vesta, please bless our hearth and home,' recited her mother, laying their gifts of vegetables and grain at the feet of the goddess. 'Favour us, Vesta, the wise and truthful. We pray that you protect this household and that the eternal flame of the family continues to burn.'

'Vesta, please guide the household members who have departed this mortal life,' said Gia. 'Keep safe their souls in the darkness, until they may live again. Keep your flame burning bright, so they may find their way out.'

With their Vestal duty done, they made room to give others a turn, squeezing their way out of the crowded temple. Gia's mother hooked her arm through Gia's, pulling them on down the road. She was good company when she was tipsy. She wasn't happy sober and she wasn't happy drunk ,but there was a medium, an in-between, in which she was the person Gia knew and loved. Right now, she provided the perfect distraction, talking incessantly about this, that and the other.

A growing murmuring noise signalled the arrival of someone important, causing them to pull up. Gia watched as a tight-knit troupe of cult members in purple robes approached, swinging incense holders that billowed smoke, followed by servants holding bunches of wildflowers and soldiers in red regalia who used their bodies to shield the woman standing in the middle.

Claudia. She was barefoot too, though she wore a long silk shroud of gold with a white silk tunic beneath, belted at the waist. She didn't wait in the line but cut ahead, 'by order of the emperor'.

Gia couldn't see her hair or face, but she recognized Claudia's hand, wearing a set of rings connected with fine golden chains. She recognized her walk. She recognized the shape of her body.

'What is she doing here?' Gia asked of herself.

Since their last meeting, Gia had been picturing her back in Rome – when she was just down the road. It made her oddly uncomfortable. She had been trying to forget their strange encounter, now here they were in the same place and time again.

'Everyone makes offering on Vestalia,' her mother said.

'Why is she here in Pompeii, I mean.'

'I heard rumours that the emperor purchased a villa here in which to spend the rest of the summer.'

It must be the Villa of the Mysteries, Gia thought, where she lost her first fight.

'He would leave Rome for that long?' Gia asked.

'Perhaps there is something back home that he wishes to avoid, like dissent among the Senate,' said her mother.

'Is that what people are saying?'

'Some of them,' her mother said. 'You know these emperors don't last long, nor their families. Perhaps it is better to be a pauper, after all.'

Claudia's party reappeared and headed back the way it had arrived, a train of opulent pomp trailing right by them. Gia could barely see her through the throng. As Claudia neared, however, her eyes were drawn to Gia's through a cloud of incense smoke.

Their gazes locked for a moment, then the group smoothly passed them by.

Gia realized that her heart was pounding.

'Come on,' said her mother.

As they walked home, they passed by the gardens of the vestal convent, where a small audience had gathered. Three vestal virgins stood at the heads of open graves, each of them with wrists and ankles bound. One quietly wept. The other screamed at the skies, begging the gods.

'Vesta, Diana, Bona Dea, anyone: please spare me from this injustice and I will worship you and only you until the end of time. I shall sing your name from the rooftops each morning! Please, I beg you, let me prove myself to you!'

'Shut up, Agrippa,' said the third girl, staring ahead passively. 'You know well the goddesses don't care about us.'

'These three vestals have broken their vows,' a flamen priest was saying to the crowd, 'and, tonight, they shall be punished for it, as you here are all witness.'

He walked along the line, addressing them in turn.

'Domitia snuck out to attend a festival with the boy who delivers grains ... Agrippa laid with a praetorian guard in the catacombs ...'

'Innocent!' screamed Agrippa. 'I am innocent, before the eyes of the gods. I didn't even kiss him, I swear.'

'Sabina attempted to run away with a gladiator,' the man said.

Sabina gave a little shrug, as if to say, 'So?'

'We should do something,' whispered Gia, though she knew it was hopeless. 'They're going to kill them.'

'What will you do, fight the imperial cult?' her mother said.

'This is a warning to any woman who thinks she can serve the sisterhood while submitting to carnal desires,' continued the flamen priest. 'You have disgraced Vesta's name for the last time.'

'We should go,' said her mother sharply. 'We don't want to witness this.'

'They will bury them alive,' said Gia. 'How can we look away?'

'The gods demand their sacrifices,' was all her mother said, ushering her on down the road as the screams of the damned vestals peaked.

'The emperor, you mean,' said Gia, trying to block it out.

'In the eyes of many, they are one and the same,' her mother said, indicating the group of cult members on the corner.

But why would the gods want such a thing? What use did they have in the heavens for young girls who'd committed the crime of a kiss?

There was hardly a man in Pompeii who stayed loyal. Every senator had a mistress. Emperors had their wives killed when they were tired of them.

But these young girls, who'd done little more than experiment, had paid for these small pleasures with their lives.

And there was nothing Gia could do about it.

Fors Fortuna was a festival held in celebration of the goddess of destiny herself. On this day, thousands of revellers crowded on boats and barges in the rivers, drinking from dawn until dusk. In Pompeii, a day's events were planned, including a variety performance at the amphitheatre.

Cyrus informed them that they'd all be working: they'd been hired to fight the students of another school in Herculaneum in the Pompeii amphitheatre, like real gladiators.

This created several problems for Gia. For one, there was a strong chance that someone she knew would spectate on the matches and realize that Viatrix was actually Gia Valerii. Her mother, for instance.

The second problem was that she would have to fight a ruthless stranger.

The third problem was that Claudia would likely be there if she was staying in Pompeii for the summer, and Gia didn't wish to set eyes on her again.

'My contact there says he'll source a girl for you to fight, Gia,' Cyrus told her. 'She will likely be untrained, inexperienced. An easy win for you.'

'Famous last words,' Gia said.

'It's never good to take things for granted, that's true, but you have to have belief in yourself too,' Cyrus said. 'Sometimes, it's that faith that leads you to victory.'

'I just want to be prepared,' Gia said.

'Then let us prepare you.'

Gia spent as many hours training as she could spare, wearing her armour to help build strength and watching as her body became more defined. She fought Cyrus one-on-one in the yard, and though she lost, despite him going easy on her, she defended well enough to earn his praise. Weights that were once a burden to carry became light, while muscles emerged that she'd never seen before. She grew stronger against the boys too. Though Gia did her best to avoid Felix, they were so often together that she had settled into a relationship of strained tolerance with him.

Things were going well. For the past few weeks, Gia's mother had abstained from the vine. She had taken back control of the family business. They enjoyed the start of summer together, eating pomegranates on the balcony and gossiping mildly about the people who passed by. Gia savoured every moment, knowing it wouldn't last. Her mother had done this before, a handful of times in the years since her father passed, worse with every dead child. Someday soon, she would retreat into her gloom and Gia would be all alone in the world again.

Juggling her duties at the taberna with her commitments for the ludus left Gia with little time to dwell on things. It also left her with little time to socialize. She hadn't seen Berenice since Maius. Occasionally she thought of Claudia in the Venus shrine with Senator Cornelius, but she always pushed it to the back of her mind.

The day before the festival, Cyrus called her into his study at the ludus. Gia had just won against Fabius for the third time in a row, goading him in the yard as she entered the building backwards, serenaded by the sounds of mocking laughter.

At least this time it wasn't directed at her.

Gia mopped her brow with a rag as she tried to cool off, but Cyrus's face chilled her right away.

'Uh oh,' she said.

'You'd better sit down.'

Gia complied, steeling herself for the worst.

'What is it?'

'I just heard from my contact at the Herculaneum school,' he said, rubbing his brow with one hand.

'Go on.'

'There's been a slight change of plans. Apparently, my acquaintance found a girl on the street willing to fight for money, but she stole from the ludus and fled. Now he finds himself fresh out of women he can train in time.'

'So, the fight is cancelled?'

'Not exactly,' said Cyrus, drumming his fingers on the desk. 'You'll now be fighting a man named Caturix of Gaul.'

'That doesn't sound good,' Gia said, after a beat.

'It's not. They say he killed twelve Roman soldiers in one go. They say he drinks blood from the skulls of his enemies. He's as tall as he is wide, like a wall of pure muscle. He hasn't lost a match yet.'

Gia blinked rapidly. 'Well, shit.'

'I didn't know they'd switch up on us like this. I fear my old enemies in Rome are hoping I make a fool of myself by backing you.'

'Is he even a student at the ludus there?' she asked.

'Technically, yes. Gladiators tend to stay with a ludus for as long as possible. It's like having free management. It benefits the school, as he's bringing denarii in.'

'*Obviously* you have to say no,' Gia said, shaking her head. 'I can fight a man, but I cannot fight a giant.'

Cyrus made a wincing expression, as if he had more bad news.

'What?' said Gia, in a flat voice.

'I'm afraid it's already arranged, against all reason and honour. Orders come from the top.' He pointed at the sky.

'The gods?'

'The emperor, Gia,' he said. 'He said he wants to see how tough you really are. He's clearly not a fan of women being gladiators.' He smirked. 'Not like his daughter.'

Gia shifted uncomfortably.

'She spared me from being killed,' she said. 'It was an act of pity, that is all. That doesn't mean she's a fan.'

'I think the emperor regrets sparing you, because all the women are talking about you now. *Everyone* is talking about you now. Many of them are planning to watch your next fight.' Cyrus patted his pocket, where coins jingled. 'The bet-makers are ecstatic. Senator Cornelius has put a large bet on you losing. I think he was the one who influenced the emperor to make the match.'

Claudia's words echoed in her mind: *'You should be warned, Cornelius is a petty man. He enjoys plotting vengeance. He'll find a way to punish you for today.'*

Claudia had warned her that it might happen, but Gia had almost forgotten about the senator until now. *Of course* he'd had a hand in it. If Gia was dead then so was the only witness to his misdeeds.

It was only Claudia's word against his, if it ever came to it.

'Don't despair,' said Cyrus, watching her face. 'Remember: Caturix of Gaul has a weakness.'

'What is it?'

'I don't know yet, but I'm sure he has one.'

'Be serious, Cyrus.'

'I am. Finding his weakness is your only hope. I'll ask around, see what I can learn. Other than that, you should probably play dirty. Play so dirty that even Felix would look at you in disgust. Your last fight was not so encouraging.'

'I got pelted with food and piss, Cyrus. You don't have to sweeten it for my pride. It was a disaster.'

'In that case, fine, it was a shit circus. Happy?'

'Not really,' Gia said with a sigh. 'I still have to fight a man who drinks blood from skulls.'

They fell quiet, both heavy with thoughts.

'You should advertise that you're accepting women students,' she said, at last. 'I shouldn't be the only one. What's the worst that could happen?'

'The praetorian guard could have me arrested for offending the emperor. They could shut the ludus down. They ...'

'You don't know that. Promise me that if I die tomorrow, you'll do it in my honour?' Gia said.

'I wish I could, but I'm struggling to afford rent on this building already.'

'I know the feeling,' she said, thinking of all the times her mother's debtors knocked at the door while they hid in the darkness.

'And all for what?' he said. Cyrus gave a wry smile, then gazed at the portraits on the wall. 'The empire needs us to put on a show. To distract the public from bigger issues. That's the only true power a gladiator has. But at what cost? So many lives lost in the name of the empire, so that the rich may be richer and the enslaved may still be prisoners. We may have earned ourselves better armour and lodgings by putting our lives on the line, but we are not yet truly free.'

Gia thought of Atticus, a broken ragdoll on the amphitheatre floor, killed for the sport of the crowd. She thought of Cassius, torn into pieces by the barbarians overseas. She could not even blame their savageness, for they were simply defending their land. It was the empire, and the emperor, who wanted more and more. No amount of death and conquest would ever be enough for him.

To rule the world was an insatiable greed.

'Soldiers and gladiators; what are we truly fighting for?' said Cyrus. 'For ourselves, or for them? Emperors come and go, and each one brings new disasters, new hardships, new debts. Power rots their hearts. If we are ever to be free of imperial rule, we must form our own army to match their own might.'

Gia cocked an eyebrow at him, surprised he would talk so openly of rebellion, but Cyrus didn't seem afraid.

'You're serious?' she said.

'A man can dream,' he said. 'Do you think me wicked?'

She slowly shook her head. 'If you are wicked, then so am I for I want the same thing. For myself, for my mother, for my brothers, for every woman in Rome.'

They held each other's gaze silently.

'There are thousands of soldiers, but there are many more men,' he said eventually. 'Add women to the ranks and maybe we could take Rome for ourselves.'

Gia scoffed. 'As if it would be so easy.' She sounded like Atticus. 'What do gladiators know of politics?'

He tipped his head towards the open archway, watching as members of the imperial cult walked down the road in their purple robes, humming a chorus about regal divinity and holding candles.

'Politics is a spectacle,' he said, 'no different to gladiators in the ring, putting on a performance so people will forget how cruel the world is.'

The cult kept a room at the macellum near the market, where they held meetings and housed their sacred books. They dedicated their lives to worshipping the emperor as a deity, believing him and his family blessed, but they were really just servants of the imperial order. They spent their days trying to convert plebeians into devotees. They commissioned sculptors to depict emperors as divinities in an attempt to win favour. For the most part, the people of Pompeii were disinterested, more loyal to the gods than the emperor.

'Sometimes I wonder what would happen if we stopped

entertaining the people,' he said. 'Would they start to look around and notice things they don't like? Or would they find a more terrible way to feel alive?'

Gia looked across the paintings on the walls. The first one was Cyrus, holding a spear and smiling. He was younger, less scarred, but a person's eyes never change.

'Hey, look who it is,' she said.

'There I am,' he agreed.

'What was your fighting name?'

'Cyrus the Silent,' he said. 'I never spoke a word. Those were the days, eh?'

'Do you miss it?' Gia asked.

'Terribly,' he said.

'You can take my place tomorrow if you want,' she joked, though she wouldn't have complained if he'd actually offered.

'I wish I could,' he said, gesturing at his leg.

'Tell me about your worst match,' she said after a pause. 'Tell me about a fight where you thought you were going to die, but you triumphed against the odds. I need to hear it. For courage.'

Cyrus was quiet, thinking hard as he gazed at his own portrait.

'Floralia, ten years ago,' he said. 'I'd just seen a man named Thaddeus lose an eye. Nice fellow.'

'I remember that fight!' said Gia. 'I was just a kid then.'

She felt guilty, for enjoying it so much at the time.

'I was in the fight that followed, against my old nemesis Corvus the Cruel. He wore a dead bird on his head. That was his thing. It was a kill-to-win game. I knew one of us wasn't leaving the arena alive. I was sick, and my lover at the time had recently cheated on me – with Corvus, of all people – so I wasn't at my best.'

'Ouch,' Gia said sympathetically.

'I couldn't get myself together, making one stupid mistake after another. Corvus cornered me and told me, in great detail, about what the two of them had done in bed together. Still, I didn't utter a word. I all but welcomed death in that moment, watching her in the audience rooting for the man currently trying to kill me. I swore to myself I would never experience that kind of pain again. Right before he was about to finish me off, he started to get cocky. He enjoyed the sound of his own voice too much. I managed to wrap my fingers around the small dagger that had fallen from his cloak and I stabbed him in the side. His face still haunts me. Ever since then, I've avoided relationships like a plague.'

'I figured that, when I saw you going at it with Senator Cornelius's mistress at his birthday party,' she said.

'You saw that?' he said, visibly horrified.

'Only fleetingly.'

'I regret it. I wasn't making very good decisions that night.'

'It sounded like she was consenting pretty strenuously.'

Cyrus groaned and buried his face in his ringed hands, each symbolizing an important match he'd won.

There was another long silence. 'There's really no other way?' Gia said at last. 'I must fight him?'

'You know what must be done,' Cyrus said gravely.

And she did. She could not drop out – she would bring misfortune to Cyrus and the ludus and make a mockery of women gladiators for ever after. Maybe no other woman would walk in her footsteps. She'd have to flee Pompeii in shame.

If she fought Caturix of Gaul, she might just die with honour.

Maybe Gia would see her brothers again.

And if, by some miracle, she *won* ... she'd be a legend. A hero worthy of the title. She would have power, in a world happy to give her none. She would be permitted into those rooms whose doors were closed to her.

Born to fight, born to die.

Gia would rise to meet her fate, to look Fortuna in the eye and say, 'Fuck you.'

As Gia walked home from the ludus, her mind was hot and full of warring thoughts that engaged in little gladiatorial battles themselves. She walked without thinking where she was going.

The skittering sound of shoes on loose stones brought her back to reality.

Someone was trailing her.

Pulse quickening, Gia pretended not to notice. She took a shortcut, but the person followed. She waited until she reached an open square with plenty of places to run to before she spun around, preparing to kick him in the sack.

'Boo,' said the figure.

It was Fabius, her nemesis, his robes pulled up over his shaven head.

'You? What do you want?' she said, already on edge.

'I hear you've got a big fight tomorrow. I just wanted to wish you luck.'

'Sure you did,' she said.

'Don't be like that. That's all in the past, right? There's no bad blood between us any more. I mean, my nose will never be exactly the same shape, but it's not really that important, in the big order of things.'

'Why do I not believe you?'

'I'm being real. I want us to be friends.'

He was definitely bullshitting her, or trying to.

Fabius held out one hand, calloused, with dirty nails.

'Peace?' he said.

'Fuck off, Fabius.'

Gia turned away, already moving in the direction of home, but Fabius was suddenly at her back, grabbing her arm and twisting it until she cried out. He didn't let go until she heard her wrist crack, falling back with a rabid look on his face.

'There's your payback, bitch,' he said.

Gia was so angry she couldn't form a full sentence, shivering violently as she cradled her wrist. 'You ... fuck you! I'll ...'

'That's the last time you'll ever laugh at me.'

'Wait until Cyrus hears about this,' she said. 'He'll kick you out of the ludus.'

'I don't care,' he said. 'I just got a nice little bonus. I would've done it for free, but it's even better that I got paid for it.'

'Someone paid you to break my arm?' she panted. 'Who?'

'That's my business. Looks like you got a lot of enemies.'

He tapped his nose and smirked. But Gia had a fairly good idea already: Senator Cornelius.

Fabius fled the scene, his footsteps fading out, leaving Gia hunched over in the middle of the road.

The pain didn't hit her right away, instead flooding her in increments until it became so overwhelming she couldn't stand. She rocked back and forth on her knees, gritting her teeth and making carnal noises. Shooting needles lanced her right arm, as a dull, nauseous ache rotted her insides.

Groaning, Gia vomited into the gutter, seized by a pain so deep she worried that it would be the last thing she felt. When she attempted to use her right hand, the small task of plucking a wild flower from the cracks between pavement stones sent lightning bolts through her entire body.

'Ow!'

Her right arm was useless.

Fuck Fabius. Fuck Felix. Fuck the empire. Fuck all men. She couldn't fight like this, and yet she had to fight.

Still on her knees in the gutter, Gia looked up at the stars.

Everything that had briefly seemed to be beautifully destined was now horribly misaligned.

7. IN HER EYES

Gia awoke that morning believing she was fated to die.

She'd had a terrible dream in which Fortuna, barefoot and blinded, had led her into a cave full of slippery eel monsters to be eaten for no reason at all. It left her feeling fearful and weakened, which wasn't ideal when she needed to fight for her life.

In the light of a new day, her wrist was horribly swollen, a masterpiece of a bruise developing like a painter's canvas. It throbbed ceaselessly, paining her with no rest, and it hurt worse with every slight movement she made.

At dawn, Gia bathed in goat's milk and rose petals – a rare treat, paid for with the last of her winnings. She lay back in the tub and cradled her arm. If this was the last sunrise she ever saw, she could at least go to the underworld to meet Pluto with soft, sweet-scented skin.

Climbing out of the tub, Gia dressed gingerly and with difficulty, changing into her armour. Its plates were engraved with chips, scratches and nicks from dozens of battles that had happened long before her. She gently wrapped her arms in leather straps, hiding the bruising. If her opponent noticed, he'd be sure to take advantage.

Gia donned a leather headband to hold last night's braid in place and struggled to put on the visored helmet that would hide her identity. Its hinge had been repaired, allowing her to see clearly enough to fight.

It was a uniform to live or die in.

Gia could do worse than dying on a blue-skied, gods-blessed day, when incense and cinnamon drowned out the smell of sulphur and shit. Many should be so lucky, she repeated to herself. It was better than dying in the rain, or the gutter.

Taking a deep breath, Gia let the sun warm her face one last time, telling herself she welcomed death. But her stomach wasn't as convinced as her head, and it lurched and ached with dread.

This was it. It was Fors Fortuna, and either the goddess was on her side or she wasn't. Based on the amount of times she'd told her to fuck off, probably not.

There was honour in dying, she told herself over and again.

By high noon, it was hotter than Vulcan's forge, drawing every citizen of Pompeii out from their sweltering villas and into the narrow, crowded streets to celebrate. Gia moved through the Forum, now heaving with people in tunics and togas, in sandals and stolas. Painted statues of the gods stood before the Forum's many columns, with offerings of food and wine scattered at their carved feet. Gia saw mimes and politicians, courtesans and orators, poets and merchants, jurors and beggars – all of them already half-drunk. Children raced through the crowd playing tag, having slipped away from the mother who called for them. Gia moved on, passing under strings of paper wheels stretched overhead, past musicians playing songs about dead emperors, past the plumes of meaty smoke that poured from stalls with grills.

Gia walked faster. Her sandals slapped across the hard ground, her sweating soles slipping across the leather.

Sudden sharp pains shot through her hand, coursing up to her injured wrist. She lifted it to her chest, biting down on her bottom lip and shutting her eyes as she waited for the agony to subside.

The boys were waiting for her on the steps near the amphitheatre, though Fabius was nowhere to be seen. Dominic caught her eye, nodding down at her swollen hand.

'You don't have to fight if you're injured,' he said.

'Who said I'm injured?'

'Fabius told me. He was boasting about it. He probably made sure to tell Caturix of Gaul, too, the way he was talking.'

'You'd better not tell anyone else if you want me to have half a chance,' she said. 'Not even Cyrus. He'll freak.'

'You should call it off. Reschedule. What good is a win anyway, if your opponent is already weakened?' said Dom.

'The emperor wills it, plus Cyrus already paid the fee,' said Gia. 'If I back down now, he'll lose his money.'

'If you lose, you'll die.'

'So I die,' shrugged Gia. 'It's in the hands of destiny now.'

'Why would you choose this?' said Dom, shaking his head.

'Didn't *you* choose it?' she said.

'It's different.'

'Why is it different?'

'Because ... every man in my family is a gladiator, ever since my grandfather was freed. There were certain expectations of me.'

'Every man in my family is dead,' said Gia.

When a loud gong sounded, the crowd flocked together, forming a tight procession as people surged into the amphitheatre.

Flanked by Lucas and Dom, Gia made her way into the tunnel

that led to the arena. A colossal ring of stone, with entrances for both nobles and peasants, the amphitheatre rose from the ground with all the presence and grandeur of a palace. One of the city's finest constructions, it was a monument to the empire.

Inside, the walls were daubed with painted posters of famous gladiators. One announced the famous Celadus, the long-haired 'heartthrob of the girls'. Another fresco depicted the end of a fight, with the losing gladiator awaiting his fate.

Gia swallowed as a wave of heat rushed up from her toes, making her feel dizzy and sickened.

She'd been here dozens of times before with her parents and brothers. She had seen gladiators bludgeoned and beaten and killed, and now she was going to be one of them. She had asked for it. As a child, she had even prayed for it.

They joined the other gladiators, where Cyrus was waiting for them. He looked at Gia with unconcealed dread.

'You are fit to fight?' he said. 'You are sure?'

'Better than ever,' she lied.

He swallowed. 'Okay, then . . . Well, here we go, gladiators. This is it. This is the big time. This is the occasion. Everyone you know, and don't, is up there watching you, so you'd better get out into the ring and impress them. If you fuck up, don't lose your cool. Count to three and think ahead.'

It was easier said than done. In the heat of the moment, it was hard enough to remain conscious.

'I'm proud of you all and I have faith in you all, but, as always, you have to have faith in yourself. Blind faith, sometimes. Blind, stupid faith. You need to step into that arena with a quiet confidence. Imagine that victory is already yours. It already belongs to you.

Follow your instincts and you'll achieve it. Half of the battle is in your own mindset.'

Another reverberating gong drew them to stand between the pillars of the colonnade. They looked out on the arena, smelling the sawdust, sweat and stale ale.

Gia watched as spectators filed up the stairs of the amphitheatre, taking their seats inside along the curved stone benches. The wealthy citizens of Pompeii sat in covered seating on ground level, while the public stood in the upper levels, looking down on the fight. They were all in high spirits about the brutality they were about to witness, laughing and drinking and making a ruckus.

If Gia wanted to join them in their freedom, she had to win. There was just one problem with that. She'd be fighting one handed, against an opponent she was unlikely to defeat with two good hands.

Gia glimpsed Caturix of Gaul on the other side of the room: a hairy mountain of a man. He caught her looking and made a condescending kissy face.

Gia felt herself shrivel, wilting like flower petals in the heat.

Her training now seemed woefully inadequate. Cyrus had done his best, but she was still slim and light. Now she was expected to triumph against a competitor three times her size.

At the sign of the emperor's arrival, the roar of a crowd of twenty thousand people filled the air, perforated by horns and drums. The citizens of Pompeii stamped their feet, making the ground shake.

The emperor took his throne in the imperial cubiculum, where wine and grapes were laid on a long table. Claudia and Decimus sat on either side of their father, wearing matching glum expressions.

Claudia wouldn't be able to intervene this time, even if she wanted to. Gia had already had her last chance.

The emperor offered an almost imperceptible nod to indicate that the frivolities could begin. The arena fell to silence, cued by the waving of a white flag. The emperor began to speak, his voice carrying confidently across the arena, amplified by the architectural acoustics of the amphitheatre.

'Citizens of Pompeii,' he said, to a cheer. 'Blessed is the day of Fors Fortuna, when the destiny of every man leads him here.'

As he spoke of Rome and of the empire, Gia's good hand clenched at her side, digging her nails into the skin of her palm as she tried to ignore the deep pain in her other wrist. The emperor spoke of victory and honour, and the great glory of the gladiators. He warned of the perils of abandoning tradition for optimistic ideals. Gia thought he turned his head in her direction as he spoke, as if the words were for her, but she doubted he could see her waiting in the shadows, in the underbelly of the structure, especially not in all her regalia.

When he had finished, and the lengthy, adulating applause quieted, a stream of supporting performances roused the crowd: wild animal fights and acts from Greek comedies before a muted voice rang out, announcing the first gladiatorial battle between Brutus Maximus and Ignatius the Impaler.

A small band played, narrating the fight with music. This first match was short and ended in a draw, neither man paying with his life. One by one, the other gladiators were called out to battle. Some returned alive but bloodied, while others were dragged out through the gates, their broken bodies to be burned. Sometimes the cries of their loved ones in the audience could be heard.

When Dominic was called up, Gia couldn't watch, remembering all the times he'd faltered in training. She paced nervously as she tried not to listen in on Felix's animated commentary, alternating wildly between euphoria and despair.

'It's not looking good ... Oh, he's done for now ... Fight back, idiot ... Fuck, he's a dead man ... No, wait ... Well, would you look at that? The bastard actually won!'

When Dominic limped back to them, battered and bruised but alive, Gia exhaled in relief.

'I can't believe I survived that,' he said, grinning broadly.

She couldn't help but grin back at him.

'Me neither, to be honest,' she said.

'Well done, man,' said Felix.

Felix was called up next, putting on his fish crest helmet. Gia felt more confident in his chances. His opponent was a short, stocky retarius, who fought with a trident and net, at least three decades older.

In the ring, however, the two men were equals. They clashed again and again as the crowd bellowed, dancing around each other like mating birds, kicking up clouds of dust. The retiarius lunged as Felix dodged, signalling a colossal groan from the audience. His opponent managed to snag him with his net, trapping one leg as he pulled back his weapon, but once more, Felix broke free at the last minute, throwing up his arms and circling the ring to win over the crowd.

'Come on, Felix!'

'You can do this, Felix!' called the boys.

Gia quietly rooted for him, despite everything, as Dominic clapped, murmuring encouragement under his breath. She moved along the colonnade, looking for the clearest view. There was already a group of gigantic spectators obstructing the best vantage point. They wouldn't make room for her, so she had to watch on tiptoes behind them, craning her neck to follow the fast-moving action.

The retiarius jutted out his beefy arm, the prongs of his weapon grazing Felix's skin, but Felix ducked and rolled, circling back around to stab the brute in his side. Blood sputtered from the wound, splattering in the dust, but the retiarius didn't give up. He lashed out at Felix, who slipped away like a fish in water. When he tried to chase after him, the retiarius became ensnared in his own net. Felix stood over him, raising his sword as he dealt some unheard insult, but the retiarius smirked, kicking out Felix's legs with the mermaid tail created by his own net-trapped feet. Felix tumbled forwards as the retarius swung his trident.

'No!'

One of its prongs poked through the soft skin of Felix's chest, blood erupting from the wound.

In seconds, he was dead, face down in the dust as the retiarius put one foot on his back, pumping his trident in victory.

'Felix,' Gia rasped, winded.

The crowd applauded, their bloodthirst growing. Felix was just another body to them, just another sacrifice.

Clutching at her mouth as her knees quaked, Gia watched as they dragged his body out of sight. He had been here just a moment ago, right by her side, and now he was worm food.

She felt a hand on her shoulder and turned to see Dominic, who shook his head. She watched a mask descend over his features, rendering them stony and still.

'We should probably get used to losing people,' he said.

Gia sank to the floor, cradling her injured arm until finally, dreadfully, they came for her.

'Viatrix versus Caturix of Gaul,' boomed the announcer.

She looked for Cyrus, but he was nowhere to be found.

Two visored soldiers approached, gesturing silently for Gia to follow. Too shocked to disobey – too proud, too desperate – she trailed them into the tunnel, stumbling through the pitch dark. Dominic shouted after her, but the ringing in her ears drowned out whatever kind words he'd reserved for her end.

A beam of light struck her in the eye, then another, bleeding into the shadows like the arms of a star. The roaring of the crowd grew louder as the mouth of the tunnel hollowed out.

It was like being born again.

As Gia emerged into the dazzling white ring of the arena, with people packed into the amphitheatre in dense layers, the deafening din trebled, underscored by a wave of whispering. Booing and jeering filled the space, drowning out the cheers and applause.

The harsh sound enveloped her, wrapping around her and rendering her senses numb.

She didn't need to remove her visor to be seen as a woman now.

Freak! Bitch! Die!

Behind her, two soldiers escorted Caturix into position, handing him his curved blade and round shield. The soldiers on either side of her did the same, passing over her sword, which was woefully small in comparison.

Caturix was even bigger and burlier than he'd looked at first sight, an eruption of hair and flesh, so scarred and weathered he resembled a human boulder. He had a wild look in his eye, as if he'd done things she could never even imagine.

She couldn't beat him on strength. She'd have to find another way to defeat him. Maybe she could best him in wit. She could be the superior shit-talker. Perhaps if she could get deep into his head, she could knock him off his game.

Gia stared out at the ravenous audience, their many faces blurring into an amorphous mass. The people of Pompeii were screaming and cheering, waving and whistling, clapping and stamping.

They were ready for their pound of flesh ... and she was it.

Gia prayed for a good death, goddess be merciful.

As the starting horn sounded, the emperor made plain his distaste by issuing a thumbs down before the competition had even begun. It was obviously for her.

Beside him, sat Claudia. Her face was unreadably serene.

'Those who are about to die salute you,' Gia recited once again, in unison with her opponent, before they returned to the centre.

Caturix of Gaul inched as close to her as he was allowed before issuing a single scoff, the foul scent of his rancid tooth-rotten breath catching her nostrils.

'So you're the little rat I've been matched up with,' he said, in the lyrical accent of the Gaul.

'I could say the same to you,' she snapped back.

'They sent me a woman as a curse.'

'You scared?'

'Don't make me laugh,' he spat.

'You should quit now and save yourself the humiliation,' Gia said, bolder than she felt. 'When you lose today, your life is over. You have nothing to go home to. No one has ever loved you – I can tell from the sadness in your eyes.'

'And I can tell from the lines on your face that everyone you ever loved is long gone,' he said.

So much for being the superior shit-talker.

'I'm surprised you can think anything at all, with such a fat head,' she said.

The crowd spluttered, laughing and gasping as they clutched each other, but Gia's opponent wasn't amused. He grabbed one of the leather straps that covered her top half, lifting her up in the air with one hand like a dumbbell.

The referee, or summa rudis, stepped in, waving his staff.

'The fight begins on *my* count,' he warned. 'Put her down.'

'I won't spare you any pity,' said Caturix.

'I hope not,' she said. 'I won't spare you any either.'

He dropped her, causing her to collapse into a heap at his feet. With one last parting kick, he retreated into his starting position.

'Enough!' ordered the summa rudis.

Gia groaned as her stomach throbbed. A broken wrist, now a bruised rib. Her odds were plummeting rapidly. She struggled to bend upright, trying to keep the pain from showing in her eyes.

The summa rudis raised the staff in readiness, then he counted them down, grabbing a handful of sand and raising his fingers to form three, two, one – letting the grains trickle back down to the ground.

The heart-stopping horn echoed.

When a drum began to beat, Gia and Caturix both moved forwards at once, meeting in the middle, both swaying slightly from side to side as they waited for the other to strike. Time slowed as every sound became muffled. Gia could hear her pulse in her ears, her breathing short and heavy as she readied herself to defend.

Caturix hung back, shifting his weight from one foot to the other before hoisting his sica. Tattooed and bearded, with missing teeth, he had an impressive girth, wider than three of Gia. Worse, he looked quite casual, stretching and whistling gaily as he took a run at her.

The slap-slap of sandals echoed and suddenly he was upon her, his blade arcing through the air towards her arm. She lunged to the left, crossing her ankles and spinning around as her sword clashed defensively against his. With brute force, he pushed them backwards, Gia sliding through the dust like a plough. Grimacing, she struggled to persevere through the pain in her wrist, but dropped her leg and rolled to one side, jutting out her ankle to trip him up.

Caturix lurched, carried by his own weight. He quickly regained his balance, driving the curved blade down on Gia's shoulder as she yelled out on reflex. The blade dug into the used metal plates, weakened by a thousand old blows to its former owner, but it still did its job, just about, serving as a barrier between the blade and her skin. The hit drew no blood.

Out of the corner of her eye, Gia saw Claudia take to her feet.

When Gia pulled away, the plate detached from the rest of her outfit, pierced through Caturix's sica like a leaf.

Caturix pulled the plate off and tossed it aside.

'Thin and cheap, like you,' he said. 'You must be the living sorrow of your mother, choosing to die like this.'

'Worry about your own mother,' Gia retorted, though his words hit a nerve. 'She must struggle to love a face so ugly.'

'Don't you talk about my mother!' he roared.

He swung at her again, but he was heavy-footed, slower than

she was. She weaved between the strikes of his blade, one shoulder bared.

I'm Celadus, she told herself. *Handsome, heroic Celadus.*

Gia didn't get many hits in, but she was tiring him out with this dance. That was her plan. She would wear him down, lull him like a big violent baby, before launching a surprise attack.

As she smirked at him, her ankle rolled over. She toppled backwards, barely holding onto her sword. Wide-eyed with delight, the man from Gaul charged again. Unable to rise in time, Gia could only block his attack, the metal clanging so hard it shook her whole skeleton.

Gia swung her sword upwards as Caturix tried to climb on top of her, catching his balls. He crumpled up with a shriek, allowing her to extricate herself from his grip. Hesitantly, hardly able to look, Gia brought her blade down on his chest, but he knocked her off her feet again by slamming his shield into her side.

Staggering, stumbling, Gia's sword clattered out of her hand as he tackled her to the ground. Mouth full of dust, they writhed like wrestlers, Gia rolling back and forth to avoid the stabs of his sica. When she kicked him in the face, he gripped her ankle and twisted it sadistically.

'Aaargh!'

Gia slipped out of his grasp and limped over to retrieve her sword.

Now she was pissed.

A well-placed kick in the back with her good leg caused him to groan. Another one on the other side and he hunched over, huffing and puffing, his stench even more fetid. But each time, he got back up with renewed vigour. Their blades clashed again, the sound ringing out. She had forgotten the crowd and the arena now. It was just the two of them.

Gia was sweating, her hands sliding down the hilt. His blade swiped her neck, slicing the skin. Before she could recover, he'd kicked her in the breast and she crashed down as his blade came for her throat, missing by an inch.

As she drew a breath, his weight pummelled against her, pinning her to the ground. Crouching over her, he raised his weapon, but a faint rumbling from the earth caused him to pause.

The ground was vibrating.

The entire arena trembled, moved by the force of the earth.

Caturix stumbled, losing his balance. This was her chance. Gia launched herself onto her knees and drove her sword into his ribs. It slid into the flesh much easier than she expected.

Caturix fell backwards, pulling her with him.

'Submit,' Gia rasped, shaking uncontrollably as she landed on top of him. 'Submit, man. Give in. I – I don't want to kill you.'

'You already did.'

Blood stained his teeth as he coughed.

Panicked, she loosened her grip. 'It's not too late. You can still get help. All you have to do is admit defeat.'

'I ... can't ... I can't lose to a woman,' he said.

He was dying. Blood gushed dramatically, more blood than she'd ever seen.

'You'd rather die than admit I'm your equal?' she said.

'I cannot lie,' were his last words.

Hidden from the crowd, Caturix heaved himself upright and pulled her outstretched sword deeper into his guts.

It looked as if the final blow was hers, but it wasn't. It was his.

His face froze to marble. His eyes dried, stuck in the excruciating moment of his death. His muscles tensed then released, making him look soft and waxy.

Gia watched him take his last breath, his last blink.

She watched the soul in his body leave him.

Instinctively, she withdrew her sword from his flesh in horror, causing him to slump backwards, a thudding dead weight. His blood ran in rivers through the dirt, covering her toes.

The cheering paled, faded out to a rumble.

'Holy gods!'

'She killed him ... She actually beat him!'

The audience wasn't sure how to respond. Some looked to the emperor, who appeared distinctly disgruntled. Gia had taken him off-guard by winning. That wasn't supposed to happen. Senator Cornelius would be most displeased.

One lone spectator clapped, somewhere near the back. Cyrus, Gia expected. Others copied, unsure if they were meant to or not. A growing cheer rang out. In response, a larger number booed, the dull monotonous sound making Gia's ears pop.

The summa rudis walked over to her and raised her good arm.

'To the victor, Viatrix the Victorious!'

A horn blared, signalling the end of the match as soldiers dragged Caturix's body away, leaving behind a trail of blood.

Gia stared at it as the band played a brief congratulatory tune, trying not to think about his family.

The crowd waited, expectant. All of the other victors had received a flower garland from Claudia, but the summa rudis now turned, without discussion, to Decimus, handing him a floral favour to give to Gia.

'A woman gladiator should receive a blessing from the male prince,' he said.

Decimus stared at it a moment. His lip curled. His chin quivered. His face put on a three-act performance. Gia couldn't hear what he said, though she sensed it was unpleasant from the expressions of those standing behind him. Then he dropped the flower as if it were poisonous and shook his head, rejecting Gia without a word.

The noise of the crowd rolled, forming a swooning, scandalized *ooh*.

Gia knew that Decimus was rejecting not just her, but the idea of her.

Beside him, the emperor did nothing but pour himself another chalice of wine, lifting it in apparent agreement.

The audience turned, cheers changing to jeers.

What did these people want from her? She'd beaten her opponent and it still wasn't good enough. Maybe she would never be enough. If they couldn't accept her now, after triumphing over a giant, they never would.

Suddenly, Claudia stood up, plucking a white flower from her own garland. She stepped forwards tentatively and held it out with a deified smile.

Slowly, Gia lowered her weapon, removed her helmet and walked over to the box. The sound of the crowd petered away again, as every head in the audience turned to them. As Gia reached out for the flower with her one good hand, she felt uncharacteristically shy. Her stubby fingers and blunt nails looked ungodly next to Claudia's, long and ringed.

'Gia,' said Claudia. 'You're still alive.'

Her voice gave nothing away.

'Just about.'

When they touched, a surge of energy moved through Gia's body, making her feel weak and hungry ... and guilty.

She resisted it, pushed it away. It didn't matter how beautiful the princess was, she was still the emperor's daughter. They would never be friends. They would never be equals. It was insanity to think otherwise.

Slightly elevated on her platform, Claudia was wearing a red silk tunic with gold embroidered trim and a white headscarf.

'I am glad. We can't have Pompeii's finest female gladiator come to harm, can we?' said the princess.

'I think I'm Pompeii's *only* female gladiator,' said Gia.

'That makes you the finest, doesn't it?'

'Do hurry up, dearest sister,' snarled Decimus. 'Unless you're planning on asking Saturn to freeze the sands of time.'

'Of course,' said Claudia, fixing on a fake smile for her brother. 'Gladiator Viatrix, congratulations on your great victory. You are the pride of the empire, in my eyes. In the name of Diana, in the name of Venus, in the name of Minerva, in the name of Fortuna – you are an inspiration to all women.'

In her eyes.

In the dark of her mind, Gia saw a lightning bolt flash, illuminating a strange scene: her in silver armour, kneeling before Claudia in a golden crown, blood-red banners stretched out behind them as the sky exploded into fire.

Both stepped backwards in unison.

The emperor looked unimpressed yet also disinterested, waving his hand to signal an end to the sparse clapping and cheering.

'I'm bored,' he said, in a child-like way, poking at his attendant. 'Where are the lions? You promised me lions, Hieronymus.'

Decimus, on the other side of him, glared at his sister with coldest loathing, but Claudia didn't seem to notice.

She was still staring at Gia, as if she had seen the very same vision.

8. A WOMAN OF WEALTH AND POWER

That night, the students of the ludus gathered to pay respects to Felix, drinking a flask of stolen wine in his honour. They sat in the atrium in the centre of the building, full of mice and bugs, where a few shaggy, browning plants curled around crumbling statues of gladiators in athletic positions. Everyone was shaken and red-eyed, telling funny stories about all the lies he used to tell.

'He said he'd slept with Lady Lando.'

'I can do better: he told me he'd once had sex with a nymph.'

'Did he really have a wife in Gaul?' asked one of the younger boys. 'He told me she was a prisoner of war.'

'I never believed anything he said,' said Dom, 'not a single word, but I'll miss hearing him talk.'

'He was a clown, but he was *our* clown.'

'That's right.'

They lifted their mismatched cups.

'Salud.'

'Salud.'

Cyrus was quiet, barely paying attention to the conversation, but he bundled up Felix's belongings into another package, just like he'd done for Atticus.

It was strange. Felix had spent most of his time harassing Gia, and the rest trying to kill her, but he was still a person. Every lost life was a tragedy. She had known him, and whether she liked him or not was irrelevant to the loss she felt now.

The memory of him trying to apologize rolled over her.

She thought about her brothers. Atticus hadn't always been very nice to her when she was a kid, but in the last few years before his death he had mellowed, becoming a different kind of brother – one who was supportive and attentive, teaching her how to cook and serve customers at the taberna.

On the other hand, Cassius, who'd been her best friend growing up, became hardened and short-tempered by his experiences at war. He had no patience for her any more. In one of their last conversations, she had complained, as she often did, that she could not join the army and serve alongside him.

'You think war is adventure and murder is glory, as if we're all off on a grand tour of the world's great wonders,' he'd snapped.

'I will never even leave Pompeii. I would swap with you any day.'

'No, you would not! You will never understand what men must live through. You don't know how lucky you are, Gia.'

Gia couldn't forget the way his face looked just then, his expression so young and soft, as if he'd temporarily forgotten what he was supposed to be, or how he was supposed to act.

'I wish ... I wish I'd been born a girl,' he said.

The last words he'd ever spoken to her.

Neither of them had been perfect, but Gia mourned their loss every day. The giant hole of their absence was so large she often fell into it.

They had been beautiful, imperfect, miraculous, human.

'Someone should make a speech,' said Lucas.

'Cyrus, do you want to say a few words?' asked Dom.

'I do pep talks,' said Cyrus, already halfway out of the door, 'not eulogies.'

'Dom, you should do it. You're good with words,' said Gia.

'But I hate public speaking. Gia?'

'Not a chance in hell.'

Lucas cleared his throat and surprised everyone by stepping up: 'Today, we lost a friend. Honestly, Felix was kind of a prick. He made fun of me quite a bit. A lot of people do, though. I guess Felix wasn't all bad. He made us laugh and he was a good guy to go out drinking with. Wherever there were women, he was happy.'

'Miss you already, brother,' sobbed one of the other boys.

'Now he's gone and we have to go on without him,' continued Lucas, as Dom patted the crying boy on the back. 'It'll be tough, but we're gladiators. When death comes for us, we go with pride. We live on the edge and we die by the sword – and through all of it, we are a family. So, let's raise a glass to our friend Felix. I hope your spirit rests in a paradise full of girls who think you're a god.'

'To Felix,' they murmured.

'To Felix,' Gia whispered, strangely moved.

'Wow, Lucas, that was actually decent,' said Dom.

When all the wine was drained, they parted ways; some heading home and others to the taberna. On her way out, Gia passed by the study where Cyrus was drinking alone. Gia knew he'd take it hard, losing Felix soon after her brother, but she didn't know how to comfort him, or herself, or anyone else.

'Let's have a look at it, then,' he said.

'A look at what?'

'Your wrist.'

'You heard about that, huh?'

'It's broken, isn't it?'

'Just a little bit,' Gia confessed, avoiding his eyes.

Cyrus stood up and came over to examine it.

'You could've died,' he said.

'You told me that was just part of the game.'

'Why would you not tell me?'

'You made it clear how important it was for me to fight today.'

'I should've been clear that having use of both hands is one of the few rules that apply to gladiator battles.'

'Felix had both of his hands and now he's gone. I didn't want to let you down. I knew how much we both needed a win. It all worked out in the end. You made yourself a small fortune, by the looks of it.'

Piles of denarii were heaped on the table.

'I cannot deny that my pockets are full, but some of these coins were earned by the death of a young man. I must spend them on something worthy of his sacrifice.'

'Ow.'

Gia retracted her hand when his thumb pressed on a particular bone. Cyrus nodded and sighed heavily.

'I'm glad it is not two candles I'm lighting tonight. You were at a huge disadvantage out there. If I'd known, I ... I could've done something to level the field. Instead, you went in there alone and one-handed to battle one of the bloodiest warriors in Herculaneum.' Cyrus couldn't help but let a small smile slip in with his frown. 'You won despite that, but, still, the point stands. You were lucky. Too lucky.'

'Is there such a thing?'

'Of course. If Fortuna graces you too much and too often, you know the balance of misfortune will ever be waiting for you. Can anyone truly be happy, knowing they will one day suffer greatly? If Fortuna made you champion today, when all was stacked against you, you owe her a great debt.'

'Maybe I'm just blessed,' Gia said impishly. 'Maybe she's doing me a favour because I'm her favourite.'

Yet the idea worried her.

Was she due some great devastation now, to balance out the fortune of surviving yet again? She didn't dare to think about it.

'This doesn't look good, Gia,' Cyrus said, still looking at her wrist. 'You need to see a physician. I'll give you the money.'

'You told me you were impoverished.'

'Not tonight I'm not. And I insist that you take it. It's yours, anyway. You earned it. After tonight, your reputation is set to go sky high. I need you in good health for selfish reasons.'

He stood and held out a makeshift sling, which he carefully fixed in place. Then he tucked a coin purse into the pocket of her regular tunic.

'Thanks, Cyrus. For everything.'

He waved one hand as if to say 'stop'. 'Rest up before your next fight.'

'Which is when?'

'I don't know yet, but the tide is turning, Gia. After watching you kill Caturix of Gaul, there are no doubts that woman can play, and win.'

Gia had often fantasized about what it would be like to have a crowd chanting her name, and yet the idea horrified her. Celadus the Handsome couldn't buy eggs without being crowded by little children asking him questions and women throwing their perfumed handkerchiefs at him.

Gia didn't really enjoy being the centre of attention, nor everyone knowing her business. She had always liked the anonymity of being a regular civilian. Nobody was much bothered about her. She came and went as she pleased. But now all eyes would be on her.

'Fabius is gone, by the way,' said Cyrus. 'I told him to never come back here.'

'I can't say I'm sad about it,' she said, after a moment.

'He's a troubled kid, but I've done enough for him. He needs to find his own way in the world, though I fear which way he will choose. Sometimes the easiest path is the most dangerous.'

'I wonder if he knows about Felix.'

'Don't worry about that,' he said. 'I'm sure he's heard already. Word has a way of spreading on the streets.'

'You're not kidding,' she said, recalling how quickly her mother had heard about Viatrix, or how she knew before Gia did that the imperial family was staying in Pompeii. Did she already know the truth? Gia had tried to pry about her plans for the day, but her mother hadn't mentioned any intent to watch the games. She could only hope her blissful ignorance would continue. 'No such thing as a secret here.'

They sat in comfortable silence a while.

'Who do you think paid him to break my wrist?' Gia asked.

'Senator Cornelius, I presume,' Cyrus said.

'His name was the first one that came to mind, but ... why would he want me to drop out? He'd already stacked the game against me. You think he'd *want* me to fight, since I was so likely to get killed. He bet money on me losing. I think the person who hired Fabius wanted to keep me from fighting.'

'I can't think who would feel so strongly,' Cyrus said vaguely. 'Unless, someone feared you would die if you fought. A broken wrist might be a welcome consolation.'

But surely there were easier, less harmful ways to prevent her from fighting?

'Do you ever think about the people you've killed in battle?' she asked.

'All the time,' said Cyrus. 'You shouldn't feel guilty about Caturix of Gaul. He could've killed you just as easily.'

'I didn't,' said Gia.

'What?'

'I didn't kill him.'

'Your sword went into his belly, Gia. You may not like to think about it, but it's important to accept reality occasionally.'

'I did stab him once, yes,' she said, 'but he threw himself on my blade rather than admit defeat.'

'Then you have absolutely nothing to feel guilty about.'

They listened to the sound of a cart passing down the street.

'What am I going to tell my mother?' said Gia. 'She's already suspicious. For all I know, she was in the audience today.'

'What did you tell her last time?'

'That a chariot reversed into me and the rich man inside gave me the money to buy my silence.'

Cyrus spluttered with laughter. 'No wonder she doesn't believe it. Okay, tell her you drank too much and fell down the steps.'

'She did the same thing not so long ago.'

'Perfect, then she'll be more sympathetic.'

'You'd think.'

He patted her on the shoulder. Suddenly his eyes opened wide.

'Oh! I almost forgot: there's someone who wishes to speak with you.'

Gia tensed up. 'Now?'

'No, no, tomorrow. At sunset. A wealthy woman who wishes to aid you on your journey, apparently. She wants to meet you at the House of Menander.'

He handed her a scroll on which the invitation was written. At the bottom, an ornate symbol was printed, a stylized kind of lioness set against a shield, along with an indistinguishable signature.

It looked official, expensive, written with brightly coloured metallic inks.

'That's right by my house. She must be one of the Roman tourists they're renovating the place for,' said Gia.

'Yes, Romans are buying up property like pigs snuffling for truffles these days,' said Cyrus.

'You don't know any more about her?' she asked.

'I spoke only to her attendant.'

'So it could be anyone?'

'Take your sword, just in case, but I believe it to be a genuine offer. It would be wise to see what she has to say, at least,' Cyrus said. 'A high-profile patron is exactly what we need right now. The idea of a woman gladiator is gaining in popularity, thanks to you, but we must ensure that it is not just a sport for commoners. Your first performance was at a senator's birthday and your second was part of official Pompeii festivities. That gives us a ring of credibility but we need the validation of a higher society audience if we're going to . . .' He hesitated. 'If we're going to be successful. Perhaps this mystery woman can help us establish support among the nobility.'

'Fine. I'll report back to you tomorrow afternoon.'

'It's been a long day. Make sure you see someone about your arm tomorrow. The longer you leave it, the worse it will heal.'

Cyrus rubbed his face vigorously. His eyes fell on the box containing Felix's things, which he stowed away under a bench before looking up to meet her gaze again.

'You should go,' he said. 'There is something terrible I must do. Go celebrate being alive, before it's too late.'

Gia didn't make an appointment the next morning. She was hesitant to spend the money and even more hesitant to consult a physician. Cassius's friend had once broken his arm playing in the ruins of an old building and the treatment for it was barbaric. The wound was filled with black ointment. A blade was used to scrape the bones. He was in terrible pain for weeks and he could never use his arm properly again. Gia wasn't keen to go through the same.

Instead, she stubbornly hoped her wrist would get better by itself. She had heard many things about the body's healing properties, mostly from Dominic.

'How will you work with one bad hand?' her mother said, when she first saw her in the sling.

She was hungover again, yet she had taken the time to lecture Gia about the dangers of drinking too much.

'We can hire someone to help us out,' Gia said, pulling out the money bag Cyrus gave her. 'Here, I have enough money to pay someone for a few shifts.'

She would find a way to get the money back to him.

'I know what you're doing,' she said.

Gia turned quickly so her mother couldn't see her face.

'What do you mean?' she said.

'You think I don't know how girls around here make money on the side? Whichever old man is paying for your company, he's a brute. First the cuts on your face, now this. He'll kill you next time. I don't want you hanging out with that brothel girl any more. She's a bad influence.'

She was talking about Berenice. At least that meant her mother didn't know she was Viatrix yet. She thought Gia was selling herself and, strange as it seemed, it was easier to let her believe that.

'I'm grown,' she said. 'It's my business what I do.'

'It's my business too, so long as you live in my house. If you don't care about your safety, then you should care about the taberna. It won't help us attract customers, if people hear what you're up to after dark. Or, if it does, they'll be the wrong kind of customers. We may as well both enter the Den.'

'All right. I won't take his company again,' Gia said, and technically it was true, because she hadn't done it in the first place.

'That's what you said last time.'

'I mean it now. I swear. I've been punished by the consequences of my actions. You think I want a broken wrist when I need my hands to survive?'

Her mother sighed. 'Please understand, Gia. I'm thankful you want to help keep the business open, but nothing is worth the sorrow. No one wants to marry a brothel girl. If you want to make money from men, you marry them. A good marriage is still my best hope for you. For us.'

Her mother raised her hands to cup her cheeks then hugged her awkwardly, hanging on as though she had something more to say, before letting go and drifting off to make lunch from the mouldy cheese and overripe fruit in the pantry.

The villa was beginning to look derelict; full of cobwebs and cracks. The plumbing made terrible gurgling noises, giving off a foul smell. Everything was falling apart, although slowly.

Gia focused on her appointment with the mysterious patron, waiting until the sun began to set before walking down the road to the House of Menander.

The garden was no longer overgrown, its hedges neat and straight, surrounded on all sides by pillared colonnades. Several statues had been installed since Gia had last seen it, as well as a small fountain with golden cherubs.

Gia knew from her father that for many years the villa had been owned by a man named Quintus, a relative of Emperor Nero's second wife, but after the last earthquake they'd moved elsewhere. Rich people thought nothing of abandoning such a palace. She was curious to meet whoever it belonged to now, particularly if they favoured female gladiators.

At the entrance, an armoured guard waited, wearing a plumed helmet and holding a shield with the insignia of Rome on it.

'Servants' entrance is at the rear,' he said.

Gia was dressed in a plain brown tunic with a rope belt, her hair braided and tied back, though small curls escaped the ponytail around her forehead.

'I'm not a . . .' She shook her head, gesturing at the sword on her hip. 'I mean, I'm here to see the, uh, the lady of the house?'

He gave her a sceptical look.

'She made an appointment with me?'

Gia handed him the scroll she'd been given.

'Hmm,' he said, looking her up and down again. 'Follow me.'

He led her through the rhodium-shaped peristyle, bordered with plants, and into the airy atrium. In contrast to the one at home, or the one at the ludus, it was blooming with exotic trees and flowers in pots, its walls painted with colourful murals of exotic animals and scenes from an epic ode, maybe the Odyssey.

'Wait here.'

The guard disappeared with the scroll still in hand.

At the centre of the atrium was an impluvium, a basin in the middle of the floor to collect rain water that dripped down from the central opening in the roof. Gia watched the droplets, so steady they formed a reassuring rhythm.

If Gia had the support of an influential Roman woman, perhaps she might survive long enough to fight again. The male gladiators had their patrons and sponsors, their fans and favourites. Why shouldn't she?

But Gia had made some new enemies lately. One had already attempted to harm her by breaking her wrist. If the emperor detested her then so would his followers, like the imperial cult. What if this was a trap?

Gia told herself that she wasn't important enough to be assassinated. The emperor probably detested a lot of people.

When the guard returned, he signalled for her to follow again.

They passed an altar dedicated to the Lares, with five wooden sculptures inside. In the main portico, a picture of a seated, serious-looking scribe looked back at her, crowned with leaves and draped in white robes. Through the tablinum, where the master of the house would conduct his business, past a marble dining table, they paused before a chamber in which a triptych displayed scenes from the Trojan War, including Cassandra trying to prevent the famous wooden horse from entering the city.

Two guards murmured among themselves, staring at her.

Cyrus hadn't been exaggerating when he called her mystery patron a woman of wealth and power, for four more armoured guards waited at the foot of a series of stone stairs, their weapons raised.

Swallowing, Gia climbed the steps that led up to a flat roof terrace and approached the hooded figure who stood at the edge looking out over the gardens.

The breeze rustled her gold silken robes.

Though Gia couldn't see her face, there was something wistful about her pose, as if she was deep in a daydream.

'You sent for me,' Gia announced shakily.

When the mysterious patron turned to face her, pulling down her hood, Gia was at once reminded that the world was an extraordinary place that could not be fully explained by any understanding of destiny.

'Claudia,' she said, stunned. 'I mean, Princess.'

'Gia.'

Gia joined her at the edge of the terrace, so close she could've touched her. The sun created a glowing halo around her body, while the light caught the ornate metalwork of her headpiece, making it look like molten gold.

For a moment, the princess said nothing, coolly appraising her.

A sudden and terrible thought made Gia's blood run cold. Gia was the only witness to Claudia's conversation with Senator

Cornelius. She knew that the princess had made some kind of deal with him, that she was working with him against her father. Cornelius had warned her that even gossip could harm her reputation. Was she afraid that Gia might talk?

Had she lured her here to kill her?

'Congratulations on your victory,' said Claudia.

'Thank you?' said Gia uncertainly, looking around. 'Is this ... Are you living here now?'

'It's just a summer palace – a holiday villa. One of many.'

The princess was now her neighbour. The princess had acquired a villa on her street. Was it merely a coincidence? They were destined to stay close, it seemed.

Claudia's eyes fell to Gia's arm in the sling. 'You're hurt,' she said.

'It's fine,' Gia said. 'It's just—'

Claudia snapped her fingers to alert the nearest guard. 'Victor, call for the imperial physician.'

He obediently trudged away.

'You don't have to do that,' said Gia. 'It's just a little—' Gia tried to flex her fingers to show how fine it was, causing pain to fill her entire body. 'Ow.' She winced.

'It is clearly *not* fine,' said Claudia. 'Let me help you.'

They fell quiet.

'You are very interesting to me, gladiatrix.'

'Am I?'

The breeze toyed with Claudia's hair, making it dance. The blue-orange sky shimmered in her pupils as she turned back.

'Do you know how many gladiators I've seen fighting at festivals and banquets?' she said. Her voice was melodic, her expression playful. 'How many times I have left the amphitheatre with the bottom of my gown speckled with the blood of fallen men? After a while, it stops having the desired effect. Life and death become one. Nothing means what it ought to any more. Yet you have stirred up something I haven't felt in years. I have been on the edge of my seat, watching you fight. I could hardly breathe in anticipation. It suddenly became of great importance to me that you won.'

Gia's mouth was oddly dry. Claudia gave her a long, curious look then sighed and shook her head, as if frustrated by something.

'Who are you, Gia Valerii?' asked Claudia.

'Is that why you asked me here?'

'You did not answer my question. I don't wish to make it an order, but I *am* the princess of Rome. Should I ask you about yourself, it's merely good sense that you should answer.'

'What do you want to know?' she said guardedly.

'How did you come to be a gladiator?' said Claudia. 'What sort of life must you have led, to be so bold?'

Gia could feel herself perspiring, though the breeze dried it.

'There's nothing exciting about me.'

'I doubt that,' said Claudia. 'What does your family do?'

'There were five of us once. Now, only two. We run a taberna, on the corner right over there. See?'

She leaned close to Claudia, to point. She could smell her fresh floral perfume again. She smelled like a tropical island at sea – not that Gia had ever actually been to a tropical island at sea.

Claudia did not shrink away from her.

'Is the food good?' asked Claudia.

They were making small talk, for some bizarre reason, as two women might do in a temple queue, or while lining up to buy bread.

'I'm the chef at present. So, no, it's not good at all.'

'I still do not understand how you became a gladiator.'

'My brother was a student at the ludus. He died. I went to fetch his things, punched a man and, long story short, I took his place and here I am.'

'Here you are, indeed. I have heard of women warriors from other lands, but I've never seen one in action. It is quite something.'

'Something?'

'The indescribable something that happens when the stars align and the goddesses on are on your side,' said Claudia airily. 'With a little more training and some better equipment, you could be a champion on the gladiatorial scene.'

'What do you know of the gladiatorial scene?' asked Gia.

'You would be surprised.'

Looking over Gia's shoulder, she steered them away from the guards with one hand, bringing them to stand on the far side of the roof and lowering her voice.

'I know all the powerful men who sit in the audience. I listen to them making commentary, making bets. I have seen every play on the tablet, every move, every kind of victory and loss. I know just as much as any of the senators who follow the games. I could supply your gladiator school with funds, so long as your tutor continues to accept women as students. That is my proposal.'

Gia stared at her. It was exactly what they needed, exactly what she and Cyrus had spoken about. Gia wondered if Claudia had some supernatural ability to read her thoughts or whether she had hired someone to spy on her.

Her face made Gia forget what she wanted to say. If she was a statue, she would've been carved from the finest marble by a sculptor so gifted they could make stone resemble silk. It was unfair, for someone to look like that. Perhaps even dangerous. In the animal kingdom, such a beautiful creature would be poisonous.

'I simply wish to be your patron. The school's patron,' said Claudia. 'I wish to support the ludus.'

'Why would you offer us such a thing?' asked Gia.

'I owe you,' said Claudia.

'No, we're even. I made that clear.'

'It is up to me what debts I owe.'

The princess was trying to manipulate her somehow, Gia was sure of it. Claudia had an ulterior motive for saving her life, and Gia had to find out what it was.

'What do you want from me?' she asked, narrowing her eyes. 'What could you possibly ever want from me, or ... anyone?'

'I want unity. I want peace. I want progress. I want to improve the lives of women in Rome and across the empire,' said Claudia, as if the answer was plain to see. 'I want to support a woman's right to fight, if only she will let me.'

'There must be something more in it for you,' said Gia. 'The imperial family isn't known for its generosity.'

'Is that how you see me, as a villain?'

'Am I wrong?'

Claudia frowned, but she didn't object. Her lips pursed as she considered carefully what she was going to say.

'Fine, then let us say I desire to rule, as any man in my position would.' She fixed Gia with a look of steely determination. 'I have spent years schooling myself on geography and diplomacy, hours learning crafts and arts and languages. I have made allegiances with my father's allies and enemies alike, using all of the gifts the gods have given to me. I am the voice in my father's ear and, on the rare occasion that he pays attention, I am powerful. I am present at every chariot race and banquet, always listening, always whispering in ears . . .'

Gia envisioned the princess sitting beside her father at the senator's birthday, and how she had convinced him to spare her, against his own will. What had she told him, to change his mind?

'People may think it foolish for a woman to rule Rome,' said Claudia, 'but the empire was built by fools. If it is wicked to want to seize power from such fools, then so be it – I am a villain.'

As if the earth itself was moved by her words, the ground began to shake, just as it had during the match.

Everything in sight shuddered, followed by the tinkle of smashed glass. The wall of the terrace, which had only just been repaired, cracked open again and a pillar collapsed, throwing up a cloud of dust as the guards assumed defensive positions.

Another strong tremor caused Claudia to fall towards her. Gia gripped onto her to catch her, their eyes meeting.

Claudia quickly righted herself, though her gaze fell to the muscles on Gia's arms. It was all over in an instant, yet their hands lingered.

'The gods are unhappy today,' said Claudia, breaking free.

The shaking faded away. Claudia signaled that she was unhurt.

A memory washed over Gia then, a memory of a dream – when she was Diana hunting Claudia as Venus, laid beneath her on the wildflower grass . . .

'What was I saying?' asked Claudia, breaking the silence.

Gia knew she ought to have been listening more carefully.

'You want to rule the world,' she said, hoping she'd understood well enough to hold the conversation.

'Women,' said Claudia. 'I want *women* to rule the world. Being born into power has its advantages, but I am still a girl. I am the child of an emperor, yet I am still less than any man.' She inspected the broken wall. 'To stand against the emperor is to stand against the gods. Perhaps the tremor is meant as a warning, but I shall not listen. The gods are no better than men.'

And Gia had thought telling Fortuna to fuck off was daring.

'The gods made the world as it is, by putting all the power in man's hands. That was their mistake and they'll realize it, sooner or later.'

'What does this have to do with me, or the ludus?' Gia asked.

'We start from the bottom. If women begin to fight with men in the ring, they may begin to take us seriously as opponents,' said Claudia. 'We may one day have women soldiers, women senators, women judges, and, at the top of it all, ruling benevolently over this society of women ... an empress. A Roman empress.'

'You?' said Gia.

'Or my future daughter. Possibly, my granddaughter, depending on how long it takes. One of us shall rule this world and spare humanity from the reckless stupidity of mankind. That is my plan, for as long as I can keep Mort at bay.'

Mort was the god of death, ever watching, ever waiting: the cold-eyed, black-winged figure of justice who terrified beggars and emperors alike. But even he would probably wilt in Claudia's presence.

'What do you expect from me?' said Gia.

'Nothing but for you to accept my offer of support. Freely. I would never use my power to force your will. This destiny is your own and you must choose it for yourself, if we are to be ... business partners.'

Meddling with fate was tricky, Gia knew that. Even the slightest decision could set dice rolling, thrusting the world into unpredicted futures. It was a fragile thing – that starry, gods-spun spiderweb of destiny. It would've been much safer for Gia to keep her head down and avoid doing anything of consequence. But it was too late. She'd already upended things through her choices.

The princess of Rome was her enemy, as any member of the imperial family would be her enemy, and yet Claudia was trapped, as Gia was. As all women were.

Gia and Cyrus needed a patron, and here she stood.

The patron of all patrons.

Gia had never imagined that she might align with the empire after all it had taken from her, but the princess's support was too valuable to refuse. It was business, she told herself. It was survival. It didn't mean anything. She wasn't sure how she would explain it to Cyrus, but she would find a way.

'All right,' said Gia. 'But I have certain conditions.'

Claudia smiled faintly. 'You dare ask me for conditions, gladiator?'

'I do, Princess.'

'Then let us hear them,' said Claudia.

'Any agreement between us should be fair, and yet you have considerable advantage over me,' said Gia, trying to sound smart. 'You are the emperor's daughter. I am a peasant and a gladiator whose death is considered a sport. You could have me killed and no one would question it. I have to protect myself.'

'What do you suggest?'

'There must be something I can do for you,' said Gia, 'so it will feel more like an exchange and less like a gift with strings.'

'Strings?' said Claudia. 'What are the strings?'

'As my patron, you will expect me to behave in a certain way, perhaps even to have loyalty to you out of duty. If I displease you, you could withdraw support as punishment. That would have an effect on the others at the ludus, so it would be in my best interests, and theirs, to please you.'

'And my word is not enough?'

'No,' said Gia firmly.

Claudia's face was impassive, making it difficult to interpret her response, but after a moment she nodded curtly.

'Fine, then. If we are to be partners in this business venture, I need to be able to trust you, and you need to be able to trust me. That may be easier if we get to know each other a little. You shall accompany me to the bathhouse tomorrow.'

'The bathhouse?' Gia repeated, unsure if she'd heard correctly.

'The male guards aren't permitted on the women's side, so a woman guard is sensible. You can guard me while I bathe, and we can speak in privacy.'

Gia had not expected an invitation so intimate.

'You can bathe too, if you wish.'

Evidently, there were things to be said that she didn't even trust her own guards with, and Gia wanted to hear them.

'I'll be there,' she said.

'This meeting, and my patronage, it must be our secret for now,' said Claudia. 'It wouldn't do well for you to be singled out as a subject of favouritism. It is always better to operate in darkness ... in shadows. That is where people like us can truly be ourselves.'

'People like us?'

Before Claudia could respond, a servant of the house appeared, coming over to whisper in her ear. Claudia nodded and turned back to Gia.

'I must go now, but Hippocrates is waiting for you downstairs. He will perform any treatment you need.' She turned to leave, her shroud swirling like the folds of destiny that curved around them, binding them together. 'My guards will see you out when you're done.'

At the arch, Claudia hesitated, addressing Gia without meeting her eye.

'Meet me in the Forum at midday tomorrow, by the toll of the bells. Do not be late,' she said.

Gia watched her depart, inwardly at war with herself.

She knew she ought to hate her, fear her, and yet she found that she was excited by the prospect of seeing her again.

Suppressing the smile that played on her lips, she went downstairs, where the physician, Hippocrates, was waiting as promised.

A small man with a frizzy halo of grey hair, he told her, without prompting, that he had previously worked as a valetudinarian, treating soldiers, and that he'd once successfully removed an axe from a skull. She nodded and listened to his stories as he examined her wrist like Cyrus had, though not so gently.

'Friend of the princess, eh?' he said, when he ran out of things to talk about. 'Never met a woman gladiator before.'

'Then I guess I'm the first.'

'Hmm,' he said. 'You should be careful.'

'Of the princess?' she said, without thinking.

'Oh no, she's the only member of her family I can stand. You should be careful of men. Pompeii men. They won't like women stepping on their toes, especially not when they're doing such a good job of it.'

Hippocrates treated her with a mixture of aloe, created a brace for the wrist out of metal and leather, and advised her to make a good offering to Asclepius, the god of medicine, for faster healing, which she did at the house altar.

Dom was right: the broken bone would heal on its own.

Alone on the street outside, Gia let out a strangled laugh, one of relief and delight, shock and disbelief. Her first patron was the princess of Rome. Her first fan was the emperor's daughter herself.

She wished Cassius was still here to tell, imagining how scandalized he'd be.

Later that evening, a group of guards and soldiers turned up at the taberna expecting to be fed. Gia's mother charged them three times the local rates and they paid without complaint, too drunk to count.

By the end of the night, they had run out of seats to fill and the money jars were full of denarii.

The men told tales of Viatrix the warrior.

9. I CHOOSE YOU

As directed, Gia wore her uniform to her meeting with the princess. Due to the heat, however, she wore only a thin band of fabric under the breastplate and a loincloth of linen under the leather skirt. Strappy sandals wrapped themselves around her legs, and a thin leather band circled her head. Her wrist was braced, her hair braided and swept up in a ponytail as usual.

Even without her helmet, Gia was recognized on every block on the walk from her house. She could hear the word running back to her mother in real time, with pitter-patter feet.

To her surprise, people were not universally hostile towards her – calling out to wave, clapping, even cheering on occasion. One little girl asked for her autograph in a loose leaf of papers covered in gladiator signatures.

'Who should I make it out to?'

'Athena,' the girl said, struggling to hold everything she was carrying. 'I'm your biggest fan. I saw you fight Caturix of Gaul. I want to be just like you when I grow up. Can I go to the gladiator school like you?'

'Maybe soon,' said Gia, wondering how old she was. 'You could probably beat me already, though. You have a warrior spirit, I can tell.'

'What's your name?' asked Athena. 'Your real name.'

There was no harm in it, was there? The news was spreading anyway. Gia could no longer resist owning the truth, and she wanted to; she was proud to be herself.

'Gia Valerii,' she said as Athena wrote it down.

Gia had the feeling she had just made a terrible mistake, but she batted it away like a buzzing fly.

She would worry about it later, along with everything else.

Bidding farewell to her fan, she advanced along a pillared walkway and under a triumphal arch. Gia entered the Forum, which was already roasting in the high noon heat. The Pompeii Forum was an epicentre of the region. It hosted many beautiful temples, along with administrative buildings and offices of law, expanding at its fringes into vast canopied markets and squares for public gatherings. It was busy at every hour of the day with people preaching and performing, praying or selling their wares. It also had a fine view of Mount Vesuvius, topped with clouds and framed scenically behind the Temple of Jupiter.

Gia was early, so she stood before the statues of the Capitoline Triad: giant statues of Jupiter; his wife, Juno; and his daughter, Minerva, on a raised platform.

As temple bells signalled midday, Claudia appeared beside her, carrying a parasol and surrounded by guards.

'Minerva is my favourite goddess,' she said, by way of greeting.

'Really? I thought it would be Venus,' said Gia.

'Why?'

'People say you look like her.'

'Physically, Minerva is more like you, being tall and athletic with enviable musculature . . .'

Gia felt herself blushing.

'But I relate to her in mind. She was her father's battle strategist. She knew the importance of words and ideas.'

Gia shaded her eyes, barely able to see through the sun's glare.

'Who is your favourite?' asked Claudia.

'Diana the huntress,' said Gia. 'She had the right idea. Never bother with men, just have drunken fun in the sacred groves with your friends. Sometimes I wish to cut my hair short like hers too.'

Claudia gazed over her, as if imagining how it might look.

'Let's go inside,' she said.

Two guards stood in Gia's way, one nodding at her sword, the other patting her down. She handed the weapon over to them reluctantly. They parted ways at the women's entrance, allowing Gia and Claudia to pass through alone.

Once sheltered from the bright light of day, in the shade of the entryway where a pair of sandals were depicted in a floor mosaic, Gia could see that Claudia's hair was loose down her back and she wore many thin layers of white silk. They put on the coverings that were provided for them.

'Your wrist. Is it healing well?'

'Oh, yes. Hippocrates is a miracle worker,' Gia said. 'I made an offering to Asclepius. I should be back to form in no time at all.'

'Good, because the people are waiting to watch you fight again, including myself. You shouldn't like to keep me waiting.'

Gia had never been to the Forum baths before, frequenting the other public thermae where slaves and servants also bathed. A newer, simpler construction, those baths were already foul and squalid. In contrast, this place resembled a palace, decorated from floor to ceiling in every room. The thermae were divided in male and female sections, each one containing a changing room, a cold bath room, a tepid bath room and a hot bath room or caldarium. The changing room was decorated with erotic art, each vignette numbered, with matching shelves for bathers to leave their clothes.

Gia's eyes caught on one of the small pictures: two couples cavorting together around a single bed, but the women were partnered together, as were the men. Gia focused on the two girls. It was as Felix had once described, one woman kissing the other between her legs.

All of the blood felt to drain out of her body, then rushed back in a sudden hot flush between her thighs.

When Gia looked to Claudia, she was admiring the same picture. Her eyes met Gia's. She did not look embarrassed, as Gia felt.

'Come on,' said Claudia.

Normally the corridors would be packed with people, some naked, others wearing modest coverings, all queuing up for their turn, but this afternoon the baths were deserted save for the two of them, giving it an eerie, timeless emptiness.

In the cold room, a fountain splashed them, surrounded by murals of frolicking nymphs. The central tepidarium was circular, with steps leading down into a round, tepid pool. This was where people shaved and oiled themselves, chatting about politics and all the dreary minutes of their lives. The thermae were as much a community centre as they were a place to bathe. This one also had a gymnasium and a library, but they moved right on to the steamy caldarium.

This chamber was barrel-vaulted with an apse at the back, decorated with fountain pillars carved like water bearers, all pouring jugs into the frothing water. Art adorned the walls, including a lifelike painting of Diana the huntress, bathing with her adoring maidens.

Claudia casually shrugged off her stola.

Gia held her breath, wondering if she might be nude underneath, but she wore a covering of the thinnest, palest fabric, which clung to her body as she lowered herself into the warm, frothing water. Gia kept her eyes on her until she submerged.

When Claudia didn't immediately re-emerge, Gia inched nervously to the edge. After a moment that seemed to drag, Claudia popped up, running her hands over her face and smoothing down her hair. As she did, her upper body rose out of the water, exposing the clinging material on her chest.

Gia averted her eyes, but not fast enough to miss the curvature of her body, soft and delicate where Gia was hard and tough.

A wave of pleasure washed over her. Gia couldn't stop thinking about the erotic murals. If there was a painting of women having sex on the wall in a public place, it couldn't be too forbidden. All this time, Gia had been thinking her desire was rare and unnatural – but here it was, immortalized in a civic building. Sure, the painted women seemed to be performing for the pleasure of the men, but who was to say they didn't enjoy it? Prefer it, even.

'Are you coming in?' called Claudia, moving her hands back and forth in the water to make waves.

'I don't think I should,' Gia said.

'Are you embarrassed? We're just two women at the baths. There's nothing indecent about it.'

'Aren't I supposed to be on duty?'

'If the traitors come for me, at least I will have died at leisure. Come, join me. It is a demand, not a request, gladiator.'

But the baths here were large and deep, like pools. They were not like the small, shallow, crowded tubs at the other thermae. The idea of going underwater like Claudia had scared Gia enough to refuse again. 'I can't.'

'I didn't have you down as a prude,' said Claudia lightly.

'I'm not, I just ... don't like to swim,' Gia admitted.

She had never learned. It had never been something she was embarrassed about before, but suddenly she felt embarrassed by everything: her hair, her body, her teeth, her skin, and the fact that her palms were already sweating. Every part of her was sweating, actually.

'You don't need to swim to use the baths,' said Claudia, watching Gia fan herself with one hand. 'I'm just sitting here. There's a little bench, right under the water. It's not too deep.'

The waters lured her like sirens, calling her to take a dip. Gia didn't want to be wet and vulnerable in such important company, but she didn't want Claudia to think she was a coward either, so she moved behind the partition. She took off her skirt, breastplate and sandals. She climbed gingerly into the water, lowering herself slowly onto the bench, leaving her shoulders and wet breastband exposed.

'See? Not so bad, is it?' said Claudia.

'Could be worse.'

She felt Claudia's eyes on her, though she wasn't looking directly at Gia, and Gia wasn't looking directly at her.

Claudia was still immaculate and glistening, wearing earrings and a necklace made of fine jewels, with no apparent fear of them floating away in the water. Gia felt bedraggled, squinting through the steam.

'Why don't you like bathing?' Claudia asked.

It sounded terrible, when she phrased it like that.

'Bathing for hygiene is fine – it's quick and practical. But bathing for leisure is boring. The water gets in your ears, your skin wrinkles, and everyone looks terrible wet ...' She stumbled to a halt. 'I mean, except you, obviously.'

'You don't need to pretend,' Claudia said. 'This is why I like nice clothes, because they cover everything up so gracefully.' She glanced enviously at Gia. 'I wish I had a body like yours, but if there is one good thing to say about being the emperor's daughter, it's definitely the desserts. Foreign diplomats bringing sweet treats just to please me. How could I resist?'

'You shouldn't worry,' said Gia. 'You should not wish to change a thing.'

Claudia's eyes widened. Oh gods. Gia shouldn't have said that. She sounded adoring, as if she thought the princess perfect.

'Not physically, at least,' she added quickly.

Shit. No, that was even worse.

'Because of my terrible, villainous personality?' teased Claudia.

'You ... know what I mean,' said Gia weakly.

The steam had clearly boiled her brain. She had complimented her beauty, then insulted her accidentally. It was a madness to even speak it aloud yet she couldn't stop herself from imagining how she might lay the princess down on towels and kiss the insides of her legs, from her ankles up.

Stop, stop, stop.

'Gia, can I ask you something?' came Claudia's voice, smaller and softer than Gia had ever heard it.

'Anything.'

'Have you ever ... enjoyed the company of a woman?'

Gia couldn't look at her. Had she read her mind somehow?

'In . . . in what sense?' she said, praying she wasn't tell-tale red.

Gia needed her to say it, in clearest terms.

'Like in the painting . . . in the changing room.'

'Why . . . why are you asking?' said Gia, too afraid to admit she knew exactly why she was asking.

'I saw the way you looked at it,' said Claudia.

She worried that Claudia had sensed her attraction and she was trying to bring it up in a roundabout way to discourage further interest.

'I hear some of the noblewomen have fun with their friends on the side sometimes, when their husbands are being boring or bothersome. It's not something I've personally considered . . . but I thought perhaps, being as you are, you know, you might . . . take an interest.'

'As I am?'

'Being a woman in a male-dominated field, of course.'

'I don't think that's what makes women want to do that. The women in that picture, they don't look like gladiators to me,' said Gia.

'True.'

'It must be something deeper . . . something inside them,' said Gia, in what she hoped was a casual tone. 'I don't know.'

She thought of herself, and how her crushes on boys were always shallow. She liked the idea of them more than the reality. She thought about the one and only time she'd had sex and how disappointing it had been. She didn't even desire Celadus, handsome as he was, but she knew that Claudia did.

'I see,' said Claudia. 'I was just curious.'

'Have you . . . have you ever considered it?' said Gia.

Claudia didn't answer for a very long time and, when she did, her response was barely audible over the sound of water and steam.

'No, I . . . I like men.'

Whatever Gia had intuited before, she couldn't have been more wrong. Claudia was letting her down gently.

'So do I,' Gia lied. 'Love . . . love the men.'

The silence between them was sore and terrible.

'What is it you wanted to discuss in privacy, anyway?' Gia asked, as a welcome distraction. 'What is it that you cannot speak of in front of your guards?'

'Right.' Claudia sighed dramatically. 'We should not be in the water for this.'

Claudia gracefully climbed out, as Gia not-so-gracefully followed, both drying off with the linens provided and redressing.

The atmosphere had shifted dramatically, taking all possibilities of desire along with it. They dried off in silence between two partitions, their every move and every breath echoing through the cavernous space.

'I know a place where we can sit and talk,' said Claudia

Gia trailed after her, her hair still damp. They passed through to the main pool, with its open oculus and high ceiling. Bare-chested terracotta men ran along the walls, holding up a heavy stone frieze. The walls were sculpted with reliefs of fish-tailed sirens and melancholy nymphs. They continued on into the open courtyard, a small green square with trees and benches. Its walls were covered in ivy, which hung down between the pillars of the adjacent portico, creating a curtain of greenery to shield them. Claudia sat down, smiling and patting the stone bench beside her for Gia to join.

'When my father departs this Earth, as he must soon enough,

my brother Decimus will inherit all the empire, based on nothing but the prematurity of his birth,' said Claudia. 'Certainly, he may be usurped by another man – a distant relative, a foreign monarch, a member of the Senate – but they will never hand power to me, due to the fact of me being a woman.'

Gia waited for her to finish, knowing she had more to say.

'Decimus is an idiot. Not just an idiot but a cruel, savage idiot. He treats his slaves like animals and his animals like slaves. He feels no sympathy, no remorse. He isn't fit to rule. If an emperor can produce an heir from their blood, it should be me, but Decimus is the one being taken under my father's wing. He has been passing off his duties to my brother for a while now and Decimus is starting to abuse that trust. He is making preparations, for when he will become ruler.'

Claudia's expression was hard as she gazed into thin air.

'I must prevent my brother from inheriting the empire, no matter what. He would be so wicked a leader, historians would write of him for centuries. I have known him all my life and he is as close to a monster as I've ever seen. He doesn't know right from wrong, and he doesn't care. He always enjoyed the executions we were forced to witness. He revels in the wickedest of punishments for even the most innocent of beasts. That is the kind of man he is.'

Gia wondered why Claudia was confiding in her. She must've had hundreds of attendants, acquaintances and friends to talk to, but she was revealing her mission to a relative stranger instead.

Gia knew there must be a reason why she'd been chosen.

'I overheard you and Senator Cornelius talking about a vote,' she said slowly. 'That night when I intervened. Something to do with standing against your father.'

Claudia bit down on her bottom lip.

'Are you ... planning something?' asked Gia.

'Decimus is making his plans, I am making mine. I need allies if I am to survive my brother's reign. That is the only reason I tolerate Cornelius. He is easy to persuade. But this strength is also his weakness. My brother could easily turn the senator's head with a few false promises. If he knew what happened on the night of the party, Decimus would find a way to use it against me. He is dangerous in ordinary circumstances, but never more so than now.'

'Why now?'

Claudia turned to look at Gia, so intently that her skin prickled.

'One evening, several weeks ago, I noticed that my father was unreasonably intoxicated after eating. He is often intoxicated, but he usually just falls asleep at the lectern. On this occasion, he was delirious, ranting and raving about spirits. I saw my brother's eyes flitting over to the amphora, watching as father drained it alone. And I swear, Decimus looked disappointed when he awoke the next day, unwell but alive.'

'You think he was trying to poison him?'

'I think he's experimenting with murder. I fear Decimus is plotting to kill me too, but I cannot prove it yet.'

'What will you do?' Gia asked.

'I will try to convince my father that Decimus is working against him, but I must tread carefully. I fear my brother will turn to more extreme methods before I can prevent it. Yet I cannot tell anyone. Decimus has many friends in many places, not all of them known by me. He may reach a point where he feels he can kill us both in cold blood and get away with it.'

Claudia gave Gia a long, hard look, as if awaiting an answer to a question she hadn't asked. It gave Gia a sinking feeling.

An idea began to form in her mind, an impression of what the princess might want from her in return for her sponsorship.

'Why are you telling me all this?' Gia asked quietly.

Claudia didn't answer for a while.

'I feel that I can trust you,' she said, toying with the hem of her sleeve. 'You risked everything to come to my assistance when I was in need, when others would have looked away in fear. Plus, my brother detests women who don't behave as he thinks they ought to. He would never stoop to making an alliance with you.'

'The feeling is mutual,' Gia said.

'If I need to make it clear, these words are not to be shared with anyone. Decimus already knows I hate him, but if he hears about these particular suspicions, he'll make things even more difficult for me. I play dumb as much as possible around him, so he won't see me as a threat – but I am a threat. Even if he does not see me as a contender, he fears what I might tell people about him, or how I might turn against him. That is why I fear he might try to remove me from the equation.'

'What is it that you wanted to ask of me?'

She suspected, but she didn't say it aloud.

'I wish for you to teach me how to fight,' said Claudia.

'Oh,' said Gia, surprised.

For a moment, she'd thought Claudia wanted her for an assassin.

'I've never learned properly. I asked many times as a child, but was always refused. It's a wicked trick, of men, to tell little girls they can't learn to fight, then give them a thousand reasons to be afraid.'

Gia thought of herself, begging her brothers to teach her.

'I've attempted to train with my guards, but they were reluctant to hurt me. Perhaps with you it would be different.'

Gia burned hot beneath her cool, still-damp skin.

'You think I would hurt you?' said Gia.

'No, I think you would know how hard to push me, and when to give in.'

Everything inside her was on fire.

'I don't expect to be able to wield a weapon as you can, but perhaps you can teach me the basics, so I can stand half a chance of protecting myself. I would rather learn from another woman, especially one who defeated Caturix of Gaul.'

Gia had barely learned to fight herself. She didn't think herself skilled enough to teach someone else. She owed her first match to Claudia and her second match to Caturix. But Claudia seemed desperate.

'Then, I will help you,' said Gia. 'You should come to the ludus tomorrow night, after it's closed. I'll ask Cyrus to leave me the key. I'll say I want to stay behind and train. It would just be the two of us.'

The air between them seemed to throb.

'I knew you would not refuse me,' said Claudia.

'I didn't know you were a prophet.'

'No, but I have communed with the goddesses. I have prayed to them and made offerings. They appear to me as visions, as pale sylphs, divinities made of light and dust. They show themselves when they wish to communicate with me.'

Gia froze, no words imminent. She did not know what to make of this. The imperial cult claimed that the emperor met with Jupiter once a moon at the top of a mountain, but she had never put much stock in it. The cult also said that the emperor didn't defecate, and that he was born under a triple rainbow as a new star appeared in the sky. But if it was true that the emperor of Rome had a special connection to the pantheon, perhaps Claudia did too.

'You have spoken to the gods?' asked Gia.

'The goddesses. Only in dreams,' said Claudia. 'I am not mad, I swear. They were the ones who warned me about Decimus. That is why I was suspicious of him right away. And it seems they were right.'

Gia had always respected the pantheon, particularly on holidays, but she didn't speak with the gods directly. Sometimes she felt as if they were listening in on her thoughts or watching from afar. Briefly, she'd sensed a certain presence in her mind when an unknown voice had aided her in battle, but no one spoke to the gods in person. No one looked upon the face of the immortal ones.

'They told me that Decimus would rule over a dark age of Rome, an era of great turmoil and suffering. They told me he would betray my father and that I must beware of him,' said Claudia.

A cold breeze wound around them like a ribbon, rustling the grass and the ivy and the leaves on the trees.

'The goddesses told me to seek a warrior. They told me to seek a fighter to protect me from the trouble ahead.'

Claudia gazed deep into Gia's eyes, until Gia felt that she might have to run laps around the courtyard to burn off all the energy building up inside her.

'A warrior? You think it's me?'

'I know it is. The goddesses told me I would know. They told me my heart would choose, and ... I choose you.'

Gia shook her head slowly, trying to confirm that she was truly awake.

'Over all of the men in the empire, I choose you,' said Claudia. 'From the moment you burst into the shrine of Venus, I knew that it was you.'

Gia could no longer deny the cosmic pull she felt towards Claudia. There was a part of her that feared the princess, but she wanted her too. She wanted her more than she had ever wanted anything.

'I ... I am glad to be chosen,' Gia said, shaken. 'I am happy to fight for you, Claudia Imperia Caesaria.'

There was a silence; throbbing, swollen, thick with feeling.

Gia felt her body drawn in as Claudia seemed to lean towards her, before the toll of a bell startled them both and they broke apart in fear.

Servants appeared in the gardens, sweeping and cleaning up detritus. Their private tour of the baths was over.

'Time for us to go,' said Claudia.

They made their way back to the Forum in silence, standing several feet apart as they said their goodbyes.

'Tomorrow night,' Gia reaffirmed. 'At the ludus. Until then, stay safe.'

'I will try,' said Claudia heavily. 'It is of greatest importance to me that I live to see you again.'

With that, she retreated with her guards in armour, drawing curious glances from the people in the Forum.

10. A MOUNTAIN OF BONES

'Do you want to explain this?'

Frozen in the act of biting into an apple, Gia watched in horror as her mother slid a piece of paper onto the table.

It was a cartoonish drawing of herself in armour, standing over Caturix of Gaul and holding aloft a sword topped with the poor man's head. The papyrus it was drawn on was thin and slightly waxy, curling and frayed at the edges, with the indents of financial calculations from the previous sheet imprinted on it.

GIA VALERII, VIATRIX THE VICTORIOUS, it read, in a large, childish scrawl.

'Where did you get this?' Gia asked.

'A little girl is selling them in the Forum, calling it official merchandise from the Viatrix Fan Club.'

Athena. Gia could only admire her entrepreneurship.

Gia slowly looked up to meet her mother's furious expression. She wasn't drunk, nor hungover, but soberly pissed.

'About that,' said Gia.

'That's how you got those injuries to your face, isn't it? And the broken arm? Because you were pretending to be a gladiator?'

'I'm not pretending.'

'Now I see my warning came too late.'

'Mother, please.'

'All this time I thought you were walking the streets with that brothel girl, and you've been in the arena instead. How? How could you sign up to die like that – after Cassius, after Atticus ...'

'Just listen, all right?' said Gia. 'Sit down and listen!'

To her surprise, her mother did.

'I'm listening,' she said, pursing her lips.

'I know it's hard to hear, but, if anything, losing father and both of my brothers made me realize how short and dull and pointless life can be,' Gia said. 'I want to do something exciting with my years, however many of them I get; something meaningful.' She reached for her mother's hands across the table. 'You say you wish me to marry and have a safe, easy life, but that is not what *I* want. I have never wanted that. We have but one life. I don't want to look back in regret.'

'And this is what you want, is it? To be a bloody brute?'

'It's more than that,' said Gia. 'I don't simply want to beat men – that's just a welcome bonus – I want to fight back. For me, for you, for everyone the empire has kept down. I've always wanted to fight like the boys did, and you always told me that I couldn't. Everyone told me women could not be gladiators, but look at where I am now.'

'They will never respect you, even if you beat them. You know that, don't you? They will only hate you more for it,' said her mother. 'You cannot really win.'

Gia threw up her good hand in frustration.

'So you think we should just sit back and do nothing? Society will never change until we change too.'

Her mother fell quiet, seemingly surprised by the passion in Gia's voice.

'I admire your optimism,' she said. 'I do. But I am older and have lived long enough to know that the world just goes around in circles. In thousands of years from now, men will still be waging wars while women watch on, kept apart from power. I know it as sure I know I am alive, as sure as I know the sun will rise, but I can't be angry at you for trying, for believing. So did I, once.'

'It's not too late to believe again.'

'It is. That ship has sailed. Just don't come crying to me in spirit when you're dead and buried. I will turn you away at the door.'

'Then I'll haunt you for ever more.'

Her mother fought back the urge to smile.

'I don't have time to talk about this now,' said Gia. 'I have to go to the ludus to talk to Cyrus.'

'Okay, but this conversation isn't over,' said her mother.

Gia departed the villa feeling lighter. Her mother was predictably unhappy, but she didn't have to keep lying any more. Not about that, anyway. She still carried the weight of the other thing.

The secret she was keeping for Claudia.

In front of the ludus, a group of girls had lined up under an embroidered banner that read, NOW ACCEPTING FEMALE STUDENTS.

In the yard, young men played with shiny new weapons and equipment, wearing golden armour that had not a single scratch on it.

'Where did you get that?' Gia asked, pointing at a shiny shield.

The boy shrugged. 'Cyrus told us to help ourselves.'

As Gia neared the entrance, someone shrieked her name.

'Gia!'

Tiny and skinny, sandals flapping, Berenice came running towards her, followed by two other girls.

'See! I told you I knew her. I'm literally her best friend.'

Berenice pulled Gia into a hug, to demonstrate.

'Wow, Berenice, you're famous,' drawled one of the girls.

'What are you doing here?' asked Gia.

'We're signing up for gladiator classes,' said Berenice. 'We're all tired of the Den. The men around here are disgusting.'

The girls *mmm-hmmed* in agreement.

Though it had been Gia's idea to accept women to begin with, the idea of Berenice fighting in the arena filled her with sudden regret. Berenice wouldn't last a minute, though that was probably what people had said about her, at first.

'What happened to the wealthy Roman?' she asked.

'Dumped me. They always do, in the end,' said Berenice. 'That's why I have so much anger inside me that I need to get out.'

'We all do, honey,' said one of her friends.

'Gia, this is Flavia and Sibyl. Girls, this is Gia,' said Berenice.

'We heard the first session would be free,' said Flavia, with a jovial shrug, 'and we thought, why not? We haven't got anything better to do today, right?'

'I heard there would be knives,' mumbled Sibyl. 'I like knives.'

Flavia had short curly hair held back by a headband, wearing an orange tunic. Around her neck hung a sprig of sacred herbs. Sibyl was a tall, sullen girl in grey, with dark hair that covered half of her face.

'Cyrus probably wants to see what you're made of,' said Gia. 'I have to go meet with him now, but good luck. I'll catch you later, Berenice.'

'Bye, Viatrix!'

They all waved goodbye in unison. As Gia walked away, she

heard Flavia say, 'Viatrix the Victorious looks a lot smaller in real life.'

Cyrus waited in his office, surrounded by crates of gym equipment and armour, his desk now completely covered in coin bags.

'Gia,' he said, standing up abruptly. 'I've been waiting for you. You said you were going to report back to me. Where have you been?'

'Entertaining the rich and famous,' she said.

He gestured around broadly. 'As you can see, your mystery patron has already been busy.'

'She did all this?'

'Apparently so. On the condition that we permit women students. Her people kindly sent over the banner outside, so I thought, it's time. Let's give this a go. Dom and Lucas are out back picking out the ones with most promise. Oh, and this is for you. It has your name on it.'

Cyrus used his arm to sweep coin bags off the table, so he could lay down a long box that was heavy enough to make him sweat. It was tied with string, with a knotted tag that read VIATRIX.

'A present? For me?' Gia was practically giddy.

Cyrus handed her a knife to cut it open, pulling off the lid and unpacking layers of straw and linen. Underneath was the most beautiful armour Gia had ever seen. It had a gold and silver breastplate that was perfectly shaped to fit her body. It looked more like a corset, yet it was not revealing, with short sleeves of finest chainmail and a leather skirt that was reinforced with thin sheets of steel. In the box was also a delicate helmet with a curved visor, a lightweight silver shield with a moulded scene of Diana holding her bow and arrow, and a perilously sharp sword, its hilt decorated with gold wings that seemed to glitter supernaturally.

Cyrus watched her carefully. 'You'd better start talking,' he said. 'Because you're looking at that sword like you're in love with it.'

Gia put it down, replacing the lid and stashing the box beneath the desk.

'Not here,' she said. 'Somewhere else.'

At the bottom of the rear yard was a barracks where students could stay if they had nowhere else to go. There were several beds, dressers and a latrine in there, with a grill outside to cook on, but it was empty at present. They sat on the porch bench, looking out at the small groups of girls who practiced moves under the tutelage of Dom and Lucas.

'How's your wrist?' he asked.

'Healing. Almost better,' she said. 'I'll have to test out my strength again soon. Here.' She dropped the coin bag he'd given her into his lap. 'Keep your denarii. I didn't need it in the end.'

'Promise me you actually saw a physician.'

'I did; he just treated me for free.'

Cyrus looked suspicious, but he let it go.

'I have some matches coming up that I'd like you to fight in,' he said. 'You're probably going to miss the next one, but Neptunalia is in a couple of weeks and one of the sponsors wants to host a variety event. It would be good to get you fit and fighting for that, while you're enjoying some public favour. Just a friendly match, nothing too serious. Look what you've started. Now everyone wants in.'

They watched as one of the girls performed a particularly impressive roll, springing up to tag her opponent with a wooden sword.

'So, tell me, who is it?' he said eagerly. 'Your mystery patron?'

Gia took a deep breath, nervously rubbing her thighs.

'She, uh, asked me not to say. She wishes to be a silent partner. I thought she might choose to reveal herself to you, but she appears to have kept her secrets, for now.'

'I see.'

'But I don't think I can keep this in and I can't lie to you, so I'm just going to make it obvious who it is and if anyone ever asks, you can say you guessed because you're so clever. How about that?'

'Flattery will get you everywhere,' agreed Cyrus, trying not to smile. 'Shoot.'

'It started on the night of Senator Cornelius's birthday party. I was spared from death and, later, I had the chance to repay that favour in kind. I ... intervened in a situation. An inappropriate situation, involving Senator Cornelius. I'm sure you can imagine. All you need to know is that I came to her aid, like she had come to mine.'

Cyrus's dark eyes widened, instantly making the connection.

'Gia,' he said warningly.

'Just hear me out,' she said. 'After I beat Caturix, she approached me again, through you. We were even, she owed me nothing then. But maybe she wanted to keep me close, because of what I knew.'

Gia was talking so fast she could hardly keep up with herself.

'I went to the House of Menander, like you asked me ... and it was her. She offered to be my patron because she wants the women of Rome to have better lives and she thinks us fighting in gladiator games is starting from the bottom up. She wants to get the people onside. I think ... I think she wants to be empress.'

'Good gods,' said Cyrus. 'She's insane.'

'She's happy to fund the ludus, and in exchange she wants me to help protect her. She said something about a chosen warrior and the goddesses and ... I don't know about that part, but she ... she's not what I thought she would be.'

Cyrus's brow rose higher.

'I already said she could come here tonight and I would teach her how to defend herself. Sorry. Can we use the ludus?'

'What are you drawing us into, Gia?' he said.

'A financially profitable business arrangement?'

'No, it's an obligation. Not just any obligation either, but an obligation to the imperial family. Imagine what will happen if you refuse to do as she asks. She can command you. If you still refuse, she can imprison you. If you continue to deny her whatever it is that she wants from you, she can even have you executed. She can do it because you looked at her wrong, or because you ruined her day, and not a single person will fight for you. That is the power emperors hold.'

'She wouldn't do that,' said Gia.

'How do you know? Even if so, her father might do it for her. He might learn what she's up to and be displeased enough to take matters into his own hands. He could level the building. He could imprison our families, or burn us alive. He can do whatever he likes because he's the emperor. That's the problem.'

'She isn't the same as him.'

'How certain are you? Enough to bet your life on it, or mine?'

Gia didn't answer directly, uncertain of the answer.

'I think she's lonely, looking for a friend,' she said instead.

Okay. Gia could hear how outlandish it sounded.

Cyrus scoffed. 'Gia, I'm sorry. I like you a lot, you're a good kid, but you are out of your fucking mind if you think someone like her can truly be friends with someone like you.'

'You don't know her like I do.'

Cyrus groaned, forming a pyramid with his hands. 'Gia, can you not see that she is playing you?'

'For what? What does she have to gain from this?'

'I don't know. Someone to kill for her, maybe?'

'No,' Gia said quickly, though she had wondered it herself. Claudia had gone out of her way to tell her about Decimus and the threat he posed to her.

'Tell that to your face,' said Cyrus.

'What do you want from me? You want me to refuse her?'

He laughed mournfully and rubbed his forehead.

'You can't say no now, after already agreeing. This is it. We're locked in. You're committed, the ludus is committed, and not only will we have to deal with the fallout from the emperor and his disapproval of woman gladiators, but also whatever Cornelius and Claudia are cooking up, probably together. If you think she's different from her creature of a father and her sadist of a brother, you're being naïve, Gia. She was raised in that family. There's very little chance that she's not a maniac too.'

Would a maniac talk about visions of deities and aspire to rule the world in woman's name? Gia asked herself. *Probably.*

'You needed the money to keep the school open and accept more students,' she said. 'We needed a patron, and here she is. We needed my introduction to be successful and, what do you know, it has been. You must admit that having the first woman gladiator be sponsored by the princess of Rome is better promotion than a thousand painted posters.'

'I thought it was a secret.'

'For now,' Gia conceded. 'Even without a name, people will still know the ludus has a wealthy patron. Just look at this gear, Cyrus! If the shine of that gold won't make us winners, then what will? How can we not succeed?'

'Only for as long as you live,' he said.

'Not true,' said Gia, looking out at the field. 'Looks like you have a few future Viatrixes to train up right over there. There's nothing special about me except the fact that I was able and willing. If I go, there will be others to replace me now.'

They fell quiet, listening as Dom gave a short speech about footwork.

'It's an interesting proposition,' Cyrus said eventually.

'What is?' asked Gia.

'Some people say Claudia is the dark horse of the family, and that she is key to their undoing because of the secrets she keeps,' he said. 'If Claudia is the key, then fine, let us open the door.'

She turned to him curiously.

'Maybe your association with Claudia can bring us closer to the real goal: to rid the world of emperors. Humanity has reached the peak of modernity. Never before in history has man had access to such vast resources and knowledge. We should not be ruled over by aristocrats but governed by those elected by the people.'

'You should've been a senator,' said Gia.

'They would not have me.'

Cyrus was silent for a long moment, staring into nothing.

'Let her be your patron, if she must. We have no choice now anyway. Let her do with you what she wishes, as long as you're willing. If she's lonely, you'll be there for her. If she wants to learn how to fight then, damn, you'll teach her. You can find out what makes her tick and how the imperial family operates. We can use that information to identify the emperor's weaknesses. All we know of him is what he chooses to present to the public, and that is bad enough.'

'We?' she asked. 'Who is we?'

'We the people,' said Cyrus.

'Do you think yourself a Brutus? A liberator?'

'A man can dream.'

'What about Claudia?' Gia asked.

'What about her?' he said. 'She'll be fine. She has plenty of money and silk cushions to comfort her.'

'I don't feel good about betraying her trust.'

'Just wait. A moment will come when you'll see who she truly is.'

Gia shook her head, silently disagreeing, but inside a voice was screaming, *He's right! Listen, Gia.*

'You are a passing fascination for her, I guarantee it, just like Celadus was. So make sure you get the most out of it, because one day she'll discard you, dead or alive, and you don't want to be left with nothing.'

Cyrus didn't even know the worst of it yet. If she'd told him what Claudia said about Decimus trying to poison the emperor, he'd be even more suspicious of what she was getting them into. Perhaps he was right to be so cautious.

He tossed the keys at her.

'For your training session this evening. If you want to use the ludus for this shit, bring me something I can use. We need to know the emperor's sins, his regrets, whatever we can get. Just ask questions and see what she tells you of her own will.'

Gia had seen firsthand the brutality that kept the wheel of empire in motion. Atticus had given his life to entertaining the rich. Cassius had died in pursuit of Rome's endless conquest. She had every reason to hate the empire and all who profited from it. There was no harm in doing as Cyrus asked. So what if she had an ulterior motive? She was certain Claudia had such a hidden motive in sponsoring her too.

'I will talk to her a little, but that is all,' she said.

Cyrus stood up, readying himself to depart for home.

'Tonight, I will pray to the pantheon,' he said. 'I will pray to all the gods that you are right – because if you are, we have the opportunity to change the course of history with our own hands.'

Gia nodded heavily. 'I will pray too,' she said.

His expression softened, regret shining through.

'If you think I'm being cruel, just remember that your new friend sits on a throne built on slavery,' he said. 'Perhaps you do not understand the indignity of enslavement, but let me put it like this: no vengeance will ever come close to the horrors that have been inflicted on slaves by so many generations of Romans, including this one. This is why I have no sympathy for the emperor's daughter. If she understood the indignity of the empire, she would not wish to rule over it.'

ACT III

DIANA

FORTUNA

MINERVA

VENUS

To avoid spying eyes and prying ears, the goddesses had established a war room, hidden away in a secret chamber of the palace of Fortuna. The four women stood together before a golden globe, which spun so fast that visions appeared on its surface. They watched, with matching expressions of gradually reducing enthusiasm, as the gladiator plotted with the man, Cyrus Jucundius.

'This complicates things,' said Minerva. 'Our chosen warrior is aligned with those conspiring to destroy the empire.'

'Aren't we doing the same, by working against Jupiter?' asked Diana.

'It is not the same. We want to install an empress. Cyrus wishes to rid the world of emperors altogether. That goes against everything Fortuna has predicted.'

'It is still possible for his actions to change the future,' said Fortuna. 'Doubts are creeping in, about the princess's intentions and character. We must ensure that he does not unduly influence the gladiator.'

'Perhaps it's just idle talk,' said Diana. 'Many men have plotted to destroy the empire and none have succeeded.'

'It endangers the princess. The gladiator is already questioning her right to rule. This Cyrus is a threat,' said Minerva.

'I will keep an eye on him,' said Diana. 'If he makes himself an obstacle, we shall do what is necessary.'

'Good,' said Fortuna. 'Let us focus. Claudia is the future we have envisioned, the destiny we have gambled everything on. Let nothing distract us from that. If Decimus fears that Claudia could threaten his rule, the boy won't hesitate to get rid of her. If we cannot fully trust the warrior to protect her, we may need to intervene more directly.'

'At least we are getting somewhere now,' said Diana. 'Gia has agreed to teach Claudia how to fight. Let us have faith and see how it plays out.'

'Yes, although . . .' Minerva trailed off.

'What?' pressed Diana.

'I fear their feelings may come between them and what they need to do. They must not allow themselves to be distracted by desires of the heart.'

One by one, they all turned to Venus, who was uncharacteristically quiet on the subject of potential romance.

'Are you well?' asked Diana, noticing.

Venus shook her head.

'My thoughts were elsewhere. There is something you should know . . .' She paused dramatically. 'Jupiter summoned me.'

Minerva startled, immediately alarmed.

'He sent Mercury to fetch me and bring me to his palace, to stand before him and answer his questions. As his children, you may evade his suspicion for a while, but he has no such allegiance to me. He has heard rumours that forces within the pantheon are conspiring to challenge his authority. He is interrogating all of the gods.'

'Oh my,' said Minerva.

'Naturally, I did my utmost to charm and dissuade him. He is not *immune to my powers of enchantment, ancient as he is.' Diana looked positively repulsed. 'But I do not think I fully convinced him,' Venus added.*

'What does he know?' asked Minerva.

'He is not yet aware of the gladiator, though he asked of Princess Claudia.'

'I am surprised she came to his attention at all,' said Fortuna, 'though I am sure he underestimates her. He is a man, after all. An immortal man, but still a man.'

Minerva grumbled darkly. 'Now I am even more concerned,' she said.

'For me, or for her?' asked Venus.

'For all of us.'

They settled into uneasy silence as the globe continued to turn.

11. PROTECT YOURSELF

'You wake up and there's a strange man in your room,' said Gia. 'He's moving quickly towards you. You're unarmed, and so is he. You're trapped and you have no way of escape. No one to hear you scream. What do you do?'

Gia and Claudia stood in the empty yard at the back of the ludus. Claudia wore a simple white tunic, though it was finely embroidered and cinched with a silk tasselled belt, while Gia wore her stripped-back uniform.

The school was empty and the moon hung high above, round and full and brilliantly bright, illuminating them.

'I would try to bribe him,' said Claudia. 'I would offer to pay three times what the person who hired him paid.'

Gia suppressed a smile. 'The assassin isn't interested in your money,' she said. 'What then?'

'I would ... beg for mercy and tell him that whatever his circumstance, he could still turn back and find a new path. I would apologize for all the pain he has ever experienced, but explain that taking my life would not bring him peace.'

'He's not interested in your sympathy. Now what?'

'I would ... seduce him?' said Claudia.

'Really?'

Claudia shrugged. 'It would be worth a shot, would it not?'

Gia was about to say something risqué like 'lucky assassin', but she held her tongue. She needed to learn to harden herself, to put up some exterior walls so she didn't fall for Claudia's potentially deceptive charms. All while getting information out of Claudia for Cyrus.

'Okay. So first thing, you're going to spring out of that bed and onto your feet, ready to fight for your life. Keep your knees bent and curl your fists – bring them up to your face, like this,' said Gia.

Claudia copied her stance, though hesitantly.

'Keep your elbows close to your body to protect your ribs. Stand with your feet slightly apart and diagonal, like this, with one foot slightly forward. It'll be harder to knock you down that way.'

'Got it,' said Claudia, moving her feet. She looked as if she was about to begin a dance performance, too graceful to be a brawler, but she lifted her chin in determination, her eyes sparkling.

'Your best chance of staying alive is staying upright. I'm going to take a few light swings at you. Dodge them while keeping on your feet, okay? Protect yourself. Better act fast.'

Gia quickly extended her arm, but Claudia was slow to move. Gia landed a light punch on her side.

'Faster than that,' instructed Gia.

'I'll do better this time.'

Claudia dodged the second strike, and the third, but when Gia came at her from alternating sides Claudia became confused, lost her centre of balance and fell, quite gracefully, onto her knees.

'You okay?' said Gia, extending a hand to help her up. She held her gaze as Claudia rose to her feet.

'I'm not usually this clumsy, I swear.'

'It was just your first try,' Gia said. 'If you fall, try to bring your attacker down with you, and while you're falling, keep your knees and elbows pointed and try to dig them in. An elbow in a soft, fleshy place will hurt, but an elbow to a hard place like the shin or the ribs can be more destructive. Basically, whatever you can reach.'

'Pointy knees and elbows, got it.'

'But maybe your arms and legs are bound. Your first defence has failed,' said Gia. 'That's when you go for the nose. Tense your neck. Then, with the hardest part of your forehead right here near the hairline, you want to drive your head straight into your assailant's nose.'

Claudia watched her uneasily.

'What's wrong?' asked Gia.

'I can't really imagine myself smashing someone in the nose with my head,' she said. 'Can you? I'd probably do more damage to myself than them.'

'That's fair. It's a last resort. There's also the groin area.' Gia demonstrated. 'Then, when they double over in pain, you knee their nose too.'

'I can do that,' said Claudia, mimicking Gia. 'Possibly.'

'If that doesn't work, then you try the kneecaps. Go for the knees and shins with short, sharp little kicks. Go on. Do the motion.'

'I feel quite ridiculous,' said Claudia.

'The world is ridiculous,' said Gia, thinking of Cassius. He had taught her first, and now she was teaching someone else – the princess of Rome, no less. 'You won't feel ridiculous when you're doing damage to your attacker.'

'Like that?'

'Sort of,' said Gia.

'I'm not doing very well at this, am I?'

'You're doing great,' Gia lied. 'It's not a test; it's just a lesson to help you.'

'Well, I like to be good at everything.'

'No one is good at everything. Not by the looks of that footwork,' teased Gia, as Claudia flashed her eyes in faux rage.

'I can have you killed, you know,' she said.

It was a joke, but it was also true.

'If none of that has worked, go for their eyes,' Gia said, miming a jabbing motion with her fingers. 'And the throat. Don't put your whole hands around their neck, like this. Put your thumb and fingers around the windpipe and dig your fingers into the notch right here.'

Gia gently took Claudia's hands and held them against her neck. She could feel her heart beating fast through the skin.

'If you press that hard enough, your attacker will be in intense pain. Right there. Can you feel it?'

Claudia swallowed. 'Yes. I feel it.'

Gia released her hands. Now her heart was pounding too.

'Let's try a different scenario. Say the attacker comes from behind.' Gia moved to stand at Claudia's back, gently pressing their bodies together as she attempted to restrict her arms.

She could feel Claudia's heat, and her own.

'If this happens, stick out your foot and trip them—'

As soon as Gia had spoken these words, Claudia did exactly as she was asked, extending one leg behind Gia's right foot and sending them both toppling. Crying out, Gia fell onto her back, with Claudia landing hard on top of her, twisting as she fell. She slowly looked up at Gia, her cheeks rosy.

Gia's breath caught in her throat.

'That wasn't meant to be an instruction,' she said.

'Oops,' said Claudia, smiling coyly. 'My mistake.'

It was like in the dream she'd had, only the other way around. If Gia was the goddess Diana, she was supposed to be on top. Claudia was supposed to be beneath her, like Venus. Everything was mixed up.

Their faces were almost touching. Gia breathed and a strand of Claudia's hair flickered, dancing as if in ecstasy.

'You did say you wished to know me better,' said Gia.

'I do,' said Claudia, not moving.

'I don't mind it,' said Gia.

As if not in control of her own arm, she reached out tenderly and tucked the wayward strand of hair behind her ear.

For a moment, they merely stared at each other.

'I . . . don't know why I did that,' said Gia.

Claudia suddenly sat back, her expression shuttered. She stood abruptly, dusting herself off.

Gia had done the wrong thing, that was obvious.

'What else can you teach me?' Claudia said, in a bright voice. 'I should like to know how to handle a weapon. A dagger, say.'

Gia stood too. 'Oh, yeah . . . of course. I haven't actually fought with a dagger yet, but we've been training with different weapons, so we're prepared for all circumstances. Let's practise knife throwing.'

They moved on quickly, papering over the awkwardness.

There was a target set up in the yard, which they'd last used during a visit from a Sagittarius gladiator. Gia took out a training knife and showed Claudia how to hold her arm and which angle to launch the knife from, demonstrating several times, once hitting the bullseye.

Then she handed the knife to Claudia.

'Every time you hit that target right there, you get a reward.'

'What kind of reward?' said Claudia, clearly perking up.

'I don't know. What do you want?'

Claudia stared at the knife, turning the blade left and right.

'How about this? Every time I hit the target, I get to ask you a question.'

Gia's stomach turned again, rolling like a barrel over stones.

'What kind of questions?' asked Gia.

'Anything I like. That's what will make it fun for me.'

Gia folded her arms. 'All right, let's see what you've got.'

Claudia missed the first shot, groaning in frustration. The second time she missed, she actually stamped her foot in temper. Gia tried not to smile at how adorable she was when she was losing.

'Are you laughing at me?' Claudia said.

'I would never.'

Finally, the knife struck the outer part of the target and Claudia whipped around triumphantly, her expression slightly wild.

'One question,' said Gia.

'Have you ever been in love before?' Claudia asked.

'No,' answered Gia.

Claudia threw the knife again, striking the board just above her last mark.

'Have you ever done it with a man?' she asked.

'Yes,' said Gia shortly.

'One-word answers only, is it?' said Claudia. 'Fine.'

Claudia threw the knife three times in short sequence, but,

on each occasion, it bounced off the target. She said a word Gia wouldn't have expected from an emperor's daughter, though it sounded like poetry on her lips.

'Your arm is too loose,' said Gia. 'You're so eager to be asking questions that you're not holding your position.'

'I'm not *eager*,' said Claudia. 'I'm a normal amount of curious.'

Claudia set her shoulders, took a deep breath and tried again. 'Ha!' she said, when she struck the ring. Claudia did a little victory dance, waving her arms in the air, before turning very seriously to Gia.

'Did you enjoy it?' she asked. 'When you ... you know.'

Gia gaped at her, her cheeks warming. 'What sort of question is that?!'

'You said I could ask anything.'

'I did. Regrettably, I did.'

'I'm only asking because ... I have never,' said Claudia.

Gia swallowed, trying to decide what to say.

'I just wondered what it was like. That's all. One day soon, I might have to ... But I've never had anyone I could trust to ask before.'

'What about Celadus?' Gia asked daringly.

'What about him?' said Claudia, in a sharp tone.

'I heard a rumour from one of the other gladiators that you took an interest in him,' said Gia, already regretting bringing it up.

'We went out once or twice, but we had little in common,' said Claudia.

'So you dropped him?'

'Actually, he dropped me.'

'I very much doubt that,' said Gia.

'It's true, and you didn't answer my question. So, did you? Enjoy it?'

Gia hesitated. 'No,' she admitted. 'I wish never to do it again.'

They fell quiet, both too afraid to look at the other.

Setting her shoulders, Claudia turned back to the board and very deliberately threw the knife. This time, it struck the middle of the target.

'Have you ever desired someone you were not supposed to?' she asked, her voice low and full of intent.

'Yes. I am guilty. Now, that's ... probably enough training for today.'

'One more question.'

Gia relented, steeling herself. 'Go on, then. Just one.'

Claudia retrieved the knife from the target and stepped back again, hard-focused on the ring. A slight motion of her arm and the blade struck the centre once more. She was fully into her stride now.

'Is there a person that you presently desire?' she asked softly.

Gia wet her lips. She avoided answering for as long as she felt she could get away with, which wasn't very long at all.

'Yes,' she said.

Claudia stared at her, lost in thought.

The silence stretched to breaking point.

Gia opened her mouth to say something, anything, to fill the growing space between them, but Claudia quickly cut in:

'I should return now,' she said, avoiding making eye contact, 'before Decimus becomes suspicious. Will there be another lesson, do you think?'

Gia tried to gather herself together. 'Yes, if you like.'

'I would like. Perhaps in a day or so I shall be free again.'

'I'll walk back with you,' said Gia.

'You don't have to do that.'

'Only for your safety. I wouldn't want anyone following you again. Unless you would rather walk alone.'

'No, no ... we can walk together.'

Gia tidied away the equipment they'd used, locking up the ludus. Claudia put on the stola she wore when she wished to travel incognito, pulling it up over her head, but Gia made sure to carry her sword just in case.

The streets were mostly empty but for night workers and drunk stragglers. A cart rolled past, its load rattling.

Gia tried to stay alert, walking ahead at every corner. She was tense and anxious, unsure if this was because of Claudia or the threat of an assassin. Claudia watched Gia closely too, her eyes barely leaving her.

'Thank you again, for today,' she said. 'I don't know if any of it will come back to me in the moment, but at least I'll have an idea.'

'There is only so much I can do. You should not be walking the streets alone without your guards,' said Gia.

'I have you.'

'Trust me, a party of four armoured guards the size of bears would be much more of a deterrent.'

'I'm not certain I can trust them, is the problem,' she said.

'Yet you trust me?' said Gia.

'As much as I trust anyone,' said Claudia airily. 'Someone has been keeping watch on me for my brother. It could well be one of my guards, though they would swear their loyalty to me on the lives of their children. I even fed them false information, a different lie for each man, to see which story became gossip on the streets, but so far, not a word. Maybe it is one of my handmaids.'

'People are unpredictable,' said Gia. 'I don't know if you can ever truly know a person's heart. Loyalty is hard to come by.'

They passed by the mural of Claudia, who stopped in front of it. Grinning, she turned around and struck the same identical pose – demure, elegant, with her hands crossed in front of her. She held her poise for a moment before bursting out laughing with Gia.

'Oh, I wish I could draw,' said Gia. 'What a picture.'

'This sight is for your eyes only,' Claudia said. She frowned. 'What's this? Someone has scratched something here. I think it says . . . mouth . . . stinker.'

Shit.

'Who would say something like that?' Claudia said, glancing back at Gia.

'Probably just some . . . jealous loser,' said Gia, quickly ushering her away.

They continued down the road until they reached the House of Menander, where two of Claudia's guards waited with red shields and cloaks.

'This is me,' she said.

The guard's visors were pulled down to obscure their faces and, though they didn't move a muscle, Gia sensed that they would be listening in, loyal or not.

'Be safe,' she said. 'If you need me, I'm right over there.'

Gia looked to the taberna, concern rising as she noted how full and noisy it appeared, with people spilling out onto the pavement.

'Looks like you have a busy night ahead,' said Claudia.

'The wheel never stops turning,' said Gia.

'I bid you a good night. The best of nights.'

They paused, neither departing, until Claudia stepped forwards, stretched onto her tiptoes and kissed Gia on the cheek.

Gia instinctively raised a hand to her face, as if trying to prevent the kiss from sliding off.

'I'll speak to you again soon, I hope,' said Claudia, falling back.

Claudia approached the guards, who opened the gates of the exterior wall. She looked back at Gia very fleetingly before disappearing.

Gia stared after her for a moment, too stunned to move, before clumsily continuing on.

Claudia had kissed her.

Claudia had *kissed* her?

It was only a friendly peck, that was all.

Although the way she'd looked at Gia as she did it . . .

Oh gods.

Gia's knees were shaky and weak, like she'd been in the ring.

She felt out of control. Her head was swollen with thoughts that pulsed against her temples, images that flew in and out of focus.

Cyrus's words broke through. *'You are a passing fascination for her, I guarantee it, so make sure you get the most out of it, because one day she'll discard you, dead or alive, and you don't want to be left with nothing.'*

No. Gia would not throw away all sense and reason for the princess who wanted to rule over a mountain of bones.

All of the wild belief and high hopes faded away slowly, until she returned to reality, sandals firmly on stone.

The door of the taberna flung open and her mother burst out, wearing a stained apron dress. She had braided her hair, pinning it up, and she was smiling toothily.

'Here she is!' she said, throwing her arms around Gia. 'The famous Viatrix is here, everyone.'

A cheer rang out. Before she could protest, Gia was thrust into the crowded taberna and presented to a crowd of diners who applauded and waved their napkins at her, all of them talking to her at once.

Gia spied Cyrus, dining with a glamourous woman in green. When he met her eye, he waved lazily.

'What are you doing here?' she called over.

'Don't you know? Everyone is talking about the Via Stabiana taberna. It's the hottest new spot in town.'

'That's right,' agreed her mother. 'Home to the finest food and the first female gladiator in the empire.'

'You've changed your tune,' Gia murmured.

'Nonsense. I've always supported your career,' she lied, because customers were listening. 'There is no mother prouder in all of Pompeii.' Raising her voice, she added: 'The Valerii family cannot be beaten; not in the kitchen and not in the arena!'

Another cheer resounded, as Gia was pushed into a chair and accosted with full plates and glasses, everyone asking her this or that, wanting her to retell her miraculous victory against the Gaul. She did her best to be entertaining, knowing that every half hour she kept them occupied, they'd buy more drinks.

'Gia, come over here and meet my friend Julia,' said Cyrus, ushering her to sit at their table. 'Julia, this is Viatrix, in the flesh.'

Dark-haired and dark-eyed, with shapely brows and a painted-on beauty spot, Julia was adorned in emerald silks, a peacock feather tucked into her headband. She was younger than Cyrus and older than Gia, probably in her early twenties, but she had the aura of a much more distinguished person.

'Well, hello.' She looked at Gia like a statue in an atrium, her eyes drifting from one curve of the sculpture to another.

'Hello,' said Gia uncertainly.

'It is my great pleasure to meet you,' she said. 'Cyrus here has been telling me all about you. I had the terrible misfortune of missing your match against the Gaul. I'm looking forward to seeing you in action, once you're back in the game.'

'Julia is a patron,' explained Cyrus. 'Her husband, Senator Quirius, sponsors the Neptunalia games. Her previous gladiator just died in the ring. She's looking for a new fighter to spend all of the senator's money on.'

Julia batted her hand at him. 'You're a wicked man, Cyrus.' She looked back to Gia. 'It's true, though,' she whispered theatrically. 'He has too many denarii. His piles of gold are taking up too much space in my house.'

'Sorry to hear about your last gladiator,' said Gia.

'He had a good run,' she said, with a shrug.

How brutal for Julia to be shopping for a new gladiator when the last one was just killed in action.

Though hadn't Cyrus done the same thing by recruiting Gia when she came for her dead brother's things?

'Cyrus tells me you already have a sponsor?' said Julia.

'That's right.'

'Well, sometimes these arrangements don't work out. Not every patron is in it for the right reasons, and more still have no idea what they're doing. If you're thinking of a change in management, you know where to find me.'

'I'm grateful for the offer,' Gia said diplomatically.

Julia winked at Gia, turning back to her conversation with Cyrus. Gia looked away but she lingered, eavesdropping.

'You were saying, about the Senate?' he prompted.

'Trouble is brewing back in Rome,' said Julia. 'Cornelius grows tired of the emperor's incompetency, but the prospect of his wretched son ruling over us is even less popular with the Senate. Cornelius and my husband rarely see eye to eye, but they are in unison on this.'

'Then now is the time to strike,' said Cyrus.

'You should go to bed,' said Gia's mother, appearing at her side. 'You're meant to be resting. I just wanted them to see your face.'

'Can you handle things without me?' Gia asked.

'Of course. We have Nicodemus now.'

She gestured at the sweaty man currently putting his head in the oven, trying to retrieve a piece of burned bread. With a yelp, he sprang back, nursing his singed fingers.

Gia's mother looked to her and shrugged.

'He's cheap,' she said.

'Goodnight, Mother,' said Gia, kissing both of her cheeks.

'Goodnight, darling.'

Gia slowly made her way towards the stairs, being drawn into four more conversations and accepting two more drinks that were handed to her on the way. She downed the first, then took the second up to her room to drink in peace.

When the glass was empty, Gia lay on the bed, room spinning. All she could think about was Claudia Caesaria.

Claudia sprawled on top of her. Claudia in her arms. Claudia, her eyes shining, cheeks glowing . . .

'Have you ever desired someone you were not supposed to?'

She couldn't stop thinking about the kiss; Claudia's soft lips on her cheek, her perfume filling the air.

Why had she asked such questions? Surely it had to have meant something.

Gia had absolutely no idea why a woman like Claudia would be interested in her. Maybe in uniform she reminded Claudia of Celadus the Handsome.

Maybe blood sports turned her on.

Maybe she was just bored and curious, like she said.

Gia didn't know, and she didn't care.

Good or bad, she wanted her.

12. A DANGEROUS GAME

The festival of Neptunalia was held during the heat and the drought of midsummer, when the people of Pompeii asked the gods of the seas and rivers and freshwaters to bless them with rain.

Claudia and her brother were carried through the streets in a litter, hoisted by guards, towards the amphitheatre, where an entire day of gladiatorial battles awaited them. Claudia waved through the window as Decimus drew his curtain. The emperor was mysteriously absent; some said he'd returned to Rome to deal with the escalating conflict with the Senate.

The matches were arranged to be friendlies, with neither party killing to win, which at least meant that Gia didn't have to contemplate her mortality for a while.

Dressed in the shiny new armour Claudia gifted her, Gia waited with the boys in the chambered darkness that surrounded the arena, shaking slightly from the cold of the stone floors and benches.

She peered out through the arches at the imperial box, where Claudia wore a gown of blue and green: Neptune's colours. Decimus looked ridiculous in a coral crown and holding a decorative trident. The siblings appeared to be bickering, talking fast and low, their faces tense.

Gia thought of Claudia's words.

'I fear Decimus is plotting to kill me too, but I cannot prove it yet.'

How much danger was Claudia already in?

'The Neptune Games will begin shortly!' boomed the announcer, as music played louder, rousing the audience.

Gia turned back to the holding area, joining Dom and Lucas. They wore matching uniforms of leather and copper, with shields that displayed the insignia of the ludus: crossed swords beneath a feathered gladiator helmet.

'I'm not sure I want to be Lucas the Lucky, after what happened to Felix the Fortunate,' said Lucas forlornly.

'At least you are not Dominic the Devious.'

'Viatrix the Victorious is so much better,' said Lucas. 'Hey, Gia, how come you don't use your real name?'

Gia considered it. 'It was supposed to be a secret, at first. But now that everyone knows, I still prefer to wear Viatrix like a costume,' she said. 'I can be Viatrix in the arena and not myself, which is good, because she is a much better warrior than me.'

Lucas looked confused.

'She makes the hard decisions. It makes me less nervous, to play a role. It doesn't feel real, so I can't be afraid.'

'I wish I'd thought of that,' said Lucas.

'I'm the opposite. When I win, I want to win under my real name,' said Dom, 'so all my enemies from childhood will remember me.'

'What enemies?'

'I have a couple.'

'What did you do to make any enemies?' teased Gia.

Despite his profession, Dom was mild-mannered, polite to a fault, the most congenial of the boys.

'I spilled someone's drink once. I called someone an idiot one time. I hit a girl in the face with a ball by accident . . .'

Gia heard a giggle. Some of the new ludus girls had been invited to watch the games, including Berenice's friend Flavia. They sat on a bench nearby and engaged in their own whispered conversations – not yet part of the group. Flavia's dark hair was braided and she wore several talismans. When she met Gia's eye, she gave her a respectful nod.

'Have you seen Berenice lately?' Gia asked her.

'Not since the day Cyrus told her she didn't make the cut.'

While Flavia had been accepted into the gladiator school, Berenice had not.

'I'm worried about her,' said Gia. 'I haven't seen her for a while.'

'She probably bumped into one of her clients and decided to go somewhere with them. She's never been the kind to plan ahead.'

'Maybe,' said Gia, unconvinced. 'She isn't normally gone so long.'

'I'll help look for her if she doesn't turn up soon.'

'Thanks, Flavia.'

Gia turned her attention to the opening acts – acrobats and pantomimes, followed by a chariot race that sprayed dust everywhere – but she was barely aware of what was going on around her. Decimus speared a boar from the imperial box. Claudia was serenaded by a travelling choir. The absent emperor was honoured through a tedious military procession.

'The Herculaneum school just confirmed your opponent,' said Cyrus, appearing through an arch. 'They weren't convinced, at first, that women fighting has any merit. But I managed to wear them down. Legend has spread about your defeat of the Gaul.

They finally found another girl who they think is ready to fight you. They trained her up, so they say, but it was all very hasty.'

Gia was oddly excited by the prospect of fighting another woman. 'What do you know about her?' she asked.

'Not much. They're calling her Dido the Destroyer. There are rumours that she's actually the pampered daughter of a wealthy nobleman who was estranged from the family after refusing an arranged marriage.'

'So she's going to be furious, then?'

'She's going to be out of her depth,' said Cyrus. 'She paid gladiators to train her before the school took notice, but they probably didn't take her too seriously.'

Gia flexed her fist, opening and closing her hand to test the strength of her wrist. It twinged slightly, but it was much better than when she'd fought Caturix.

'This is her first real fight, so go easy on her,' said Cyrus. 'Don't finish her off in the first quarter-hour. Make sure it's an entertaining match. The Neptunalia crowd is always heavily intoxicated, so prepare yourself for some interjections.'

'As long as it's not piss, I can handle it.'

Cyrus patted her shoulder, then stepped back to admire her.

'That armour is really taking your image to the next level. Remind me to get some posters of you painted around town. The head of your fan club has done a great job, but I think we need something a little more dignified.'

'Oh, I don't know ...'

Gia pulled out Athena's drawing, which she kept on her person at all times as a good luck token, holding it up for Cyrus to smile at. 'I think it's pretty dignified.'

She looked down fondly at the caricature.

'I take it back,' he said. 'It's a perfect likeness. Your enemies far and wide will be shaking in their sandals.'

'They'd better be,' she said, tucking it away again.

'You're up first – so stretch, drink some water, say your prayers, whatever you have to do. They'll announce you soon.'

Cyrus talked to the others briefly and disappeared, off to do whatever he did before fights – taking last bets or sweet-talking sponsors – Gia wasn't sure. Cyrus inhabited all the spheres and circles of Rome without truly belonging to any of them.

In a quiet corner, Gia prayed to herself.

'Fortuna, please bring me to victory,' she whispered. 'I look to you, Fortuna, goddess of all that is and isn't, all that will and won't be, for favour on this day.'

When Gia looked up, Dom was watching her and listening in.

'Whatever works, right?' she said.

He gave a small smile at the side of his mouth before turning back to Lucas. Flavia was telling a story about a gladiator she'd seen killed by a bull, in a so-called 'battle of the beasts'.

'The horns gored him right in the balls,' she said. 'Then the bull trampled him. He looked like a vomit bowl by the end of it. Not even the gods of death would claim him.'

'Isn't it bad luck to talk about death before a fight?'

'I always make offerings to the deities of death before I do something dangerous,' said Flavia. 'They're the only ones that can save me. Jupiter won't do a damned thing for me unless it can get him laid with a mortal woman.'

Gia chuckled along with the others.

'You all know it too,' Flavia added. 'Don't pretend you don't.'

'When you're right, you're right,' said Dom.

'My family only prays to Jupiter and Juno on special occasions, when our relatives are staying over,' said Lucas.

'My mother only prays to the emperor,' said Dom.

'My parents used to pray to all the gods,' said Gia, 'just to be sure.'

A flurry of trumpets and drums signalled a shift in the atmosphere, creating an expectant stirring. Saluting the others, who wished her good luck, Gia headed towards the tunnel, ready to make her entrance in the arena.

'Please, everyone, take your seats. I insist.'

The noise of the crowd lulled, interspersed with boos, shouts and whistles.

Gia walked towards the light, breathing steadily and tensing her muscles, more centred than ever before.

'Now, for your viewing pleasure, we present the battle of the babes,' said the announcer, who wore fur-trimmed red robes. 'For many years, only men have battled in the arena—'

'Get on with it!' someone yelled.

'Not one but *two* female gladiators will fight for the right to call themselves the greatest,' said the announcer. 'But only one shall triumph this afternoon. Only one shall be blessed by Neptune.'

He nodded at Decimus, who wore the coral crown. Gia was certain he would not be blessing her, win or lose. He looked as sour and sinister as he always did.

'Our first challenger is not, as you may have heard, from Amazonia after all, but right here in Pompeii. You may also have heard legend of her battle against Caturix of Gaul, who died brutally by her sword.'

Gia still had not mastered the art of carrying both a shield and a sword, preferring to use just the gladius. She locked her hand around it now, ready to swing into action as soon as the match began.

'She is a student at the Pompeii gladiator school and her patron is none other than the princess of Rome, Claudia Caesaria herself!'

Shock hit Gia like a punch. Wasn't that was meant to be a secret?

A gasp rang out in stages, followed by a growing murmuring.

Gia's eyes flew to the imperial suite. Claudia looked startled, while Decimus's face was frozen somewhere between a sneer and a scowl.

Not even the boys at the ludus knew that. Who had told the announcer?

Gia felt smaller now, more vulnerable, at the mercy of not just the gods and the imperial siblings but the people. The crowd, however, responded positively, cheering the news that the emperor's daughter loved the games as much as they did.

Claudia forced a smile to her lips, waving gracefully.

It wasn't uncommon for members of the imperial family to have favourites, even personal gladiators they paid to remain at their side all day and night. It was only because Claudia was supporting *women's* sports that the announcement drew any attention at all. Gia noted many women in the audience cheering in favour, engaged in the games in a way they hadn't dared to be before.

'We love you, Princess Claudia!' called one.

'So, please, put your hands together for our reigning champion, Viatrix the Victorious!' bellowed the announcer.

The crowd roared, this time in delight.

Many of the people of Pompeii had changed their minds about women gladiators, it seemed. To know that the princess herself was a supporter was a white flag, signalling for others to join in. It was an entertainment, and the people loved nothing more than being entertained. They welcomed Gia as if she was their hero, though Gia knew if she displeased them, they'd turn on her just as quick.

'Her opponent today has travelled here from Herculaneum with a thirst for blood,' said the announcer. 'She heard that another woman was gaining renown in the arena. She gave up all the riches and privilege of her birth to get dirty in the ring. She believes herself to be the greatest woman fighter in the empire and she will tolerate no competition. She's here to prove herself superior and she won't quit until her opponent submits. So, please, put your hands together for . . . Dido the Destroyer!'

A Titan emerged from the tunnel on the other side.

Gia wasn't sure what she was expecting, but it was surely not the woman who appeared before her. This was no lady of leisure playing at gladiators. Dido had short hair like the goddess Diana and she was every bit as muscular as the strongest of male gladiators. Not only was she taller than Gia, she was broader and more intimidating in every way. Worse, she was carrying both a sword and a shield.

An easy win, Cyrus said.

Go easy on her, Cyrus said.

Dido looked Gia up and down, and laughed.

'*You* are the one they told me to be afraid of?' she said, in a voice that was higher and more delicate than her frame would suggest. 'I could break you in half.'

'Just wait until you see me fight,' said Gia.

'I've beaten boys five times your size back at the ludus. I have left them weeping and begging for their mothers.'

'I'm sure just your presence is enough to cause that,' said Gia.

Dido lowered her voice. 'You're a fraud. You didn't even kill the Gaul. He fell on your sword and you claimed victory.'

Gia tried not to show that she was rattled.

'You dishonour me,' she said, even though it was true.

The crowd was quiet, trying to listen in.

'Present yourselves to the emperor— uh, I mean, to the imperial children before we begin,' said the announcer, encouraging them to follow.

Dido and Gia stood before the box, looking up at Claudia and Decimus as they made their oaths.

'If I must watch these two donkeys beating on each other, they'd better be battling to the death,' said Decimus, standing up and raising one arm. 'Kill to win!'

His voice rang across the amphitheatre. The sudden change in plans rippled through the audience, some in favour, others in opposition.

'No, Decimus,' said Claudia, placing one hand on his arm. She was smiling, but her voice was firm. 'Gladiatorial games have rules, darling brother. You know that as well as I. It has all been arranged. You can't just change things now.'

She didn't even glance in Gia's direction, every bit the Roman princess she was supposed to be.

'Why not, dear sister? When I am emperor, I shall do what I like.'

When I am emperor.

'Well, you are not emperor yet, so sit back down and stop making a scene, lest Neptune be grievously displeased,' said Claudia.

The crowd hushed, a soft hissing of surprise, but they were not hostile to this show of power from Claudia. They were not yet loyal to Decimus.

He glowered at Claudia, his gaze slipping to the nearby trident, but he didn't act on the rage that caused his cheek to twitch. Slowly, he returned to his seat.

'Please, do not let my spoilsport brother interrupt your fun,' said Claudia. 'Let the fight begin.'

When Claudia applauded, so did the audience, as Dido and Gia returned to the centre of the arena.

As much as Gia had enjoyed witnessing it, Claudia was playing a dangerous game, humiliating Decimus in public like that. Yet for the first time, she understood it: Claudia was angling to be the people's princess, to win the allegiance of every woman in Rome. They could not vote or occupy the Senate, but they had a quiet, persuasive power of their own, just as Claudia had saved her life by whispering in her father's ear. It was a secret and underestimated strength – one they could use to their advantage.

The fight began the same way it always did, with drums and a handful of sand. Before she knew what was happening, Gia was in the thick of it, fending off an attack from an opponent with everything to prove. Dido was strong and solid, but also fast and flexible, keeping up with Gia's speed. Clashing metal rang out as they sparred, lunging back and forth in the rhythm of a dance, but almost all of her hits were defended by the shield.

'When I return to Herculaneum as a hero, I'll be sure to tell everyone what a disappointment you were,' said Dido. 'Look at you, dressed up in your fancy armour, princess's pet.'

'Jealous?'

'You know what people say about you?'

'Enlighten me,' said Gia. 'I love it when other people tell me about myself.'

'They say you're just a paid whore for the empire,' said Dido.

'Aren't you a nobleman's daughter?' scoffed Gia.

'I gave up everything to be free.'

'You speak as if you were enslaved.'

'And what did you sacrifice, to be here?' said Dido.

Gia didn't have a clear answer to that. She had lost her brothers and her father, but not in pursuit of freedom. She had not been arranged in marriage, though she was sure her mother would try, given half the chance. It wasn't her family who had held her down, but Roman society.

'You know, the princess was a fan of another gladiator last summer,' said Dido, 'buying him gifts, attending his matches . . . Some even say they were intimate.'

Gia faltered, Dido's sword crunching into the breastplate as she narrowly avoided serious injury.

'One day, he lost a big fight and she just dropped him,' continued Dido. 'Left him in the dirt. Every now and then, she gets bored and picks up a new toy to play with before she discards them. You'll be next.'

Hadn't Cyrus given her the same warning? It was hard to tell the truth from the rumours and lies.

Gia shook off her words.

'I don't support the emperor,' she said. 'The emperor took my brother to war and let him be ripped apart.'

'Then why are you accepting their gifts? Their patronage? Shame on you. You're a traitor, which is why . . . I . . . have . . . to win!'

Dido ran at Gia, swinging her sword so fast Gia could hardly keep up. The blade nicked the bare skin on Gia's arm.

'We don't have to be like the men, you know,' said Gia. 'We

don't have to tear each other down to build ourselves up. We don't need to play dirty or talk shit.'

'I know what game you're playing. When the men fight, they hold nothing back. They go for the throat. They step into the arena with the goal of winning by whatever means, and so should we.'

Dido suddenly pivoted, causing Gia to trip over to herself.

The balance of the fight was tipping in Dido's favour. Gia needed to strike out, before the scales weighed against her. She picked up pace, keeping Dido at arm's length as she forced her to run around in circles. She did it long enough that they began to follow a familiar pattern, a figure of eight in the dust. Gia waited until she knew Dido would move left, following the well-trodden pattern, then she darted right instead, swinging around to bring her sword to Dido's back with a clang. They began to spar again, faster this time, their movements more furious, until a rolling sound overhead caused them both to fall back.

The skies opened, releasing a cloud of pouring rain that swept down to the arena and soaked them both instantly.

The crowd exploded into joyous song and reverent chanting, praising the god of the waters.

'Neptune has blessed us!' cried the announcer. 'He recognizes our devotion and spares us from the drought!'

But her opponent had little time for the majesty of nature. Through a slick of rain, Dido struck again, hitting Gia's right arm.

'That's the one that's injured, right?' said Dido.

Gia hissed and cursed, biting down on her bottom lip.

'Does it hurt?'

'Not as much as this is going to,' she fumed, spinning on the spot so she could bring her sword to Dido's knees.

Her opponent lost balance and fell, with a clash of armour. Every action sprayed water, the soft percussion of rain syncing with the endless beat of drums.

Gia struck out at her again, again, again. Her sword was raised, held up over Dido's head, but her opponent kicked out at Gia's unprotected ankles, using her shield to jam into Gia's shins. Not even the knee pads she wore could protect her from the blunt edge of a heavy metal shield. As she collapsed, Dido retrieved her own sword and jutted it out, Gia barely stopping it with her own weapon.

Swords crossed like a gate, they both struggled to their feet. Metal sliding on metal, weapons dripping, they stood face to face, separated by a curtain of fine rain.

'Submit,' yelled Dido, over the noise of the downpour.

'I can't do that,' Gia cried back.

Possessed with renewed determination, Dido pulled away her sword and attempted to drive it at Gia. Gia met the strike with her own vigour, then jabbed Dido in the space between her shield and her sword. It struck the leather part of Dido's breastplate, causing her to cry out.

When Dido charged, Gia didn't move until she was right on top of her then she jammed out one foot, causing her opponent to stagger.

Just like with her brother Atticus, Gia felt the need to prove herself.

She struck again, lancing Dido's shoulder. Dodging her sword, Gia pushed her competitor back to the centre of the arena. Dido made one last run at her, abandoning her shield for speed, but Gia ducked low and Dido toppled over her.

Extricating herself, Gia kicked away Dido's dropped sword, crawled onto her opponent's back and held her weapon to her throat. Dido tried to throw her off, bucking like a mule, but when the blade cut into Dido's skin, she growled and threw up one arm in defeat.

'I submit,' she said.

A whistle sounded.

'Viatrix the Victorious is the winner!' called the announcer.

The crowd roared energetically, celebrating the victory of their home hero. Gia stood up to bow, spreading her arms to thank them for their applause. Claudia was on her feet, clapping above her head.

The sound of the crowd reverberated, an overwhelming din,

I'm Viatrix, she told herself, pumping one fist boldly. *I'm Viatrix.*

The crowd cheered harder.

Gia wasn't so much a person to them as a symbol of their own desire for victory. She represented Pompeii now, or women, or even the empire. The higher she climbed, the harder and further she'd fall.

Waving, she turned back to shake hands with Dido and was met by a face of hot, glaring hatred.

'Fuck you,' said Dido.

'That's not very sportsmanlike.'

'They told me I was certain to win.'

'They always do. That's their job. If they can't make you believe you have a chance, you won't have one.'

'How will I find a patron if the first fight on my scorecard is a loss?' said Dido, her face twisted in defeat.

Gia sighed, her shoulders relaxing in sympathy.

'My first fight almost ended in me getting my skull caved in,' she said. 'If not for the intervention of the princess, I'd already be in company with Pluto. My second fight was ... lucky. Caturix chose death rather than submit to a woman. If not for his own bigotry, he might still be alive.'

They exchanged a knowing look. Despite their differences, both knew the shortcomings of men.

'You put up a good fight. You almost had me there. You're already a gladiator. You'll have no trouble attracting a patron.'

Gia saw Cyrus and Julia moving through the crowd.

'In fact, I know someone you should talk to. Come with me.'

Though uncertain, Dido followed behind her.

'Well, if it isn't our winner,' said Julia, embracing her. 'And ... our loser,' she added, when she saw Dido.

'It was a close thing,' said Gia.

'That it was,' Julia agreed.

'Dido is looking for a patron.'

'I see.'

'And wouldn't you know it? Julia here is looking for a gladiator to sponsor.'

'Subtle,' said Dido, under her breath.

Gia left them to discuss business in the hope that they'd both found what they were searching for. She turned to face Cyrus, whose gleeful victory faded rapidly on seeing her stony expression.

'That announcer knew about Claudia?' Gia said, when he patted her on the back. 'You wouldn't happen to know anything about that, would you?'

He flashed her a guilty look.

'It was you?' said Gia.

'Look, people were going to find out soon enough and, like you said, it's the kind of promotion one cannot keep quiet about. Your profile in Pompeii just ascended to the next level, which puts you in a great position, not just as a gladiatorial competitor but as a person of importance, with access to the imperial family.'

'You should've told me what you were planning.'

'You might've talked me out of it.'

'This puts us in danger,' she protested. 'We'll have a target on our backs now – from the people, from Decimus, and definitely from the emperor when he catches wind of it. I didn't think you'd want to draw so much attention, with what you have in mind.'

She gave him a sharp look, referring wordlessly to his dreams of revolution.

'You'll have to trust that I know what I'm doing,' he said. 'The benefits and opportunities far outweigh the risks. Speaking of what I have in mind, you told me you'd bring me some information.'

Gia faltered. Truthfully, she did have information – about Claudia's fears that Decimus was a poisoner. But she was reluctant to betray Claudia's trust by disclosing something so dangerously personal. If the princess had confided in her alone, she would know who to blame if word got out.

'Be patient. I'm working on it.'

'We cannot wait too long. Dissent grows in the Senate. If there is ever a good time, it may come sooner than we think.'

With that enigmatic statement, he moved away.

'So, the princess, huh?' said Dominic, appearing at her side. 'You kept that quiet. Lucas was so excited he had to go take a shit.'

'Classic Lucas.'

'He thinks we'll get to meet her now. He really thinks he has a shot there.'

'I promise you, he does not.'

Gia was more than ready to go home and get changed, to wash off the blood and try to repair her armour, when a dull horn sounded, long and low, bringing the amphitheatre to silence.

The praetorian guard swept in, swarming into the arena in formation. Some stood at the centre, staring out at the crowd with their visored faces, while others approached the imperial box.

They handed Decimus a scroll, which he delicately unfurled.

A tiny smile flickered at the corner of his mouth before he dabbed at his eyes, weeping without tears.

'It's father,' he said, in a voice that demanded attention. 'He has taken ill. We must return to the villa at once.'

The news spread through the crowd, morphing as it did.

'The emperor is sick.'

'The emperor is deathly ill.'

'The emperor is on his death bed.'

Decimus handed the scroll to Claudia and followed two of the guards out of the amphitheatre. She read it over quickly, her hands trembling so much it shook the paper up and down.

Gia looked up at her from the dirt of the amphitheatre. In Claudia's pale face, Gia saw fear, but also something else, something she couldn't quite discern. The expression passed before Gia could process it.

As the princess turned to go, she looked down and caught Gia's eye.

Gia placed one hand over her chest, holding her gaze. She hoped the gesture conveyed her loyalty ... her devotion, even.

Yet Claudia simply nodded, a blank expression on her face, before she drifted away, out of sight.

When Gia turned back to the amphitheatre, Julia was watching her.

13. ENTER THE LABYRINTH

According to the rumour-mongers at the taberna, who sat at the counter and drank too much wine, the emperor was too ill to return to Rome. He continued to rule from his bed at the House of Menander, though he hadn't been sighted for weeks. The villa was guarded constantly. Loyal subjects and cult members filed up to leave offerings at the gate, chanting and praying as if he was already a god.

Officially, spiritually, death in Pompeii was not something to be feared but a continuation of mortal life, particularly for an emperor who was likely to be deified. When the time came, they would make a mask of his face after his last breath and cast him in stone, to attend all further ceremonies until the fall of the empire as a bust, just like all the other emperors. His advisors would tell the people that the emperor dined with Jupiter and danced with Venus, that he would continue to watch over the empire from the realm of the gods, putting fear in the heart of the next man.

But everyone knew that death was actually wretched, even emperors, who went out withered and shitting themselves. Everyone feared the unknown that waited beyond the end, especially those, like Gia, who had seen their loved ones cruelly snatched away in an instant.

Life went on. The Senate and the courts were responsible for the day to day running of society. But Decimus had already assumed his father's ceremonial role, wearing his golden crown of laurel and ivy leaves, waving from the balcony of the villa. He was seen around Pompeii in the company of brothel girls, getting pig drunk and demanding that the tabernas serve him for free.

He was just as terrible as Claudia had described him to be.

Gia hadn't seen her since Neptunalia. Donations continued to arrive at the ludus and her guards continued to visit the taberna. But there was no word from the princess herself. Gia began to worry. She even went to the villa, but was told that Claudia was not receiving visitors.

Claudia was alive, it seemed; she just couldn't – or wouldn't – contact Gia.

She thought again of Cyrus's words. *'You are a passing fascination for her, I guarantee it.'* Dido, too, had warned her of this.

Had she been discarded so quickly?

No. A real warrior would be patient. There must be a reason Claudia was hiding away. When Claudia was ready, Gia would be too.

Julia, on the other hand, was making her presence deeply felt, sending gifts for Gia to the ludus in hopes of luring her away. Knee guards. Spices. New sandals. A musky perfume that appeared to have been made for a man. Gia piled them with all the other gifts she'd received from fans and potential patrons.

Soon the month of Augustus came, bringing festival season with it. Public sacrifices were made daily on Decimus's orders, along with what was deemed 'the punishment of the dogs'. Decimus had decided that there were too many strays in Pompeii, charging his guards to round up every canine he could find and putting them down. This made Decimus deeply unpopular with everyone, from senators to slaves. The people did not stand for such mindless cruelty.

On the thirteenth day, Pompeiians usually celebrated the Nemoralia of Diana, but Decimus deemed it unnecessary. Signs were put out to state that it was cancelled at short notice, for Decimus had deemed it 'disrespectful and disruptive'. Even private celebrations were expressly forbidden.

Nemoralia was mainly a women's festival, which was perhaps why Decimus was so opposed to it. The hunting or killing of any beast was forbidden on Nemoralia and, according to those same taberna rumour-mongers, Decimus wanted to go on a boar hunt that weekend, which was why he'd cancelled the festival. He had robbed a goddess of her sacred day, just so he could kill beasts for bloodsport.

But the women of Pompeii were not to be dissuaded so easily, particularly when word spread that the princess would personally defend anyone who celebrated the festival of Diana. Secret meetings were arranged, to be held out of the sight of male eyes, attendants passing messages through servants as they waited in line, or through the children who ran from house to house.

Just after midday, Gia received a message at the taberna, left on the doorstep and tied with string.

The scroll was unsigned, wax-sealed and richly decorated with illustrations of the goddess herself.

You are invited to an elite and most of all discreet celebration to honour the sacred mysteries of Diana at the House of the Labyrinth this evening.

Gia's heart sang and screamed. Claudia. It had to be.

Finally, Gia would see her again. She clutched the invite to her chest and closed her eyes.

The invitation demanded a mask as part of the dress code. She didn't have a mask, but she managed to track one down by asking her mother, who asked the woman next door, who asked Lady Lando. She said the brothel girls wore them sometimes with clients who got off on a little humiliation. None of them asked any questions.

It was a brown leather eye mask, the kind that exposed the bottom half of her face. Gia teamed it with her one good set of robes, which she'd acquired for her cousin's wedding a few years past. A cream tunic with an embroidered trim and a matching stola, it set off her dark hair and tan skin. She was barely recognizable as Viatrix like this. She looked not even like herself, but someone completely different.

'Gia!' said her mother, startling when they crossed paths in the portico. 'I thought you were a cult member.'

'All hail the emperor,' Gia said, in monotone.

'At least you're not dressed to fight,' she said.

'Not on Nemoralia; I'm taking a day off from being a mindless brute.'

'You look nice. Where are you going?'

'I may or may not have been invited to a secret mystery party, hosted by a woman of society,' she said, in the loftiest voice she could put on, 'but I issue no comment on whether I'll be attending or not.'

'Be careful, won't you?' said her mother.

'A woman can only be so careful.'

'You don't know what that monster Decimus will do when he finds out people have defied his orders. Look what he did to those poor dogs.'

Everyone feared Decimus, even her mother, who rarely made mention of the incumbent emperor. But very little felt frightening compared to standing in the arena fighting Caturix or Dido. Nothing scared her more than the hot, racing thoughts that filled her head with concern for Claudia.

'What will you do tonight?' Gia asked.

'A group of us will gather together here, in the cellar, and make our rituals. Maybe also drink a bit. Not too much, of course.'

'A group of who?'

'Just ... Lady Lando, and some of the girls,' she admitted reluctantly.

Though her mother had strictly forbidden her from joining the Den, she had no such objections to being friends with them.

She was, like most people, a contradiction.

'Then you'd better be careful too. Have a good night.'

Her mother kissed her. 'Love you.'

'And you.'

Gia was quietly concerned about the state her mother might get in under the influence of bad company, or whether this would push her to relapse, but she knew she couldn't control her, just as her mother couldn't stop Gia from fighting. They were both responsible for their own decisions, their own direction on the path of life.

Ever since she became a gladiator, Gia had assumed she'd die in the dust of the ring, at the hands of a challenger. If she died otherwise, so be it. She would be careful, as she'd promised, but nothing would keep her from the secret mystery party.

Nothing would keep her from Claudia.

The House of the Labyrinth was so named due to a mosaic that showed the Greek hero Theseus grappling with the Minotaur as Ariadne watched on.

Gia was greeted at the door by a robed figure holding a sword, handing over her invitation and cloak. When they nodded her in, she stepped through thick clouds of incense smoke that made her cough and choke.

Inside, there were women reciting poetry, women playing instruments, women dancing and chanting and laughing. Gia inched her way into the atrium, where a priestess in black robes drew symbols in the air with her fingers. Gia nervously accepted the silver goblet passed to her by a half-naked servant wearing a tiger mask, moving between the groups of people conversing, unsure how to participate. She took a sip, but it tasted as foul as Tartarus.

She made a noise of disgust, then took another swig.

'Gia, so glad you could join us,' said Julia, swishing over to her in a green silk robe and elaborate peacock feather headdress.

So it wasn't Claudia who'd invited her, but Julia. Gia's face must've reflected her disappointment, for Julia frowned.

'Why so gloomy? Didn't you hear? We're having a party.'

'These people look rich and learned. I have nothing to say that will impress them.'

'Nonsense. They should be so lucky to be acquainted with you.'

'I don't know about that.'

'Then you're lucky you have me,' said Julia. 'I can be your guide. You're going to have a marvellous time. I have so many interesting people I want you to meet. Drink up, it will give you courage.'

'What is it?' Gia said. 'It's foul.'

'Libation.'

'For a ritual?'

'Of sorts. Go on, drink up.'

Gia braced herself and downed the whole thing, which seemed to please Julia greatly. 'That's the spirit.' She put her arm around Gia, steering her through the smoke towards the nearest group and introducing her. 'Can I be ever so rude and interrupt you for a moment? I'd love for you to meet Viatrix the Victorious.'

'Viatrix! Oh, we've already heard of you, of course. Yours is the name on everyone's lips lately,' said one woman.

'It's you I have to thank for the fact that my young daughter now wants to be a gladiator when she grows up,' said another.

'Perhaps I should like to fight a man with my bare hands too.'

They all began talking at once, as Gia struggled to keep up.

'How often do you train?'

'Did you really kill the Gaul?'

'When is your next fight?'

The same questions, over and over. Julia repeated this routine three more times until Gia had greeted every artist, every senator's wife, every courtesan, acrobat, poet and mystic in the room, including Flavia, from the ludus.

'Guess who I bumped into the other day?' she said. 'Berenice!'

'You did?' said Gia, relieved. 'That's good news. How is she?'

'She seems well enough. She said her Roman man came back to town so she's reconciled with him.'

'Hmm,' said Gia, her concern not yet fully satiated.

'She's been staying at some villa on the outskirts of town with a group of Den girls, says he comes to call for her every now and then. Sounds like he's creating some kind of harem.'

'Do you know anything about him, this Roman man?'

'Only that he cries after sex.'

'I'm glad she's alive, at least,' said Gia.

'Happy Nemoralia, anyway,' said Flavia. 'Oh, wait.' She reached into her robes, pulling out a spring of herbs tied with string, like the necklace she wore. 'You should take this. Don't ask me why.'

'Why?' said Gia instinctively.

'I'm a big believer in dreams. Last night, you were in mine. I got the feeling I'm supposed to give you something, as a token, to protect you. It doesn't make sense, but the mysteries of the gods rarely do.'

'Oh . . . Thanks, Flavia.' Gia lowered it over her head, letting the herbs hang in the middle of her chest.

Julia forcibly moved her on, introducing her to another group of women in colourful robes, their masks brightly painted and studded with jewels.

'The princess's gladiator herself, in the flesh,' said one.

'Yes, I'm trying to convince Viatrix here to let me be her patron instead, but so far, she is loyal,' said Julia.

'What happened with Dido the Destroyer?' asked Gia.

Julia gave her a blank look.

'Who?' she said.

'The gladiator I introduced to you, from Herculaneum.'

'Oh, it . . . it didn't work out.'

'Why not?'

'She simply wasn't what I was looking for.' Her eyes lingered on Gia. 'It seems I might just have to be patient, if I'm to get what I desire.'

Gia swallowed, afraid to ask.

Julia leaned in, as if to kiss her or tell her a secret – Gia wasn't sure which. 'I could teach you some things, you know.'

'Such as?'

At this precise moment, like a portent of the great mockery of fate, a figure appeared in the doorway behind Gia, casting a shadow.

'Princess!' said Julia, falling back and paling. 'I'm so glad you were able to come, after all.'

'How kind of you to extend your hand,' said Claudia icily.

Gia turned to see the princess, accompanied by several handmaidens and wearing a gold mask to match her white-and-gold robes. Her long golden hair was braided and decorated with flowers and she smelled as heavenly as usual.

A server drifted past and Julia lunged for him.

'Here,' she said, passing it to Claudia. 'Drink this. We will get underway in just half an hour. I'll, uh ... leave you two to catch up.'

She shot Gia a significant look and slunk away.

Left alone together but for the handmaidens, Gia found that Claudia was reluctant to look at her.

'You look ...' blurted Gia, though she was afraid to finish.

'What?'

'Divine,' said Gia, though she really meant 'furious'.

'And you, you also look ... different,' said Claudia, her cheeks colouring. 'I have never seen you like this.'

'Bad different?'

'Just *different* different.'

Gia swigged awkwardly at her drink.

'So, how do you know Julia?' Claudia said, seemingly fascinated by a series of carved occult figurines.

'Through Cyrus, at the ludus. What about you?'

'She's a senator's wife,' said Claudia. 'We have often been at the same banquets. I didn't know you were so well acquainted. She was sure to brag about how close the two of you are, in her invite to me.'

'We're not,' she said.

'You *looked* quite close, just then.'

'She was trying to lure me away from you by offering her patronage,' she said. 'I told her I'm not interested.'

'I see.'

Claudia sipped her drink, pulling a face.

'Tastes like piss, doesn't it?' said Gia. 'But I'm starting to get a bit of a buzz.'

'I could do with losing my head for a while,' Claudia said. 'This past week has felt like an annum.'

'How are you? Tell me honestly. How's your father?'

'Not tonight,' said Claudia, shaking her head. 'I wish to talk about anything other than my mounting problems.'

Gia burned all over, restless in her own skin.

'You didn't return any of my messages,' she said.

'It isn't safe. My communications are no longer private.'

'I've been worried.'

'You have?' said Claudia.

'If you have found another warrior to serve you better, all you need do is say,' said Gia. 'I will not betray your trust, no matter what.'

Claudia took a long swig of her drink, then a deep breath.

'The problem is ... that you are also becoming a problem,' she said, staring at a point over Gia's shoulder. 'A problem for me.'

Gia frowned.

'In what way?'

'The fact that you don't know is the problem,' said Claudia.

She held Gia's gaze. There was a fierceness to her expression, a hard resolve in her sea-glass eyes.

Before Gia could enquire further, a gong sounded.

'Everyone, please follow me – it is time to begin,' called Julia.

They all funnelled into a well-decorated reception room, its ochre walls painted with scenes of maenads and satyrs.

The longer Gia looked at them, the stranger she felt, as if they were coming out of the wall and staring at her, specifically.

'Welcome, neophytes, to the Mysteries of Diana,' said the priestess in black. 'On this fine Nemoralia, we shall descend into the labyrinth in search of illumination. We shall look to the past, to the future and to the world beyond time, as we seek to be reborn and renewed in the eyes of the divine.'

The half-naked servers gathered up the empty goblets. Gia's had some kind of sediment at the bottom.

The goblets. Fuck. There was something in the drink, something that made all the lights of the candles bleed into the shadows, something that made the room sway, something that filled Gia's body with pulsating waves. She turned to Claudia to warn her just in time to see her drain the glass.

Too late.

'You are about to enter a realm of visions, journeys, monsters and gods – a world in which trees may talk and animals may change their shapes,' said the priestess. 'You may encounter the shades of the dead or spirits who will guide you. You may see things you cannot describe, or feel things you have never felt before. You may be euphoric or terrified, but your journey into the darkness is your own. You are in control and you alone can decide your fate.

Remember, you must never speak about what you are about to witness, so seal your lips before you descend.'

As the priestess spoke, her voice seemed to grow louder, deeper, echoing. It sounded primordial. It was reverberating through Gia's body, until the voice seemed to come from inside her.

'The goddess Diana is not just the patron of wilderness, of wildlife, of hunters and gatherers, but also of the night and the moon. She is the light-bearer, the wanderer, the warrior and the maiden. Blessed Diana, please light our way through the wilderness of the soul.'

One by one, the attendees were given torches, descending the stony staircase in the corner into the cellar beneath the villa. Yet it was no ordinary cellar, painted in bright reds and golds with carved mystical symbols. It had many paths branching off from the main room, like a series of caves. It smelled ancient; freezing cold, even with thirty people in there.

'Choose your paths wisely and choose for yourself. You must complete this journey alone, just as we are born alone,' said the priestess.

Several women disappeared at once into the darkness of open doorways, as if it were a race. Panic stabbed at Gia's chest.

'Good luck on your voyage,' said the priestess. 'There will be trials and tribulations on your way, fears and temptations you must face, but the goddess is waiting for you at the heart of the maze. Don't keep her waiting, ladies. Now, it is time to enter the labyrinth.'

An indistinct sense of dread began to grow inside her, though Gia couldn't put her finger on why.

The priestess joined Julia and some of the most colourfully

dressed women in a monotonous chant, all holding hands while servants circled them, wafting incense and banging skin drums.

The thought suddenly crystallized: Claudia.

Gia whipped around to look for her but she'd already vanished, taking one of the many paths solo as instructed.

'Claudia?' she called out, but no answer came.

'Shhh,' said Julia, lifting a finger to her lips. 'We journey in silence.'

Left without answers and with no way of knowing which path she'd chosen, Gia picked the one straight ahead, walking through the narrow tunnel until she was alone in the dark, her sandals slapping on the stone below.

Gia walked for so long that it felt as if a year had passed. She walked for so long she never thought she'd see light again.

At times, she felt unusually calm and detached, as if she was merely dreaming. At other times, she was seized by the claustrophobic panic of being lost in a cave in the darkness below ground.

Sometimes she heard someone running on the other side of the wall or crying out for help in the distance, calling out to them with no response, but for the most part, the labyrinth was silent and suffocating, blocking out all the rest of the world. It swallowed her whole. She was a small rodent being digested by a snake, sliding down through the belly of the beast.

Gia was carried forwards by a force beyond herself. She could feel herself unravelling and the world deconstructing until nothing solid or physical remained, leaving only the ideas and impressions of things.

A faint scene bloomed in the distance, growing larger and

brighter. She drifted towards it. Gia found herself standing in an atrium, painted white and surreally open to the skies, full of exotic trees and plants. There was a small shrine here to the goddess Diana, sculpted in clay. Based on the scattered ashes around the shrine, Gia sensed that she was supposed to make an offering. How foolish of her not to bring anything.

She was about to leave the room with dishonour when she remembered the sprig of herbs that Flavia had given her. Perhaps the dream was a sign, and the offering a good omen. She removed it from around her neck and burned it over a waxy candle.

'Diana, goddess of the hunt and the moon,' she whispered, 'please lead me to the truth. Let me know my purpose in the world. Please protect me from the dangers that await and . . .' She hesitated. 'Please protect Claudia Imperia Caesaria.'

The herbs emitted a scent both harsh and heavenly, its grey smoke seeming to form a serpent that wound around her before dissipating. All of the candles in the room flickered wildly as a shaking, skittering noise filled her ears, like something enormous moving beneath the ground below her feet.

Gia now had to choose between the left path and the right. She tried to listen to her intuition, but her thoughts were clumsy and scrambled, random words and concepts connecting together in ways that made no sense.

She picked the left, for no other reason than it was wider than the right, but soon regretted it when she passed a series of grimacing stone heads, their faces twisted by unknown torments. Her torch illuminated many more statues lining the wall, a mixed-up zoo of creatures both real and mythical, all of them watching as she passed, looking as if they might come to life at any moment.

Her head was swimming now, every part of her alert and on fire. The sound of her own breathing was heavy in her ears. She felt herself falling, tumbling and stumbling, tossed from one room to another, and in each, she found a strange treasure.

A painted tree, its branches climbing up to the stars, its roots stretching down into the underworld. An Egyptian sphinx. A cave, with an elder man crawling out of it. Phases of the moon.

'Gia!'

Claudia's voice echoed, from somewhere far away.

Gia tried to follow her, but the sound bounced around, changing directions. Eventually, the fearful cry morphed, turning into a wicked, monstrous noise, like mocking laughter, before fading out.

Strange groaning noises moved through the walls as Gia staggered forwards, choosing between two more branching paths.

Suddenly, there she was. Claudia, standing still at the end of a tunnel, illuminated by a shaft of light from the surface.

'Claudia,' she gasped.

Claudia fled, disappearing into the enveloping dark again.

'Claudia, wait!'

Gia followed, trying to keep up, listening for the sound of Claudia's footsteps as they echoed through the tunnels. As she closed in on her, her fingers grasped at the folds of Claudia's billowing robes but they passed right through.

When she rounded the corner, Gia was alone once more.

She realized she was hallucinating and that she no longer knew what was real or not. Her body seemed to float unnaturally near the stony ceiling, looking down on herself, so small and scared and lost.

Stay calm, Gia, she told herself. *Get a grip. Don't give in to fear. You're in control. This is all just in your head.*

Time stretched and shrank and became incalculable, flowing around her like water. People appeared at her side and disappeared again, speaking without sound. Julia. Cyrus. Her mother. Her father. Berenice. Felix. Cassius. All ignited into existence and extinguished again by the power of her ragged breaths.

Gia was dizzy, disorientated.

Every now and then she had a moment of sobering lucidity, finding herself slumped against a stone wall or standing in an empty cavern, but the slippery visions kept drawing her back into their madness.

A Minotaur charged past, chasing another initiate.

In a small hollow, a woman nursed a baby with cloven feet.

A winged creature with a human face perched on a beam.

With a sudden sizzle, her torch was extinguished by dripping water leaking from a pipe. Panting, Gia waited for her eyes to adjust to the darkness, scrambling along the wall through the pitch black until she saw a distant speck of light. She moved towards it, shaky on her feet.

The light grew large and bright, forcing her to shield her eyes. She followed it to a shining temple of marble and gold, where a giant statue of Diana waited, captured in the act of the hunt.

She'd made it to the heart of the labyrinth.

Exhausted, Gia collapsed at the stone goddess's feet, gazing up at her.

Forever frozen in time, with one hand the goddess reached for an arrow from the quiver she carried on her back, and with the other she held a bow.

Gia reached out to touch the cold earth herself, trying to calm down.

The skin on her fingertips vibrated.

The grinding sound of stone on stone.

The statue came to life at her touch, turning its head. A light seemed to shine from within, while streaks in the marble resembled golden veins.

The sculpted deer at Diana's side came to life too – trotting over and sniffing at Gia's hand curiously.

Gia petted its smooth marble head as it bowed before her.

'I have been waiting for you,' said the statue of Diana, in a voice that seemed to emanate throughout time.

14. THE GAMES WE PLAYED IN THE HEAVENS

Gia stared, shaking and speechless, unsure if she was still hallucinating or not. What else could possibly explain this? Whatever was in that goblet – the damned libation – had turned her mind inside-out and upside-down. She had imagined herself standing before the gods occasionally, picturing them as they might show themselves to a mortal like her, but it had never been like this.

Staggering backwards, she watched as the statue shattered into tiny pieces, revealing the human form of the goddess beneath. Her chiton was made of some unearthly fabric, glittering unnaturally, while her eyes glowed white and hot like stars, without pupils, burning into Gia's.

For the rest of her life, Gia would look twice at all statues.

'Gia Valerii,' said Diana, in a slow, drawn-out way.

'You know my name?'

'I know the names of all of my followers, but yours is more important than most. Yours may yet be written in history until the end of time. We foresaw a warrior who would serve the princess of Rome. We foresaw a man, but even deities make mistakes.' Diana gave a wry smile, all too human. 'It is better that you are not. I am confident that a woman will do a better job.'

'A better job ... of what?' asked Gia, her voice trembling.

Diana appeared to regard her with interest.

'You have reached the crossroads of destiny, Gia,' she said. 'Now you must make an important decision.'

Diana stepped off the podium and began walking towards her. Gia shrank back in awe and in fear, watching as Diana retrieved her arrow and fired her bow, striking a nearby pillar.

A shimmering vision appeared there, like a painting. It was a landscape, a scene of the Bay of Naples.

The sky was as red as rage, the sea like spilled blood.

The ground trembled beneath Gia's feet, as it did during the fight with the Gaul. Her eyes blurred. She saw the ocean drawing back like a blanket. In the vision, Mount Vesuvius erupted. The mountain blew its top with an energetic boom, bursting into a plume of black smoke that blocked out the light of day, rivers of liquid fire running down its sides like waves.

'Humanity stands on the precipice of a great disaster,' said the goddess. 'At first, the signs were unclear. We knew only that civilization was doomed to a dark age of ruin. We saw only an eruption of fire and smoke. But now, we have seen the truth. One disaster shall befall another. The death of the emperor will lead the pantheon to war.'

Gia stared at her in slow, drugged, bewildered horror.

A war on earth was frightening enough, but a war in the heavens could be the end of all things.

'When Tiberius is murdered, as us goddesses have predicted, Vulcan's forge will be ignited in fury. Pompeii will burn in vengeance. Buried beneath a sea of fire, it shall be lost for thousands of years, becoming a tomb. Every person left in the city shall be buried along with it.'

Gia shook her head vigorously, not wanting to believe it. But what reason had a goddess to lie?

Diana shot another arrow, this time at a different pillar. An image appeared: fire spreading through the streets of Rome as amphitheatres crumbled, as the great temples were ransacked and soldiers executed citizens at mass. Decimus watched from the balcony of his villa, serenaded by a fiddle player.

Many more scenes bloomed in the window Diana had created, rising and setting like suns. Gia saw the emperor spitting up foam, Decimus carrying a severed head, Cyrus toppling to the ground in the arena. She saw Claudia crying tears of blood, standing alone in the imperial box, wearing her father's crown. She saw Pompeii burning. Rome falling.

The visions faded out again, leaving Gia to simmer in fury and in fear.

'I don't understand,' she said. 'How can it be?'

'The eruption of Vesuvius will catalyze a series of events that will lead to the fall of the empire ... and at the helm of it, will be the dark king: Emperor Decimus Tiberius Caesaria,' said Diana. 'The devastation of Pompeii will cast ripples throughout the empire, weakening the bond between an emperor and his people. Under Decimus's control, that divide shall grow deeper. The entire empire shall crumble. Rome shall be dust, never to rise again.'

'There are many who pray for such a thing,' said Gia, thinking of Cyrus. 'The empire has spilled much blood.'

'The empire is flawed, as is every empire that ever existed and perhaps ever will, but its loss will topple many other civilizations. Much knowledge and skill will be lost for ever. Much history will be unwritten, many mythologies corrupted. There will be unrest and revolt, usurpers vying for control, a breakdown of law and order . . . Chaos, of the most dangerous kind. Humans will suffer, far more than they suffer now.'

'What does this have to do with me?' Gia asked, trembling uncontrollably. 'What can I do to change destiny, that a goddess cannot?'

'Every deity sponsors mortals of importance whose life to influence, much like gladiators have patrons,' said the goddess. 'They represent our will on earth. It is a game of the gods, to shape human empires. But no destiny is set in stone. Even the smallest diversion from a plan can disrupt the work of fate. Mortals are difficult to control, and even more difficult to predict. The future is becoming less certain. We are losing our hold over the civilization we created once again.'

Gia still didn't understand. Diana sensed it, elaborating:

'Vulcan is the patron of Emperor Tiberius. He has guided him since he was a boy. Jupiter is the patron of Decimus, his heir. When Tiberius became emperor, Vulcan gained power. But Jupiter is the king of the gods, and he cannot stand to share his throne. He resists the spirit of democracy and he will do whatever it takes to put Decimus in power. Combined, they shall destroy the world.'

It was too much to hold in her mind all at once.

'If Decimus does not become emperor,' said Gia, 'if he were to, say, die violently at the hands of a female gladiator, can Pompeii still be saved?'

'Pompeii's destruction is as inevitable as the emperor's death, but in the void left behind by the disaster, a much greater danger will blossom. Decimus's ascension to power can and must be prevented, no matter what the cost.'

Yet Gia refused to accept it. Not Pompeii, her beloved home, her graveyard, her temple, her life's great love. Not where her father and brother were laid to rest. Not where so many innocent souls dwelled. She would not allow it.

'What about Fortuna?' asked Gia. 'Can she not be persuaded to tip the scales of fate and save Pompeii?'

'Even she is bound by rules. Laws of nature, of order, of tradition and authority. She is the one who has led our rebellion.'

'There must be something you can do.'

'Not I, you,' said Diana.

Gia laughed, reflexively, thinking it a joke. But the goddess's face was severe and serious.

'Me? Why me?' she said.

'It was not I who chose you, but the princess herself. That is how we know you are the one.'

'You have spoken to Claudia?' Gia asked, recalling what she'd said about communing with the goddesses.

Diana nodded solemnly. 'Minerva is her patron. She has been entrusted with an important mission, just like you.'

Gia had doubted the princess, but the truth shone clearly now. Claudia was right. She was telling the truth, about everything.

They were in this together, irrevocably so.

'Us goddesses have conceived of another future, one in which Claudia Caesaria becomes empress. The alliance between gods and mortals could be strong again, women working in union, both above and below. Should this future come to pass, Rome will not fall in a year, or in a hundred years. It will endure. Eventually, a new world will be born, a better one, with women at the helm.'

Diana turned, walking back towards her podium, as the stone deer followed.

'For now, the gods have little interest in you or the princess of Rome,' she said. 'They are certain that men will be the main players in the new era, yet again. But they will soon learn of our visions and that we stand against them. They will learn that we are backing Claudia, against the will of Jupiter.'

She gradually resumed the position her statue took, slowly reaching back to grab her eternal arrow.

'The princess's life is in danger. You must protect her long enough that she can rule. Claudia must become empress for Rome to survive this century and only you, the warrior she chose, can do that.'

Gia was weak, winded.

'Where? When will she be in danger?' she said.

'That I cannot see. Only you will know, when the time comes.'

Diana was stiffening, calcifying, only her eyes moving now as she said: 'I am *your* patron, Gia Valerii. Do not let me down.'

Her skin was hardening, becoming marbleized. Every hair and muscle of her body turned to stone, until she became a statue once more.

The light that had shone so brightly, dimmed. Gia was returned to a cavernous room with torches fixed to the wall. She was kneeling before a small replica of Diana with an altar behind it, barely taller than herself and certainly not capable of talking or moving.

Gia swore, once and again.

It had felt like so much more than a dream. She was not capable of imagining such complex things. It was more like glimpsing beyond the veil of reality. Many men talked of visions they'd had after drinking this or smoking that, but they were random, nonsensical, occasionally profoundly symbolic, but never as detailed and coherent as what she'd just witnessed.

Claudia said she'd also spoken to the goddesses in dreams. They had that in common now. It wasn't that Gia hadn't believed her before, but only by experiencing it herself did she truly feel the power of it. The realness of it. The undeniable magnitude of such a thing. The goddess herself was instructing Gia to protect Claudia.

She couldn't deny her feelings a moment longer. It wasn't foolishness. It wasn't lunacy. It was destiny.

It took Gia an extraordinarily long time to make her way back through the maze, meeting many dead-ends and taking just as many wrong turns, but at least she felt better rooted in reality now, her hallucinations withering away to mere phantom sounds and inexplicable sensations. With every step, she became more eager to set eyes on Claudia, so she could tell her what the goddess had said.

After what felt like a lifetime, she found herself back in the red-and-gold cellar room where other girls were recovering from their journeys, glugging at water and wrapped in shrouds. Several applauded her return.

Looking around, Gia drank from the bowl that was handed to her, after being assured that it was only water. But Claudia was nowhere to be found.

'Good to see you again, friend,' said Flavia.

'Flavia! You really saved my neck back there,' said Gia.

When Flavia looked confused, Gia mimed the necklace she'd given her.

'Ah, I had a feeling you'd need it.'

'This isn't your first mystery party, is it?'

'My mother was a priestess. I'm something of a veteran.'

'How was your journey?' Gia asked.

'I have been on many journeys,' she said, 'but this was not one of my favourites. I saw myself buried in the earth as a statue, posed in action, as if something had petrified me on the spot.'

Gia thought of the volcanic eruption she'd seen and Diana's prophecy of Pompeii entombed.

'Gia!' said Julia, appearing as if from a cloud of smoke. 'You made it. How was your descent?'

'Illuminating,' she said vaguely.

'I hope you got the answers you were looking for.'

'Only more questions, I fear.'

Her meeting with the goddess already felt floaty and far away, like a dream she was struggling to remember.

'Such is the way. The first time is always a gamble, a leap into the dark,' she said. 'I remember mine well. I communed with the spirits of nature themselves—'

'Have you seen Claudia?' asked Gia.

Julia seemed annoyed that this was her most pressing thought.

'Not yet. I'm sure she'll return to us soon. Some journeys are short and others are long. Perhaps the princess is grappling with herself in a dark place, consumed by the vastness of her own undoing.'

Julia said this brightly, as if she hoped as much.

One by one, Gia watched the party attendees make their way out of the maze, some of them cheering and laughing, others sullen and haunted. She waited until only Claudia was left, before she began to panic. The imperial handmaids also seemed rattled, whispering to each other furtively.

'Did the princess go in alone?' Gia asked them.

One girl nodded. 'She instructed us to stay behind.'

'I told you we should not have abandoned her,' said another.

'How were we supposed to refuse?'

'Has Claudia still not emerged?' said Julia, eavesdropping. 'I do hope she's not having a terrible, *terrible* time.'

Gia started to get a bad feeling, deep in the pit of her gut. Julia and Cyrus were no fans of the empire. Was she capable of harming Claudia? Was she part of some sinister conspiracy?

Gia stood up abruptly.

'I'll go back in and look for her,' she said.

'You needn't do that,' said Julia.

'I'm doing it anyway. There is no argument.'

Julia stared at her a moment, then sighed. 'Then here, take this.' She reached into her pocket and handed her a ball of twine. 'To find your way back.'

'At least this time I shall be sober,' said Gia, tucking it into her robes. 'You might've warned us that the drink had herbs in it.'

'What else do you think happens at a secret mystery party?'

Though the thought of returning to the labyrinth filled Gia with trepidation, the memory of Diana's warning and the vision of Vesuvius shone so brightly in her mind she didn't dare to ignore it. Claudia could not be empress if she was dead in a labyrinth. Gia had to protect her.

That was her job, her destiny.

Tying the string to a nail near the door, Gia entered the maze, trying her best to remember the path she'd taken before. She hadn't planned on coming back so she hadn't memorized the route, though some of the weird statues and paintings she passed looked vaguely familiar.

For a time, Gia thought she was making progress, only to find herself back in a place she'd already passed, string trailing along the ground. She was getting herself tied-up in loops and knots, trying to search every cave and crevice.

'Help!'

A distant cry.

'Hello?'

'Is someone there?'

The sound bounced around, making it hard to trace.

'Claudia?'

'Gia?'

The voice sounded close, and yet she couldn't locate her.

'Where are you?'

'I don't know!'

With a warm rush of relief, Gia spied her, hunched on the floor in the corner of a cave on the other side of the stony wall.

'Claudia!'

Gia flew over, kneeling in front of her. Claudia startled at Gia's entrance, deathly pale. Her pupils were as big as moons.

'Gia . . . Is that really you?'

When Gia sat beside her and touched Claudia's shoulder, it was solid and fleshy, like a real person should be.

'It's me. It's you.'

'You're here.'

Neither of them spoke for a moment.

'I fucking hate labyrinths,' said Claudia.

'What happened?'

'I got lost. I went over on my ankle. I can't walk on it.'

She gently touched the swollen flesh.

'I tried to crawl my way out, but whatever was in that drink sent my head to some very strange places. I can't remember how I got here. I have no idea who I am, or what I'm doing. Everything ... is falling apart.'

Gia put her arm around her, pulling her closer. She didn't care if it was appropriate or not. 'It's okay,' she said gently. 'I'm here now.'

'I saw some dark things, Gia,' said Claudia gravely.

'So did I. Seas of blood, skies on fire, the whole parade. But I also saw Diana. She told me to protect you, that you're important ... I think I knew that already.'

Claudia looked up at her. Gia wasn't sure if it was the libation or something else, but it was a look of adoration.

'As are you,' she said. She leaned her head against Gia's shoulder.

Gia tried to act casual, though her chest was drumming again, the blood rushing in her ears like waves.

'Last night, Minerva told me to do whatever it takes to become empress ... but I don't know if I can.'

'Of course you can,' said Gia. 'Of course you will. I saw the way you held the attention of the crowd at Neptunalia. They respected you. You commanded even your brother. You're capable of anything.'

Claudia stared down at her lap, softly shaking her head.

'Not this,' she said.

'Come on,' Gia said, standing up. 'You'll feel better when you get some water and some fresh air. I'm sure there's someone here who can look at your ankle.'

'How am I supposed to get out if I can't walk?' said Claudia.

'I'll carry you.'

'Bodies are heavy, you know.'

'I shall not ask how you know,' teased Gia. 'I carry swords, shields and armour, sometimes all at once. Trust me, I've got you.'

She pulled up her stola to reveal her arm, where the muscle was sharply defined when she flexed it.

Claudia smiled, still sorrowfully, but it was an improvement.

'Okay, hero. Let's go.'

'Here, hold this,' said Gia, passing her the ball of twine. 'We will be like Theseus and Ariadne.'

'I hope not,' said Claudia. 'Didn't he abandon her on an island and run off with her sister?'

'Oh, no, I don't remember that part,' said Gia.

'That's what I heard.'

'Now we just have to follow the twine back along the path I took. I, uh, may have made some detours.'

'As long as we're together,' said Claudia, 'we'll be fine.'

Gia bent down and scooped Claudia up, carrying her across her chest as men did to their wives on festivals sometimes, using one knee to hoist them upright before taking to her feet. One of her hands was tucked into the soft area behind Claudia's knees, while the other supported her back.

They traversed the labyrinth. Gia found it difficult to walk, talk and carry her all at once, so they wound their way in silence. Gia soon lost track of the twine, which had been severed somehow – possibly by one of the many rats. She began to suspect that they were lost, but she was too proud to admit it, saying nothing when they passed the same mural twice and hoping Claudia didn't notice.

After a time, Gia grew tired.

'I need to rest my arms a moment,' she said, depositing Claudia gently on a stone bench. They sat with their backs against the wall, gazing out at the dizzying folds of the labyrinth.

'We're lost, aren't we?' said Claudia.

'Only a little, sorry. I'll figure it out.'

'I don't mind. The longer we're stuck in here, the longer I can put off the rest of the world. I am grateful you came back for me, of course. I should not like to be here so much, if I were alone.'

Gia dared to catch her eye.

'I would not abandon you,' she said.

'I know,' said Claudia, staring into her deeply. 'It's not in your nature.'

'What do you know of my nature?'

'Not as much as I would like. If I had my way, I would know everything, right down to what you ate on your eighth birthday.'

'A cake my father made,' said Gia. 'With fig jam.'

'You really remember that?'

'He died not long after.'

'My commiserations. What was he like?'

'He was a good father. He liked to teach us things. He loved to joke and entertain people. I know no better man in all of Pompeii.'

'What were you like, when you were young?' asked Claudia.

'Energetic. I had brothers, so I learned how to act tough. I had a happy childhood . . . until it wasn't. What about you? What were you like as a child?'

Claudia laughed ruefully, her eyes drifting off into the thin air.

'I was precocious. Annoying, probably. I wanted to be the best at everything, even then. I remember trying to hold my own at grown-up events, thinking I was a woman by the age of ten. I don't really remember being *happy*, though. Perhaps when my mother was alive, though I hardly remember her now. Mostly, what I remember is my brother making my life miserable with his wicked tricks.'

'Such as what?'

'If ever I had a pet, it ended up dead somehow. Anything I loved, he would lose or destroy. He delighted in making me cry or lose my temper. Nothing made him laugh more than seeing me humiliated.'

Gia's brothers had teased her often. Sometimes they had even been cruel, but this was something else, something infinitely more disturbing.

'There was this one particular bird that used to come to the balcony and I would feed it,' said Claudia. 'Such a cute little thing, with fluffed up feathers and shiny black eyes. Sometimes it would perch on my hand.' She imitated the gesture. 'One day, I found its head on the ledge, cut clean and wiped of blood. I picked it up and turned around, and there was Decimus, smirking in the doorway. When I told father, he denied it. A stray cat was blamed. My brother delighted in dropping the word *bird* into conversations after that. That is just the beginning. There are memories I have of him that I can never speak of, memories that will die with me.'

Gia's chest was tight.

'I don't like to think of you alone at night with him.'

'Perhaps then, you should stay over and keep me company?' Claudia said.

They were dipping their toe into that pool again; that dangerous unspoken pool that neither had fully been submerged in.

'To keep me safe, of course.'

'I could do that,' said Gia.

'He isn't a strong fighter. You could probably floor him with a single hit.'

Their eyes locked and the moment stretched, taut, both acknowledging what wasn't being said.

Gia could kill Decimus. Physically, she could kill him.

Claudia hadn't asked in so many words, but that didn't mean Gia couldn't take her own initiative. The goddess had told her that Decimus must be stopped at any cost. His death was not just wise, but necessary. And yet, she would be sacrificing her own life to do so.

'What if we never escaped?' said Claudia. 'Would that be so bad? We could just stay here for ever and never have to face our problems.'

'I thought you hated labyrinths.'

'Not any more.'

'We wouldn't last too long, I fear,' said Gia. 'Personally, I should like to see the sky again, and feel the breeze.'

'If you insist.' Claudia sighed.

'We should continue on, before it gets too late,' Gia said. 'I think we're making progress. I remember that statue over there of Bacchus and his giant phallus.'

'I am officially traumatized,' said Claudia.

They eventually picked up the trail of severed string, following its winding, criss-crossed path to the dark mouth of the labyrinth.

'Something terrible is going to happen to Pompeii,' Gia said bluntly. 'Diana has shown me what is to come.'

Gia readied her explanations, thinking Claudia would have many questions before she would be believed, but she simply said: 'I have seen it too.'

'What do we do? The goddesses say it cannot be prevented, but we must try.'

'We do not know when it will occur, or even *if* it will occur, but we will watch the mountain closely, for signs.'

One of the labyrinth's many entrances opened up ahead, promising freedom and escape, but Gia was reluctant to let this moment end. On the other side, the real world awaited, terrible and doomed.

As they moved to cross the precipice, Claudia said: 'Wait.'

'What is it?'

'I just want to savour this moment, before we return.'

Claudia closed her eyes. Instinctively, Gia held her tighter, but the dreadful feeling she'd had before had not gone away.

'Okay. I'm ready now,' said Claudia.

When they reappeared in the cellar, Julia jumped up and made a fuss, calling everyone over to tend to the princess. Claudia was installed in the atrium with blankets, water and grapes, her foot propped up on a low stool. The house had emptied out, leaving Julia to entertain the last stragglers, while Claudia waited for a chariot.

Gia reclined on a bench, forming a cushion with her hands and putting them behind her head, staring up at the stars. Only when they were alone did Claudia speak.

'When I lost my head back there, I had so many visions and, yes, most of them were of rotting corpses piled up in pyramids and giant bird heads calling out in my mother's voice, but some of them were of you,' she said.

'Oh?' said Gia, lighter than she felt.

'It made me think... I want you around more often. I want you around as much as possible. I feel safe with you, Gia, and I don't think I've ever felt safe around anyone since my mother passed.'

Gia felt her cheeks burn, but she didn't move from her position, laid on her back. It made it easier, not to look at her as she spoke.

'I am glad of it,' she said. 'I want you to be safe.'

'Soon my father will die, so says Hippocrates. The people don't know it yet, but they already suspect. My brother will return to Rome and I... I will be expected to return with him.'

Gia had always known it, but the confirmation was still brutal.

'If I were to employ you as a bodyguard, what would you say to that?'

Gia sat up abruptly.

'You could be my own personal gladiator,' said Claudia.

'You mean I'd return with you to Rome?' said Gia.

'That was the idea.'

Gia risked glancing at Claudia's face, struck by how beautiful she looked in the moonlight.

She hated how vulnerable she felt, how weak.

'What about the ludus?' she said.

'I will continue to finance the ludus. If you wish to fight in the amphitheatre of Rome, I am sure that can be arranged. But as my most trusted, most honoured guard, I would want you to remain at my side for as much time as you can spare me.'

Fate was aligning again. Gia had been told to protect her and here Claudia was, asking for her to stay close.

She imagined them walking together under the Roman sun, standing before the Pantheon. People talked of the city's colossal statues, its fountains, its food. An entire life unravelled in Gia's mind, rich and full of feeling. So many turns of the year, so many festivals, so many trips and activities and milestones, and all of them enjoyed together until death parted them. She wanted nothing more, right then.

Gia already knew that she would go to Rome. She was sure that Cyrus and her mother would have much to say about it, but wherever Claudia was concerned, destiny took over. There was no fighting it.

She was on the brink of saying, 'Wherever you are, I will be,' when Claudia suddenly said: 'My father received a message from the man I am engaged to yesterday. My brother opened it and told me.'

The words assembled in Gia's head but they did not make sense. She didn't respond for so long, she forgot how to speak.

'You are engaged?'

'It was arranged when I was still a child. He is a prince.'

'Right.'

'I am expected to marry him.'

They sat in silence, listening to the laughter of distant revellers.

Gia leaned forwards on the bench, her hands clasped, legs apart as if steadying herself for a fight that hadn't started yet.

'I should've told you sooner,' said Claudia quickly.

'It is quite an important detail to leave out.'

'It is a business arrangement. A marriage of convenience. We have never even met,' Claudia said. 'That's why he's writing now: he says he's preparing for marriage and he wishes to visit with me as soon as possible. Perhaps he has heard that my father is ailing and he hopes to secure his position at my side.'

'And what about what you want?' Gia asked.

'It doesn't matter what I want,' she said.

'That's not true. It matters to me.'

Claudia's eyes were shining, filled with tears that did not spill.

'With my father on his death bed and Decimus poised to replace him, I have to forge strong alliances if I am to prevent my brother's wildest impulses. A marriage with a foreign prince is what I need to protect myself. To protect Rome.'

Gods, Gia had been a fool, thinking this was some star-crossed romance.

A servant of the house appeared, signalling that an imperial chariot had arrived to collect the princess.

'Take some time to consider it, please,' said Claudia, in her public-facing voice, as Gia helped her up.

They hobbled over to the open door, Claudia resting on Gia's arm. Claudia looked to her, but Gia did not return the glance. Her heart was slowly breaking the whole time, though she didn't speak a word of it.

'We'll be staying in Pompeii until Vulcanalia,' said Claudia. 'You have until then to decide.'

Vulcan, god of fire. It was his fury at the emperor's death that would cause Vesuvius to erupt, so Diana said.

Gia felt that she had no choice: she had to serve Claudia in Rome, to protect her as the goddess had destined. She had to put her hurt aside.

'I don't need to think about it,' said Gia, standing in the doorway, between one world and another.

'No?' said Claudia.

'I will do it.'

Claudia smiled, reached out and gently squeezed Gia's hand.

'You would really sacrifice all of this, to be with me?'

'It looks like it,' Gia said. 'I am surprised myself.'

This new silence between them took shape, sprouted wings.

'Do you want a ride back to Menandro?' asked Claudia.

'No, I think I'll walk,' said Gia, avoiding her gaze. 'It's not far. I could do with the fresh air. To clear my head.'

'You are sure?'

'I am.'

'Then ... I shall see you tomorrow?' said Claudia hesitantly.

'As you wish.'

A praetorian guard carried Claudia to the chariot and they galloped away into the night, leaving Gia in the dust. She stood there not moving for a long while before making her own way home.

With every step, the conversation repeated in her head, more and more dreadfully each time.

Gia hadn't cried since Atticus died and she didn't cry now. All of the tears just froze to ice inside her, making her feel hard and heavy.

Claudia had a fiancé, a man she was indebted to marry, but she couldn't walk away. Claudia's survival, her victory, was crucial to the very existence of Rome.

Before Gia knew what she was doing, she was running as fast as she could, just as she had on that first day at the ludus.

Gia couldn't risk falling in love with Claudia.

Yet she was beginning to fear it was too late.

15. MURDER IS ITS OWN VOCATION

When Gia turned up at the ludus the next day to tell Cyrus, he was waiting for her in the office, his feet up on the desk.

'Do I know you?' he quipped. 'I don't think I recognize you.'

'Very funny,' said Gia. She sat down opposite him. 'Did you miss me?'

'A bit. You look like you have news.'

Gia cut straight to the chase: 'Claudia asked me to be her personal gladiator, and I have agreed. I will return with her to Rome.'

Cyrus put down his feet, frowning as he leaned across the desk.

'What about our arrangement?' he said.

'Perhaps the ludus can expand its horizons and I can fight for you there.'

'There is no changing your mind, I sense.'

'None.'

'Gia . . .'

'Cyrus.'

'I cannot pretend I'm not concerned for you.'

'I am concerned too, for all of us.'

'What are you saying, Gia?'

'Listen.' She fixed him with a grave look. 'Decimus is dangerous.'

'Everyone knows that.'

'He's been poisoning his father.' Cyrus did not appear surprised. 'He is planning to kill the emperor and seize power. If he takes the crown, it will be the end of everything. We *have* to stop him – whatever it takes.'

Cyrus raised his eyebrows. 'Whatever it takes?"

'I will do it myself, if I have to.'

'Don't be ridiculous, Gia.'

'I've never been more serious.'

'You would do this just so Claudia can be empress?' he said. 'How do you know she'd be any better for the world than her brother?'

'Because he's a monster and she is not,' she said.

'You know only what she has shown you.'

'I have seen all I need to see,' said Gia.

Cyrus opened a bottle of amber liquid that looked as if it had been sitting on the shelf for a thousand years.

'Do you even know what you're asking of me?' he said.

'Don't you want the same thing?' said Gia. 'To rid the world of another rotten emperor? Well, now is your chance to actually do something. If you wish for the empire to change, well, this is change.'

'I assume you have some kind of plan.'

'I do.'

'Then I am listening.'

'We must do it soon, here in Pompeii where he will have less protection. As Claudia's gladiator, I'll have access to the House of Menander. I could let you in unseen. At night, the guards come to the taberna and drink. We could do it then.'

'If Decimus is murdered, Claudia would be the immediate suspect,' Cyrus said. 'Decimus might be trying to set her up already by choosing poison to murder his father. It is seen as a woman's weapon, after all.'

Gia hadn't considered that.

'Then it would be better that she is out of the villa, in another place where she can be witnessed, so she can't be blamed for it,' she said.

'They could still suspect her. She could have hired someone.'

Cyrus finally poured Gia a measure, replenishing his own.

'Here's my version of the plan,' he said. 'Gia, you are a fine gladiator but murder is its own vocation. There are men in Pompeii with a lot of experience in the business and they would be much better suited to the task. I happen to know a couple of them. Don't ask questions.'

'I didn't say anything,' said Gia.

'Once the current emperor is dead, and only then, you will alert us when Decimus is home and grant us access to the building. You and Claudia should then go elsewhere. I'm sure you can come up with a reason. My associates will befriend the guards who visit the taberna and make sure they get good and drunk, then one man shall enter the house wearing a guard's armour, which shall be forfeited in a game or otherwise stolen. He will suffocate Decimus in his sleep. It will leave no mess. The physician will not be able to make judgement on the cause. Everyone in Rome knows that Decimus smokes opium and worse. My associates will leave out some detritus to that effect, to really stage the scene. The Senate and the imperial cult will want to cover it up to spare him shame.'

'This isn't the first time you've thought about this, is it?'

'Hell no it's not,' he said.

'They depart for Rome after Vulcanalia. By the time they arrive, it will be too late. The emperor doesn't have long to live, and when Decimus is crowned as emperor he'll receive the full protection of the praetorian guard.'

She thought of the thousands who would perish in Pompeii if the goddesses were correct, and drew a breath.

'There is more. Something really bad is going to happen, Cyrus.'

'Yes, you said: Decimus will be ruler of the world,' said Cyrus.

'Something worse.'

'What could possibly be worse?'

'I can't explain it, not in any way that makes sense ... but I think a disaster is coming, and a lot of people will die. Maybe we can't stop it, but if Decimus survives it, the death will not end there.'

'I didn't know you were superstitious,' he said.

'I'm not, not usually. This is different. I have seen things. I have ... heard things. I have had visions of Mount Vesuvius erupting, and a war in the heavens.'

Cyrus didn't ask her to elaborate, of which she was glad.

'Even if I'm wrong, Decimus must not rule. His poison will spread through Rome, through the empire and beyond. I can't say what will be left of the world if we let him place that laurel crown atop his head.'

'What if the current emperor is still alive by then?' asked Cyrus.

'No one will rule until he has passed over.'

'It sounds like he's on the raft down the Styx already.'

'Let us just hope that he doesn't take too long to pass through the gates,' he said. 'We have only a brief window of time.'

'So you are in?' she said.

'I've been waiting for this my whole life,' he said. 'You bet I'm in.'

Cyrus clinked their brass goblets together.

'To the death of the emperor,' he said.

'To the death of the emperor.'

Three days later, and the emperor still had not died. Claudia confidently assured Gia that he looked worse each passing minute and that Hippocrates was sure he wouldn't recover from whatever mystery illness was ailing him. He was still dying, just slowly – slowly enough to put his affairs in order. He had signed an imperial decree naming Decimus as his heir. They had no choice but to wait.

That evening, the people of Pompeii were celebrating one of many festivals dedicated to wine, so the streets were full of merriment. Decimus was out being debaucherous and Claudia was watching over her father, along with several guards, meaning that both were safe, for now.

Gia was free to join the celebrations with the ludus students, sharing a bottle purchased for them by Cyrus. One of the boys had been left heartbroken when a girl rejected him. Cyrus was trying to cheer him up, telling stories of all the romantic devastation he'd experienced in his life, including the story about Corvus the Cruel.

'One day, she was gazing into my eyes, the next she's with him and she won't even look at me!' he said, gesticulating. 'It took me a long time to get over that. Perhaps I still haven't, or ever will.'

'I'd love to get my heart broken,' said Lucas, 'because that would mean a girl gave me the time of day in the first place.'

'Be careful what you wish for,' said Cyrus. 'It changes you for ever. You can never again be the innocent person you were before.'

'Who said I'm innocent?' said Lucas.

'You have the face of a cherub and the brain of a baby bear. If ever I learn that you've slept with anyone, I shall throw you a party.'

'You're on,' said Lucas amicably.

Gia stayed silent, thinking of Claudia's fiancé. Her head was swollen with questions. When would he arrive? What would he be like? What did he want? And the most pressing question: might Claudia care for him?

'Are you fighting at the Vulcanalia games?' asked Flavia, sitting down next to her. 'I've been matched up against Dido the Destroyer.'

'Uh, I don't think so,' said Gia.

'Too bad. It won't be the same without Viatrix the Victorious. Got any tips, to help me with the Destroyer?' asked Flavia.

Gia considered it, draining her cup.

'She's desperate to prove herself, especially after losing to me. A patron has also rejected her. She'll probably overexert herself and get frustrated easily. She likes shit-talking. Brush up on your insults and bring them to your game.'

'The runaway bride won't know what hit her,' said Flavia. 'She'll be back to old Daddy Denarii before we're through.'

'Nice,' said Gia.

She turned to the boys, who were playing a game of Twelve Lines on a board brought by Dominic, rolling dice.

'What's new with you, Lucas?' Gia said.

'My dog ran away. Nothing much.'

'Oh, I'm sorry.'

'She'll be back,' he said. 'She always comes back. I haven't seen her since the day Decimus killed all those stray dogs, though.'

Gia opened her mouth, but Dom very slightly shook his head at her, eyes wide. She shut it again.

If Lucas hadn't put the two together, it was better to let him believe she might just have run off.

'Fuck Decimus,' she said, raising her cup.

'Cheers to that,' said Dom.

'What about you, Dom? How are you doing?'

'I'm pretty well. I've been enjoying teaching the new recruits at the ludus. I think I prefer it to the arena.'

'I guess you think you're too good for us now,' said Lucas.

'Did I say that?' said Gia.

'You're never around these days. I'm not even mad. If I was the princess's gladiator, I'd spend all of my time with her too.'

'What Lucas is trying to say,' said Dom, 'is that we've missed having you at school. There are a couple of other girls at the ludus now, but it's not the same.'

'Hey!' joked Flavia, taking a seat at their table.

'Present company excepted, of course,' said Dom.

'I do have something to tell you, though,' said Gia.

'Uh oh,' said Lucas.

'I might be ... moving to Rome.' Cyrus met her eye. 'It's not set in stone. I haven't even told my mother yet. When I do, I'll never hear the end of it.'

'You can't leave,' said Lucas. 'Why would you leave? Rome is expensive, and full of Romans.'

'It's just something I have to do. I'll return to Pompeii as often as I can, or you can fight in the games in the capital. I'll see you all again. It's not the end.'

'I guess I saw it coming,' said Dom, after a moment.

'It's the end of an era. You've been like our little sister,' said Lucas.

'Little? I'm older *and* taller than you.'

'We'd never had a girl fight with us before. We took you under our wing—'

'You mostly just insulted me.'

'No, we took you under our wing and we looked out for you, like a little sister,' Lucas insisted.

Gia laughed, resigned.

'When destiny calls, you have no choice but to listen,' said Flavia. 'Good luck in the capital. You're going to need it.'

They raised another cheer to her news. Gia wished she could tell them everything – about the visions of the goddess, about the plot to kill Decimus or the erupting volcano – but it was too much for anyone to process, especially her, and she could only bury it down deep, sinking it with another goblet of wine.

It all bubbled up again as she walked home, pushing through crowds of drunken stragglers and narrowly avoiding being vomited on from an upper window.

People recognized her as Viatrix, cat-calling her to draw her attention, but she acted as if she couldn't hear them. She didn't want to be Viatrix tonight, just Gia.

She stopped and stared at the dark mound of Vesuvius in the distance. She was sure it didn't normally smoke so much.

Still, the emperor lived. Still, the people of Pompeii were unaware of their imminent fate.

Further along the road, she passed by a small shrine to Venus, which was full of barrels of wine, crates of grapes and other offerings. She left the only thing she had in her pocket: a single coin.

Claudia wouldn't leave her mind, intruding on every thought like a stone in her sandal, and the more she thought about her, the worse she felt.

As Gia turned away, she felt a sharp jolt that jiggled her insides.

For a moment, nothing happened, then a great shaking began. Every shutter and sign along the road began to clatter. Roof tiles and bits of brick scattered the pavement as Gia ducked into a doorway for shelter.

She watched the statue of Venus crumble, spraying the road with her broken stone body.

Vesuvius groaned, a hollow dying moan.

16. ALL MY HEART LONGS TO WIN

A cacophony of roaring and creaking sounded, filling the sky, as everything in sight shook violently.

Gia waited for fire to burst from the peak, but it didn't. The shaking ceased, followed by a nervous quiet.

A wave rolled under her feet, making the buildings sway and the pavement appear to breathe. It lasted just a few moments before fading out.

People came piling out onto the streets, shouting and laughing from the animal exhilaration of the quake.

'That was a big one!'

'Praise the gods, I thought we were done for.'

'The length of time between tremors is shortening,' said one scholar to another, bustling past Gia. 'I believe it to be a sign that eruption is imminent.'

'What kind of damage would be done, should it erupt?'

'The most catastrophic kind,' said his acquaintance.

The two scholars hurried off, continuing their conversation.

Gia continued on, heading towards home, but as she passed the House of Menander she pulled up, debating whether or not she should try to check on Claudia.

All seemed peaceful at first glance, despite the quake dust

showering the courtyard, but some strange intuition compelled her to look closer.

Gia stared at the scene for a long time before she realized that something was wrong with it.

A bloody handprint on a fallen pillar. Just a faint smear.

She spied a body in armour, just one foot visible behind a wall that had partially collapsed.

No. This wasn't the night the assassination was supposed to happen. This wasn't Cyrus. This was someone else.

Breathing heavy, head swimming, Gia approached the villa.

Not a noise rang out from the house, which was softly illuminated from within. The columns stood solemnly, the statues silent, the sound of running water from the fountain making Gia's skin creep.

She approached the murdered guard, bleeding from the neck and glassy-eyed. She crouched down, pushing up his sleeve to feel for a pulse. He had none. She used her palm to gently close his eyelids.

Gia gingerly retrieved the man's sword, holding it out in front of her as she crept towards the villa. In the portico, she found a second guard, stabbed in the head. Gia repeated the ritual, checking for life and closing his eyes.

Her heart pounded so violently it shook her body like the earthquake, making her unsteady on her feet. Every small sound and movement caused Gia to twitch, swinging the sword from side to side as she moved through the villa.

The third dead man was crumpled at the bottom of the stairs, his neck apparently broken. Gia stumbled past him woozily.

Opening a door, Gia walked into a room filled with incense and flowers, presumably to cover up the stink of the dying man in the canopied bed.

The emperor's room. He was dressed in fine robes and surrounded by many cushions. The chamber was full of gifts and offerings, figures carved from wood and bone that were meant to protect his soul on its journey into the afterlife.

Gia crept closer, noting how much smaller and more pitiful he looked when he wasn't sitting on a throne, surrounded by flags and shields and soldiers in armour. Here, he was just a yellowish, oozing, fleshy flap of a man, red-nosed and pock-marked, his festering breath wafting out as his throat rattled with phlegm. The sheets were stained with blood and piss and bile.

He could not have suffered a greater indignity.

She considered finishing him off, just the two of them alone in this room and with a killer in the house to take the fall, but she needed to find Claudia first.

A shadow moved past the door. Gia held her breath, pausing until the figure passed out of sight before following. Clearly, they were not here to harm the emperor, but someone else.

She trailed behind the cloaked intruder, treading as lightly as she could. Gia watched as he kicked open a door, revealing Claudia standing behind a podium in an attempt to hide.

As Claudia screamed, the man raised his sword and lunged at her.

The princess was the real target – that was clear.

Gia kept out of sight as Claudia ducked, but the attacker was large and strong, pulling her into him. He wrapped his arms around her, holding the blade to her throat. As they struggled, Claudia managed to stamp on his foot. She sunk her teeth into his hand, which Gia had *not* taught her, and kicked out at his groin, which she had.

The man cursed and staggered backwards in pain, and Gia was ready to jam her sword into his back.

When she withdrew it, he toppled forwards, slamming face-first onto the ground at Claudia's bare feet and revealing Gia's presence.

'Gia,' whispered Claudia, eyes wide as she saw her.

Gia put one foot on his back, driving in her heel.

The assassin grunted in pain.

'Tell me who sent you and I'll give you a blessed death,' she said. 'You will float off to the Fortunate Isles with drunk, giggling nymphs at your side. If you don't, I'll make it last. It'll be like being dragged screaming into the underworld by Valkyries who haven't trimmed their talons for a century. Your choice.'

When he didn't answer, Gia ripped back the hood of his robes, revealing a young man with closely shorn hair.

'You,' she breathed.

It was Fabius, her nemesis. Fabius, whose nose she'd broken. Fabius, who was paid to break her wrist.

'Tell me who hired you, Fabius,' said Gia, driving the point of her sword into the wound she'd made.

'Fuck off,' he grunted.

'One last chance,' she said. 'Speak up or the next words out of your mouth will be you begging me for mercy.'

Fabius laughed and gurgled, looking at Claudia.

'All ... hail ... emperor ... Decimus,' he said. His last words. His face fell still, his eyes frozen open.

When Gia looked up, Claudia was already gazing at her, just like their first meeting in the temple of Venus.

They both stood, unmoving, panting slightly. Gia looked around the room, in case the assassin hadn't come alone.

The bedsheets were rumpled and there was a manuscript open.

'Who sits across from you, face to face, close enough to sip your voice's sweetness?' said Claudia. It took Gia a moment to realize she was reciting a poem. 'And what excites my mind, your laughter, glittering. So, when I see you, for a moment, my voice goes, my tongue freezes.'

Gia had the sensation that her life was about to be shipwrecked.

'Fire, delicate fire, in the flesh', said Claudia. 'Blind, stunned, the sound of thunder, in my ears. Shivering with sweat, cold tremors over the skin. When I see you, I'm an inch from dying.'

She stepped closer, and Gia dropped her sword.

'You came, and I was mad for you, and you cooled my mind that burned with longing. Come to me now, free me from aching care. Win me all my heart longs to win.'

Gia did not remember moving towards Claudia, nor did she remember Claudia moving towards her, but suddenly they were upon each other, their bodies compelled together as if by an invisible pair of hands.

They pushed up against each other as Claudia's soft lips met hers, as if their bodies were attempting to absorb each other, to become one body.

Gia's arms were around Claudia's waist, trying to pull her ever closer, while Claudia's hands were looped behind Gia's neck, tickling the soft hairs there.

It made Gia shudder, shiver with pleasure.

Claudia kissed her again. It was a hungry, grasping, pained, passionate sort of kiss, stained with both joy and sorrow.

Gia kissed her back just as furiously, as waves of heat and vibration moved through her like aftershocks.

'Gia,' Claudia moaned softly.

Gia knew this could be the one and only time she'd ever experience this, that Claudia might merely be acting out her wild fantasies before submitting to a loveless marriage with a prince, but she didn't care. Nothing in the world could have stopped her then, not even if the goddesses themselves descended to tear them apart by force.

Gia now copied something she'd once seen her brother Atticus do to a girl, winding her hand into Claudia's hair and gently bunching her fist at her nape, then she kissed Claudia's neck with just the faintest trace of her lips.

Claudia moaned. They stepped over the dead man on the floor and collapsed onto the bed, their bodies entwined in some inextricable knot. Claudia's mouth was warm, even warmer than the bare skin that brushed against her own – skin so soft and sweet-smelling, Gia could've devoured it.

'I have desired you so desperately,' Claudia gasped. 'I have desired you since the moment I first saw you.'

Gia's lips moved to Claudia's ear, kissing the lobe before moving down to the neck again, to the collarbone.

'I have desired you for longer still,' she murmured in a low voice, drifting to the space between her breasts.

'Not possible.'

'It is so. You were the girl painted on the wall that I secretly fantasized about, before we even met.'

'Tell me more,' Claudia purred.

Gia kneeled over her, gently taking her wrists and pinning them above her, watching as Claudia stirred in pleasure beneath her. Gia kissed every part of her face, from her forehead and eyelids to her nose, kissing along the line of her jaw.

'I have dreamed of you, Princess. I was Diana and you were Venus.'

'I see.'

'And I was chasing you.'

'Well, you caught me,' said Claudia. 'I am captured.'

Heavy footsteps clattered in the hall, causing them both to gawk in horror. They exchanged one panicked glance, then Gia sprang off the bed, standing next to the body on the floor with the sword outstretched, while Claudia reclined as if woozy.

Decimus appeared, flanked by two guards. By the look on his pallid face, he expected to find a different corpse.

'How wonderful to find you alive,' he said in a flat voice. 'Thank all the gods of the pantheon. It's a miracle.' He nodded at one of the guards. 'Go, inspect the rest of the villa. Make sure none of these cowards are still lurking around.'

Decimus had none of Claudia's beauty or charm. He was ghoulish-looking with pointy cheekbones and flat eyes, his greasy hair slicked back in a style that made him look severe, adorned in an ostentatious gold tunic.

'I'm sure you're delighted to find me unharmed, dear brother,' said Claudia, in a voice that suggested she was anything but certain.

'Of course, sister. I see your manly peasant friend here has made short work of the killer too. Such a shame that we can't interrogate him now.'

'Yours was the only name he spoke as he died,' said Claudia. 'He called you Emperor Decimus.'

'Did he really? How curious.'

Gia cursed herself inwardly. If only she'd let Fabius live, he could've helped to prove that Decimus was behind the attack. She had acted too hastily. She had destroyed all the evidence in her eagerness to spare Claudia.

And she would do it again.

'Imagine if you had been slain, with father on his death bed too. I would've been the only survivor of the family. What a terrible tragedy that would've been.'

'And yet, here you are, arriving home so soon after the fact, with your guards in tow, ready to come to my aid, though you would have been just a few minutes too late. Tragic indeed,' said Claudia.

The atmosphere was as thick and solid as flesh, Decimus gazing emotionlessly at Claudia, who stared calmly back.

Decimus turned to his guards.

'Get that body out of here,' he said. 'Leave it out front, see if anyone knows who he is.'

Gia had no doubt that Decimus knew who he was, that he was the one who had hired him. But he had to keep up pretences, for now. His guards dragged Fabius's body out of the room as Gia watched, thinking about what Cyrus said, about the path the boy's life might take if left to his own devices.

'You should get some sleep, dear sister,' said Decimus. 'Say goodbye to your little friend now. Tomorrow will be a big day. I'm going to need you looking your loveliest and most enthusiastic ready for the announcement ceremony.'

'Of course. How could I *not* be excited to see my dear brother crawl blindly into the utmost position of global power?' Claudia said.

She narrowed her eyes to a squint, pressing her lips together in the falsest smile Gia had ever seen.

The siblings gave each other one last look of unbridled hostility before Decimus turned and left.

They listened for a moment as the footsteps faded, waiting until they were sure they were alone. Then Claudia turned to Gia.

'If you hadn't been here tonight . . .' said Claudia. She shook her head.

'Thank the goddesses I was. Venus herself sent me a sign,' said Gia, sitting down on the bed beside her. 'She shook the earth. I think she's trying to warn the people of Pompeii. I was nearby when the earthquake hit, so I came to check on you.'

'He broke into the house right after the tremor.'

Gia looked around Claudia's chambers again, noting the brass sculptures of the moon and sun on one wall, the purple drapes with a golden fringe, the bookcase full of leather tomes in one corner and a small shrine to Minerva with a carved statue of an owl in it. This was not even her home but a holiday villa, and still it had been decorated to the highest standards.

'Gia,' said Claudia. 'What are we doing?'

'I don't know. You tell me. You're the one with a fiancé.'

'I don't care about him,' said Claudia.

'You said you liked men.'

'So did you.'

'Well, I was lying. Obviously. Were you?'

'I have desired men, but none so much as you.'

'You still plan to go through with it,' said Gia. 'He will still be your fiancé, whether you care for him or not.'

'Anything could happen between now and then. Destiny is unpredictable, as we have seen for ourselves.'

Claudia tentatively reached out to touch Gia's hand. Their fingers entwined as Gia felt the room tilt.

She struggled to catch her breath.

'There are a great number of things that could prevent he and I from marrying, if you think about it,' said Claudia. 'He could die on the journey to Rome, or be whisked away by an enchantress, or take one look at me and leave immediately.'

'I doubt that,' said Gia.

'Perhaps, by the time he arrives, I shall be in a better position to refuse him. If I can survive that long, of course.'

'I will make sure of it,' said Gia.

'Even without a fiancé, it is not as if women can simply marry each other,' said Claudia. 'An empress certainly could not have a wife, just as an emperor could not have a husband.'

'How can this be wrong? How can it be wrong for me to kiss you, when nothing has ever felt so right in my whole life?'

'Who said it was wrong?' asked Claudia.

'No one talks about it, other than to make fun. It may be something women do in private, to be painted on the walls of bathhouses, but it isn't something people do in public, for . . .' She almost said 'love'. 'It isn't like this. This is . . . different.'

'We do not know what people desire behind closed doors,' said Claudia. 'Perhaps it is more common than we think.'

That was true. The people of Pompeii were probably full of secret passions they didn't dare to share with others.

'I don't want you speak for you,' said Claudia, 'but, for my part, I fear that I am falling for you, and I don't know what to do about that.'

Gia reached forwards, gently stroking her hair.

'I fear I have already fallen,' she said.

'Please tell me of your feelings,' Claudia urged.

'We should run away, leave Rome to rot,' said Gia.

As the words left her lips, Gia knew it wasn't possible. The goddesses would forsake them, or they would be first to be slain by the hand of Emperor Decimus, or everyone she knew would die. If a deity asked you to do something, there were few ways to avoid it – and even fewer reasons why you should.

'I meant more, your feelings towards me?' said Claudia.

Gia blinked at her in surprise.

'Is that not clear?' said Gia. 'I thought you figured that out long ago.'

'I suspected, but I could never be sure. I feared that I was delusional with lust and seeing only what I wanted to see.'

'Delusional with lust?' said Gia, cocking one eyebrow.

'I said what I said.'

'I have agreed to move to Rome with you,' said Gia, raising Claudia's arm to kiss down the inside. 'I am here because I feared for your life.' She slid off the bed, kneeling at Claudia's feet. 'I have kissed you, and desired you, and begun to dream of you as if you belong to me,' she said, lifting Claudia's leg and slowly kissing her way down to the top of her thigh.

Claudia arched her back, throwing back her head.

'Oh gods,' she said, clutching the sheets on the bed.

'I did this, all the while knowing I am unworthy in the eyes of society, and that you could discard me at any moment.'

'I would never discard you,' Claudia said, cupping Gia's face. 'You are worthy; worthier than me.'

'I did all of that with no expectation of my feelings being returned,' continued Gia. 'I knew it would be worth whatever moments of peace I could steal with you, however brief they might be.'

'Gia,' said Claudia softly. 'You could take on Sappho, with words like that.'

'Be serious.'

'I am!'

'It hurts to know you will one day marry another,' Gia said, 'but it does not change my feelings. It only urges me to hold back, for fear of losing you.'

'I don't want you to hold back,' said Claudia. 'I want all of you, even the parts you don't like, the parts you're ashamed of or afraid of, just as I would hope you would love me too for all my flaws.'

Love.

Claudia had said the word love, as if that was obvious.

But guilt weighed on Gia's mind.

There was still a secret between them, keeping them apart. For a moment that evening, she had wondered if Cyrus had been behind the assassination plot. In colluding with him, might she have endangered the princess?

'There's something I must tell you, and I hope that you can understand,' said Gia, her voice quaking.

Claudia instantly sat upright, her face creased.

'I dread to hear it if it will break my heart,' she said.

'There is a plot to assassinate your brother,' Gia whispered. 'It is arranged to happen once your father dies.'

'How did you find out?'

'I ... have been involved.'

Claudia paled. 'No, I would never allow it. Your hands are the very last hands I would want to commit that crime. I would not wish for you to carry that in your soul. I would've killed him years ago if I thought I could get away with it.'

Gia marvelled at her casual tone.

'Who is behind this plot? Is it senators?' she asked.

'Common men.'

'They will kill me too,' said Claudia.

'No. They won't have the opportunity. I'm to accompany you out of the villa.'

They sat in silence, listening to the ruckus in the gardens as the bodies of the slain guards were removed.

'I know well that my brother is a monster and that he must die for Rome to survive,' said Claudia. She looked anxiously at the door. 'And yet ... I am afraid. Afraid this plot will fail, that it will be exposed, that we will be torn apart. Even speaking of such things is dangerous.'

'That is why I hesitated to tell you. I didn't want to put you in even greater danger. But I cannot lie to you,' said Gia. 'Not now.'

'I don't know if I trust that the plot will be a success. Decimus is wily. He is paranoid. He has his little spies in places – brothel girls and slaves he pays. If he learns of this, it shall be all of us who will suffer for it, and the price will be high indeed.'

'What other chance will we get?' said Gia. 'You have communed with the goddesses and so have I. Decimus cannot become emperor or Rome will fall. Once, I would have prayed for the empire's downfall, but now I believe in a better Rome, in better Romans. I believe in you, as empress.'

'And I believe in you. You are right – it must be so.'

Claudia leaned into her like she did in the labyrinth, and Gia put her arm around her again as if they had been doing this since time began.

It felt as though they had.

'There are sure to be many men who would like to kill my brother. I just hope these assassins are trustworthy,' said Claudia.

'My contact is trustworthy.'

'How will they do it?' she asked.

'Suffocation. No trace. They will stage the scene so that it appears to be an accident, the tragedy of Decimus's own undoing.'

'What about Pompeii? Vesuvius is already restless,' said Claudia. 'If I were empress, I could issue an order of evacuation, warning the people to flee. I could say the gods themselves told me and no one would question it. But I will not be able to persuade my brother. He cares nothing for the people here. Whether they burn is irrelevant to him. No, it is imperative that he dies. If we are to stay away from the scene, we should not be in Pompeii at all.'

'What are you thinking?' asked Gia.

'When the time comes, let us take a trip to Herculaneum and stay overnight. I have been planning an excursion there for a while. A family friend lives there, and she's always inviting me to visit. I will send a message ahead of us.'

'What of the emperor? We cannot act until he dies.'

'My father hasn't moved in days. He cannot stand or talk or read. He may be clinging on longer than expected, but the end is near. I am certain of that.'

They quieted again.

'You should go,' said Claudia. 'I don't trust Decimus not to try to pin what happened here tonight on you.'

'You can't stay here alone after what happened,' said Gia.

'I doubt he will try again tonight. I will put furniture in front of the door. I have done it many times before.'

Gia gently ran her thumb across Claudia's cheek. Claudia raised her hands to catch Gia's, holding them in place near her face.

'I wish for you to be safe in bed and dreaming of me.'

'Of that I can oblige.'

'Come, I'll show you the back way out.'

They descended the stairs together, their warm bodies pressed together. Gia relished every time their hands brushed clumsily, or when Claudia's hip bumped into hers, flashing shy, secret smiles at each other. Through the servants' quarters, Gia stepped out into the blood-splattered gardens, pausing between two pillars.

'I will meet with my contact tomorrow and return here after,' she said, 'then we'll set off for Herculaneum. It's over an hour on the road. I'm assuming you have a carriage we can use?'

'I will arrange it all.'

Claudia inched towards Gia, standing on tiptoes to kiss her.

'I know I am putting you in danger, just by letting you close to me,' she said, 'but I am selfish. I can't wait to get away from all this, even if it's just for one night.'

Gia took Claudia's hand, raising it to her lips to kiss.

'This will be just the beginning for us,' she said.

Though there was a part of her that still didn't believe it.

Gia returned to the taberna, falling quickly to sleep. Hours later, she awoke to the sound of clashing bells. It was still dark, the sun only peeping out from the rim of the horizon, but bells were pealing across Pompeii.

Half-climbing, half-falling out of bed to stand at the window, she watched as a procession of robed cult members holding candles walked slowly down Via Stabiana.

'The emperor is dead. The emperor has ascended,' they chanted. 'The emperor dines on the isles of the Fortunate and Blessed.'

ACT IV

DIANA

FORTUNA

MINERVA

VENUS

When a mortal soul passed over, they arrived in the underworld on a boat across a dark, winding river. The wicked dead were ushered to the right, into the eternally sunless pits of Tartarus, while the heroic dead were ushered to the left, into the permanently sunlit uplands of Elysium. Those who lived mediocre lives continued ahead into Asphodel Meadows, where pallid flowers grew infinitely.

The late Emperor Tiberius expected to be met at the shore by a welcome party made up of his ancestors and dead servants, but he found himself terribly small and alone after death instead, just an old body on a boat that was crammed to burst, squashed between a slave and a soldier.

It was so cold he felt it in his bones, though he was certain he no longer had any bones to speak of.

The emperor was roughly pushed forward by a cloaked, faceless figure, joining the queue of miserable-looking people who followed a snaking path towards a mountain.

Numb and dazed, he trailed them, thinking the line might lead to a fine feast at which he was the guest of honour, like a birthday surprise. Perhaps even he, as powerful as he was, needed to complete *some form of pilgrimage before his greatness would be recognized and celebrated.*

But the warm glow of Elysium faded into the distance as he was shepherded into Tartarus, and Tiberius realized that he would not be dining with the gods on the Fortunate Isles as the imperial cult had promised.

'No, wait! What's going on? I don't belong here. Don't you know who I am? I'm the emperor of Rome!'

'Not any more,' came the reply, from the hordes who pushed him on.

They cared not that he had, until this night, been the mightiest man in the world. Now, he was just another disembodied spirit, another lost floating soul, condemned to toil in the pits with the other monsters.

When Vulcan learned that Tiberius had died at the hands of Jupiter's protégé, he set alight his great forge in fury.

Jupiter would say it was just a game, that Tiberius was just a mortal, and not a very impressive one at that, but that wasn't the point. Vulcan had spent many years manoeuvring Tiberius into power. He had endured Jupiter's selfishness and greed for millennia, waiting for his turn at ruling. Tiberius had been a fool, but he was Vulcan's fool and Jupiter had taken him, just like he had taken everything else. The fire inside him bled out with a guttural roar, as his rage set fire to the building around him.

As the blacksmith to the gods, Vulcan had made every weapon, every throne, every piece of armour. He even created the lightning bolts wielded by Jupiter. He had built mechanical soldiers and automated beasts and many other inventions made of iron and steel, which melted together now to form a thick molten substance that poured out into Tartarus, creating rivers of fire.

Dense black smoke cloaked the underworld. These ominous clouds drifted over to Elysium, interrupting a performance of the muses held in honour of Jupiter. The gods in attendance began to cough and choke, including Minerva, Diana and Venus.

The lightning staff of Jupiter shone bluish-white through the clouds of acrid smog from which its maker now emerged, fully armoured and limping.

'Emperor Tiberius is dead,' said Vulcan.

Jupiter laughed, the sound ringing loudly.

'Why else do you think we are celebrating?' he said. 'Come, friend, join us. Do not be a sore loser.'

'He was murdered,' said Vulcan.

'Your candidate was past his prime, just like you,' said Juno, queen of the gods, seated in the peacock-shaped throne he'd made for her. 'I know fire runs in your veins, Vulcan, but you really need to learn how to cool your head.'

'I did not engineer it,' said Jupiter, 'but his death will benefit me. I do not deny it. I have broken no rule. I am merely playing the game. I am the king of the gods, and my rule is final. For your insubordination, you must pay a price.'

The crowd stirred. The gods warred occasionally, often bickering over mortals, but it was different, more serious, when Jupiter took umbrage with someone.

'How will you punish him?' asked Juno.

'We will battle, to the death, on the day of Vulcanalia,' said Jupiter as the gathered audience gasped. 'As the humans celebrate with gladiatorial games, so shall we fight one-on-one in the Arena.'

The room erupted into pandemonium.

'Vulcan must be punished,' said Mars, the god of war.

'Kill him, my king!' cheered Invidia, goddess of vengeance.

'Please, can this not be resolved over a diplomatic banquet?' said Concordia, the goddess of peace.

As the pantheon continued to bicker, Minerva, Diana and Venus snuck away.

'Do you think Jupiter suspects us?' whispered Venus, afraid the breeze itself might eavesdrop on them. 'Perhaps he knows about Gia and Claudia, and their plan to kill Decimus. Why else would he insist on gladiatorial games?'

'Perhaps he heard that I appeared to her on the Nemoralia,' said Diana.

'If he knew the whole of it, I don't think we would be allowed to walk free. He may be close, on our tails, so to speak, but he cannot be certain yet,' said Minerva.

'If he learns the truth, he'll have us fighting in the Arena too, and I don't much like our chances,' said Diana.

'That is why it is so important that we carry through with our plan,' said Minerva. 'Decimus must die without a successor so Claudia will be free to make her claim. Let us meet again when the deed is done, and no sooner.'

The three goddesses parted ways at the Orchard of the Dawn, where fruits in the gradient shades of sunset hung from leafy trees, oblivious to the spying eagle concealed by its branches.

17. EVERY EMPEROR'S LAST WORDS ARE A LIE

Gia washed and dressed quickly, running down to the taberna to find her mother passed out, slumped at the counter.

'Mama.' She shook her gently. 'Wake up, good news: the emperor is dead.'

But she was out cold, her lips stained red from wine. An empty chalice lay beside her, its grainy dregs gathered at the bottom.

Gia blamed herself. She hadn't been around lately and this was the result. Her mother was back on the drink and she didn't even know the worst of it yet. How would Gia tell her they had to leave Pompeii, to abandon the taberna and the graves of her husband and sons?

Leaving her to sleep, Gia swept up and cleaned the tables before heading to the ludus to meet with Cyrus.

As she moved through the city, Gia saw people celebrating, continuing their vinalia festivities from yesterday with renewed vigour upon hearing the news, though they quietened immediately as a group of praetorian guards came through on horseback. There was a hard edge to the atmosphere that morning, with even the soldiers seeming jittery. Society could turn on a coin at the hands of the wrong emperor, and Decimus seemed to everyone to be the wrong emperor.

The role was promised to him as Tiberius's only son, but people didn't like it. They didn't like *him*. He was unpopular before he was even in power, and such emperors tended not to last for too long.

'You won't catch me kneeling for that little shit,' someone said. 'Not after he killed all those poor dogs.'

'Nor me,' agreed his companion. 'You know he rents a villa just for his harem of girls? Gets them drunk and high so he can beat them.'

'Doesn't surprise me.'

'I hear he buys slaves just to hunt them in the forests.'

Maybe Cyrus was right and the people were ready to turn.

He waited for Gia in front of the ludus building. He silently signalled for her to follow, taking her into the atrium with its brass statues of athletes in motion. They sat on the bench, looking up at the dark clouds overhead.

'Today must be the day,' she said. 'We cannot wait any longer.'

'Agreed. Decimus is already rounding up senators. He wishes to be confirmed as soon as possible, but the word on the street is that many of the senators despise him. They are procrastinating, waiting to see if another claim to Rome should emerge. There are rumours about a nephew.'

'A nephew?' Gia repeated. 'Who? Could he be a threat to Claudia?'

'I know no more. You should proceed with the plan to go to Herculaneum. I'm assuming Claudia isn't too devastated by her father's passing to travel.'

'She has been watching him decline for days. His death

will be a relief. He isn't suffering any more, not on earth anyway.'

They listened to the bells tolling again.

'How will you get in, if I'm not there to give access?' she asked.

'We will intercept some of the guards, like I said, and enter the villa in their armour.'

'What if Decimus isn't home this evening? He might wish to celebrate his imminent rise to power. What then?' asked Gia.

'Then we will have to improvise. I'll have one of my associates track him. He will be stabbed in the back in an alley instead. The Senate can speculate, but they will never be able to identify the culprits, and perhaps they will not be too interested to find out. There were only so many men who stabbed Caesar, but there were many more who were quietly glad of it.'

'I pray you're right.'

'Speaking of praying, let's make an offering, for luck.'

In the atrium was a small altar, dusty with ash. Cyrus lit a candle, pouring out a goblet of wine for the gods.

Gia cut off the straggly bottom of her braid, burning it in the fire.

'I pray to Fortuna, the sword of destiny. Please let us be fortunate in our endeavours,' she said.

Cyrus retrieved a small piece of dried seaweed from a jar on the shelf nearby.

'I will make my pleas to Neptune, god of the seas.'

'Why?' asked Gia.

'No reason. He's just my favourite.'

Cyrus closed his eyes. 'I was born by the sea and one day I shall return to it, but let it not be today, my god,' he said. 'Please keep my pupil safe as she makes her way in the world and let her never forget the great wisdom of her tutor.'

Gia smiled and rolled her eyes.

'It is done,' he said.

'So, this is it,' she said.

If their plan failed, Decimus would become emperor, Claudia would be in danger, all would be lost. But if their plan succeeded, Claudia would be empress – and what then? She would live a life consumed by the responsibility of millions. Would Gia ever see her again?

Perhaps the goddesses viewed Gia as a kind of sacrifice, to serve a purpose in a singular moment, to tip the scales of fate before promptly being forgotten. What use would Claudia have for her when she was ruling the world? The longer Gia thought about what it would mean to win, the more she feared victory.

'Cyrus, can I ask you a question?' Gia said.

'On the blessed day of the emperor's death? Anything.'

'Have you ever felt love, for another man?' she asked. 'Not just desire, but love, of the romantic kind?'

Cyrus looked at her oddly, his brow creased, trying to work out why she would ask such a thing.

'Just once,' he said, drinking the wine they'd offered to the gods. 'I was a young man. Well, younger. One summer, I befriended another young man and we hit it off. We did everything together. At first, it was just us chasing girls and getting wasted, going on adventures and pulling pranks, but as time passed, I realized I preferred his company to any of the women we were involved with. One night, I expressed to him these feelings and to my great surprise, they were returned. I began to fear I could not be happy without him by my side. Each time we slept together, we grew closer. Then suddenly summer was over and he left to fight in the war. I never heard from him again.'

'That's so sad,' said Gia.

'I moved on. I loved again. There were many women who came after, but never another man. An all-consuming love only comes once in a lifetime, if it comes at all, and it almost always ends in tragedy.'

'That's exactly what I'm afraid of,' Gia said.

'Can I ask why you're asking?'

'You can probably guess, can't you?'

She watched his face fall, inch by inch.

'Don't tell me you think you're in love with the princess?'

Gia didn't answer, which was, in itself, an answer.

'Gia,' he said softly.

'I know.'

'She cannot love you back, not in the way you deserve.'

'That's not what she says.'

'What has she said?' he asked, in a gentle, paternal way, as if certain that Gia had misinterpreted things.

'That she has desired me since the moment we met and that she can't live without me,' Gia said.

Cyrus's expression danced, conflicted: he was surprised, curious, suspicious, optimistic and downright frightened all at once.

'You couldn't just fool around with your friends, huh? You had to go after the emperor's daughter?'

'I didn't *go after* her. She came after me, if anything.'

'I know Claudia is said to have the beauty of Venus – I prefer a woman with darker features, but that's just me – but, sometimes, you have to think with your brain and not what's between your legs. Use your head, Gia. I beg you.'

'It's not like that,' she said. 'It is not just lust. For the first time in my life, I feel like I was made for something, that I was meant to be here.'

'I don't trust her,' Cyrus said, 'and you know that. People say she is charming but manipulative, that she is poison presented as a flower.'

'They don't know her like I have known her.'

'She will marry a foreign prince, they say.'

'I know.'

'You will accept that?'

'We could still be lovers. Who cares who she is promised to, for convenience and politics? I would be the one in her heart. Maybe it seems foolish to you, but love is always a gamble, isn't it? Even if you're lucky enough to find it, in a world that seems so absent of it at times, it might not end happily,' she said. 'One of you could die too soon, like my father, or fall out of love, like your ex who ran off with Corvus.'

'You speak no lies,' he admitted mournfully.

'There are no guarantees with Cupid.'

'I have given you my advice, I have given you all the experience of my youth, but you must make your own mistakes,' said Cyrus. 'With so much at stake, you'd best enjoy whatever time you get together.'

It wasn't his blessing, but it was the best she was going to get from a man who wasn't her father.

'Go to Herculaneum with her and live as if you are truly free for one night,' he said, 'because when you return, it will be to chaos, even if we succeed.'

Cyrus saw her off at the door, patting her on the back.

'Next time we see each other, Decimus will be dead,' he said.

'He'd better be,' she said.

When Gia arrived at the House of Menander just before midday, a horse-drawn chariot was waiting for her. It consisted of a red-and-gold box with a rounded roof and curtained windows that were open to nature.

It looked like the litters in which the imperial family were often transported, but it was attached to wheels and two white horses instead of carried by slaves. Gia marvelled at its construction and at the decorative gold wings on either side, gently stroking the mane of one of the horses, which were also draped in red and gold.

Claudia emerged between two pillars, walking towards her all dressed in black. A gaggle of advisors trailed after her, scurrying to keep up with her strides. They wore robes of varying colours, which indicated their role within the house.

'Princess, please, we need your assistance—'

'You will have to speak to Decimus,' Claudia said. 'He is the one in charge, after today. I am leaving Pompeii to mourn in private.'

'But your father... what are we to do with his body? There must be a memorial, a ceremony, we must have coins printed, and flags sewn, and arrange for him to be officially recognized as a deity...'

Claudia caught Gia's eyes.

'Like I said, Decimus has called himself emperor, not me.'

'Your brother can't be located.'

'Call the Senate for help if you must. My father just died. I implore you to be respectful and grant me my privacy.' Claudia dabbed at her eyes with a black cloth. 'I was the one who had to bear witness to his last words. What else must I endure?'

'Yes, Princess,' said one advisor, urging the others to back away. 'We will ... figure something out.'

The advisors went back inside. A guard sat atop the chariot, ready to drive.

'What *were* his last words?' Gia asked.

'Mostly just gurgling noises, but I've been telling everyone he said, "Let a new Rome be born from my demise".'

'You are lying?' said Gia, surprised.

'Every emperor's last words are a lie,' Claudia said. 'I'm sure he would prefer to be remembered that way.'

Gia nodded at the chariot.

'Fancy,' she said. 'It'll attract attention. It might be the fanciest thing I've ever seen – besides you, that is.'

'I borrowed it from a noblewoman friend of mine, so that we can travel *incognito*,' said Claudia, fluttering her lashes. 'And I'm not that fancy.'

'You are so fancy that if you told me you cried diamond tears, or that your daydreams were stitched as tapestries, I would believe you.'

'Oh, stop,' said Claudia, though she actually looked pleased. 'Everyone in Herculaneum is wealthy. Most of the people there are Romans on their summer seaside retreats. It will not stand out.'

'What about him?' Gia whispered, nodding at the driver.

'He is the most trustworthy man I can find. It was not easy. When we arrive, he will take us to Rectina's villa, then he will spend the evening at a nearby inn before returning in the morning to drive us home. I have paid him well for his discretion. Wait until you get a look at the place. It has more statues than you've ever seen.'

'Statues, huh?'

'Wonderful ones! Are you not a fan?'

Gia held out her hand, helping to lift Claudia into the carriage. She took it and smiled, gracefully climbing up and reclining on the covered bench there.

'I can't say I've ever seen a sculpture more beautiful than the vision before me right now.' she said.

Gia climbed in after her, ducking to avoid making contact with the ceiling.

'Perhaps you just haven't seen the right sculpture yet.'

Someone had prepared the chariot for what looked like a romantic date, with cushions and blankets, an ice bucket with wine and fruit juice, and a spread of bread and cheese.

They set off down the road, rolling over scattering stones.

'How do you know this Rectina?' asked Gia.

'When I was a child, my parents threw lots of parties. She was one of the people invited. She is a friend of Pliny's.'

Gia only vaguely knew who that was, certainly not enough to comment, so she just nodded.

'Sometimes she would get bored of the adult conversation, as would I, and she would let me ask her all the questions I liked,' said Claudia. 'I knew she had one of the finest libraries in Rome, full of scrolls. She knew a lot about a lot. She often went on travels and brought back little trinkets for me. I visited her over summer. She kept in touch with letters. She was a kind of mother figure to me, I suppose.'

Gia thought about all of the things she didn't know about the world – about geography and history, politics and art. How could she keep up with Claudia, who had grown up immersed in those matters? Gia knew only a little about a little.

'What are you thinking about?' asked Claudia.

'How simple my life has been, compared to yours.'

'No life is simple.'

'Did you ever visit Pompeii, when you visited Rectina for the summer?'

'Once or twice, in secret.'

'I wonder if we ever passed by each other on the street. I remember seeing the imperial litter once.'

'Maybe I waved at you,' Claudia said, smiling. 'Maybe I glimpsed you on the street and thought *that is the most beautiful girl I've ever seen.*'

Gia scoffed. 'No, that's what *I* said when I looked up at your mural on the wall. You know, it's nice to think you were always there in a way, watching over me.'

'I was; I saw everything,' Claudia joked.

Gia thought about confessing to the graffiti she'd carved, but she didn't want to ruin the romance of the moment.

They travelled along the paved highway, occasionally passing another cart or chariot. The journey lasted for several hours, but they didn't draw the curtains, enjoying the scenes that passed by quickly: endless fields of hay bales, tangled woods, small settlements and isolated villas, surrounded by trees and walls.

'Do you ever think about what you would be like if you'd been born a commoner?' asked Gia, as they passed a small village where people washed their clothes in a stream. Nearby, a group of children played a game of tag.

'It is hard to imagine,' Claudia said. 'In some ways, I would have more freedom. In others, I would have less. I think I would be a different person completely. Wouldn't you, if you had been born the emperor's daughter?'

'I would be a total rotter,' Gia joked. 'All of that power and privilege would go to my head, I'm sure.'

'I can't do anything that regular women do. I have always had servants to do those things for me. I can sew and paint and sing, I can dance and recite poetry, but I'm not sure how useful those things would be in the real world.'

'You can sing?' said Gia, smiling.

'A little, but what good will it do me? Whether I am a fugitive peasant or an empress commanding battalions, I cannot see how singing will be useful. I would have been better off learning metalwork, or carpentry.'

'Perhaps you can rouse the troops with a ballad.'

'You are teasing me,' said Claudia.

'I can't do any of the things *you* can do. I wouldn't know how to deal with senators, or make speeches at games. But I can cook. I can wash and clean and fix things. Comes with the territory, growing up in a taberna.'

'I'd be relying on you for survival, should we ever go on the run together,' said Claudia, in a voice that suggested she found the idea enchanting.

'And I would be glad to be relied on.'

They couldn't talk about anything to do with Decimus because of the guard, but they passed the time by talking about everything and nothing, from their favourite instruments (Claudia, the lyre and Gia, the cymbalom) to their favourite labour of Hercules (slaying the nine-headed Hydra and cleaning out the Augean stables in a single day, respectively).

'If you could be any creature, what would you be?'

'Hmm. I can't say I've ever thought about it too much. Maybe a wolf, or a fox. Something a bit wild that might bite,' said Gia.

'I don't see you that way. I think you would be a loyal and loving creature, like a dog,' said Claudia.

'You think I am like a dog?'

'In the best way.'

'What about you?' asked Gia.

'I think I would be a spoiled house cat, one of those extremely fluffy ones that are perfectly delightful until you piss them off.'

'A dog and a cat, huh? We might be in trouble here,' said Gia.

'Dogs and cats get along fine, in the right circumstances.'

Gia closed her eyes a moment, enjoying the feel of the breeze tossing the strands of hair that had broken free of her braid and listening to the song of the summer countryside.

Birds were singing, insects were buzzing, the shoes of the horses were clip-clopping in a soporific rhythm that made her feel slow and sleepy.

When Gia opened her eyes again, Claudia was gazing at her, her chin propped in the palm of her hand as she lazily ate grapes.

'You're cute when you sleep,' she said.

'I wasn't asleep,' said Gia, drowsy.

'You definitely were because you snored a little.'

'I don't snore.'

'Then my ears must be deceiving me,' said Claudia.

'If I snored, my brothers would have had something to say about it.'

'You're clearly in denial,' said Claudia, in a sing-song way.

'I am not!' Gia crossed her arms in a fluster.

'You're cute when you're embarrassed too,' said Claudia.

'I'm not embarrassed,' Gia huffed. 'I'm annoyed by this great injustice, this campaign of falsehoods.'

They both let loose of the laughs they were holding in.

'You are very unserious,' said Claudia.

'Do you wish that I was different?' Gia said.

'Not in a single way.'

'Good, because I'm not sure how to be anyone else.'

They fell quiet, exploring each other's palms with their fingers, tracing the life lines that were etched there.

When a large aqueduct passed overhead, the driver called out: 'We're approaching Herculaneum now, Princess!'

'Thank you. We shall stop in town and walk to the villa.'

Vesuvius loomed large, closer than Gia had ever seen it. It appeared peaceful today, slumbering in the heat along with everyone else, but its colossal size against the small villas of Herculaneum was intimidating.

Gia blinked and for a moment she saw it erupting, plumes of fire arcing up from its summit as rivers of lava streamed down its sides.

Her heart hammered, her ears ringing.

Avalanches of burning dust swept through the city starting fires, blocking out the light of the sun as rocks rained down.

Gia blinked once more and the blissful summer day returned.

18. YOU ARE THE WORLD

Herculaneum was named after Hercules, a hero of mythology famous for his many adventures. Hercules had always been a favourite of her brothers, and Gia's too. They revelled in the many stories associated with him, speculating about his great strength. When Gia was older, she learned that women were banned from worshipping him in clubs. Later still, she learned that the unsung hero of the story was truly Minerva, who had found Hercules wandering the wilderness as a baby and raised him as her own, imbuing him with power through the milk of her breast.

The grid of criss-crossing streets was lined with luxurious houses cladded in coloured marble, many of them painted with intricate scenes of gods and monsters, with boat houses that bumped along the jetties that stuck out from the rugged coast. The town's walls were painted with red and blue murals, visible through arches and columned walkways.

The chariot pulled up near a local inn, just a stroll from the town forum. A mural of Hercules was painted on its side, holding his club in one hand and wrangling a snake in the other. It had red and blue awnings and tables set up outside under parasols, where customers in fine robes sat drinking and dining.

Claudia lowered her veil to hide her face. 'Incognito,' she said.

'Let us hope no one recognizes you either. Our cover will be blown if Viatrix the Victorious has to stop to sign autographs.'

'I'm more concerned about you,' said Gia. 'Your presence would cause a far bigger stir on this, the day of the emperor's death.'

The news had already reached Herculaneum. A small group of cultists huddled in front of a noticeboard which displayed a confirmation of his passing, chanting in monotone.

Wherever they walked, the subject was being discussed.

'Emperor Decimus, good gods,' said one man, shaking his head in disgust. 'Rome must really be falling if that's the best ruler they can offer us.'

'How long until that wretched idiot is confirmed?' complained one woman to another. 'Surely there must be someone else to lead us?'

'I dare say even a dog would be better, if there were any left in Pompeii.'

'I didn't like the last man either,' said the merchant, who shook hands with a trader from foreign lands, 'but we'll soon be begging Pluto to return him.'

Yet, for the most part, the people continued about their day, unmoved.

'I suppose I am an orphan now,' said Claudia.

'Will you mourn him?'

'There is nothing left to mourn,' she said. 'One day I will tell you more about my life and perhaps then you'll understand why.'

'You don't owe me any explanation,' said Gia. 'Whatever you feel is yours to feel, and you are entitled to it. I just want to be sure that you're not putting a face on.'

'I am always putting a face on,' she said, 'but not with you. I cannot hide myself from you.'

When their driver disappeared into the local inn, they kissed hungrily under the veil in the shade of a large palm, almost getting caught by a cultist. They strolled through a marketplace full of people in colourful togas and robes, where food and garments were being sold. They passed crates of glistening fish, vegetable bouquets, rolls of fabric and jars of spices, pretending they were regular customers.

'Imagine if we were normal,' Claudia said, putting up her parasol, 'and we were here shopping for our evening meal. What would we eat?'

'What about oysters in a wine sauce?' said Gia. 'Lemon cake for dessert.'

'That sounds divine. We would eat on the terrace of our villa as the sun set over the bay, talking of our plans for tomorrow,' said Claudia.

'Perhaps you can sing for me.'

'Maybe on a special occasion, such as your birthday,' Claudia said. 'Speaking of your birthday, when is it?'

'The Ides of March,' said Gia.

'The day Caesar died? Is it really?'

'Slaying emperors is in my blood. I already know your birth date, of course, being that it is a public holiday.'

'What would you like for your birthday gift?'

'It's months away.'

'I like to be prepared.'

'You are my gift,' said Gia.

'You already have me. What else?'

'I don't desire some precious object,' said Gia, quickly kissing her hand when no one was looking, 'but maybe we could celebrate with some kind of activity.'

'Activity?' said Claudia flirtatiously.

'There are many things I would like to do with you,' said Gia.

'Such as what? Do tell.'

Make love to you, was the first thing that came to mind.

'To make dinner together, or, more likely, to make a mess. Me in an apron and you with flour on your face.'

'What else?' said Claudia, smiling.

'To wake up early together and listen to the birds while watching the sun rise. Or to cuddle together at night as rain pounds the roof, wrapped in blankets.'

'I would like to see a play, or go to a dance,' added Claudia. 'We could go to a gallery or a museum to see the Greek and Egyptian artefacts.'

'To walk on the beach . . . How about it?' Gia said, gesturing to the shining strip of the sea. 'We can do that one right now.'

'Who would refuse?' said Claudia, smiling.

They ambled down to the sea front, where blue-green waves lapped the shore, removing their sandals to feel the sand squishing between their toes.

'It is not just the good things I look forward to,' said Claudia. 'I also want to care for you when you're sick. I want to comfort you when you're sad. I want to endure the world's great and terrible weathering together, for better or for worse.'

Gia's only answer was to take her hand. The mere grazing of their skin, the gentle tangling of their fingers – it felt illicit.

They waded into the waters, and jumped the waves as they came in. They splashed each other, watching the birds circling overhead and imitating their cries.

When they tired in the afternoon heat, they took shelter behind a dune, cuddling close together where none could see them as their hair whipped back and forth and their robes rippled.

'If I were a god, I would wish to be like Saturn, with the ability to cease the flow of time, stopping it like a dam,' said Claudia. 'I would put a stop on all the world, birds frozen in the sky above, just so I could kiss you for as long as I liked.'

Their lips met again, soft and warm, melting into each other.

'I think I would rather be like the messenger Mercury,' said Gia. 'He walks on the earth, above and below. He is a traveller of all realms. That way, I could always find you, wherever you were, whatever you were. Goddess, woman, shade of the underworld. I always fancied myself a little winged hat and sandals to match too.'

'I like the sound of that,' Claudia teased, before sighing.

'What's wrong?' asked Gia.

'I would be so happy, if not for the fact that the world is about to end,' she said. 'If a disaster will plague Pompeii, I must do everything in my power to stop it. Should we fail to prevent Decimus from being named emperor—'

'We will not fail,' Gia cut in.

'Should we fail,' Claudia insisted, 'I may have to take more drastic measures, to ensure the people are protected.'

'Such as what?'

'Make a claim against him. Present the Senate with evidence as to why he should not be ruler. I don't know if him poisoning father will be enough. The people are already against him, but it will be dangerous. I fear I am unlikely to survive any kind of rebellion. He will not spare me as his flesh and blood.'

'We could still kill him, even if they announce him,' said Gia. 'He wouldn't be the first. If it happened to Caesar, it can happen to him. The goddesses have willed it, so it must be so: you must fulfil your destiny.'

'I know that when we return to Pompeii, I shall remember why I wanted to be empress, but, right now, I cannot think of a reason,' said Claudia. 'You are all I want. If we were just two ordinary women, we'd be free to be together. No one would care what we did, though our lives would be hard.'

But it was just a distant fantasy, out of reach.

'Once you've lived the life of an emperor's daughter, I don't know if you could ever be happy in common society. You would always be thinking of what you'd lost,' said Gia. 'It would be like turning down a feast to feed on scraps. You would for ever be hungering for the sweet nectar your tongue still remembered the taste of.'

'There is only one sweet nectar I know of,' said Claudia, kissing her, 'and I intend to keep drinking it until my dying day.'

Time passed too quickly. Soon, the sun was beginning to set, though the heat of the day remained.

'We should head over to the villa now,' said Claudia sadly. 'I told Rectina we would be there before nightfall.'

The white-painted Villa of the Papyri was parallel to the coast, accessed by a columned portico that looked over the sea. The gardens hosted a gallery of busts, as well as small marble and bronze statues, which were spaced out between columns and around the edge of a large rectangular swimming bath, immaculately laid in mosaic.

Claudia retrieved a bottle of wine and a small bunch of dainty white flowers from a chest aboard the chariot.

'Gifts for our host,' she said, as explanation. 'My mother always brought gifts when she visited someone, no matter who they were.'

An older woman dressed in blue robes waited between palms, waving them in. She had a well-worn face, with sparkling eyes.

'Claudia,' she said, rushing up to embrace her. 'I didn't know if you would still be coming. My deepest condolences.'

'It was his time,' she said. 'Please, take these.'

'That's sweet of you. You didn't have to.'

'It's nothing.'

'I worry for you, darling.'

'I worry for me too.'

'And your brother?' she said, her face curdling. 'Is he ... well?'

'Unfortunately.'

'I assume he is still ... the same?'

'Worse. He is set to become emperor, though not if I have anything to do with it,' said Claudia. 'That is why I am here.'

Rectina raised one dark brow curiously. 'Oh, well then it sounds as if you should come inside right away.'

Her gaze drifted to Gia.

'Oh! This is Gia,' said Claudia. 'Gia Valerii.'

'The famous Viatrix,' Rectina said, kissing her cheeks warmly. 'I know you. You fought our girl Dido on Neptunalia.'

'Please, call me Gia. Thanks for welcoming us into your home.'

'It is my pleasure. An elder like me always longs for visitors. I've heard so much about you. You've started quite the fashion.'

'Fashion?' asked Gia.

'Young girls playing with wooden swords, wanting to wear armour and beat up local boys. I'm very much a fan.'

Rectina ushered them inside.

'Come. Have you eaten yet? I've put out a spread for you.'

She led them through the villa, along a peristyle full of sculptures. Gia noted murals of Bacchus, Venus and a seated Mercury, his winged sandals on display. Claudia nudged her and smiled, pointing. The walls of the house were painted with lavish cherubic frescoes, with ornate mouldings in every nook and cranny. They passed a large library, its shelves full of rolled scrolls placed in capsules, stretching up to the ceiling.

'The pride of the house,' said Rectina. 'I have Sophocles. Aristotle. Horace. I have Strabo. I have Virgil. I have Epicurus, the writings of Chrysippus, and parts of the *De Rerum Natura*, by Lucretius.'

Gia nodded, pretending to be impressed by these names.

'Almost two thousand works in total,' said Rectina. 'It is one of the largest libraries in all the empire.'

'I miss spending long summer days in your library, learning about plants and gemstones and other fascinating things,' said Claudia.

'That reminds me. Did you enjoy the papyri you asked me to send?' asked Rectina. 'Pliny's work on herbs?'

'Oh, yes,' said Claudia. 'It was most useful.'

In the triclinium, they reclined on cushioned dining couches as servants brought bowls of figs and platters of cured meats. Rectina talked briefly about her studies, about her parties, about her friends in politics, before turning the conversation back to their sudden arrival.

'Oh dear, listen to me bending your ear!' said Rectina. 'Can you tell I haven't had company for a while? Please, let us talk about you now.'

'I am very grateful you let us stay on short notice,' said Claudia. 'You know I wouldn't normally impose.'

'Any time, though I must admit, I am curious to know what brings you here, on this of all days.'

Claudia looked to Gia as if for assurance, though she was the empress and Gia her attendant. Gia nodded, gently patting her hand in what she hoped was a platonic-looking way.

In a quiet, careful voice, Claudia filled Rectina in on her plan to seize power from her brother. She spared no details, confessing the assassination plot, though she didn't say who was involved.

'Oh, Claudia, you are playing with fire,' said Rectina. 'We both know how dangerous Decimus is.'

'I am aware, but the people must be protected from him.'

'You might be able to remove him, but they will simply replace him with another man. I hear some of the senators are convinced your cousin Marcellus will return to Rome and challenge Decimus. They might be able to convince him.'

'I doubt that. Marcellus has no interest in ruling.'

'And you do?' asked Rectina.

'You know I do.'

They exchanged a long look that Gia couldn't interpret.

'It might all be for nothing. I doubt the Senate will suddenly allow a woman to claim power. Yes, times are changing, but not so quickly.'

'It is fated,' said Claudia.

'Fated?' repeated Rectina, with a sceptical look.

'I have visited with the goddesses. Minerva chose me herself. They are trying to save Rome from collapse. They saw me wearing my father's crown.'

Rectina looked doubtful, her face wrinkling.

'Are ... are you quite well, my dear?' she said.

'I know you are a woman of science and not faith, but you must trust me now when I warn you of what is to come,' said Claudia.

'I am sceptical. Visions of gods have led many clever minds astray. Many scholars have claimed to be guided by deities, but no such claims were ever proven.'

'We have envisioned an eruption of Vesuvius,' said Claudia. 'It will mark the beginning of a new era. Pompeii will be destroyed, buried for centuries. Thousands will die. Gia has seen the vision too.'

Gia expected that Rectina would dismiss this, but the elder woman grew pale, her face grave.

'It is as I feared,' she said. 'I have read many works on the subject of vulcanology. I have observed unusual activity from Vesuvius in the past few days,' she said. 'The birds have fled. The river smells of sulphur. There have been an increasing number of tremors in recent weeks, each growing in strength.'

Gia and Claudia exchanged a harried glance.

'I've been reading about the eruption of Etna and the signs that were recorded beforehand. I think you may be right. It has certainly been a subject of interest in the preceding years. Vesuvius is thought to be dormant, but clearly it is not completely at peace.'

Gia found herself wishing Rectina didn't find the idea so credible, if only so she could soothe herself.

'If Vesuvius were to erupt, Herculaneum would be threatened too,' said Rectina. 'This library would be destroyed. Centuries of research would be lost.'

'There is more. If my brother survives the event and returns to Rome as emperor, the empire is prophesied to die along with him,' said Claudia. 'He will reign in tyranny and stupidity, worse than any emperor before him, with all the power of Jupiter at his back. Everything will be lost. He must not get that chance.'

Rectina nodded, thinking deeply.

'I have powerful friends, as you know – connections in Rome that may be useful – but you will have an uphill battle ahead. Your life will be in great danger.'

'We are all in danger, so long as we remain in Pompeii.'

'I will write to Pliny,' said Rectina. 'He has an entire fleet of ships at his disposal. I will urge him to send a party as soon as possible – one to Pompeii and one to Herculaneum – in anticipation of a great catastrophe. If the worst happens, he may be able to mount a rescue.'

'Tomorrow is Vulcanalia,' said Claudia, 'and Vulcan's forge is located beneath the mountain. I don't think it a coincidence. The eruption could occur as soon as then. We are due to return to Rome the day after, although I may be able to delay that, now father is gone. But Decimus must die tonight. Perhaps, it is already done.'

'I do hope so,' said Rectina.

The conversation reached a lull as servants busied around them.

'It's an early night for me,' she said. 'If you are correct, we have a busy and perhaps dreadful day ahead of us tomorrow. I will have the servants begin packing up the scrolls. I have prepared rooms for both of you, but –' she glanced between the two of them, smiling coyly – 'you are welcome to make your own arrangements.'

Rectina kissed Claudia on the forehead, like a mother.

'I shall see you in the morning.'

Rectina hurried off to speak to her servants, while Gia and Claudia were chaperoned to their separate quarters. Each room Gia passed was beautifully appointed, with statues of satyrs pouring water pitchers, or portraits of Amazons.

Gia barely laid down her bag and cloak before she took off to Claudia's room, finding her waiting expectantly at the doorway.

'I missed you,' she said breathily.

'You saw me mere seconds ago,' said Gia.

'That is all it takes to miss you.'

They were drawn together forcibly, their bodies tangled in a passionate clinch. Gia's hands moved through Claudia's hair, tilting back her head to kiss her face, while Claudia's hands roamed the muscular plains of Gia's stomach, her fingers lingering at the hips.

'I want you,' said Claudia.

'The feeling is mutual,' said Gia.

She hoisted Claudia up. Instinctively, Claudia wrapped her legs around Gia's waist, her arms looped around Gia's neck as their kisses became deeper, more desperate. They staggered backwards, clutching at each other hungrily, fear and desire mirrored in their eyes. Acutely aware that this could be the one and only chance they had to steal such a moment together, set against the backdrop of the end of time, Gia kissed her as if the world was ending ... which it very likely was.

The pair fell backwards onto the bed and Gia crawled on top of Claudia as she grasped at her tunic, trying to tug it off over her head. Gia made quick work of the fastenings on Claudia's outfit, removing her clothes smoothly despite her trembling hands.

In a heartbeat, they were both naked as the day they were born, as if their garments had blown right off, their limbs impossibly intwined.

'You are exquisite,' said Claudia.

Gia kissed her body, trailing down from her plump lips to her breasts, her belly button and the soft, rounded part of her stomach. Gia gently spread her legs, recalling the picture she'd seen painted on the wall, and kissed Claudia in the most intimate place.

'Oh!'

Gia circled the tip of her tongue slowly, gripping Claudia's thighs. Claudia moaned, bunching the material of the sheets up in her fist.

'Oh . . . oh my goddess,' she said.

'I am not a goddess,' Gia said. 'I am a gladiator.'

'The first time I saw you in the arena, I desired you,' said Claudia, her voice ragged. 'I desired you more than any man I'd ever set eyes on. A strong woman, wielding a weapon? I was weak for you. I am still weak for you.'

Gia's right hand moved up Claudia's thigh, her fingers delicately tracing the area of pleasure between her legs.

'You have seen nothing yet,' she said.

Claudia gasped and covered her face with a pillow.

'Gia,' she said. 'Gia, Gia, Gia.'

'Claudia, my Claudia.'

Moving her hand slowly, Gia leaned back down to kiss Claudia intimately, her tongue meeting her fingers in unison as Claudia's moans grew louder.

Too loud, perhaps.

She wondered what Rectina would think, if she knew what they were doing. Perhaps she wouldn't mind the idea.

'How did you know?' gasped Claudia as Gia continued to explore Claudia's most sacred space. 'How did you know it would feel like this?'

'I was born to do this,' said Gia.

Claudia was breathing heavily now, her hands desperate for any purchase she could get on Gia. Gia's tongue moved faster, causing Claudia's soft moans to increase in volume and intensity, forcing Gia to clamp one hand over her mouth. This only seemed to increase the princess's desire. Gia's hand drifted down to her breasts, cupping one tenderly as her other hand worked to serve her.

Claudia's body tensed and trembled until she threw back her head.

'Gia!' she cried, followed by a low moan. She jolted in a kind of shock that made her eyes wide, then hooded, her lids closing as her body melted into liquid.

Dazed, Claudia lay panting against the pillows as Gia reclined next to her, lying on one side, her fingers still dancing over Claudia's skin.

'I am shaking,' said Claudia. 'I cannot stop shaking. That was life changing.'

Gia laughed, blushing, flattered. 'That good, huh?'

After a long moment, Claudia sat upright, gazing down at Gia. 'I want to make you feel like that too,' she said.

Claudia straddled her as Gia had before, though she seemed nervous, eager to please. She lowered herself to kiss Gia's earlobe, her neck, her collarbone. There was no mole or stretch of skin left unkissed as Claudia teased her endlessly.

Gia groaned, writhing pleasurably.

'I don't know what I'm doing,' Claudia said, pulling up when she reached Gia's pelvis. 'I don't know if I'll be any good.'

Gia cupped her cheek, her heart pounding.

'It will be good because it is you,' she said.

With renewed confidence, Claudia gripped Gia's ankles, smiling devilishly.

The princess kissed her between her legs, as red-hot fireworks exploded inside Gia's head.

19. DECIMALIA

It was the twenty-fourth day of the month of Augustus, in the year 79 AD.

The morning of Vulcanalia.

It had been a sweltering hot night. Gia's nightmares had been full of fire and beasts, with groaning skies and crumbling columns that resembled the goddesses.

She woke to find herself in bed with Claudia, the bed covers twisted and wrapped around one of her legs.

It took a moment for the details to fill in.

They were in Herculaneum. Decimus had hopefully been assassinated. The future empress was still fast asleep.

The future empress she'd made love to last night.

Gia rolled over, kissing Claudia's shoulders and stroking the golden waves that spilled down her back. She murmured but didn't wake.

A slither of pink shone in through the closed shutters. Gia stood up to open them, beholding the red morning sky.

Red, as far as the eye could see, reflected in the sea, as if Decimus's blood had been spilled from the heavens above. It was a sinister omen. Gia had never seen a sky like that before.

The peak of Mount Vesuvius appeared dormant as usual,

but the air smelled different. It felt thicker, more dangerous to breathe in.

A faint rumble passed below her feet, causing her stomach to roll, though it wasn't strong enough to rouse Claudia, a smile playing on her lips as she slept.

Gia was rocked by a wave of sorrow, imagining all of this land scorched and blackened. She knew they had to get back to Pompeii as soon as possible. If Decimus was dead, then the empire had no ruler. It was time for Claudia to make her presence known and felt, to organize the people of Pompeii and warn them of the impending disaster. Everything rested on this day, this moment.

It was time, and Gia was as ready as she'd ever be.

Claudia stirred, rolling onto her back and smiling invitingly when she saw Gia. Gia climbed on top of her as Claudia pulled her down to meet her lips.

'It is dawn,' said Gia, stroking her hair. 'We must go.'

'Just a moment more,' begged Claudia, lifting up one knee. 'We have time. If this is the last day of the world, there is something I must do one last time.'

'But—'

Claudia lifted her right index finger to Gia's lips.

Half an hour later, they re-emerged from beneath the sheets, pink-cheeked.

'Now we really have to get up,' Claudia said.

They readied themselves quickly, enjoying a breakfast of fresh fruit with Rectina. Their cups and bowls rattled slightly with tremors.

They all looked to Vesuvius in unison.

The reddish hue that Gia had observed had faded to a greyish-blue.

'Be safe,' said Claudia, hugging Rectina as they departed.

'I'll be fine; don't worry about me. I have already sent a message to Pliny.'

She kissed them both on the cheeks and bowed her head.

'I will make offerings and pray for your safe return,' she said.

'I wonder if my brother is ... truly gone,' said Claudia quietly, as they walked to the chariot. 'I wouldn't put it past him to cheat and lie his way out of dying.'

'He is gone,' said Gia. 'They will not fail. They cannot.'

Back on the road, they travelled in uneasy silence. The earth was scorching, sweat dripping down Gia's back. It was quiet in the countryside between the two settlements, eerily so. She heard none of the summer chorus she'd enjoyed yesterday.

'It's quiet,' said Claudia, mirroring her thoughts.

'I noticed that.'

The journey home was long – longer that it needed to be. Claudia was sick with nerves, asking the driver twice to pull over for fresh air.

'I'm nervous about hearing of his death,' she whispered as they stood beside a river, pretending to admire the view. The driver took a leak against a tree several feet away. 'How should I react? I don't want to draw suspicion.'

'It will be suspicious if you act like it was a great tragedy when everyone knows how terrible he was,' said Gia. 'You should say nothing. When my brothers died, I was in a stupor. The grief didn't hit me for a while. And I actually *liked* them.'

Claudia gripped her hand, her eyes shining.

'I wish I'd had chance to meet them,' she said, 'especially Cassius. He sounds like a fun character.'

Streaks of greyish-white cloud hung around the peak of Vesuvius in a ring, like winged guardians.

Gia glanced at Claudia, her heart tossing and thrashing like wild seas. If time was running out, there were certain things she needed to say. She could barely contain the words that arose inside her, but she repressed them.

Not now, she told herself. *Not yet.* Love came quick, but if it was strong, it would endure. It could wait.

Save the world first, tell Claudia she loved her later.

Past the Pompeii city walls, a great pyre was burning in a field, casting a plume of spiralling smoke into the sky.

Vulcanalia, the festival of fire. Every year, there were sacrifices.

Gia could just make out three blackened bodies tied to stakes. A group of cultists gathered around the fire, raising their fists.

'All hail Emperor Decimus!' they chanted.

'Did they just say Decimus?'

'They must not have heard the news yet,' said Claudia. 'They will worship whoever is emperor without question, no matter how terrible, but I suspect they will not support me, based solely on me being a woman.'

'All hail Emperor Decimus!'

Further into the city, they saw people dressed in Vulcanalia costumes and regalia, all heading towards the amphitheatre for the day's entertainments, though the celebrations seemed subdued.

Everywhere Gia looked, small groups of imperial cultists were visible, some holding elaborate flags, standards and banners, swinging incense holders.

In the Forum, people were also beginning to gather, but not to celebrate. They appeared disgruntled, arguing back and forth with the guards on patrol.

Their carriage pulled up, at Claudia's request.

'What's going on?' Gia heard someone shout.

'Why is there no water?'

'The aqueduct system has failed,' announced a man in ceremonial robes, reading from a tablet. 'It will be back up and running in just a few hours.'

'The wells and taps are all dry.'

'I can't do business without water.'

Gia turned to Claudia, who looked shaken.

'Do you think it is related?' Gia asked.

'Rectina said she'd recorded signs of a volcanic eruption, including changes to the rivers and waterways,' said Claudia.

'What if Vesuvius erupts before you can be confirmed?'

Without answering, Claudia exited the carriage, approaching the crowd.

'Claudia,' Gia hissed. 'What are you doing?'

Gia climbed out after her, following behind and drawing her sword.

The people parted, creating an aisle, but their faces were hard and whispers carried through the mass.

'Princess Claudia,' said the man with the tablet, reverently.

She turned to the public, raising her voice: 'People of Pompeii, please heed this warning. You can see the signs for yourself. Even the gods have seen. I believe Mount Vesuvius is going to erupt and every life in Pompeii will be under threat.'

The crowd erupted into a cacophony, a chorus of fear and disbelief.

'How do you know?'

'What's she talking about?'

'She must think she's the emperor now.'

'The scholars have observed worrying signs in the preceding days, signs that remind them of the historical eruption of Etna,' Claudia said, louder now. 'We don't have much time. If Vesuvius erupts, it will destroy Pompeii. We must do the unthinkable and evacuate. Gather your loved ones, take whatever you can carry and flee. Travel as far away as possible, before it is too late.'

The direction was not well received.

'You want us to leave our homes? Our farms?'

'What about livestock? How am I to transport thirty cows?'

In the sweltering heat, the frightened crowd risked becoming a braying mob, exploding into disarray as half of them scrambled to save themselves and half turned on the man with the tablet, ignoring Claudia's warning.

'They're just trying to distract us.'

'Get the water back on now!'

'Please, you must remain calm and listen,' Claudia pleaded. 'As the princess of Rome, I implore you to evacuate.'

Praetorian guards approached, some on horseback.

'Halt, in the name of the emperor!'

The guards descended, detaining them both. Gia's arms were wrenched behind her back.

'Unhand me!' cried Claudia. 'Who commands you?'

'Your brother.'

Claudia looked grey and sunken before recovering herself. 'He is well?'

'Well enough to give his orders.'

Fuck. That bastard was still breathing somehow.

Gia attempted to fight them off, stamping on a foot and using her elbow to crack a nose, but it did no good: they quickly cowed her.

A soldier in a tufted helmet produced a scroll.

'Claudia Imperia Caesaria, daughter of Tiberius, you have been accused of arranging the attempted assassination of your brother, Emperor Decimus Severus Caesaria. You will be held at your brother's mercy ahead of a public trial.'

Claudia was momentarily speechless.

'Fuck off,' ranted Gia, pretending to be outraged. 'We weren't even here. Who told you that? Because if it's Decimus, everyone knows he's a fucking liar.'

This earned her a fist in the ear.

Claudia was calmer than Gia expected her to be, calmer than she herself felt inside. She merely shook her head and lifted her chin.

'You are mistaken,' she said. 'My own life was threatened by an assassin.'

'We have orders, Princess.'

'Let me speak to my brother.'

'He is about to appear at the Vulcanalia games, where his ascension to emperor will be celebrated.'

'My brother is not yet emperor. He has not been officially approved by the Senate. He may be my father's named successor, but he does not have this authority. Please, unhand us both. You are making a mistake.'

A hushed silence fell upon the scene.

'Your brother was confirmed by the Senate last night,' said the soldier. 'Senator Cornelius led the commencement in an emergency ceremony.'

Cornelius.

'That traitor,' spat Claudia. Gia looked to her for an explanation. 'He was supposed to delay the confirmation until I returned. After everything he ... I should've known.'

She trailed off, her face twisted in horror.

'I should've killed him when I had the chance,' lamented Gia.

Now it was too late. It was Vulcanalia, Decimus was emperor, Claudia was in danger and Gia had failed the goddesses. Everything was forsaken.

The guards hustled Claudia away as Gia cried after her.

'Claudia! *Princess!*'

Claudia turned, looking hollow, like she was no longer present in her body. Gia had the horrible feeling it was the last time she'd ever see her face. Pain spread out from the middle of Gia's chest. Why hadn't she said it? Why had she waited? She had always been too slow, too late, too hesitant. Too afraid to say what she really meant. She could not die, nor let Claudia die without knowing.

'Claudia!' she called again, but she didn't turn back. She didn't hear.

'What about the eruption?' someone was asking.

The crowd burbled, growing thicker and more hostile.

'What eruption?' said the guard, gesturing at the perfect blue sky.

Gia struggled against the guard's restraints again, but they held her tight.

'The princess told us Vesuvius is going to erupt.'

'The princess is no longer trustworthy. Please, return to your homes.'

If she and Claudia were detained, they could not organize an evacuation. They could not warn their friends or family. Everyone would die. When Gia's knees buckled in shock and grief, the guards dragged her upright again.

'Gia Valerii, also known as Viatrix the Victorious, you have been accused of conspiring to assassinate Emperor Decimus, with the assistance of Cyrus Jucundius and the Pompeii gladiator school.'

No.

'That's bullshit,' she said. 'They are innocent. Shame on you all, doing the bidding of a monster like Decimus. Have you not seen what he is capable of?'

Several of the guards exchanged glances.

They had heard.

'We all are in danger. Vesuvius is going to erupt. All of you will die, every last one. And for what? For a man like him?'

The rest of the guards chuckled, thinking her mad and wild, though people in the crowd who had heard Claudia's warning did not seem as convinced.

'Every emperor is just as wicked as the last,' said the soldier. 'As long as I get paid, that's all I care about.'

Gia felt as weak as a child.

'Says here that you are to be transported to the amphitheatre to fight in the Vulcanalia games, by the order of the emperor,' said the guard, reading a tablet. 'You should save your strength for the arena.'

'He wants me to fight?'

'You heard me, come on.'

A part of her wanted to scream and struggle, to try to take down the guards who marched her through the streets, but the larger part of her knew it would be pointless, if not entirely disadvantageous. In the short time it would take her to kick one of them in the groin and attempt to steal his weapon, one of the others would spear her with their sharpened swords.

They passed the taberna, which was worryingly dark and empty, and the ludus, which appeared to have been ransacked. Guards carried out crates of equipment, including that which Claudia purchased, along with scrolls bearing her lioness insignia.

Gia thought of her father and her brothers. Soon she would get to see Cassius and Atticus again. It would be a blessing, yet she feared being taken from Claudia. She wasn't ready for them to be parted yet.

For as long as she lived, she would attempt to protect her – until her very last breath. She would do it not because the goddesses had prophesied it, but out of love. There was nothing more powerful than that, not even in the heavens, for even the gods were victim to it. It was all she had now.

As they trudged through the streets, people cheered and booed at the sight of a prisoner, their expressions souring when they recognized who it was. Whispers multiplied rapidly as children spread word through the streets. One face in particular stuck out from the crowd. Athena, the young founder of her fan club.

'Gia!' she cried, running alongside them. 'I'll fight for you, Gia!'

One of the guards struck out, catching her face with his fist.

'Shut up, stupid kid,' he said. 'Didn't your mother teach you not to cheer the enemies of the emperor?'

Athena fell back as Gia's stomach turned over and over.

Gia's life would end in the ring, just as she had dreamed when she was a girl Athena's age. But she couldn't regret the path she had chosen. If she hadn't become a gladiator she wouldn't have met Claudia. She would not have known the euphoria of exploring a woman's body. Life was short and brutal, just like a fight in the amphitheatre, and despite her wounds and losses she had found meaning in it. She had found joy in it. That was enough, she told herself.

That was enough. It had to be.

Everything had gone to shit. She had failed her mission. Fortuna had turned on her, or Fortuna had lost control – Gia wasn't sure. But she was marked for death now, she was sure of that. The volcano was soon to blow, and she couldn't stop it. The goddesses had abandoned her – or else they were losing their own war against the gods, powerless to prevent the dark future from unravelling.

The amphitheatre loomed on the horizon, like a giant tomb, getting bigger and bigger as they advanced towards it. Every fight she'd ever witnessed flashed through her head; every loss and win, every drop of blood. The beginning and the end of her life.

Inside, it was packed with people dressed in black and red, but there was a palpable nervousness in the air, as word of Claudia's warning spread.

'What if the girl is right?'

'These tremors have me worried.'

'What can we do about it? It's in the hands of the gods now. Let's just try and have a good day, shall we?'

Though she couldn't see the speaker, Gia could hear a voice, echoing through the cavernous space.

'Today is a historic day indeed,' crowed Decimus. 'This shall be the last time we celebrate Vulcanalia.'

The audience groaned in disappointment and disapproval.

'From now on, we will celebrate Decimalia instead, not a festival of fire but a festival of military and might.'

There was a low murmur of discontent. Gia saw a blur of troubled faces – speculating on the consequences of denying a god his festival and replacing it with a celebration of self.

Gia was led on, into the covered area that ringed the arena at ground level, which had been converted into iron-barred cells in two rows. The end of the room was open to the arena floor, allowing them to spectate on the event. It was currently empty, switching between opening acts.

As Gia was forced roughly into the nearest cell, the door clanging shut, she heard someone faintly speak her name. She peered through the darkness into the next cell, where a familiar figure was huddled on the ground, looking raw and purplish.

'Cyrus!' Gia flew to the bars between them, kneeling on the ground. He crawled over to her, grunting.

'Are you well?' she asked.

He gave her a classic Cyrus look, raising one brow.

'Okay, stupid question,' she said.

They clutched hands through the bars, holding on tight.

'I've been better, it must be said.'

'What happened, Cyrus?'

'We trailed Decimus to a villa, near the Vesuvius Gate. He was hosting a gathering there with a group of brothel girls, but the plan was interrupted. Someone knew we were coming. I think someone must have been spying on our conversation at the ludus. We were betrayed, Gia. We were intercepted by the praetorian guard, beaten and brought here. They know about Claudia. They know about everything.'

'We?' she said. 'You said *we* were brought here. Who is we?'

Cyrus turned his head, indicating the cells beyond. Gia saw

a frazzled, dirty-faced Julia and a distinguished man in blood-stained robes, huddled together – her husband, Senator Quirius, Gia guessed.

She also spied two grizzly looking men with beards who she didn't recognize. She assumed they were Cyrus's assassin friends.

Across the aisle was another row of cages. Gia saw two familiar faces, though drawn and fearful.

'Dom! Lucas!'

'They arrested all the students at the ludus,' explained Cyrus. 'The emperor is saying we were all involved in the plot to kill him and we cannot fight his word.'

'Do something, Gia,' said Lucas, clutching onto the bars. 'I don't know what, but I bet you can think of something.'

'Please, gods, I cannot die today.' Dom prayed, over and over. 'My work on this earth is not yet done.'

'What of the others?' she asked.

Trumpets sounded, startling them all.

'Flavia is about to fight for her life out there,' said Cyrus.

Gia moved to the other side of the cell, trying to make out the two figures walking towards the centre of the ring. Flavia wore only the most basic of uniforms, just patches of leather strung together with no protection, and she had only a wooden sword, while her competitor carried a mace. Decimus's doing, no doubt.

Gia pushed up against the bars, searching the crowd for her mother's face, but she wasn't there. She tried to see into the imperial box. Claudia wasn't there either. Decimus was flanked on either side by Den girls. Gia narrowed her eyes, trying to figure out where she knew one of them from when she realized it was Berenice.

Oh no.

She had changed her hair and her eye looked bruised.

A pained cry rang out as Flavia took a hit. Then another. Gia clasped her hands together, barely able to look as the mace struck Flavia's face.

Flavia had come to her aid when she needed her, without her even needing to ask, but now Gia could do nothing to save her.

Flavia toppled backwards, crashing down on the dusty ground as her opponent threw up his arm and claimed victory.

Just like that, it was over. Gia prayed for a good death for her.

Two guards dragged her body away as Gia backed up, retreating into the far corner of her cell and slumping to the floor.

Flavia's words at the House of the Labyrinth rang in her ears.

'I saw myself buried in the earth as a statue, posed in action, as if something had petrified me on the spot.'

This, then, was not the death that Flavia had envisioned.

Did that mean the future was now changed? Unpredictable and unseen? Maybe they still had a chance to stop it all.

Gia looked around the cell, seeking a way out. She asked herself what she needed to do to escape, how they all might work together to secure their freedom. But she could not squeeze through the bars, or kick open the door. She had nothing to use as a weapon, nor even to smash open the lock.

'What are we going to do?' asked Lucas again.

'I'll be honest, it's not looking good right now,' Gia said.

'That's what I thought.' He sighed.

One by one, the others were called up to fight. Julia and the senator were penned in with a bull, whose horns gored them both, their entrails pulled out and dragged along the ground.

Gia turned away, but the sound still haunted her.

The two bearded would-be assassins were torn apart by lions. Other students were trampled by horses or under the wheels of chariots, until the sand that covered the arena floor was stained like a map, with continents of blood. So much gore and death that Gia could barely process it all, let alone grieve for anyone.

By the looks of the audience, she was not alone in her horror. The gladiator school was once the pride of Pompeii, known for miles around, and now Decimus was killing them off like those dogs.

'I guess this is it,' said Lucas, when he and Dom were called up. They were to fight each other. 'Only one of us can survive and I'd rather it be you. You have more to live for than me. I'm just sort of ... here.'

'Don't say that, Lucas,' said Dom.

'You all know I'm lucky to have made it this far. My family always said they expected me to die years ago. I had a good run.'

'I don't want to come back without you,' said Dom, welling up.

Lucas patted him slowly on the back, avoiding his gaze.

'Lucas,' said Cyrus, shaking his hand. 'It's been an honour.' He turned to Dom and did the same.

'See you around, big brother,' said Gia, as Lucas grinned.

'See you, little sister.'

Dom reached through the bars, squeezing her hand.

'Whichever one of you makes it out, flee the city,' she told them. 'Take as many people with you as you can.'

'Why?' asked Dom.

'A disaster is coming. Even worse than this. Something more terrible than you can imagine. You must leave today, do you understand?'

Dom nodded, though his expression was uncertain. Lucas looked oddly carefree, as if he'd already accepted that death was coming for him today.

She watched them depart in heart-stopping dread.

The fight began, signalled by the flare of horns and the terrible pounding of drums, but Gia couldn't watch, turning her back and pressing her hands against her ears, chanting to herself to drown out the sound.

Yet the stupidest, most animal part of her could not look away.

She had not been in the amphitheatre on the day Atticus died, and a part of her regretted not being present in his last moments. Cassius too had died far away, with no one to comfort him or even know what happened for sure.

No. She had to watch the last moments of her friend's life, so they were not alone when they died. She had to witness, so the world would know. So their legends would not die with them.

The fight didn't last long. She saw Lucas fall and not get up. The summa rudis moved over to him, bending down to check his pulse. Then he summoned Dom over. Lucas wasn't dead yet. They were making Dom finish the job. Oh gods.

Dom raised his club . . .

At the last second, she closed her eyes by instinct.

Lucas. Poor Lucas.

Dominic didn't return to the cells. Gia hoped he was running free, as far from Pompeii as he could get.

Now only she and Cyrus were left.

When the guards came for him, he fixed her with a devastating look – one she had no name for.

'Goodbye, Gia. You know, you really were my favourite.'

'Cyrus.'

She reached out, trying to hold onto him, but she couldn't prevent the guards from dragging Cyrus away to his fate.

'Goodbye,' she whispered after him.

Alone in the cell, Gia rocked back and forth, waiting for the sounds of the battle to begin, wondering what terrible beast the emperor would make her face.

Perhaps he would fight her himself.

When her name was called, she was hauled upright and forced to change into the uniform dictated by Decimus, a skimpy bundle of leather straps that barely covered her body. She had no helmet, no shield, and only the wooden sword still splattered with Flavia's spent blood.

It felt heavier in her hand than steel.

Gia stood in the dark, trembling, terrified.

This was it. This was how she died.

The thought had barely formed before she was hauled out of the dark cell and pushed headfirst into the light.

20. YOU NEVER FORGET HOW TO KILL A MAN

'Today, you will enjoy the final fight of Viatrix the Victorious,' bellowed the announcer, as the amphitheatre fell quiet. 'Emperor Decimus has declared that women gladiators are to be banned across the empire.'

Gia heard someone booing, a sound that was swiftly cut short.

A high-pitched scream followed.

Thud, thud, thud.

A man's head rolled slowly down the amphitheatre steps, coming to rest at the bottom next to a woman who promptly fainted.

A guard retrieved the head and brought it to Decimus, who held it in his hands while grinning.

'Does anyone else have any objections?' he said.

But the amphitheatre was unusually silent.

Gia recognized the man's staring face from the vision Diana had shown her, when she warned her of what was possible if she failed. Parts of the prophecy were still intact, then, despite what had happened to Flavia.

The future was just a bundle of tangled threads. She had no way of knowing how it would end.

Gia looked around the arena, searching for signs of Cyrus, as the realization of what was about to happen dawned on her.

'Both of our fighters have been charged with crimes against the empire, but the winner shall walk free, thanks to the emperor's great generosity,' said the announcer. 'Today, they will fight for freedom. They will fight for their lives. So, please, put your hands together for Gia Valerii, and Cyrus Jucundius.'

Cyrus. She had to fight Cyrus.

The haunted look on his face was like a knife to her throat.

They were led to stand before the imperial box, vowing to be beaten and burned, unable to look away from the other.

When it was Gia's turn, instead of reciting the words as instructed, she shouted up at Decimus: 'Where is she? Where is Claudia?'

'That is none of your concern,' he drawled.

'It is the people's concern.'

'People do not make requests of their emperor,' he said, loud enough that all could hear. 'Their emperor makes requests of them.'

'Shouldn't it be the other way around?' Gia shouted back.

The audience responded with a soft hiss, a low murmur, though subdued by the beheading.

'You must salute the emperor,' said the attendant nervously. 'You must say, "Those who are about to die salute you, Emperor Decimus". Please, I beg you to say it.'

Gia looked deep into the emptiness of Decimus's eyes.

'I refuse,' she said.

'I also refuse,' said Cyrus.

Gia nodded at him, in appreciation.

'We refuse to salute you,' she continued, turning back to Decimus. 'You are no emperor. You are barely a man. You are as cruel and as corrupt as you are cowardly. You wouldn't last a moment in the arena against me.'

The crowd rippled.

'Fight me one on one. Then we'll see what kind of ruler you are.'

Decimus's expression didn't change. It didn't twitch or shift.

'Or are you scared to lose to a woman?'

The crowd murmured as Decimus consulted with his robed advisor before turning back to them with a sinister smirk. For a moment, Gia thought he might take her up on the offer.

'Let the games begin. To the death!' was all he said.

As Gia and Cyrus marched back to the centre of the arena, she knew without doubt that Decimus would kill both of them, win or lose.

'Look at you, threatening to beat the emperor,' chuckled Cyrus. 'If I'm going to die today, I am glad I at least got to witness this.'

'How can you make jokes now?'

'What else can I do? I will not let them take my sense of humour too.'

Those infernal drums sounded as the summa rudis let sand slip through his fingers. A brash horn signalled the start of the match.

Gia immediately laid down her wooden weapon.

'I won't fight you,' she said.

'Gia,' he said sadly.

'I cannot fight you.'

Cyrus copied, but his expression was solemn now.

'If we don't fight, he'll kill us both,' he said. 'You know that. He might do so anyway, but at least this way you'll stand a chance.'

'Then let him,' Gia said, sitting down on the ground to a chorus of boos. 'I would rather die with you than take your life.'

'Don't be stupid, Gia,' said Cyrus, towering over her. 'You still have a chance to do something. It's not over yet.'

The booing increased dramatically, reaching a thundering crescendo.

'It looks pretty over to me.'

'Decimus still lives. It's not over until he's dead.'

Two soldiers approached, carrying swords horizontally.

'It appears that our gladiators refuse to fight without proper weapons,' said the announcer. 'Emperor Decimus has generously allowed them an upgrade. The more bloodshed the better!'

When one of the men offered the hilt to Gia, she shook her head.

'Take it, Gia,' ordered Cyrus.

'No.'

'Maybe we can still fight our way out of this,' he said, in a low voice. 'Take it.'

Gia complied, looking around the amphitheatre, but guards ringed the arena in thick formation, lining along the stairs and crowding the entrances.

'There are too many guards. We'd never make it to Decimus.'

They watched him, sitting sour-faced in his box, surrounded by all the pomp and circumstance that made even a creature like him appear regal.

'We won't even make it out of the ring,' she conceded. 'He is well protected, now that he is emperor.'

'Then we must fight,' said Cyrus. 'We have no choice.'

'I will not kill you, Cyrus. You won't change my mind.'

'This isn't just about you,' he said. 'This is about them.' He looked to the audience, some of whom were currently booing them. 'If we both die, who will kill Decimus? Who will save the people from the disaster you warned about? Maybe I was wrong about Claudia. Maybe you can still find her and stop him. Maybe the goddesses can aid you. You must kill me, so you can live to kill him.'

'No. Never.'

'If this is our last fight, then let's make it count. I will come for you and I will mean it. I will do some damage, but you will survive it. Then, when it is time and I tell you I'm ready, you're going to take that sword and drive it into my chest, here, just to the right. Right through the heart.'

'I can't,' Gia said.

'You have to.'

'I won't do it, Cyrus.'

'If I have to force you to fight me and save yourself, so be it.'

Cyrus roughly yanked her upright, grabbing the leather strap at her shoulder and planting her on her feet.

'Hey!' she objected.

'It's been a while since I've been in the arena,' said Cyrus, stretching his dark limbs. 'But I was a fighter too. It still runs in my blood. They say you never forget how to kill a man if you've done it once.'

He struck out at Gia again, lancing her shoulder.

'I'm sure it applies to women too.'

'Cut it out, Cyrus,' Gia complained, as he swung for her again.

'At some point, you're going to have to fight back.'

Grunting, he tried once more, forcing her to fling herself dramatically to one side to avoid his driving blade.

'Stop it,' she said.

'Let Decimus think you've fought for your life,' Cyrus said, moving towards her swiftly. 'He may take sympathy if the crowd calls for it.'

Gia staggered backwards, avoiding his advance.

'Let them murder us in cold blood but not by my hand,' she cried. 'No. Not by choice will I take your life.'

'There is a chance, however small, that you may live, and I am determined to give it to you,' said Cyrus. 'You said the goddesses were on your side, that they chose you to defend Rome. It's not too late. You can still do what you were destined to do.'

His words caused her to pause. He came at her again, more aggressively this time, his face twisting bitterly as he kept up pace, sweeping his weapon. He jabbed his sword at her, which she defended with hers.

'Stop!' she begged.

Their swords met again as they circled each other, sliding up and down with the ring of metal on metal.

'I need you to get angry, Gia. You should know the truth about me. I used you. I put your life on the line. I took advantage of you when your brother had just died. You could've died many times, and I would've gotten over it, just like I did with Atticus, and with Felix. If you die, it is because of me.'

They were both sweating already in the baking heat.

'I made my own choices,' she said.

'I'm the one who sent Fabius to break your wrist,' he said.

Gia faltered, shaking her head as her blood ran cold.

'I don't believe you.'

'Of course it was me. Who else would have motive to spare your life, but stop you from fighting? I thought you would figure it out. I can't believe you didn't. You had too much trust in me.'

'You're lying.' The words caught in her throat.

'I thought it was the only way,' he said. 'Believe me, Gia.'

Gia met his gaze.

'I didn't think you'd last a moment against Caturix. I needed a way to excuse you from the fight. I didn't count on you being so stubborn. When I first saw you at the amphitheatre, I thought Fabius had failed somehow. I didn't realize you were hurt until a few thrusts in and, by then, it was too late to intervene. I sent you into the arena with a broken wrist. It was only by your own merit that you survived.'

'Not mine. Claudia's.'

Cyrus's expression flickered.

'Oh yes, dear Claudia. Since I am about to die, I must speak my opinion.'

'I don't want to hear it,' she said.

'I never had you down for an idiot, far from it in fact, but the princess is making a fool of you, Gia,' he said. 'If you think you will live happily together in Rome, or that she will ever come close to ruling the empire, you must've taken a knock to the head in one of your matches.'

'It doesn't even matter,' she said, her voice thick and choked. 'He took her. I don't know where she is. She could be dead already.'

'It would be better if she was.'

'What did you say?' Gia murmured, setting her jaw.

'You heard me.'

'I need you to say it again.'

'I hope that bitch is dead.'

Gia's temper swept her up against her will, filling her body with energy. She thrust the sword towards Cyrus's neck, cutting the skin.

His dark eyes twinkled as he dabbed at the blood.

'That's more like it.'

With a loud 'Ugh!', Cyrus attacked, driving her back.

This time Gia fought against him, her heels driving into the dirt as she used her whole body's weight to keep him at bay.

'Everything you love, she will destroy,' he said.

'Shut up!'

'Let's say, by some miracle, that she does become empress. Do you think they will allow you to stand by her side? She will take a husband and you will be resigned to the servants' quarters. Your whole life will pass you by – watching, waiting, wanting something you can never truly have.'

Cyrus left himself open, but Gia didn't take the bait.

He set his face, closing his eyes a moment before he lunged forth and stabbed Gia in the shoulder.

She roared in pain and shock, watching the blade sliding out of her flesh, her blurry form reflected in the metal.

'Do you hate me yet?' he said. 'Or do I need to do it again?'

He struck out, as Gia ducked.

'Your turn,' he said. 'Come on. Hit me back.'

Gia winced as the pain crested, moving through her in waves.

'You could never make me hate you, Cyrus.'

'You're a disgrace to the school. I didn't train a coward.'

His words echoed across the amphitheatre as the audience watched.

'You wanted to prove that a woman can fight. So do it.'

'I already did,' she said. 'I don't have anything to prove.'

'You're wrong. You do. Everyone knows the only way to be the best is to kill the one who taught you.'

The sky above rolled, the sound of a thousand stones shaking. The whiplash crack of lighting briefly illuminated them.

'The gods are at war,' said Gia, pausing to look up at the darkening summer sky, gloomy despite the oppressive heat.

'They always were, and they always will be,' said Cyrus. 'It changes nothing.'

'I need you, Cyrus. I need your help.'

'You don't need me, and I cannot help you. I know in my heart that I am destined to die today. In the name of Fortuna, I revere it.'

Cyrus struck again, this time cutting her thigh.

'Fuck!' Gia cursed.

'FIGHT BACK,' he roared, beneath the sound of thunder.

Screaming in frustration, Gia took advantage of his exposed flesh and drove her sword into his upper arm.

'There. Are you happy now?' she sobbed.

Cyrus smiled through the pain.

'Again,' he said. His skin was dripping sweat. 'This time, in the chest.'

'Please,' she begged.

'Do it, Gia.'

'No,' said Gia, tears streaming from her eyes.

'If you cannot hate me, then you must love me enough to give me a good death. Do not let me be torn apart by whatever beasts they still have waiting in cages for us. Be a hero, and take my life like a man.'

'I am not a man.'

'No. You are better,' said Cyrus.

As Gia stuck out her sword, Cyrus changed position. He took her off-guard, performing a half-twirl and holding his sword to her throat.

'Nice move,' she said.

'Kick out at my bad leg, quick. The right one.'

This Gia did without question, obeying her tutor. He cried out gutturally, clutching his thigh, grabbing her leather skirt as he fell, so that he brought Gia down too. She straddled him, one foot on either side, with the tip of her weapon touching the skin on his chest between straps. He dropped his sword, writhing in pain – Gia wasn't sure if it was real or imagined.

'Kick it away,' he whispered.

Gia paused only briefly before complying.

'Damn. This hurts like a bastard. Now I really want you to finish me off,' he said, gritting his teeth. 'There's no way back now.'

She hesitated, tears stinging her eyes.

'You must kill me now, Gia, or you will also lose.'

Gia's hand shook, straining with the effort of keeping the sword in position.

'Everyone will lose,' he insisted.

'Maybe they already did,' she said, thinking of Vesuvius. 'Maybe it's already too late and your death will be for nothing.'

'It's never too late,' he said. 'You can still change fate. If you love Claudia, then you must go find her.'

'I thought you wanted her dead,' she said.

'I said what I had to say to make you angry, but it was also the truth. It *will* end in tears, but most love affairs do. Maybe that's the beauty of it. Or maybe I am just bitter. For here I am, old and alone. After all those lovers, I will still die on the ground.'

'You are not alone,' said Gia.

'We are all alone,' said Cyrus. 'We are born alone and die alone, and all that happens between is only a passing phase.'

He nodded, very slightly.

'Do it,' he said.

'Cyrus,' she begged, pleaded.

'I'm excited to see what the underworld is like after hearing so many stories. I do hope they have wine there. I am certain they do.'

Gia hesitated, swallowing down bile.

'Take this,' he said, ripping off his necklace and pressing it into her hand. It had a brass fish pendant hanging from it. 'May Neptune protect you, in my absence.'

Gia gazed at it, tucked it into the straps of the uniform for safekeeping, then leaned down to kiss his clammy forehead.

The audience whispered in interest.

'Now. Before it's too late.' He raised his hand to his forehead. 'Those who are about to die, salute you.'

Sobbing, aching, ravaged by a thousand fears and regrets, she held his gaze as she raised her sword again.

'Let your memory live eternal, Cyrus Jucundius,' said Gia. 'In strength. In honour. In victory. In love.'

She drove the blade straight through his heart, crying out in shared pain. The fearful look on Cyrus's face melted away, his dry lips curving, his eyes softening as the life drained out of him.

'I will see you again,' Gia said, her tears sprinkling his skin.

His shaking hand reached up, grasped at hers. She covered his fist with both of her own hands.

'I think ... I am becoming a god,' were his final words.

Pain coursed through her body – not the kind caused by a sword, but the stab of grief, of hurt, of soul-tearing agony.

Cyrus fell silent, and then still, as the arena erupted in applause. Shakily, Gia stood up, still sobbing and heaving.

What a show. What a spectacle. And people were entertained by it.

She retrieved the necklace and put it on, holding its pendant between her fingers and kissing it as the crowd roared. Dazed, she looked up to the imperial box as two men dragged away the limp body of her beloved mentor.

Decimus glared down at her coldly, whispering to his advisor: an imperial cultist in a hooded robe. Senator Cornelius was there too, though he didn't look happy. Hadn't Julia said he loathed Decimus? Yet here he was, standing at his side.

'Viatrix the Victorious is, once again, victorious!' cried the commentator, lifting Gia's arm and throwing it up in the air.

Yet there was nothing left to celebrate.

Decimus began a sardonic slow clap, his face twisted.

'Yes, yes, very good,' he said, projecting his voice so the audience fell quiet. 'Unfortunately, no win can spare you from justice.' He raised his arms. 'The gladiator will be sacrificed to Vulcan in celebration of the last Vulcanalia. Consider it a special festival treat from me, your new emperor.'

Gia was surrounded by praetorian guards, their swords stretched out to prevent her from fighting. Her own weapon gathered dirt on the ground, still covered in Cyrus's blood. One of the guards snatched it up.

A group of slaves carried in a pyre, with a stake in the middle. The guards dragged Gia towards it and tied her to it with thick rope.

They were going to burn her alive, a death so terrible she would've brought herself down on the sword like Caturix if only she still could.

The slaves brought in stacks of wood tied with twine, starting a dozen small fires that soon coagulated into one growing inferno that crackled and spat.

Some of the crowd watched in anticipation, but others fled, ushering their children out of the amphitheatre.

Once, Gia had thought it worse to die without ever knowing love. Now, all too late, she realized it was much better. She had tasted desire. She knew what it meant to be alive. And now it was over. The crushing bitterness of all that was being stolen from her stopped her from struggling too hard.

In her mind, Gia retraced Claudia's soft skin, her sea-glass eyes, her golden waterfalling hair ... She would be the last image on Gia's mind before all went dark.

All the world could burn but for her.

She was the empire.

She was the world.

A vibration, beneath Gia's feet. A distant rumble.

It built in strength, causing the pyre to partially collapse, the fire hopping, dancing, spreading across the dusty floor.

A gust of hot air tore through the amphitheatre, shaking every flag and banner. It was like putting her head in a furnace. Gia was a piece of meat, roasting on a skewer. Unable to free herself, she could only endure the great wave of pulsating heat until it subsided.

For a moment, no one stirred, too shaken to speak and with half the audience already fallen to their feet, but then a distant boom sounded, a double bang of the likes Gia had never heard before.

The noise was so loud that it was heard as a thud in Rome, over a hundred and twenty miles away.

21. A MONSTER OF A DIFFERENT NATURE

A plume of darkened smoke, flattened at the top like a tree, stretched up into the sky above the mountain.

'The gods have given us a sign!' crowed Decimus. 'Great Vulcan has blessed us. He is happy to welcome a new emperor!'

The growing plume blocked out the sun, causing the audience to whisper fervently. It darkened the amphitheatre, creating a palpable sense of impending doom.

Gia nervously watched the flames of the pyre creeping closer. She could hear shouts and screams outside the amphitheatre now.

'Vulcan is happy with our sacrifice,' said Decimus, though based on what the goddesses had told her, Gia highly doubted it. 'He has blessed the city of Pompeii on this day, as a reward for our reverence.'

Another violent rumble rattled the stadium.

'Vulcan's day is almost over. Now it is time for Jupiter to guide us. He has chosen me, above all others, to work his will on Earth. The king of the gods and the emperor of Rome, hand in hand, walking as equals. Together, we will remake the world. We will bring about a new era of conquest and fealty. Let Vulcanalia end with a bang, for tomorrow, the world is born again from the ashes of the old.'

The volcano roared again, like the low drone of an out-of-tune messenger horn, to exultant cries from the cultists.

Outside, a growing ruckus sounded, as a group of panicked people pushed into the amphitheatre, staggering and stumbling, crying out.

'The wave!' was all Gia heard.

She could hear rushing water too, like a river during a storm.

With an ear-splitting groan, the ocean inexplicably crested over the top of the building, spilling down the insides of the structure and turning the seating areas into vast waterfalls.

The great weight of the water created a deafening drone, which drowned out the sound of screaming.

Decimus and his party, including Berenice, were being hurried from the stands, him pushing and shoving his subjects out of the way. The spectators who hadn't already been washed away began fleeing the amphitheatre too, pouring out into the street in a crush.

The flames on the pyre snuffed out like candles, one by one, as the giant wave crashed down before her.

Water washed away the fire, submerging Gia completely.

Darkness. Infinite and ancient.

Plunged below the surface of the thick, briny ocean, Gia couldn't breathe, couldn't move, couldn't see. Cold water poured down her throat. She closed her mouth instinctively, but she needed air. She struggled to free herself, clutching desperately at the knots that held her in place, but they were tight and hard.

Gia felt her chest constricting, her body burning and aching as the water thrashed around her. Her lungs felt like they were about to pop. Any strength she had left was rapidly trickling away.

She was dying. She was ...

The water darkened as her consciousness faded.

Suddenly, she was awake again as her head popped out at the surface. Light burst through the blurry, salty slick that clouded her eyes. She gasped, coughing wetly, puking up seawater as she struggled against her bounds.

The wave peaked with a groan, residing quickly as the water was drawn back towards the bay, but the amphitheatre was still flooded with a pool of dirty water and she was still tied to the stake, unable to get away as the wave rolled over her again.

Gia filled her lungs just before she was submerged once more, holding her breath in terror as the world underwater fell dark and silent. Unknown debris bumped against her, but she couldn't avoid it. She could only squeeze her eyes tighter.

She counted, waiting for the wave to recede.

At the count of thirty, the water retreated. Gia squinted out at the amphitheatre, sodden and spluttering.

The necklace Cyrus had given her floated in front of her, its little fish pendant attempting to swim away.

With another heart-stopping jolt, she saw it. A column of fire and rock rose up to the heavens with a thundering roar.

Burning clumps of rock rained down, hissing as they fell into the water.

A large burning boulder plunged into the pool. The ocean rose up over Gia's head again, dragging her under. Beneath the surface, the water churned, getting warm as the arena began to warp and crack.

Gia worked busily at the ropes that held her in place. The water must have softened the knots, for at last they loosened and fell apart, drifting into the water.

Blessed Neptune.

Gia blinked, trying to peer through the dark greenish haze.

Fuck. She didn't know how to swim.

She frantically kicked her feet, cycling her arms, but this did nothing. She could not seem to rise.

Gia thought of the debris she sometimes saw carried by the ocean, floating on the surface as the water brought it to shore.

She would not die. Not yet, anyway.

She closed her eyes and ceased struggling, letting her body still like a corpse in the hope that she would float. Her chest was straining again, her limbs weakening for lack of air. Gia counted until her head broke through the surface. She felt herself bobbing up and down like a sitting gull.

She gasped, breathing in lungfuls as the giant pool in the centre of the amphitheatre tilted violently, swinging back and forth and making it hard for her to stay above water. The force of the water created a whirling, swirling motion that pulled her into its current, floating past the balconies where spectators once sat. The stands above her were almost empty now, while the floor of the amphitheatre was a seabed.

The summa rudis floated by with his staff still aloft, his face blank with shock. There was a terrible smell of sulphur in the air.

She floated like the rest of the scum that covered the surface of the water: dead animals, armour, hats, goblets.

When the right moment presented itself, Gia clutched at one of the hanging banners with Decimus's face embroidered on it and hauled herself onto a large piece of wood that had broken off from the imperial box.

Gia heard a terrible *crack*, a noise that seemed to reverberate from deep beneath her feet. The amphitheatre crumbled under the weight of the water, pillars toppling, arches collapsing.

The empire was falling with it.

When her makeshift raft floated close enough to one of the broken arches near the main entrance, Gia hurled herself off, climbing into the stands, over the benches and hanging on the side of the building.

She looked out over flooded Pompeii, the air thick with smoke as that terrible pillar of fire split the sky in two. Though much of the water had pooled into the bowl of the amphitheatre, the ground below was sodden, with people wading through waist-high water, dirtied with sewerage and littered with debris.

Gia dropped down with a yell and a splash, dragging herself up and moving as fast as she could.

She didn't need to tell people to evacuate now. People were pelting towards the bay with sacks on their backs, carrying their children and their livestock.

In the distance, Vesuvius blared, its beam of fire rising higher.

The sea of wet bodies became impossibly dense as it moved downhill towards the port, creating a crushing stampede in the slushy puddles left behind by the great wave. Someone kicked Gia in the ankle. An elbow ploughed into her side. Another tremor shook the earth. People were trampled as they fell to the ground, shouting and screeching, begging and praying.

Gia was engulfed by the swarm and dragged along the flooded road, soaked through and shivering. The crowd thickened still, clogging and pooling in every square, too many people trying to flee at once, trapping them all in the middle of it. She saw a child go underfoot, disappearing into the body of the mob, but, before she could do anything, they were gone and she was pushed on.

Time slowed. Everything felt hazy and numb. The part of her that thought and felt things was far away now.

The panicked crowd passed the apparently abandoned taberna. Impulsively, Gia ducked and forced her way out of the crowd, getting kicked in the stomach as she did, then slammed up against the wall, but she managed to push open the splintered taberna door, sliding in through a narrow gap and slamming it behind her. She pushed a large lectern up against it, afraid the mob would follow.

After disaster came disorder. It wouldn't be long before people were looting and killing each other.

Gia called out for her mother, the sound echoing. She could hear only her own feet, her own shaky breaths.

'Mother?'

The floors were wet, or dusted, or both. Rocks had piled in through the open windows. Vases had been smashed, coins scattered across the floor. Bread was still burning in the oven. Gia fished it out, tucking it into a small sack, along with any other provisions she could fish out of the mess.

Panting, she pushed on through the villa, listening to the faded screams of the people and the roaring of the volcano.

'Mother?'

No answer came.

Gia finally found her, buried under a pile of rocks in the atrium before the gravestones of her husband and sons.

'Mother!'

Gia scrambled through the pumice to free her, trying to shake her awake. When she drew her hand away, she saw blood.

'Mama?'

She turned her mother over, revealing the deep gash on her

head, her once-warm brown eyes now cold, staring at Gia without blinking. A little breath escaped Gia's lips, followed by a raw, strangled, animal sound.

Her mother was dead. The last of her family, gone.

Pomegranates. Nemoralia. Gossip and wine. A thousand memories washed over her at once, making it hard to scream.

The sky overhead groaned louder as her eyes caught on a bloodied piece of rock, with her mother's flesh still attached to it.

This was not the work of Decimus but of the gods. Of nature. A single rock. A single rock had fallen from the sky and taken her mother's life, and thousands more were about to pummel down on Pompeii.

Gia dragged her mother's body away from the open atrium, and howled, shaking her again and again.

'Why?' she begged.

A thunderous crashing shook the building, spraying her with fresh dust.

'Why did you let them die?' she screamed, delirious. 'You could've saved her. I couldn't save her. I couldn't save ...'

All the will and spirit drained out of her.

It didn't feel real. She prayed she would wake up at any moment to her mother fussing, but she was gone and the world was ending and there was nothing she could do about it, because the pantheon had abandoned them.

The sky turned black overhead.

Just as before, Gia swallowed down her pain like vomit and banished it from her mind. It was too late to save her mother, but she could still find Claudia. She could still save others, and herself.

Gia covered her mother with a sheet. She prayed for her spirit and left her with the lares and the shades, the household dead, hoping they would carry her to the underworld to reunite with the rest of the family.

She went to the door, pushing aside the lectern she'd used as a barricade. She paused only a moment to sob raggedly, bent over at the middle, before continuing on.

Outside, the world was on fire.

Swept up again in the crowd, Gia struggled to a stop in front of the House of Menander, which had been half demolished in the quake. She knew Claudia wouldn't be there. The villa was barely standing. Decimus would be keeping her close, as far away from here as he could get in the time since he'd fled the amphitheatre.

Gia believed he'd keep her alive long enough to punish her. From the stories Claudia had told her, he delighted in torturing her. Or maybe he'd try to use her as leverage somehow, persuade her to support him in exchange for her life. Gia feared that Claudia would rather die, more so if she thought Gia was also dead.

Decimus had fled, but to where?

Perhaps he would try to travel outside the city, to the Villa of the Mysteries or to Herculaneum. Or maybe he'd be sensible enough to head for the shore?

BOOM.

The earth shook again, as ringing and rattling filled the air. When it ceased, it was replaced by a terrible silence that gradually filled with roaring screams.

In the distance, Gia saw clouds approaching, racing across the sky towards her like a dark curtain.

Something struck her in the head, bouncing off her temple.

'Ow.'

Rubbing the sore spot, she reached down to pick it up. It wasn't a cup of piss this time, but a rock.

Another hit the ground in front of her, breaking apart into dust.

Gia realized the clouds were not clouds at all, but stone: a solid wall of stone was hurtling unstoppably through the air, pushed out in a ring by the force of Vesuvius.

Everything inside her told her to run, run, run, so she did.

Servants and slaves gathered on the balustrades of every building, watching as the rock curtain moved towards them, some of them calling out to unknown gods. It began to rain – a fine mist of hot sand that stuck to Gia's skin.

She skidded to a halt as a giant burning boulder hit the road in front of her, splitting the pavement as the ground opened up.

Gia tried to listen out for the whistling sound of falling rocks, ducking and diving in blind panic. Another hurtled towards her, forcing her forwards as screams tore through the growing darkness. It hit the poor man behind her instead, consuming him with falling fire.

In the chaos, Gia glimpsed several familiar faces: Lady Lando, buried by rocks. Her mother's employee, Nicodemus, his head covered in blood. The imperial doctor, Hippocrates, crushed by a fallen pillar.

He looked right at her, opening his mouth as if to call her name, but before she could help, another boulder landed on top of him.

Yelling incoherently, Gia fixed her eyes forwards. Don't think about it. Don't think about it. The screaming of the crowd increased, as did the frantic trampling as everyone attempted to climb over each other. The hot rain became a bombardment, darkening the sky further.

Dust in her eyes, Gia watched as hailstones the size of chariots rained down from above, crushing people and buildings between blinks.

She swerved, stumbling, winding around the rockpiles and fires, no longer sure of which direction she was facing.

One giant rock struck a red-tiled roof, causing a nearby villa to cave in. Another struck the pavement in the middle of the mob, creating a gaping crater.

Something inside Gia snapped.

She passed beyond panic, into a state of mind she'd never experienced before. She was no longer afraid or grieving or in pain. She was as cold and impassive as a god, walking through the burning streets unflinching.

The fleeing citizens were covered in dust, their hair whitened, their faces baked in clay-like masks. The roads were covered with ash. A group of pale, ghostly cats bounded along a wall. A donkey lay dying at the side of the road, unable to see for all the grit and dirt in its face.

On a lonely corner, two elders sat down hand in hand.

Gia managed to duck into a doorway, cutting through a stranger's empty villa to the rear yard. She climbed over a wall, keeping low as she tracked the dirt road that ran behind the row of properties.

Down in the harbour she saw ships being loaded, ready to flee across the sea. On the horizon, fishing boats sailed peacefully past the giant grain ships that came from Egypt, as yet unaware of the unfolding disaster in Pompeii – but closer to land, the waves were frothing and boiling, full of rocks.

Gia tried to identify the imperial ship, but the waters were heavy with traffic as the first refugees set out to sea, frantically trying to navigate the obstacles that still fell from the sky. More and more ships were drawing in, perhaps including the fleet sent by Pliny, though they could not reach the shore for all the pumice in the waters.

Yet a handful of them had already escaped the crush in the port. Not everyone would perish today.

It was a small comfort, in the predicament she was in, for Decimus would still destroy the world if she let him.

For a fleeting moment, Gia considered running to shore, swimming out to one of those ships and climbing aboard.

But Claudia wasn't here. Gia had sworn to protect her. She couldn't abandon her now. Maybe all was already lost, which was why the goddesses were so silent.

If destiny had chosen her, she would die trying.

If the world was ending, they would depart it together.

Gia turned back the way she had come, against the grain of the fleeing crowd, running not towards the harbour but away from it, back towards Pompeii.

A grey cloud materialized as another storm of soft, warm pumice battered the surface of the earth.

A terrible noise prompted her to look back over her shoulder.

One of the raining boulders tore through a ship, causing it to snap in half with an ear-splitting shriek. Another took on water, leaning dangerously to one side.

If the sea was no longer safe, the people were trapped.

Gia pushed on, away from the harbour as the remains of her life washed over her, both good and bad.

The delicious cooking smell of the taberna. Her mother's lifeless stare. Her father's tight embrace. Hiding in the dark from debtors. Cassius's melodic laugh. Atticus's fresh grave. Cyrus clinking goblets with her ... then begging her to kill him. Her mother linking her arm. Fabius dead on the floor. Berenice running up to her ...

Several memories clogged together.

Berenice, talking about her Roman man. Flavia, telling her about the villa where the wealthy Roman kept a harem.

Berenice standing at Decimus's side.

It all fell into place. Berenice and her mysterious wealthy Roman man who returned to Pompeii, the one who cried after sex and gifted her a necklace, the one who kept a villa just for brothel girls. The one who dumped her.

It was Decimus. It was fucking *Decimus*.

Hadn't Cyrus said he trailed him to a villa where he'd been entertaining women? Maybe that was where Decimus was hiding out now. If only Gia had asked where it was, but she wasn't thinking clearly at the time.

The bombardment of pumice thickened, falling harder and forcing Gia to shelter in a shrine to Minerva. Tremors pulled her to her knees. When she looked up to the statue, she saw the goddess blink, the marble of her face becoming fluid in motion as a creaking noise sounded all around her.

'Seek the Vesuvius Gate,' she said.

Minerva was Claudia's protector. Decimus's villa was near the Vesuvius Gate. Claudia had to be there, and it wasn't far.

'Decimus must die,' said the goddess. 'There is still time.'

'It's not too late?' said Gia.

'As long as she lives, there is still a chance. Heroes don't give up.

That is what makes them heroes. You must be the hero the world needs, Gia Valerii.'

The statue returned to stone as the ground continued to tremor.

Gia struggled uphill towards the north, through the swampy flooded streets, the raining rocks and sweltering heat, the terrifying rumble of the earth and the droning horn of the volcano blowing its top. She could barely see the red-black sky overhead as the air filled with ash. Every few moments, a figure emerged from the dusty gloom ahead, their whitened faces only briefly visible as they glided towards the Forum or the harbour, neither of them acknowledging the other. Body parts stuck out from the piles of rock, entombed in the places where they'd died. This was what Gia imagined the underworld would be like: dark and hot and horrifying and lonely.

She had to find that villa.

Pumice covered the ground like snowfall, coming up to her shins. It was as difficult to move through as water, slowing her down. The rock was light and full of holes, but there was so much of it that it threatened to suffocate the entire city, coating everything in sight with a grey, foamy substance.

Gia struggled on, until the stone reached her thighs.

Near the Vesuvius Gate, the streets emptied out, the rock forming thick drifts, but people had ploughed paths through the pumice. A handful of slaves pushed wheelbarrows full of rolled carpets and marble busts down the street. Disembodied footsteps reverberated in the distance, accompanied by frenzied shouts and the incessant calling of names.

The fleeing people seemed to be coming from all directions except one, a villa where many torches burned within.

Beneath the sounds of the volcanic blizzard, Gia could hear

music playing faintly. She raced across the courtyard and into the atrium of a lavish villa.

Like all the villas of the rich, it was decorated with murals of the most rampantly nude gods, its floors laid with mosaics. In one room, a quartet of musicians played a dire tune. Many rooms were piled with bags and boxes, as if the act of packing up the house had been started, then abandoned.

Gia followed the sound of voices onto the colonnade. It overlooked the water in the distance, where a dirty, swirling storm rolled in and the tides thrashed furiously.

Gia peered around a pillar, spying Decimus and his advisors standing at the balcony. In the large room behind them, a crowd of people had gathered, as if waiting for a celebration to begin, though their expressions were morbid.

The sky continued to groan and roar.

Gia glimpsed Berenice, her face sunken as she comforted another girl.

'We must set sail,' begged Senator Cornelius. 'They are saying the city will be buried in just a few hours.'

The memory of their confrontation flashed through Gia's mind. He was a ruddy man with a combover hairstyle, pompous and simpering, and, by the look on his face, he was rapidly regretting his life choices.

'Do you think the gods would kill such a man as me?' said Decimus, gazing off into the distance. He took a sip from a golden goblet. 'This is a warning to the people of Pompeii that they should obey my rule and fear my wrath.'

'But the scholars say—'

'Don't talk to me of scholars, of scientists, of readers of scrolls. They are mere mortals, blind to the desires of the pantheon.'

'I really must insist that we be allowed to evacuate.'

'Oh really? You insist, do you?'

'Just because you are emperor, doesn't mean you're not also an idiot,' said Cornelius, shaking his head. 'Ever since you were a child, you were an insidious little creature. I have known bad men. Damn, I *am* bad men, but you are a monster of an entirely different nature.'

'Perhaps you are correct, Senator,' mused Decimus.

He nodded at his guards, who picked up the protesting senator and threw him over the balcony without a shred of hesitation.

His screams died out, finished by a terrible *thud*.

'Jupiter has shown himself to me,' said Decimus coolly, to the remaining senators. Most were frozen in horror, though a couple of the men were rapt, attentive to his every word. 'He has instructed me. If you think he would let me perish while I am in possession of his power, you are as much mistaken as poor Cornelius here.'

He leaned over the balcony, giggling at the sight of the senator's smashed flesh against the rocks.

'What a mess a man makes when he dies,' he said.

A bolt of red lightning split the sky behind him, causing several of the senators to shrink back in fear.

'We will go ahead with our celebratory dinner in the triclinium. Jupiter wills it. Guards, fetch my dear sister. She has one last chance to swear loyalty to me.'

Gia's heart throbbed at the mention of Claudia.

Hidden behind a statue of Romulus and Remus, she held her position until the coast was clear.

Gia located the servants' quarters, rooting around in search of a disguise. The rooms here were empty, with any remaining staff waiting on Decimus and his guests. Most had already fled, leaving their belongings in disarray.

She found a plain sackcloth tunic and put it on over her still-damp gladiator uniform, covering her hair with a headscarf. As long as Decimus didn't look directly at her, he wouldn't recognize her.

She trailed the servants into the kitchen, where she attracted several curious glances. Gia pulled a knife into her robes, fixing it in place under the strap beneath her tunic as one servant watched her curiously.

'You should arm yourselves too, if you want to get out of here alive,' she said.

The servant copied, instructing her friend to do the same. The friend then commanded another woman in another language. The last recruit retrieved the knife she used to cut meat, holding one finger up to her lips.

'When I say now, we attack together,' said Gia.

The women did not question it.

22. A CORONA OF FIRE

The grand dining room had been painted pitch black, even the floor and the ceiling. A large, right-angled banquet table had been laid some time ago, its meats and fruits already rotting in the heat. In one corner, a senator had been slashed with a thousand small cuts, hung up by his wrists and left to bleed out. In another corner, a pond of dark water writhed with eels.

The centrepiece of the table was a small gold statue depicting Decimus as Jupiter, holding a lightning bolt in his hand. Gia presumed the imperial cult had commissioned it, based on the unlifelike sculpting of his physique that made him taller, firmer and more handsome than he really was.

Gia laid a tray of bread and olives on the table and retreated to the edge of the room, where servants and slaves lined up against the freshly painted walls. She was lucky the lighting was so dim and the sky so dark; the shadows helped to hide her face.

She watched as Claudia was brought in by guards, taking her seat at the table between a brothel girl and a cultist.

Her face and hair were mussed and dirtied, still wearing the same clothes she had been detained in. She appeared defeated yet unharmed, gazing expressionlessly at the empty seat that would have been occupied by Senator Cornelius.

Gia stared at her hard, willing her to look up, but she didn't.

Berenice was there too, her hands shaking as she poured a glass of water, spilling some, which she wiped up fearfully with her sleeve. Two of the other brothel girls held hands under the table, squeezing each other occasionally as rocks bounced off the roof with a terrible shuddering and thudding.

There were twenty-three seated guests at the absurdly long table, including Claudia, Berenice, brothel girls, senators and cultists, none of them appearing to be in the mood for a party. Dusty and dishevelled, they exchanged furtive looks in the silence. The exits were blocked by stone-faced praetorian guards, preventing anyone from leaving. The heat was deep and suffocating, causing the reluctant guests to sweat and fan themselves. They startled at every crunch and creak of the villa under assault.

Every revolt had a boiling point, when a tyrant's followers were most likely to turn their backs on him. Gia knew the moment could not be far away.

She waited for the new emperor to show himself. The large golden throne at the head of the table had been left empty for him.

One of the senators refused to be seated, standing before the guards.

'Please, I must go and find my wife,' he said.

'Who is more important? Your wife or the emperor?'

'What about my children?' he tried.

'Sit down, Senator,' snapped the bulky guard, his eyes wild, 'before he returns and sees you trying to leave.'

'Please, let us flee before it's too late.'

The senator's face was dripping with sweat.

'We have orders.'

'Forget your orders. Pompeii will be destroyed, and us with it!'

'Let them go,' demanded Claudia. 'If this is the last night of our lives, we should be with the people we love.' Her composed expression flickered, fear tugging at her features for a moment before she reassumed her stoic demeanour.

The guards crossed their weapons, blocking the exit.

'Emperor Decimus says none can leave,' said one.

'Is there nowhere you would rather be than here, doing the bidding of a man who would spare no sorrow for your demise?' asked Claudia, in a voice that was firm yet gentle. 'Where are your own families? They might be trapped or injured. All of us here will die, but those who leave now may still live.'

The guards didn't reply, staring out vacantly like carved pillars.

'Go, save yourselves,' she said, but it was too late.

At that moment, Decimus bustled in, wearing a gold-leaf crown and white silk toga with a purple cape, followed by the small orchestra Gia saw before.

Decimus took his seat, a lavish throne with golden-eagle wings sprouting from its back. He surveyed the guests with a cool stare, the corners of his mouth upturned with macabre excitement.

'Salute me,' he ordered.

One by one, the guests raised their hands. He looked to the servants, who copied – even Gia.

He pointed at the man who had begged to leave.

'Have Senator Quietus flayed and strung up, like the other.'

His guards dutifully obeyed, pulling the screaming man out of his chair and fixing him into the cuffs on the ceiling.

'Decimus, no,' said Claudia. 'Why must you be so cruel?'

'Because I can be,' Decimus said. 'You should try it sometime, sister. You're far too soft for a world like this.' He smiled. 'Most of the time, anyway.'

'What's that supposed to mean?' she said, scowling.

'It means you have secrets just like everyone else,' he said, 'and if you wish for me to keep them, you will hold your tongue or risk me cutting it out.'

Claudia bit down on her lip, eyes blazing. They were no longer the colour of sea-glass but of the raging volcanic seas outside.

When a giant hunk of rock hit the roof, everyone startled except for Decimus ... and Claudia. Claudia did not shrink at the noise of another bombardment. She did not tremble in anticipation of what Decimus would do next. Other than the erupting volcano, this was her normal, Gia realized. This was her world. This was the life she'd known all these years, living in fear of her brother.

'Please, tuck in,' said Decimus, gesturing at the feast.

The guests looked over the mound of sweaty, festering food as the crack of a whip echoed repetitively and Senator Quietus screamed. Several senators nervously piled small mounds of slop onto their plates before Decimus gave a cackling laugh, clapping his hands together in glee.

'I'm just jesting with you,' he said, as the men quickly dropped their plates. 'It seems Vulcan's fury has ravaged the delicious dinner I had prepared and let it rot. A shame, but it shall not stop our fun. It can feed the grateful peasants who flock here when the sky clears and the golden dawn begins.'

Gia again willed Claudia to look at her, but her gaze was fixed straight ahead.

'When I emerge unscathed from the wrath of the eruption, all will know that I'm endowed with the gifts of Jupiter,' Decimus said. 'That I am not just an emperor but a god. They will recognize me as destiny's chosen ruler. I alone shall change the course of history and be remembered as the greatest ruler of all time.'

'Yes, emperor,' murmured the robed cultists. 'It shall be so.'

'All hail Emperor Decimus!' someone shrilled tremulously.

'If I am now emperor, then I ought to be treated as one.'

Decimus signalled to Berenice, gesturing under the table.

Still shaking, she disappeared beneath it as Decimus rearranged his robes. Gia tried to block out the rhythmic grunting that followed.

She snuck another look at Claudia, who still hadn't sensed her presence. She was glaring at her brother with utmost hatred. Everyone else stared down at the table, afraid to look at each other.

Decimus panted through his nostrils, climaxing with a dull grunt before he righted his clothes. Berenice reappeared from beneath the table, her face coloured with shame as she took her seat again. Yet Decimus was oblivious to the simmering atmosphere in the room.

'Let the festivities begin with a sacrifice to Jupiter himself.'

'Not Vulcan?' said one of his advisors, in a small voice.

'I shall choose which gods we honour, and which we don't.'

'Apologies, my emperor. I spoke out of turn.'

'Perhaps I shall pass a law that only Jupiter can be worshipped across the empire,' mused Decimus.

This drew a soft gasp from one of the brothel girls.

'One god is a stronger symbol of authority than an entire pantheon. I've always found that there are far too many goddesses.' He looked to Claudia. 'The only thing they are useful for is creating more gods—'

There was another terrific *crash* as something large struck the roof again. Several guests squealed as the sound of falling rocks intensified.

Unbothered, Decimus drained his goblet. He clapped his hands at a group of slaves who huddled in the doorway. Two freed the prisoner hanging from the ceiling and dragged him across the room to stand before Decimus.

'You all know Publius here. My right hand, or so I thought. I caught him trying to run away,' said Decimus.

'My sister,' Publius rasped. 'She cannot walk. I must go to her.'

'How immoral must a man be to abandon his emperor in his time of need?' said Decimus. 'He must be punished for his disloyalty, but his life will not be in vain. He will die a most interesting death for our entertainment. I heard about a man who fed disobedient servants to the eels and I thought, what an enchanting idea. They are drawn to the smell of blood, and the more places for them to feed from, the better.' He held out his hand to one of the servants, who gave him a dagger.

'Please, forgive me, Emperor,' Publius begged in high pitch. 'I was weak. I will stay. I will never leave your side. Until death. Let me honour you again—'

He broke off with a cry as Decimus etched a deep cut in Publius's left cheek, before kissing the right.

'You know not the meaning of honour,' he said.

Publius made a gut-wrenching moaning noise as the slaves forced him to stand on the ridge of the eel pond. They attempted to shove him in the hole as he clung on to them, still begging for his life.

'Please, have mercy on him,' cried one of the senators.

'Decimus, stop this right now,' demanded Claudia.

'Silence,' boomed Decimus. 'You're ruining the moment.'

Publius ceased fighting, weeping instead.

'Perhaps you could play something a little more cheerful?' Decimus asked of the band. 'To really set the scene.'

The musicians launched into a lively tune utterly unsuited for the act of feeding a weeping man to the eels, as if any such piece of music existed. Decimus bobbed his head back and forth, drumming his fingers on the table as he wet his lips.

'Go ahead,' he said.

Poor Publius hung on for a few more moments, his screams filling the room before he slipped, plunging into the pool. Gia could hear him shrieking beneath the water as blood and bits of flesh began to rise on the surface. The slippery, knotted, snaky mass in the centre rose up to feed on the human scum, their biting mouths gaping open until there was nothing left but small floating bones.

Decimus was the only one who laughed. He turned to see the stricken faces of his guests just as one of the senators leaned out of his seat to retch on the floor, making an obtrusive splattering sound.

'Repulsive,' Decimus said, pulling a face.

'Skinning a man for the eels you're fine with, but a bit of vomit is disgusting to you?' said Claudia. 'You're pathetic.'

'It's rude. It sullies the nature of this fine party we're having. Not everyone gets to witness a human body consumed entirely by eels and their lives are much poorer for it, I assure you.'

'This isn't a party; it certainly isn't a *fine* party,' Claudia said, her voice wavering. 'The food is rotten, your guests are hostages, and the volcano on the horizon is about to erupt and bury us all beneath a sea of fire!'

'Oh, do cheer up, sister. You're being very ungrateful.'

'*Ungrateful?*'

'I could've killed you as soon as I learned about your treachery.'

'Then why didn't you?' Claudia asked. 'I'm curious. I know it can't be because you hold love for me in your heart.'

'There is still a part of me that remembers the adorable child you once were,' he said, 'but those days are long past. The only reason you're alive is because I consider it a fun pastime to tease you. It thrills me, to see you shiver and quiver.'

'You tormented me,' Claudia said, 'even when I was small.'

'You grew up fine, didn't you? Aside from your taste for poets from Lesbos.'

Claudia flushed.

'Do you think I don't know what you get up to with that gladiator friend of yours?' he said, in a playful voice.

Statuesque against the wall, Gia tried not to let fear show on her face.

'My spies saw you cavorting together like lovers in Herculaneum yesterday as her associates set out to murder me.'

The senators and brothel girls gawked at them, their eyes flitting from side to side as the siblings batted back and forth.

'You have it all wrong as usual, Decimus,' Claudia said. 'The gladiator and the others – Cyrus and the ludus students – they were not involved. I acted alone. You must free them so they can survive.'

'It's a little late for that, I'm afraid.' Decimus pulled a mocking, pouty face. 'We had ourselves a fine Decimalia.'

'What do you mean?'

'I'm sure you can figure it out, can't you? I arranged some gladiatorial games. Kill to win. Your lover was victorious . . .'

Gia watched hope catch on Claudia's shifting face, like when Pandora opened that box.

'I couldn't have that,' he finished.

'You killed her?' Claudia whispered. 'You killed Gia?'

'Did I not mention that?' said Decimus lightly. 'Oh, well. Better that she is gone, so you can't embarrass me further with your strange inclinations, sister.'

Gia fumed silently, but she could not reveal herself – not yet.

'She and father can club together to pay the ferryman of the Styx on their way to Tartarus,' he said.

'How?' Claudia demanded. 'How did she die?'

'I burned her at the stake, if you really wish to know. I didn't get to see the end of the show, regrettably, but if that didn't finish her off, she would've drowned when the great wave rose over the amphitheatre. It's been an eventful day. It's tragic that you didn't get to witness your beloved's final moments, but I'm sure you will keep her memory well ... in your perverse little fantasies.'

In a heartbeat, Claudia leaped to her feet, grabbed the gold statue of Decimus as Jupiter and smashed it into her brother's face.

'I will kill you myself!' she screamed, launching herself at him.

Guards pulled her off, prying the statue from her hands, but Decimus had an unsightly gash across the nose, skin sliced open by the decorative lightning rod.

Decimus surprised Gia by laughing, a genuine, hearty laugh.

'There's the real Claudia no one else gets to see,' he said. 'I know you, sister. You forget this. I know you better than anyone else in this room.'

'You know nothing but yourself.'

'They all think you're such a sweet, precious princess, but I know the truth. Shall we tell them what you did, Claudia?'

Claudia stared at her brother, chest heaving, saying nothing.

'All right, let's see what they think of this.' He smiled maniacally, looking around the dining room. 'You were the one who killed our father.'

Gia fixed her eyes on Claudia, watching her carefully.

The most terrible of silences fell between the siblings, though the world outside continued to rage and riot.

'Liar,' Claudia said, at last. She had recovered her temper, assuming a stonier, colder demeanour again.

'You must think me stupid,' he said, dabbing at his wound. 'You can't fool me like you fool everyone else, Claudia.'

'You were the one who sent an assassin after me, or did you forget?' she said.

Decimus didn't acknowledge this, smiling slowly.

'You were waiting for him to die. Admit it. You and I both knew he was sick, that Hippocrates said his heart was failing. You hated him as much as I did, so you quickened the process. I see right through you, sister. You did it for yourself, just as I would've done, but you have only benefited me.'

'You're wrong,' said Claudia, coldly holding his gaze.

'I know you snuck out undercover to buy black henbane from some slutty cult woman,' said Decimus. 'She told me herself, when I held a knife to her throat. Black henbane, to free the spirit of the dead.'

'It sounds as if you know far more about it than me,' said Claudia.

Gia's head swam, unable to keep up. What was it that Rectina said, about sending Claudia a papyrus on herbs?

No. She could not trust a word that left Decimus's lips. That was exactly what he was hoping to achieve.

'I don't judge you for it,' he said. 'Poisoning father might be the most interesting thing you've ever done. If only you would stop pretending to be so good, we could have a little fun.'

'Are you done?' Claudia sneered.

'You were the only one with him that night. You insisted on it, sending the servants away. The guards will swear it before the Senate.'

The guests exchanged suspicious glances.

'I know you gave it to him, sister. You are a pretender, a poisoner, no better than me,' said Decimus.

'I knew you would try to pin some made-up charge on me, but none of it shall matter unless we make it to a ship,' Claudia replied. 'At least let these people free, if not me. I don't care if I live or die any more.' She glared at him spitefully through narrowed eyes. 'Everything I have ever loved, you have already taken from me.'

Gia longed to run to her, to speak out in her defence, but she was just one warrior with one small knife. She couldn't kill all of them. She had to bide her time, and wait for the breaking point.

Decimus signalled for the slaves to free Senator Quietus. For a moment, the blood-soaked politician looked relieved, but then Decimus jerked his head towards the dark pond in the corner.

'Oh no. No, no, no.'

As Quietus stood on the edge of life and death, Claudia's arms were twisted behind her back by guards. She was forced to stand closer to the pool. Decimus approached her, looking her up and down and smiling, a sinister slit.

'You will watch this,' he said, squeezing her face with one hand. 'You will see this and remember your place.'

Nodding to his guards, Quietus was thrown into the pool. Like his name, he did not make a sound as he died.

Hear me now, Fortuna, Gia prayed silently.

When all the gods seemed to have abandoned the people, they turned to Fortuna. She was the last hope, the only one who could snatch victory from the jaws of defeat. Fortuna had turned for Gia, and against her.

If there was ever a time to intervene in my favour, it is now. I know you still have power. I know you are greater than Jupiter, or any of the gods.

'Are you ready to swear allegiance to me now, sister?' asked Decimus, as Quietus dissolved into a cloud of blood and flesh that gradually reduced to nothing. 'If you refuse to bow for me, I don't have much use for you.'

Claudia's expression hardened further.

'I would rather die,' she said.

'Then you have chosen your own destiny,' he said.

Please, Fortuna, prayed Gia. *Please hear me.*

'The only question that remains is how to do it. Should I slit your throat, throw you off a cliff or feed you to the eels? So many options.'

A roaring sound heralded, the ground shaking again as thick black smoke filled the sky. The landscape around them disappeared, leaving only a murky shroud that smelled like cinders. A soft *boom* resounded, shaking the tableware.

Looking out through the arches, Gia saw a corona of fire in the sky rising from the peak of Vesuvius. She didn't know if it was the rage of the gods or the intervention of the goddesses.

The fiery light illuminated the faces of the servants who she knew hid knives in their robes, their expressions hard, hungry for survival.

It was time.

Now or never, the moment to fight had arrived.

ACT V

DIANA

FORTUNA

MINERVA

VENUS

On the day of Vulcanalia, Minerva, Diana and Venus sat apart in the amphitheatre of the gods, watching as Jupiter and Vulcan battled. Shielded by their respective servants, followers and maidens, each dwelled on the failed assassination of Decimus. Diana mourned the impending death of the candidate she'd backed. Venus mourned the loss of a love with the potential to be great. Minerva mourned the future.

Half of her was present in the arena of the gods, spectating on the immortal games, but the other half of her was seated in the Pompeii amphitheatre, watching with growing horror as Gia and Cyrus entered the ring. Minerva applauded when expected, but her stony expression concealed the tempest of thoughts that filled her head.

Decimus would be emperor, despite their efforts. The power of Jupiter would protect him from harm. Claudia was imprisoned; Gia was set to die. They had failed to change the course of history. Not even having Fortuna on their side had assured them victory. They had betrayed the gods, and soon they would be punished for it. As things stood, the battle was lost.

Like most deities, Minerva had not always worked in the name of good. For some of her past misdeeds, she was wracked with guilt.

Yet she had been alive for millennia, and her views about the world and the nature of gods had changed many times over. She understood enough about her father to know that he was close to unmasking her, that he had pieced together the shattered fragments of the plot that had been concealed from him.

A bright flash tore through the ring, drawing Minerva's attention.

In one last act of vengeance, one last attempt to kill Decimus in revenge for the murder of Tiberius, Vulcan's fury caused Vesuvius to erupt on Earth, causing even the realm of the gods to shake.

With a thunderous roar, Vulcan broke apart into hunks of burning rock.

A shocked murmuring passed through the crowd of gathered gods, though Jupiter did not seem concerned.

'Vulcan has been defeated,' he boomed, growing ten times in size, his voice echoing. 'Let it be recorded in the annals of history that none shall stand against me.'

Subdued applause resounded.

'Untrue,' came a voice.

Jupiter turned to see Neptune, god of the seas.

'Not all of us are loyal to you alone.'

He raised a trident to match the lightning staff held by Jupiter.

'My own brother would move against me?' said Jupiter.

The divine crowd gasped and murmured among themselves. Even Minerva was shaken. Fortuna had not predicted this. They were in uncharted territory now.

The goddesses made eyes at each other across the arena. Perhaps all was not yet lost. The thread of fate was still spinning.

'Who else can stand up to you? Decimus cannot rule. I will not allow it.'

'You know not what you say, brother.'

'The boy is a menace, just like you.'

'Be careful now. Do not make a terrible mistake,' warned Jupiter.

'Vulcan was one of us, and you destroyed him. It wasn't enough for you to proclaim yourself king of the gods. You could not let anyone else possess power. You wanted it all for yourself. This is no longer a pantheon, but a dictatorship.'

Jupiter seemed to be steaming, his staff crackling.

'Weak! You were always the weakest of us,' he roared. 'Who else was strong and wise enough to lead but me? Certainly not you, and certainly not Pluto, who chooses to live among the dead.'

Pluto looked back and forth as if to say, 'Who, me?'

'Then let us fight,' said Neptune, 'and we will see which of us is the strongest. We will prove it, once and for all.'

As the two gods exploded into battle, water erupted from the prongs of Neptune's trident. A great wave flooded through the arena and trickled down to Earth in a giant waterfall, where it doused the burning amphitheatre in Pompeii, freeing the gladiator from her binds.

Minerva released a breath. Venus clasped her hands to her chest. Diana curled her right hand into a small victory fist.

The prophecy was in ruins, the future uncertain, but, for now, the warrior and the princess lived.

23. MAKING HISTORY

It was almost midnight on the last night of Pompeii.

Fire formed the shape of a sickle as it fell from the mountain's peak, shining bright through the darkness. It lit up the sky as streaks of flame glided down the hillside, thick and fluid, leaving a patchwork of blazes behind them, razing the landscape to cinders.

As the fire swept closer to the city walls, the air filled with the acrid stench of sulphur, causing them all to cough and choke, spitting and spluttering. The guests staggered to the colonnade in panic, watching the eruption across the Bay of Naples, their hysterical screams like a terrible symphony.

Red lightning flashed through the darkness.

'Surely you see we must leave now,' begged Claudia. 'Not even you can be so stupid as to ignore such a warning.'

Decimus chuckled, amused by the fearful faces before him.

'Oh, no one is leaving! This is better than I could've hoped for. What greater way to welcome a new emperor than with an act of the gods. Some men may dream of reigning peacefully, ruling over an era of stability and peace. Not me. No, I wish to be moved. I wish to be entertained. I wish to ... make history.'

Gia caught the eye of the servants, sliding her own knife into her palm.

'Now,' she said.

As Vesuvius boomed once more, Gia swung her arm, throwing the small knife across the room.

It grazed the side of Decimus's face. He recoiled, crying out.

At the same time, the servants began stabbing guards in a bloody frenzy, pushing their way out of the room. Some of the guests climbed out of the colonnade in their eagerness to escape, taking their chances on the steep, burning cliffs.

Gia swiped another knife from the table as one of the praetorians came at her. Her blade was small but she knew the right spot to target: between the bottom of his helmet and the top of his breastplate. Jamming the dagger into his throat, she used his body to defend against the other guard, swiping the dead man's sword as an upgrade. She thrust it into the thin chainmail that covered the second man's stomach.

Both guards dropped to the floor in unison.

Decimus whirled around, clutching at his bleeding face.

'Who did it?' he raged. 'Which one of you tried to kill me?'

Gia pulled off her headscarf to reveal herself, giving the emperor a little bow.

'Gia?' Claudia exclaimed, struggling against the remaining guards.

Gia paused to take in the beauty of her face from afar, waves of love and desire coursing through her body. Claudia's expression was reverent, as if witnessing an ecclesiastical event.

'He told me you were burned at the stake then drowned,' she gasped.

'I was,' Gia said casually, before lunging furiously at Decimus.

'Look who's not dead,' she said.

'Pests are so hard to kill,' he said.

'Tell me about it.'

The two guards holding Claudia released her to defend the emperor, their swords crossing above her head as Gia ducked. With a well-timed kick in the back, one man toppled over the balcony, sliding down the smoky folds of the hill and leaving his weapon behind. The other man was shaken enough to pause, giving Gia the opportunity to skewer him against a wall. The sword sliced through the metal of his armour like a pin through linen.

The room emptied, as those who survived fled for their lives.

All except Decimus, Claudia, Gia ... and Berenice. She was hiding under the table, too scared to come out.

Gia met eyes with her, exchanging a look of horror.

'Very good, gladiator, very good,' said Decimus, as Claudia moved to stand beside her, clutching her hand tight. 'Perhaps I didn't give you enough credit. I did say I wished to be entertained and you are funny, I'll give you that. I tell you what. I'm feeling generous, this being the day of my own festival. I will let you leave alive, on the condition that you never return.'

'I'm not going anywhere.'

'Why are you here? For my sister? She isn't worth it,' spat Decimus.

'She is worth a hundred thousand of you,' Gia returned.

'She doesn't care about you, gladiator. She doesn't care about anything.'

'That's not true,' said Claudia.

'It's over, Decimus. We're here to fulfil the prophecy,' said Gia.

'What prophecy?'

'Didn't you hear? You're going to die tonight.'

A bone rocking *boom* shook the villa while plumes of fire filled the sky.

Berenice emerged from beneath the table and tried to run, but Decimus saw her. He grabbed her by the hair and raised his dagger to her neck, holding her in front of him as a shield as she begged him to free her.

'Let her go,' demanded Gia.

'Oh, that's right. She's your friend, isn't she?' he said as Berenice whimpered.

'Let her go, or I'll make you regret ever breathing her way.'

'She's been very helpful to me,' said Decimus. 'Not very loyal to you, though.'

Gia's eyes flicked to Berenice and back. 'What do you mean?'

'Why do you think she tried out for your ridiculous gladiator school? I had her spy on you,' said Decimus. 'She was the one who overheard your assassination plot. She brought the information straight to me, of course. She was so loyal, like a dog. If I'd asked her to jump off a cliff, she would've done it.'

Gia and Berenice locked eyes as her friend's face collapsed in on itself.

'I would,' said Berenice, nodding in terror. 'Anything for you, my emperor.'

Gia wasn't angry; she knew Berenice was as much a victim as anyone with her bruised face and her sunken sockets, her shaking hands and bare, bloodied feet. But it would be difficult to kill Decimus when he had a knife to Berenice's throat.

'Decimus, please,' begged Berenice. 'What about the baby?'

'Baby?' Gia echoed in horror. She didn't want to believe it, but if Berenice was bluffing, she was braver than any gladiator.

'What fucking baby?' said Decimus.

'I prayed for it,' said Berenice. 'I prayed to Venus. She made me fertile, and your seed is strong, master.'

Wide-eyed, her face open in innocence, Berenice raised a hand to caress Decimus's cheek, even as his knife dug into her neck.

'We could be a family, a proper family, just like you said you wanted. You need an heir, and I can give one to you. I think ... I think he's a boy.'

Decimus stared at her a moment. His face softened. His lips curled in a smile. Berenice smiled too, in relief. Then the emperor began to laugh.

Gia watched fear clouding Berenice's expression as Decimus rocked back and forth in amusement.

'Do you ... do you really think the emperor of Rome would have some whore's baby?' he managed, at last.

'Please,' was Berenice's last word.

He slit her throat with a flourish, her blood splattering dramatically. As Berenice slumped to the ground, rivers of fire began to race towards them down the hillside, branching into little streams and tributaries.

Just like her blood on the floor.

'You didn't have to kill her,' Gia snarled at Decimus.

'Boo. But I wanted to.'

'That is precisely why you cannot rule, why you *will not* rule,' said Claudia, shaking with rage. 'Soon you will be dead, dear brother, and another, far better, ruler will lead Rome while you toil with the shades in Tartarus where you belong.'

'Who? Go on. Entertain me,' said Decimus.

'Me,' she said.

He looked to his sister and made a disbelieving noise. 'You?'

'Yes, brother,' said Claudia. 'While you were busy drinking and smoking and swinging your dick, I was learning about statesmanship. I have been convening with senators and meeting with foreign diplomats. I have been educating myself on the matters which hold an empire together, while you have been lavishing attention on yourself. You crave power to tyrannize, but I crave power to better the world. That is the difference between us; one of many. That is why the goddesses have chosen me as your successor. I will not let you return to Rome alive.'

'You won't *let* me?'

'You heard her,' said Gia.

'How are you planning to stop me? Oh, I really must be having a nightmare if any of this is to be believed.'

Another large hunk of rock slammed against the roof, causing all of the tiles to fall and shatter on the ground.

In the brief moment when Gia was distracted, Decimus threw himself upon her, knocking her to the ground. He stomped on her bad wrist, causing her to cry out and drop her weapon.

'Not so tough now, huh?'

Decimus kicked the sword away. It slid across the tiled floor and off the balcony, tumbling down the hillside.

'You really thought you had me beat.'

He pulled out his dagger, but before he could bring it down Claudia swung a candelabra against his head.

Decimus barely flinched, calmly wiping the hot wax from his face.

The air around them was steaming. The heat was increasing, both of them reddened and wet with sweat as Gia lurched to her feet, dodging the blade that swiped through the air towards her.

'This is your last fight, gladiator.'

Decimus no longer seemed human. Wild-eyed and snarling, there was a carnality about him, free of pity, free of mercy, free of humanity.

The villa pounded and shook, until her vision blurred. Time slowed as the room around them darkened.

'Today, you will lose for the last time.'

The scene pulsed and burned bright, filling Gia's eyes with golden light.

24. THE AMPHITHEATRE OF THE GODS

Gia awoke in the labyrinth she'd traversed on Nemoralia.

She was unharmed and unarmed, but her head was slow and heavy, pounding like those rocks on the roof.

How had she arrived here? The last thing she remembered was Decimus trying to kill her, a flash of gold light—

Bile rose in her throat as her hands flew out, searching for any sign of Claudia. But she was alone.

Panicked, Gia scrambled up and began to run, her sandals slapping and splashing through shallow puddles as she called out, her unanswered cries echoing through the twisting, curling paths of the vast stone maze, its walls painted with familiar mystical scenes.

Gia passed through a crumbling arch and suddenly she was standing before what she knew to be the gates of the underworld, stretched open like two black wings of a bird. She could see all the shadowy fields and meadows of pale flowers beyond it too. They were terrible and beautiful and she wanted to pluck them, even though she knew instinctively that if she touched them, she would never be able to leave this place.

Beyond, all of the trees were bare, with dark curls of smoke coming off them, and when the wind blew, the sky groaned as if it were also dying slowly. On the horizon, a thousand fires burned.

The path before her was crowded by people with no shoes on, following a winding path into Tartarus in pilgrimage, as black-winged beings swooped down from the sky, snatching up bodies like owls catching mice.

In the distance, to the east, Gia could see the glowing towers on the isle of the Fortunate across a dark sea. Here lived the souls of the honourable dead: all the good kings and heroes of history, socializing with the gods themselves.

Gia turned and found herself in a chamber of a colossal stone amphitheatre with rows of curved seating, thirty times as large as the one in Pompeii, though it was enclosed by a dome like the Pantheon of Rome.

A tremendous cheering, clapping, stamping noise filled the titanic arena, reminding her of the start of a gladiatorial match.

The stadium was crowded with otherworldly beings wearing starry crowns and robes that floated around them like silk on water. They were glowing, glittering divinities, and yet their beautiful faces were twisted in bloodlust as they watched two figures fighting in the centre ring.

One was Jupiter himself, bearded and muscular, engaged in battle with Neptune, the sea god. Gia recognized them from their statues, though they were much bigger and less human than she'd imagined, their features strangely angular and sculpted, their eyes without pupils. Armoured and crowned, each carried a weapon, though Jupiter's cast lightning bolts and Neptune's spewed ice and steam.

Light and heat streamed in arcs around them as they danced, floating between strikes like leaves in the breeze.

Gia recognized some of the lesser deities from myths and legends: the two-faced god of doors, Janus; the cloven-footed god of farms and fields, Faunus; the eternally teenaged Juventas. Even Hercules was present.

They didn't seem to notice Gia standing there. They were all transfixed on the fight. Some of them looked afraid, while others roared in delight.

Jupiter struck the final blow, causing the universe itself to tremble.

With a reality-shattering groan, lightning pulsed through the body of Neptune, who broke apart into a million fish and corals.

Jupiter's booming voice rang out as he turned to address the pantheon of deities.

'To those among you who have worked against me: your rebellion has failed. Now, divine justice must be done.'

The amphitheatre dimmed, illuminated only by the starry crowns of the gathered gods.

'Decimus is destined to rule the world. It has been written in the stars. Yet some of you saw fit to intervene,' said Jupiter. 'Some of you think yourselves greater than fate. You have meddled with destiny. For this, there must be a price.'

The amphitheatre silenced in fear and awe.

'Next, I call to the ring ... Minerva.'

Her name echoed through the crowd.

A great chorus of cries and whispers rang out.

Minerva emerged from the audience of gods, disappearing momentarily before reappearing in front of him. She wore her feathered helmet, her face solemn.

'Minerva, you are the goddess of wisdom, yet your actions

have shown none,' said Jupiter. 'You have broken the laws of our immortal games and brought the pantheon of the gods into disrepute. What have you to say for yourself?'

'Decimus is no leader,' said Minerva.

'That is not for you to decide.'

'You are ancient, father. You no longer understand the ways of humans. Mortal civilization is not a game. The only disrepute is the cruelty of the old gods.'

'You dare to challenge me?' roared Jupiter.

'You summoned me here to fight, and fight I must.'

'Then let me show you how small and insignificant you are compared to the king of the gods.'

With a terrifying clamour, Jupiter and Minerva began to spar, with Minerva fending off the bright bolts her father threw at her. A helmeted battle owl swooped down from the ceiling, clawing at Jupiter's face as his lightning singed the feathers on Minerva's helmet, before an eagle flew in to tussle with it.

Gia felt a comforting hand at her shoulder. Looking up, she saw Diana – not a statue this time but a shining, star-crowned deity, with a bow and arrows at her back.

A small speckled deer nudged Gia's hand with its snout.

'Come, maiden,' said Diana.

Maiden?

'I need to see what happens,' said Gia, gesturing at the fight.

'We won't know the outcome for some time yet.'

'How much time?'

'They are gods,' said Diana, ushering her out of the amphitheatre. 'They can fight for millennia. Let us hope it does not take that long.'

Gia shuddered, thinking about how hard it was to keep fighting for an hour.

'Why am I in the Villa of the Labyrinth?' Gia asked.

'You are not,' said Diana.

'Then, where am I?'

'You are nowhere, and everywhere. Your mind is architecting scenery for you; a stage set upon which our communications can take place.'

Diana's grove assembled around them, blooming into being like flowers. It felt so real. Gia could smell the perfume of the pines and hear the trickle of running water. She could feel the hazy sun beating down on her.

'Mortals cannot look upon the divine in their true forms, so we wrap ourselves with the shrouds of your consciousness instead. That way, your tiny human brains can make sense of our existence.'

'Tiny, huh?' Gia said.

'If it helps, us deities aren't too smart either,' Diana said. 'Some think we should've given up on humanity long ago.'

'Do you agree?'

Diana looked at her and smiled. 'Not I. I have a secret soft spot for their mortal foibles.'

Gia followed Diana through an archway, into a white-walled courtyard. The skies overhead were cloudy and brilliantly blue.

'In here,' said Diana.

In a chamber within, the goddess Venus waited, wearing a crown of flowers, along with a hooded, white-eyed woman Gia identified as Fortuna by the spinning orb in her hand.

On the wall behind them, an enormous golden wheel revolved

slowly, its shining spokes separating animated scenes, like living tapestries.

'It is your time to fight, gladiator,' said Fortuna.

'I'm still alive?' Gia said.

'Vividly so,' said Venus, circling her curiously.

'The wheel is spinning, the pantheon is at war,' said Fortuna. 'A new future will soon be decided. We will equip you for the final battle, but I cannot sway fate in your favour this time.'

As Fortuna spoke, Venus gently stroked Gia's arm, causing the pain to fade away. Gia flexed her fingers, awed.

Diana dressed her in otherworldly armour – silvery and slightly translucent at first, but, as it moulded to Gia's body, it turned to burnished gold.

A shining sword materialized in her grip. It had a round golden globe for a hilt, like the one Fortuna spun in her hand.

'You must return to fight for the life of the empress, but you were not just chosen for your combat skills, Gia Valerii,' said Fortuna. 'You were also chosen for your fortitude and tenacity, for your bravery and valour. Not every fight will be in the ring. Some wars are fought in the heart. Your virtues will aid you now, in the final hours.'

'We will keep the wicked gods at bay,' said Venus, kissing her on both cheeks. 'But you must do the rest, handsome girl.'

'If Minerva is successful, you must still reach Rome for the prophecy to be fulfilled,' said Fortuna. 'You must not fail.'

'And if she loses?' asked Gia.

'She will not lose,' said Venus.

'Go forth, Gia, and be victorious like Viatrix,' said Diana, raising a salute.

'I believe in you,' said Venus gently, though it was normally mortals who believed in deities.

The three figures drifted away, towards the horizon. At the same time, Gia felt herself floating back past the pantheon where Minerva was on the brink of defeat, but she kept falling, faster and faster, until all the world was a blur.

The vision bled, pooling to reform the image of Decimus, looming large before the reddening sky. Claudia stood behind him, illuminated by the fire's light.

The black-painted dining room trembled, but Gia's hand was steady as she held out her sword and parted her feet, assuming a fighting position.

When Decimus blinked at Gia in confusion, she realized she was still dressed in the goddess's divine armour, and holding the sword with a globe-shaped hilt.

'How—' Decimus began.

The volcano blared like a horn, announcing the fight.

'You're not the only one who has the favour of the pantheon,' Gia said.

Claudia watched on with wide, glittering eyes.

'The goddesses have foreseen your reign of terror,' said Gia. 'They know the empire will crumble to dust in your hands.'

'They told you that, did they?' snarled Decimus, picking up the sword of a fallen guard and holding it out. 'Do you expect me to believe that the goddesses would commune with a worthless peasant like you?'

'"*Worthless peasant*". Fine words from the ruler of the people. You think we're less than you. Less powerful, less cunning, less ruthless. But you're wrong. The people are more terrifying than you will ever be.'

'You are nothing,' he spat, 'and I am the world.'

'I was chosen. How else do you think I survived both the fire and the water?'

Decimus's confident veneer momentarily faltered.

'The goddesses want me to win – for Claudia, for Rome, for the empire ... for the future of civilization, lest another millennium of fools rule over us in your image.'

'There isn't a man alive who can kill me,' he said.

'Then it is a good job I am not a man,' said Gia, advancing.

Another storm of pumice battered the building, causing a rhythm that reminded Gia of beating drums in the arena. Smaller stones rained down too, mimicking the sound of applause.

'Are you sure the gods are still on your side?' she said.

Lightning flashed again on the horizon, and Decimus paused to behold the violent sky show. When he was distracted, Gia quickly struck out with the sword, slashing him across his cheek as he had done to Publius.

He hissed at her like a snake and drove out his sword. It hit the goddess-made armour, bouncing off harmlessly.

'Try again.' Gia smirked.

As the villa creaked and tilted, they burst into combat. Decimus was more agile than Gia expected, dancing around the blade of her sword. He moved fast and she struggled to keep track of him, blocking his frenzied blows.

'You call yourself a fighter?' he goaded.

'I'm just warming up.'

'You are wasting your time,' he said. 'You can't stop me. No one can.'

'Kicking the shit out of men like you is never a waste of time,' said Gia, delivering a hit to his shoulder.

Gia slashed at his arms, at his chest, at his legs, but none of these wounds seemed to pain him. It was as if he felt nothing at all.

'See?' he said. 'You can't wound me.'

Gia tried again, but her strikes were ineffective.

'I AM A GOD!' he roared.

He lunged at her with a terrifying strength. Gia was overpowered, pinned against the painted wall.

His face was contorted into a monstrous mask.

With one hand, he clamped her broken wrist, forcing her to drop the sword. With the other, he held his own sword to her neck.

Her weapon fell between her legs, propped upright by the wall behind her, its hilt only inches from her good left hand.

Decimus had always had strangely flat eyes, but now they seemed to darken, his pupils shrinking to pinpoints as his face twisted into inhuman hatred. His hand tightened around her neck and she strained to grasp the sword, just out of reach.

Claudia took another run at him, this time armed with a bust of their father, but he flung out an arm that sent her driving into the table with a clatter.

It was unnatural, as if Jupiter himself had possessed him.

'No woman will ever rule Rome,' he said, in a voice that shook the ground, 'and no man nor god shall ever be greater than me.'

His eyes gleamed red, reflecting the volcano's fire.

The fingers of Gia's left hand stretched out, blindly groping down the wall at her back until she felt them brush the hilt of the sword.

'Nice speech, shame about the ending,' she said.

'What ending?' he said.

'This one,' she cried.

With a ferocious roar, Gia brought her sword up, left-handed, underneath his chin to slice through flesh.

But there the sword stopped, as though it had met impenetrable metal.

'Huh ...'

She watched in horror as the sword of the goddesses shattered like glass, breaking into a million useless tiny pieces that scattered on the ground.

Decimus smiled, his lifeless eyes boring into her.

'Gods never lose,' he said, as the villa creaked and tilted.

Held in place by his suddenly superhuman strength, Gia could only watch as he raised his weapon. She took a deep breath, anticipating a sudden and painful death. Decimus brought the blade down in one swift movement, and then ... he stopped.

Gia held still. Decimus continued to stare at her, his arm frozen in position a mere hair from her chest.

The weapon slipped out of his hand.

His fingers clawed uselessly at Gia as his eyes popped.

Gia saw the tip of a blade, bursting through his chest. A rose of blood stained the front of his white toga.

Claudia.

Gasping, the princess withdrew the sword, hesitating a moment before she drove it through him again, and again, crying out each time she stabbed him in the back, until she was sobbing and he was lifeless, his weight slumped on top of Gia.

She shoved him off, watching as a bubble of blood burst between his lips.

His body thudded to the ground.

Gia gently prised the weapon from Claudia's hands and embraced her as she shook and sobbed.

The emperor was dead, but no bells tolled this time. It was the end of the world and there was no one to mourn him.

'I killed him,' murmured Claudia.

'He deserved it.'

'I have his blood on my hands ... literally.'

'Don't think about it.'

Claudia wiped her palms on her robes.

Another *bang* threw them off their feet. The villa shook, columns collapsing and walls crumbling as the foundations gave way.

'Gia,' Claudia breathed, her eyes on fire. 'I didn't know if I would ever get to touch you again.'

Gia embraced her, tasting the ash that clung to her eyelashes and lips.

'I will never let you out of my sight' said Claudia.

'We must go to Rome,' said Gia. 'We must leave now, so you can be empress.'

'Wait,' said Claudia, staring at her brother's body. 'I need some proof that Decimus is dead.'

Claudia kneeled down over his corpse, removing the golden crown of leaves. She gazed at him, her face oddly serene, then closed his eyelids before climbing to her feet.

Framed by the reddish skies, splattered in blood, Claudia looked as if she'd just crawled out of Tartarus herself.

She placed the crown on her head, and the earth shook again.

25. A MERCIFUL DEATH

Gia and Claudia had barely stepped out of the villa when the roof sagged and fell in, throwing up another cloud of dust and burying the bodies inside, including that of former emperor, Decimus.

Gia staggered backwards, shielding Claudia behind her.

Outside, the garden had set alight, flames forming connecting strings of fire like daisy chains.

They fled through the broken building and out into the scorching heat, staring in horror at the apocalyptic scene that awaited them; this wasteland of burning ash Gia once called home.

Pompeii.

Her heart ached.

'Where are your family?' Claudia asked.

'I have no family,' said Gia, her eyes stinging. 'Cyrus, my mother, the ludus boys – all dead.'

'Gia, I'm so sorry,' said Claudia, reaching for her hand.

'I cannot think about them now,' she said. 'I am afraid I will fall down and never get up.'

'I will keep you upright,' said Claudia, supporting her weight as Gia's knees sagged, swimming through the shin-high stone.

As they made their way through the streets, past the Vesuvius Gate and the equestrian monument, the noise was roaring and tremulous. The howling winds whirled around them, hot as burning sand and spreading the flames of a hundred fires. The air was a peculiar brown colour – fizzing, grainy and stinking of sulphur.

Every building in sight was collapsing, shedding tiles as the stone creaked and groaned. Everything was covered in fluffy pumice and dust, dulling the shapes of things and making the city unrecognizable.

They watched as a ball of lightning moved through the darkness, toppling a column. The Forum was in ruins, the statues fallen, the temples crushed.

It was only by the grace of the goddesses that they had lived this long, for Pompeii had been levelled and submerged in six feet of stone, yet there were other survivors of good fortune too, emerging from the sewers and the cellars of houses, caked in dirt and blinking through the gloom, holding all they could carry.

Gia and Claudia scrambled down towards the harbour where the seas were still smoky and frothing. The wrecks of a dozen boats bashed together, some sunken so that only a single mast could be seen.

'There is an imperial ship hidden in a secluded bay, waiting to bring Decimus back to Rome. Follow me,' said Claudia.

Panting, weak with shock, they picked their way along a barely visible path down to the bay to find – nothing but the violent sea.

Claudia stared at the empty ocean before falling to her knees, letting out a ragged scream of fury.

Gia waited a moment for her to calm, then sat down beside her.

'How could they just ... leave?' Claudia howled. 'They can't have known Decimus is dead yet.'

'Maybe they just assumed as much. What now?'

They could not fly to Rome, not unless the goddesses produced a chariot driven by Pegasi, and they could not sail without a boat.

'If Rectina wrote to Pliny as she promised, there should be a fleet of ships approaching to rescue people,' said Claudia. 'Perhaps they were unable to reach Pompeii. Maybe they are waiting in Herculaneum.'

'Then we must travel there,' said Gia, helping Claudia to her feet. 'We have no other choice.'

The sky was darkening again. They paused for a brief kiss, clutching hands harder than was necessary, but the desperation of the situation made even love seem bleak. Exhausted, they headed back the way they had come.

Gia's throat was sore and scratchy. It was hard to draw a full breath. Claudia coughed on and off, choking on the acrid dust. They pulled their robes up over their mouths, trying to keep the fumes out as they scrambled down towards the sea, hoping to follow the trail of the coast.

The great lake of pumice stones carried them downhill in little landslides as the volcano gave another low, trembling drone, causing all of the stones to shiver.

'It's not over,' said Claudia.

Something warm and wet grazed Gia's head. She glanced up as the skies opened, expecting a swell of rain but met instead with falling rocks, small at first but rapidly growing larger, the air filling with their percussion.

'We must get under cover,' Claudia shouted over the noise of the storm, but they were horribly exposed.

One of the rocks struck Gia in the head, causing her ears to ring.

The stones were harder, heavier now. The volcanic bombardment was intensifying.

'Run!' she said, throwing her arms up over her head.

They pelted downhill through the scramble of stone.

Gia sighted a small cave and flung them into it. They huddled together in the trembling, smoke-scented darkness, shaken by every tremor that threatened to collapse the hollow they were sheltered in.

Pumice began pouring into the hole of the cave, a wave of stones that rose higher, the air thick and hot. Gia kicked through the opening as it filled with rocks, using a misshapen boulder to create airholes.

She didn't know how long it would hold up or whether they would suffocate in the earthen womb. The rock storm showed no signs of ceasing, raining down in an endless torrent.

Gia stroked Claudia's hair to comfort her as they listened to the otherworldly roaring, as wild and as raw as anything they had ever heard before.

'All those people,' Claudia cried, wiping her eyes.

'Don't think about it,' said Gia, tensing up.

'The ships will be damaged,' said Claudia. 'We are trapped here. This is it. There is no way out. We will surely perish.'

'No,' said Gia stubbornly. 'We're going to make it. We got this far. We have to make it. We have to.'

'I cannot believe I thought I could save the world.'

'We can still save Rome,' said Gia. 'We can't give up. Why would the goddesses allow us to succeed in killing Decimus, only for us to die here in a cave?' Gia was trying to convince herself as much as Claudia. 'I refuse to believe it ends like this. They have kept us alive, all so you can rule.'

No. The optimism wasn't working. Gia still felt oppressively doomed.

'Not even the gods can fight nature,' said Claudia. 'Decimus was Jupiter's own protégé, and now he's cold and dead. The deities are not always victorious in their ambitions. We may be on our own now.'

'Decimus cannot become emperor,' said Gia. 'We won.'

'Maybe so,' said Claudia.

'We may die, but Rome will survive.'

'Yet the war in the heavens goes on. Will humans ever be free of the whims of the gods playing games?'

'We did all we could,' said Gia. 'We are only mortal.'

They quieted, listening to the sound of the world ending.

'Many times I have imagined my own death,' said Claudia. 'I saw myself getting sick after eating poisoned food, or being slaughtered in my bed, even being beheaded by my brother and brandished around the city on a stick ... but never this.'

'It is hard to believe,' agreed Gia. 'I was fairly certain I would die in battle. Imagine signing up to be a gladiator but it's a volcano that gets you in the end. What are the chances?'

She smiled at Claudia, but Claudia did not return it.

'It was all for nothing,' she said.

'No,' said Gia fiercely. 'Not for nothing. It still means something.' She gripped Claudia's hand. '*This* means something. Us. You, and me. We loved, we lived, we existed. We were here.'

'There are worse ways to go, I suppose,' said Claudia. 'If there must be a last place, I would choose to be in your arms.'

Gia kissed the top of her head, pulling her closer.

Though they were filthy, terrified and cursed, squatting in a cave as a volcano erupted beyond, they had each other to hold as the ground shook and split open and the world caved in, binding them so tightly together that they were no longer themselves. No longer separate beings. No longer apart.

They were not alone. They would not die alone.

The sound of falling rocks startled Gia awake. Awake. Alive. Unsure how much time had passed, she blinked through dust clouds to see the hole she'd made growing larger, revealing a white, featureless sky.

'There's someone in there!' came a voice.

Staggering up, Gia shook Claudia, who stirred.

'Who is it?' she whispered.

'I can't see yet,' said Gia.

They inched fearfully towards the hole as a group of people emerged, all of them covered in blood and dirt.

'There are two women in there!' said one man.

'Quick, dig them out.'

A shuffling avalanche of stones poured into the cave, making the opening wide enough to step through. Gia assisted Claudia first, listening to the gasps of surprise when the rescue party saw who it was.

'It's the princess of Rome!'

Gia followed as they flocked around Claudia, realizing she was still wearing the armour made by the goddesses.

'And Viatrix, the gladiator!'

The eruption was over, or so it seemed. The survivors of the disaster had gathered on the beach. Many of them were injured, wrapped in makeshift bandages. Some had dirty faces, tear tracks visible through the dirt. There were kids lugging sacks and elderly women giving out water and bread. Sailors and scholars and soldiers and slaves, all standing together as equals on the edge of history. Here, Gia spied Celadus the Handsome, in the flesh. She saw Rhea – the girl Atticus once had a crush on – and even the shopkeeper who'd yelled at her for vandalizing his wall.

'Claudia! Gia!'

It was Rectina, hurrying towards them in the company of a sickly looking elder man wrapped in a dozen blankets. She pulled them into an embrace that reminded Gia of her mother at her best, weeping tears into their hair.

'I have never been happier to see your face,' said Claudia.

'Thank the goddesses you warned me,' said Rectina. 'It was your visit that pushed me to reach out for help. If not for Pliny here, we'd be dead too.'

'We took a battering, though,' the man said. 'Two of our ships didn't make it, but the skies are clearing and one is still afloat.'

A dusty dog appeared, yipping as it ran circles around them. It was a tall, lean, thin-faced thing, slobbering into Gia's hand.

She imagined, for a moment, that the dog was Lucas's.

'And your brother?' asked Rectina as a group gathered curiously. 'What news of the emperor?'

'Dead,' said Claudia. 'He did not survive the eruption.'

'Viatrix!'

Something small and fast came hurtling towards Gia, wrapping their arms tightly around her middle.

'You're here! You're okay! I knew you'd survive. I told everyone you would.'

It was little Athena, though she looked much younger than Gia remembered, shaking with fear.

'They . . . they're gone,' she sobbed, clutching at Gia. 'They're all gone, except us. My parents, my sisters, everyone.'

Gia didn't know what to say at first, so she merely hugged her back.

'We're family now,' she said. 'You and me. Come with me to Rome. We can't stay here. We'll look out for you, I promise.'

Gia looked to Claudia, who nodded.

'As empress of Rome, I shall make it my top priority,' she said.

Athena merely stared at her in awe.

Gia looked out into the growing crowd, seeking familiar faces. She knew she wouldn't greet her mother or Cyrus, the two people she most longed to see, but when she caught sight of a young man, his hair grey with dust, she broke out into a run.

'Dom!' she cried, sweeping him up into her arms.

'Gia, thank the gods.'

'The goddesses, really,' she said.

He buried his face in her shoulder.

'Lucas . . . I killed him. I killed Lucas,' he said.

'You had no choice. You must know that. He knows that.'

The dog, which had followed her, sniffed at Dom until he petted her head.

'I'm glad you're still here, friend,' Gia said. 'Lucas would be too. He wanted you to live, so that's what you're going to do. Will you come with us to Rome? We can make another home there.'

'There is nothing left here for me now,' Dom said.

Gia watched as more survivors gathered on the beach, catching snatches of arguments and reunions. One man wanted to return to his house and retrieve his money, but the scholars were holding him back.

'You cannot go back, sir, please. It's not safe!'

Another woman wept for her daughter.

'She lives,' she said. 'I know she lives. We must turn over every stone.'

But Pompeii was ash, and many would be buried beneath its ruins.

Gia greeted two of the brothel girls and the stray cat they'd rescued, before she shared the bad news about Flavia and Berenice. There weren't many survivors of the disaster, but each life saved was precious indeed.

A group of soldiers approached, carrying more of the wounded, calling out for assistance. Some of the brothel girls ran up to help them.

One of the soldiers removed his helmet, staring hard at Gia.

Gia's first thought was that the rock had hit her a little too hard on the head, for she was looking in the eyes of a dead man.

Her second thought was that it was a gift of gratitude from the goddesses, because her brother had been resurrected from the dead.

'Cassius,' she whispered, in numb shock.

Claudia's head whipped around at the sound of his name.

He had short hair now, and he looked older than before, his skin weathered by the sun and lined by whatever he'd seen at war, but it was unmistakably him, breaking into a clumsy run as his face hung slack.

'Sister,' he said, sweeping Gia up just as her knees gave way.

'How is it so?'

They fell down onto the sand together, as Gia gasped, unable to form words, or even believe what she was seeing.

'You are here ... You are alive ... I am not dreaming,' she said.

'Gia,' was all he said, tears falling down his face.

'They said you'd been torn apart by barbarians. Mother arranged your grave. She mourned you ... We all did.'

'Where is she? And Atticus?'

Gia slowly shook her head.

'Atticus died in the arena, Mother in the disaster.'

Cassius buried his head in his hands.

'I am too late,' he said, his voice breaking.

Gia held him tighter.

'Where have you been? All this time? The army sent us your ring.'

Cassius wiped his eyes, shaking his head.

'My own men took my ring and left me for dead on the battlefield. I was taken hostage by a local tribe,' he said. 'Nice folks, as it turns out – not too happy about us invading their country. They patched me up. I told them I couldn't give two shits about Rome, that I just wanted to return home to see my baby sister. They ...' He looked over her shoulder, momentarily distracted. 'They let me go.'

'I'm so happy I get to meet you after all,' came a voice, and Gia realized what Cassius had been distracted by. 'Gia has spoken so highly of you.'

He stood up, bowing unsurely. 'Princess.'

'Empress,' she corrected. 'But you can call me Claudia.'

Cassius looked to Gia for some kind of explanation.

'I ... I am her gladiator. Her bodyguard,' she said, suddenly embarrassed in the way only older brothers can inspire. 'We ... A lot has happened.'

'I see that,' said Cassius warily. He probably thought Gia was a prisoner.

'She's not ... We are friends.'

'Friends?' said Cassius.

'Friends?' said Claudia, with an edge to her voice.

It was far more complicated than that. Their relationship was a secret and Claudia was engaged, but this wasn't the time to have that particular conversation.

'We will talk, all of us, later.'

The skies seemed quiet now, as if even the gods had reached an armistice. It finally felt safe to breathe.

Gia had survived. Claudia lived to rule. Her brother was back, and she was not alone. She would let nothing ruin that peace.

The people on the beach looked around uncertainly, knowing neither where to go nor who to turn to for direction.

Claudia had noticed too, stepping onto a crate someone had rescued from the ruins and clapping her hands to draw their attention.

'I know there will be objections,' Claudia said, raising her voice, 'many of them legitimate. Who am I to you but a girl who sat at the emperor's side? What right have I to rule over any other? We can discuss it with the Senate upon our return, but, right now, the only leader Rome has is standing before you. I appeal to you to recognize me as empress, if only to keep at bay the chaos of an empire unattended. We must steer these people to safety, so we may one day rebuild the city.'

The crowd murmured uncertainly.

'More ships will be sent from Rome, to search for survivors and retrieve any valuables that can be salvaged. You will need to resettle, but this will not be the end. Every single one of us standing here is greatly fortunate to be alive.'

'Then let us get you to Rome,' said Pliny the Elder.

No one immediately protested.

'It is thanks to Claudia that I am alive,' said Celadus the Handsome. 'I heard her warning about the volcano in the Forum.'

The crowd hummed, talking among themselves. Gia exhaled, trying not to worry as Celadus and the princess conversed.

For now, the plan was working, but who knew what awaited them in the capital. It was an uneasy, tentative peace.

Pliny called for his servants to begin preparing the ship that bounced in the dirty, foam-filled bay beyond.

As Cassius tended to the wounded, Gia joined Claudia aboard the ship, standing at the bow. She didn't stir at Gia's presence or say anything, staring off into the murky distance.

Gia marvelled at the perfect art of her thinking face.

'What's on your mind, Princess?' she asked.

Claudia reached for her hand without looking at her.

'My own brother,' she said, after a moment. 'Would you think me ridiculous if I said that I mourned that monster?'

'No. He may be a monster, but he is still your blood.'

'The world is better off without him, as am I, yet I mourn the person he could've been ... and perhaps, too, the person *I* could've been, if he had never existed.'

The sailors were preparing to cast off, raising the damaged sails and clearing the deck of debris as the last passengers climbed aboard, including Dom and Cassius, in company with Athena and the dog.

'You are exactly the person you are supposed to be,' said Gia.

'Do you think the people will accept me as their ruler?'

'They must,' said Gia. 'There is no other.'

'Not unless my cousin Marcellus makes an appearance. As my father's nephew, some might view him as the legitimate heir.'

They fell quiet.

'What will you tell them, about what happened last night?'

'I will say my brother was crushed by the collapsing roof ... as both of us witnessed,' said Claudia, after a beat.

'I remember it well,' said Gia quickly.

Claudia turned to face her.

'Gia, there is something I must tell you.'

These simple words caused Gia's stomach to turn, her chest rising and falling as many terrible possibilities made themselves visible.

'What is it?' Gia asked, as the sailors raised the anchor.

Claudia lowered her voice as they both faced out to sea, letting the grinding noise of a ship being launched drown out her confession.

'Decimus was not the first man I have killed.'

'No? Who was the first?' Gia asked lightly, thinking she was joking.

The ship began to drift, the sailors using oars to navigate the giant lumps of pumice like icebergs.

'Decimus is a maniac; a danger to all man and womankind. I feared he would try to kill me, and I was right, but ...'

'But what?' Gia urged.

'He never poisoned our father.'

Gia's heart raced.

It was one of the first things Claudia had ever confided in her: her suspicions of her brother's plot to rule.

'That was me,' she said.

'He was being truthful, back at the villa?'

'About that, yes.'

'You were the one poisoning him?' she said. 'All along?'

Claudia broke away from the bow, pacing back and forth in agitation.

'It is not that simple. My father had been senile for years. His heart was failing. Rome was already collapsing under his rule. He'd lost the confidence of the Senate. I knew he would lead the empire into ruin, and, with every chalice of wine, he grew more belligerent. He has hated all women since my mother died. It sickened me to know that the world turned on the whims of such a cruel, ignorant man. It sickened me more how much he worshipped my brother, how much he was willing to forget to protect his heir. Not once did he ever defend me from Decimus.'

'So . . . you killed him?'

Gia had always known that Claudia had a ruthless side, that she was a rose with thorns, but she had not predicted this. How believable Claudia had been, telling her a false story.

'He made my life a misery. He and Decimus both. I was born inferior to them and I would've died as such if I hadn't . . . done what I needed to do.'

Gia swallowed, unspoken words stuck in her throat.

'It was them, or me. That was what it boiled down to. If I couldn't kill them, I would kill myself and be rid of this forsaken world.'

'You lied,' Gia rasped. 'You lied to me.'

'I did not love you at first – though soon after, I did,' she said. 'The lie seemed small, not too far from the truth, but it became bigger as my feelings for you grew.'

Gia shook her head and took a step back.

'If I didn't love you, I would continue to let you believe the lie, but I cannot, even if it means you will never love me back,' said Claudia.

'You should've told me.'

'Did your friend Cyrus not ask you to get close to me? To spy on me for him?' she said. 'You didn't tell me that right away, and yet I love you still.'

Gia could not deny it.

'It is a terrifying thing, to share your darkest truth,' said Claudia. 'I couldn't be sure if I could trust you. I have been betrayed many times by the people closest to me. Yet there is one person I trust with all of my soul, and it is you. Not the Senate, not the gods, not even myself. You.'

'You offered to be my patron,' said Gia. 'You saved my life in the arena. Why? What did you want from me then, before you loved me?'

'The goddesses told me to seek a warrior, and you are the one I chose.'

'But why?'

'I saw something in you. I wanted you. I longed to know you. My intention was ... you. Just you, Gia. You are all I desire.'

'Me, and the world,' Gia said.

'If you asked me to, I would give the world up.'

Gia's shoulders relaxed, though her hands were still clenched at her sides.

'Did you hope I would kill Decimus for you?' she asked.

'I would never ask that of you. I meant it when I said not by your hand, not on your soul. He did mean to have me killed. That part was true. He sent the assassin, I am sure of it. But he was my problem, and I intended to handle it. So I did.'

She gazed into Gia's eyes.

'I am glad, that I did it myself. He was mine to kill.'

Waves roared around them as they navigated the rocky shore.

'Emperors rise and fall,' said Claudia. 'Even the old gods were overthrown by their children. I knew what was required of me, and I did it. I just needed people to think I was innocent long enough to get away with it.'

'Do you regret it?' Gia asked.

'I do not,' said Claudia, and she was fiercer now than Gia had ever seen her. 'My only regret is that I have hurt you.'

'I would not have judged you for wanting him gone,' Gia said.

'Which one? My father or Decimus?'

'Either of them, honestly.'

As the ship sailed out into open waters, the waves thrashed around the vessel, scattered with the debris of many shipwrecks.

'Do you judge me now?' asked Claudia.

Gia hesitated. The true answer was complicated. There were certain worries Gia had, certain quiet creeping worries she barely dared to voice even to herself, about what Claudia wanted and what she would do to get it. She feared the shadow of an unknown prince and all the terrible burdens of ruling an empire of bones yet to come. But the goddesses had selected Claudia for a purpose. They had enabled her and laid the path. They saw what Gia did not, and she trusted in their vision.

Hadn't a part of her already suspected, and hadn't it made Claudia even more fascinating to her? Hadn't she watched her stab her brother a dozen times in the back and kissed her thereafter?

Gia had killed, and spared no mercy. They were the same. She no longer wanted anything but the raw, naked truth between them. More frighteningly, she found that she didn't really care. Good, bad, soft, brutal: she wanted Claudia anyway.

She wanted all of her.

'Your silence is the most terrible sound I have ever heard,' said Claudia, 'and yet, I know I am undeserving of your forgiveness.'

'I am just trying to find the right words.'

'Should you dare to trust me once more, I would never lie to you again. But if you do not, I shall love and protect you all the same. You owe me nothing and if ever you wish to be free of me, I will not stop you.'

'Claudia,' Gia said gently.

'But you must understand, whatever I am, I cannot be anything else now. I did this, I chose this ... and I would do it again—'

Gia silenced her with a kiss – as sweeping as the rough waters, as warm as the rivers of lava that streaked through blackened hillsides.

She could not hold her tight enough, or long enough, to express the depths of her affection, which was endless.

For a moment, there was nothing but them. No carnage. No destruction. No terror. In a world of gods and mortals and monsters, love would save them and bury them whole, all in one.

Gia broke away from Claudia's lips, gasping for breath.

'Your destiny is my destiny,' she said. 'Our fates are entangled now.'

'You are sure?'

'As sure as I am that you will rule Rome,' Gia said.

In the distance, Vesuvius continued to smoke, but the sun broke through the thick blanket of cloud overhead, casting a single ray that shone upon Claudia. The crown glinted like molten gold as the green, sea-glass eyes of the new empress glowed with unworldly light.

She carried the power of not just one goddess, but four.

Gia lifted Claudia's hand to kiss it, then bowed before her.

'All hail the empress of Rome,' she said.

Rectina noticed and did the same, moving towards them.

'All hail the first empress of Rome,' she said.

'You will have to imagine me bowing,' said Pliny the Elder. 'My back will never forgive me if I do. But all hail the empress, yes.'

Cassius awkwardly copied, though he did not seem entirely convinced.

Some of the sailors and scholars fell to their knees in reverence, repeating the chant, as did Dom and Athena.

Others held back, their expressions fearful, resentful. This was a new world. A woman would rule Rome and not everyone was ready for it.

Gia saw light dancing in Claudia's eyes as the people chanted her name.

Many people spoke of revolution, but few acted on it. Even Cyrus had failed to kill the would-be emperor. Claudia alone had succeeded. She had taken destiny into her own hands and made it hers.

No wonder the goddesses had chosen her.

She was furious and unknowable, greater than any man who had ever lived.

Gia could not have been more dangerously in love with her.

EPILOGUE

A terrible peace had fallen upon Pompeii; the haunting quiet of the aftermath of a disaster. But, in Elysium, the skies burned red with fire as lightning coursed through Asphodel Valley. The war of the gods raged on.

Neither side had lost, or won. Jupiter wasn't dead, but neither was Minerva. Unable to kill the other, the two had reached an impasse – unstoppable force meets immovable object – until both were exhausted into submission.

Jupiter retreated to the stars to recuperate, watching over Earth and Elysium from above. But Minerva knew he would soon return to enact his revenge, and the game of the gods would begin once again.

Minerva liked to win. She had once turned a mortal woman into a spider when she beat her in a weaving contest. Perhaps that was why she had regressed into her animal form and flown away, leaving Diana to face the future alone.

As she and Venus approached the palace of Fortuna, Diana was quiet. Venus lightly gripped her hand, urging her on.

'What do you think will happen now?' asked Diana.

'Good things,' replied Venus.

'How can you be so optimistic?'

'Because even in the worst of times, even when all is lost, even on the last day, in the last hour, on Earth and in heaven, there will be love. There will always be love. It is undeniable, inescapable and indestructible, no matter what horrors are brought upon us by men or gods. Love is all we have; our one true freedom. That is why I am the most powerful deity of all, because love is truly immortal.'

'I don't doubt it.' Diana smiled.

Within the palace, the goddess of fortune and misfortune spun her wheel once more, its ricocheting sound echoing.

'You sent for us?' said Venus.

'Things have not gone quite as planned,' said Fortuna, after a moment. 'I didn't predict that Claudia would be the one to poison her father, nor that she would be the one to kill Decimus. Her actions, unexpected as they were, protected her from the foresight of Jupiter. He didn't see her coming, and so he was unable to prevent her. If we had known, he also would have known. That is our great fortune. Claudia may still become empress.'

'And yet the war rages on,' said Diana. 'Jupiter's allies are rallying against us. Soon the pantheon will be irrevocably divided. With Minerva absent, we need your guidance more than ever.'

'Tell us, Fortuna, what do you see?' said Venus.

Fortuna nodded and turned to her wheel, waiting until it stopped its revolutions – but it didn't stop. It just kept on spinning and spinning, until it broke off its hinges, shattering into pieces.

The goddesses shrank back with a cry of surprise.

Fortuna turned, her face pale, her clouded eyes searching as she raised her palms in hopelessness, gazing into them as if she expected to see a vision there.

'Nothing,' she said. 'I see nothing.'

ACKNOWLEDGEMENTS

Acknowledgements are usually written at a strange, liminal time for the author, when the book is finished but doesn't fully exist yet. It's a period of uncertainty. There are people I need to thank for things that haven't happened yet. In that way, to write an acknowledgements page is to look into the future, which is apt for this story.

The first person I want to thank is you, the reader, for choosing this book. There are a lot of excellent books you could've picked instead but this is a story about fortune, and it is my great fortune that you found me. Thanks for sticking with me this far, whoever you are. You're probably pretty cool, in my professional opinion.

Speaking of good fortune: this is my third published book, my third time writing an acknowledgements page, and I'm thanking three people for the third time also. First, to Hannah Sheppard, who has represented me throughout my entire career, often going far above and beyond to guide me through the labyrinth of publishing. I would've given up years ago if not for you. I couldn't ask for a better agent.

To my editor, Yasmin Morrissey, whose belief in me is so great I'm often left speechless by it: thank you for everything, literally everything. Thank you for making this such a fun, inspiring process. Thank you just for being you. I can't wait to do it again very soon.

To Genevieve Herr, whose edit transformed this story and took it to dizzying new heights: thank you for always knowing what I'm trying to achieve, even when I fail to execute it the first time around. I am forever wowed by your ability to elevate and illuminate a story.

To the incredibly talented Tom Roberts, who made Gia and Claudia real. To Holly Macdonald, whose vision brought it all together. To Jesse Green and Patrick Knowles: thank you for bringing this story to life in such a beautiful way. It's such a privilege to have a cover like this one, and I thank the assembled gods for it every day.

To Tierney Holm: thank you for some of my favourite funny editorial notes. To Millie Monaghan, a brilliant sounding board and all-round good soul: it's my great honour to have you on my team. To Simi Toor and the rest of the S&S team: what a dream! You've made me feel so welcome and put me at ease. I've been so buoyed by your excitement, pushing me through my usual anxiety to create an unforgettable experience. To Rachel Denwood, Ali Dougal, Laura Hough, Alice Twomey, Danielle Wilson, Alesha Bonser, Sophie Storr, Lizzie Irwin, Ellie Curtis, Arub Ahmed, Maud Sepal and MRules – thank you so much.

Thank you to Mom and Dad for your enduring belief in me. Not every author is privileged to have a support system like I do. Thank you for our trips to Rome and Pompeii, which you planned years ago without knowing I'd ever write this book. We're so blessed to have spent so much quality time together as a family.

Thank you to my extended family too, for your ongoing enthusiasm. Thank you to the friends who are there through celebrations and commiserations. Thanks for the lols and the memes that make the bad days pass faster. Thanks to my raccoon triad, to my Discord pixel sisters, to the assembled authors of Strap in Patricia. Thank you to the writers whose books line my shelves. Thank you to every bookseller, book blogger, bookstagrammer, booktuber and booktoker, to every reviewer and reader I haven't met yet.

Because this is a very gay book, it also feels right to thank all of the queer women in my life. Even though this story is set in 79 AD, many of my own formative experiences went into it. It's the epic sapphic fantasy I wanted to read as a teenager, but it's also the product of all of my own queer coming of age. So, this one goes out to my best mates. To the TV lesbians who showed me the way (thank you, Bad Girls!). To all the literary sapphics who taught me how to love. To the activists who fought for our rights and continue to fight to this day. To my former wife. To the exes who are still good friends and the exes I'll probably never speak to again: all of you made my life, made me who I am. No Ragrets.

Finally, a special thank you to Mary Beard, to Sappho and to Xena: Warrior Princess.

CONTENT WARNINGS:

Sexual assault and implied threat of sexual predator, p.111, p.398
Cruelty/implied cruelty towards an animal, p. 253
Torture, blood and gore, death and violence, Chapter 22
Scenes of a sexual nature, Chapter 16, Chapter 18